MADNESS
TREADS
LIGHTLY

D0958095

MADNESS TREADS LIGHTLY

POLINA DASHKOVA

TRANSLATED BY MARIAN SCHWARTZ

amazon crossing

Text copyright © 1998 Polina Dashkova

Translation copyright © 2017 Marian Schwartz

Previously published as Легкие шаги безумия by Eksmo in Russia in 1998. Translated from Russian by Marian Schwartz. First published in English by AmazonCrossing in 2017.

Published by AmazonCrossing, Seattle

www.apub.com

Amazon, the Amazon logo, and AmazonCrossing are trademarks of Amazon.com, Inc., or its affiliates.

ISBN-13: 9781477823460
ISBN-10: 1477823468

Cover design by Damon Freeman

Printed in the United States of America

MADNESS TREADS LIGHTLY

CHAPTER 1

Moscow, March 1996

Lena Polyanskaya wrestled the stroller through the deep March slush and lumpy melting snow like a Volga boatman. The narrow street was lined with tall, hardened snowdrifts, and any speeding cars splashed the pedestrians with thick brown muck.

Two-year-old Liza kept trying to stand up in the stroller so she could walk on her own little feet. She thought she was too big for a stroller, and anyway, there were so many interesting things to look at: sparrows and ravens making a racket as they fought over wet bread crusts, a shaggy ginger pup chasing its own tail, and a bigger little boy walking toward them, gnawing on a bright red apple.

"Mama, Liza wants an apple, too," the little girl informed her mother seriously, standing up yet again.

A big bag of groceries was hanging off the stroller handle, so the second Lena lifted Liza to seat her properly, the stroller tipped all the way back and the bag split open.

"All fall down," Liza summed things up with a sigh, gazing from her mama's arms to the groceries strewn through the muck.

"Yes, my love, all fall down. Now we'll pick it all up." Lena had carefully set her daughter on the sidewalk and was picking the groceries out of the slush and brushing them off with her glove when she noticed someone in a dark blue Volvo parked across the street, watching her intently. The tinted windows reflected the snowdrifts and pedestrians, so Lena couldn't see exactly who was watching her, but she could feel that person's gaze.

"We do make an entertaining spectacle." She grinned as she managed to reattach the bag to the stroller handle, get Liza seated, and shake the dirt off her leather gloves.

When she turned into her own courtyard, she spotted the Volvo again. It drove by very closely, at minimum speed, as if the people in it wanted to remember exactly which door the young mother with the stroller entered.

There were two of them—a woman behind the wheel and a man in the passenger seat. Lena didn't get a good look at them, but they got an excellent one of her.

"Are you certain?" the woman asked quietly after the door shut behind Lena.

"Absolutely. She's barely changed in all these years."

"She has to be thirty-six now," the woman observed. "And that young mama couldn't be over twenty-five. And the child's so young. You haven't mixed something up? It's been a few years, after all."

"No," the man answered firmly. "I haven't mixed anything up."

The telephone trilled in the empty apartment.

"Can you talk now?" Lena barely recognized the voice of her dear friend and former classmate Olga Sinitsyna. The voice in the receiver was so strange, hoarse and very soft.

"Hi, Olga, what's happened?" Lena pressed the receiver between her ear and shoulder and started untying the ribbons on Liza's cap.

"Mitya's dead," Olga said very softly.

2

Lena thought she'd misheard.

"I'm sorry. What did you say?" she asked, pulling off Liza's boots.

"Mama, Liza has to go," her daughter solemnly informed her.

"Olga, are you home right now? I'll call you back in fifteen minutes. I just walked in. I'll get Liza undressed, put her on the potty, and call you right back."

"Can I come over right now?" Olga asked quickly.

"Of course!"

Olga and Lena were the same age—thirty-six. Mitya Sinitsyn, Olga's brother, was two years younger. How could a perfectly healthy thirty-four-year-old man full of strength and plans for the future who didn't drink, use drugs, or have any connections to crime, drop dead?

Before Olga arrived, Lena managed to feed Liza lunch and put her to bed, wash the dishes, make a pot of cabbage soup, and start the laundry. Today she planned to translate at least five pages of a massive article about the latest psychological research on serial killers, "Cruelty and the Victim," by the trendy American psychologist David Crowell.

Even though Liza was scarcely two, Lena worked a lot and still ran the same literature and art department at *Smart* magazine as she had before her daughter's birth. The editor in chief had done his best to accommodate her and let her come in just two days a week. The lion's share of her work she took home to finish at her computer at night. On her two in-house days, she left her daughter with a lonely old neighbor, since neither Lena nor her husband Sergei Krotov had living parents. Liza was growing up without grandmothers or grandfathers, and for Vera Fyodorovna, a well-educated pensioner, spending the day with a calm, loving child was sheer joy. And the money Lena and Sergei paid her came in handy, given her miserable pension.

"Don't you think of sending my little Liza to day care!" Vera Fyodorovna would say. "As long as I'm on my feet and of sound mind, I'll stay with her as much as you need."

For Lena, having Vera Fyodorovna in the apartment across the way was a godsend. It wasn't only that Sergei's salary as a colonel in the Interior Ministry—he was deputy chief of the Criminal Division in the Domestic Counterintelligence Administration—barely supported them, but also that Lena herself couldn't live without work. She realized she'd be replaced the instant she eased up even a little.

Lena's time was scheduled down to the minute, and she was beyond exhausted, sleeping five hours a day at most. Now she only had one of her two precious hours of Liza's afternoon nap left, that is, a good two pages of translation. But Lena didn't even bother to sit down to her computer.

Ever since Olga's call, all she could think about was Mitya. She imagined what must be going on now with his parents and his eighty-year-old grandmother, Zinaida Lukinichna, who, despite her advanced age, still had her wits and a keen perception of life . . . and death.

What could have happened to Mitya? An accident? Did a car run over him? Did a brick fall on his head? But everyone knows a brick doesn't just fall on anybody's head.

Lena had just turned on the electric kettle and poured coffee beans into the grinder when the doorbell rang.

Olga was standing in the doorway wearing a black kerchief, her grandmother's, probably. Tousled, bright gold locks poked out helter-skelter. It was obvious at first glance that she hadn't combed her hair or washed and had thrown on whatever was at hand. The news of Mitya's death had caught her unawares. So it was an accident?

"He hanged himself," Olga said in a dulled voice as she took off her coat. "He hanged himself last night, in his apartment. He looped his belt around the gas pipe above the kitchen door."

"Where was his wife?" Lena asked quickly.

"Sleeping. Sleeping peacefully in the next room. She didn't hear a thing."

"Who found him?" Lena wanted to say "his body" but faltered. It was hard to refer that way to Mitya, who recently had dropped by for a visit and sat right here, on the kitchen sofa, sparking energy, health, and plans for the future.

"His wife. She woke up, went into the kitchen, and saw him."

All of a sudden Lena noticed that Olga had stopped calling her brother's wife by her name. Before she'd had nothing but praise for her.

"What happened next? At least have some coffee. Do you want me to ladle out some soup for you? I just made it."

"No." Olga shook her head. "No, I can't eat anything. Or drink. Open the window a little and let's smoke while Liza's asleep. What really happened, no one saw." Olga shrugged nervously and took a deep drag. "We only know what she said, and she doesn't remember anything. She pulled Mitya out of the noose herself."

"Wait a sec," Lena interrupted her. "But Mitya was six feet tall and solidly built. Katya's like Thumbelina, half his weight and three heads shorter."

"Yes, she said it was very hard. But she couldn't leave him like that, and she was hoping he might still be alive. Don't worry, I'm thinking straight. I realize that anything's possible, but out of the blue like that, without even a note. And Mitya had always considered suicide a terrible sin. This is not enough to tell the police, of course, but Mitya was baptized, he was Orthodox, he went to confession and took communion. Rarely, but still. Now there can't even be a funeral because suicides don't get funerals. Any sin can be prayed away—except this one."

Olga had dark circles under her eyes, and her hand holding the dead cigarette was trembling.

"He dropped by to see me about a month ago," Lena said softly. "He had so many plans. He was telling me he'd written five new songs, he'd gotten in to see some famous producer, and now he said he'd have one music video after another coming. I don't remember exactly what we talked about, but I got the impression Mitya was doing great. Maybe a little too excited, but in a good way. Did some hopes he had connected with that producer fall through?"

"Those hopes of his were born and died ten times a month." Olga grinned sadly. "He was used to it and took it totally calmly. All kinds of producers, big and small, were endlessly popping up in his life. No, if we're talking about what truly worried him, then it was his own art, not in terms of popularity and money, but whether he could—or couldn't—write. The last month he'd been writing like never before, and for him that was the main thing."

"You mean you're not ruling out that Mitya didn't do it himself?" Lena asked cautiously.

"The police assure me he did." Olga lit another cigarette.

"Have you eaten anything at all today? You're smoking like a chimney. Want me to make coffee?"

"Go ahead." Olga nodded indifferently. "And if I can, I'll take a shower here. I haven't even washed today, and I've already been to the morgue. Forgive me for showing up here with this nightmare, but being home right now is so tough. I have to get my bearings and then take care of my parents and grandmother."

"Come on, I'll give you a clean towel."

"Lena, I don't believe he did it," Olga said softly, standing in the bathroom door. "It's all so bizarre. Their telephone was out all day. I checked at the station, and the line was completely fine. Something happened to the phone itself, and this morning a neighbor fixed it in a minute. His wife called the ambulance and police from their neighbors' at five in the morning. It was the neighbors who called me. By the time I got there, they'd already taken Mitya away. You see, that night his wife was . . . well, high. They told me Mitya was, too. They said it was suicide from drug psychosis. They found needles in the apartment and tracks on his arm. So the police didn't try too hard. 'Ma'am, your dear brother was an addict,' they told me. 'So is his wife. It's perfectly clear!'"

"Mitya wasn't an addict," Lena said slowly. "He didn't even drink. And Katya . . ."

"She'd been shooting up for a year and a half. But not Mitya. Never."

"Did you see him in the morgue?"

"No. I couldn't. I was scared I'd faint. He was already in the cold locker. They said there was a line for viewing. There are an awful lot of bodies. If I write a petition to the Prosecutor's Office, he'll stay there, waiting his turn."

"What have you decided?"

"I don't know. But if he's going to lie there in the cold locker, my mama and papa and my grandmother are going to have heart attacks over my brother. And they explained to me that a petition wasn't going to do much. They'd hand the case to some girl working off her Moscow residency permit in the District Prosecutor's Office, since they don't have enough investigators. She won't go and do any digging. It was so clearly a suicide. They have so many unsolved murders now, and this one, just some addict . . ."

She made a hopeless gesture and closed the bathroom door.

While Olga was taking a shower and putting herself in order, Lena stood by the window, holding the buzzing coffee grinder, and thought about Mitya Sinitsyn. What had they talked about then? He'd been over for a couple of hours, after all. He'd been telling her that he'd written five new songs and he'd even left a cassette. Lena had never gotten around to listening to it. She had to find it.

Yes, yet another megaproducer had appeared on his horizon. But Mitya hadn't said his name, he'd said, "Terrifically famous, you wouldn't believe it! I'm afraid I'll attract the evil eye!"

Then they'd eaten dinner and talked about something else for a long time. *We were just reminiscing about our student days,* Lena thought.

Mitya graduated from the Institute of Culture and studied to be a theater director. It was an odd major, especially these days, and he never did work in his field. He wrote his songs, sang them for a small circle of friends, and had some gigs in clubs in the late 1980s. He was always in talks about some record, or some CD, or music videos for television.

Nothing ever came of the talks, but Mitya never gave up. He believed he had good songs, that they just weren't pop. But there was demand for more than just pop. Mitya wasn't counting on stardom, but he wanted to find his audience, and not through concerts in underground crossings but through more respectable channels—radio, television. For that, though, he not only had to compose good songs and perform them well, he also had to build up the right acquaintances and contacts, hobnob with producers, and offer himself as a product. And Mitya didn't know how to do that.

Lately he'd been working as a guitar teacher at a children's drama school. The money was pathetic, but the kids loved him. That was important to Mitya because he and Katya couldn't have kids, though they'd wanted to badly.

If Lena was to assume what Olga said was true, and Mitya had been murdered, then her first question had to be who benefited? Who could have felt threatened by someone who taught kids classical guitar and wrote songs?

She had to find that cassette and listen it, only not now, around Olga. That might be painful for her. As it was, she was barely keeping it together.

Wet snow was falling outside. Looking into the courtyard, Lena mechanically noted that Olga hadn't parked her little gray Volkswagen very well. She was thinking about how Olga was going to have a hard time getting out and might get stuck in a snowdrift when her gaze slipped over the dark blue Volvo, parked only a few meters from Olga's car and already lightly sprinkled with snow.

⋆

"There, you see?" the woman sitting behind the wheel of the Volvo said quietly to her companion. "I never doubted they were still in touch, and pretty close touch, too. Close enough that after what happened, she rushed straight here."

"I'm afraid," the man murmured with dried lips.

"It's all right." The woman fondly ran her short, well-manicured fingers over his cheek. "You're doing great. You'll calm down and realize that this is the last push. Then it's all over. I know how scared you are right now. Fear comes from deep inside, it rises from the belly to the chest. But you're not going to let it rise any higher. You're not going to let it into your head. You've been able to stop that thick, burning, unbearable fear lots of times. You're strong now and you'll be even stronger when we make this push—difficult and essential, but the last. I am with you."

Her short, strong fingers slid slowly and gently over his smooth-shaven cheek. Her nails were polished a matte red, which looked garish against his very pale cheek. While continuing to speak quiet, lulling words, the woman was thinking that she mustn't forget to remove this polish tonight and use something more muted, more elegant.

The man shut his eyes. His nostrils flared slowly and rhythmically. His breathing was deep and calm. When the woman felt his face muscles relax, she turned on the engine, and the dark blue Volvo slowly left the courtyard, came out into the side street, and from there onto the main road, where it got lost in the crowd of cars speeding under the slow, wet snow.

Olga Sinitsyna had been Lena Polyanskaya's best friend all five of their years together in the journalism department at the university. Afterward they lost track of each other and only reconnected eight years after graduation, totally by accident, on a plane.

Lena was flying to New York. Columbia University had invited her to lecture on modern Russian literature and journalism. In the smoking section, an elegant, well-groomed businesswoman wearing an austere and expensive suit sat down next to her.

It was 1990, and businesswomen like that were still a rarity in Russia. Lena took a quick glance at her and was amazed that a rich American was flying Aeroflot rather than Pan Am or Delta. But right then the woman sadly shook her light blond head and said in Russian, "You take the cake, Polyanskaya! I keep waiting to see whether you'll recognize me."

"Olga! Olga Sinitsyna!" Lena was ecstatic.

It seemed incredible that a successful businesswoman would hatch from that ephemeral, sublime creature she always remembered in jeans and a sweater. Olga had been a typical smart Moscow girl of the late 1970s who could argue all night long over Russia's fate and sacrificial mission and the vicissitudes of existential consciousness and then stand in line for hours, not for boots at the department store, but for the basement exhibit hall on Malaya Gruzinskaya Street or for tickets to a Richter concert at the Conservatory.

Olga Sinitsyna, known all over the journalism department for being scatterbrained and impractical and for her absurd, ill-fated love affairs, and this cool woman with the sparkling American smile, so self-assured, seemed like beings from different planets.

"In the end," Olga told her, "I was left on my own with two little boys a year apart. I did marry Givi Kiladze, you know. Remember him?"

Givi Kiladze had studied journalism with them and was—unrequitedly—in love with Olga all five years. A Muscovite whose family had come from Georgia two generations before, he only remembered his native language when he wanted to slit someone's throat. As a rule, the only people whose throats he wanted to slit were Olga or anyone who dared get closer to her than three meters.

"Passion ends quickly. Our life went bad, and we were practically starving. Givi couldn't find a job and started drinking and dragging hordes of tramps into our home, after which the towels and teaspoons would disappear. Everyone had to be fed and given a place to sleep. He has a generous soul, and there I was with a belly and toxicosis. When little Gleb was born, he sent for his great-aunt to come from their mountain village and help me. His great-aunt was followed by his great-uncle and then another uncle and another aunt. Eventually, I grabbed Gleb and fled to my parents'. That's when the drama started. Amateur drama: 'I'll kill myself! I'll kill you!' Basically, we made our peace. At the time I firmly believed a child needs his father, even if he's crazy.

"My Gleb has dark hair and eyes, but my younger, Gosha, was born blond and blue-eyed. That idiot started howling that Gosha wasn't his son. You know what I did to keep my sanity? Started learning Japanese! Picture this: a nursing mama with an infant at her breast loudly reading Japanese characters while the father of her children runs around with a dagger shouting, 'I'll murder you!' while Gleb, at two and a half, is sitting on the potty and saying in Georgian, 'Papa, don't kill Mama, she's good!' It was his mountain relatives who eventually set him straight.

"Meanwhile, there wasn't so much as a coin in the house. We lived on what my parents gave us. They couldn't give us a lot but they gave us everything they had. Packages would come from the mountains, too—homemade wine, figs, nuts. Basically, I went back to my parents again—took the kids and left. For good. Givi would show up in the middle of the night, drunk as a skunk. It's a good thing Mitya was there and could step in. Otherwise Givi would have killed me without batting an eye. He was jealous, even of my own brother."

"You could have called." Lena sighed. "Why did you totally vanish?"

"What about you?" Olga grinned. "Why did you?"

"Things happened." Lena shrugged. "I have my own skeletons in my closet. Did you learn Japanese after all?"

"Did I ever! You know, I'm actually grateful to Givi. If he hadn't driven me to Japanese, I wouldn't be the manager of the Russian branch of Kokusai Koeki. I started translating the manuals for the computers and office equipment they sell without having the foggiest idea what they were. But I had to feed my children, and mama and papa, and my grandmother, and Mitya. My little brother—he's still a deadbeat—writing all his songs and playing his guitar, and not doing anything he doesn't want to do. But he does like to eat.

"So I had to earn the money, and I turned out to be pretty good at it. I got hooked on it and pretty quickly started earning a lot. Mama and Grandma stayed with the children while I built my career. I'll be senior manager soon, then deputy director, and then the sky's the limit. Everything's great now. I'm making tons of money, and sometimes I look in the mirror and see this woman I don't recognize. Remember the poems I used to write? And my paper on Kafka? That was when I used my brain, whereas now . . . No, of course, I use my brain now, too, but sometimes I get the feeling that instead of a brain, there's a computer in this crock of mine spitting out decisions."

"Come off it, Sinitsyna." Lena started laughing. "Everything's going great for you, and not just kind of, but for real. The Kafka and the poetry, they're still in there, they didn't go anywhere; it's just your youth that's passed. There's a time for everything."

"But your youth hasn't passed," Olga said, looking into Lena's big, smoky-gray eyes and her skinny, makeup-free face. "Polyanskaya, you look exactly the way you did in our first year."

"Stop it!" Lena shook her head. "I'm just skinny, so I look younger. Also, business suits and makeup are by no means required in my work. I am in journalism, so I can get away with the same old jeans and sweaters. Your position requires more of you, you're our businesswoman."

Six years had passed since that meeting on the plane. Olga had become deputy commercial director for the Russian branch of Kokusai Koeki. Lena ran the literature and art department at the joint

Russian-American magazine *Smart*, and two years ago she'd gotten married and given birth to a daughter, Liza. But Olga Sinitsyna hadn't remarried. She was disillusioned from her first experience of family life. She spent the crumbs of free time she had left after work on her sons and younger brother.

For those six years, Lena and Olga stayed in touch, calling each other and getting together fairly often. Each realized that the older you get, the harder it is to make new friends. You have to treasure your old ones. You have to have someone you can call at any time, day or night, someone who'll be glad to hear from you. Someone who remembers you young, carefree, and defenseless. And when you're together, you too can remember what that felt like, if only for a few minutes.

CHAPTER 2

Tobolsk, September 1981

He liked recalling his childhood. Each time he would drag up an especially hard, painful episode and start reproducing it mentally in all its details. The more agonizing the details, the longer he dwelled on them.

He'd grown up a quiet, dutiful boy. His mother watched his every step, his every breath.

"You're the grandson of a legendary Red commander," she would repeat. "You have to be worthy of your grandfather. He was a great man."

The little boy didn't really understand what it meant to be worthy of his grandfather. A stern, broad-faced man with a blond mustache wearing a leather jacket and a shoulder belt gazed at him from the many portraits, large and small, hung all over the apartment. There was nothing else on the walls—no pictures or calendars, just portraits of his legendary grandfather. On his mother's desk there were small bronze busts of the two great leaders, Lenin and Stalin. Venya Volkov always gave his all, dusting their small, cold faces and scrubbing their bronze eyes and mustaches with tooth powder. Venya Volkov always tried his hardest. Cleaning the apartment had been his chore since he was seven, and his mother assiduously checked the quality of his work.

Once, noticing a white spot under Stalin's eye—tooth powder—she'd slapped the boy's cheeks. He was ten at the time.

He wasn't surprised at the punishment. He considered it wholly deserved. But for the first time he was struck by his mother's perfectly calm, indifferent face. Methodically dealing those ringing slaps, she stared into her son's eyes and repeated, "There are no accidents in life. There's always an intention behind carelessness. Carelessness is a crime."

Lots of his classmates were beaten by their parents, but it was mainly the fathers doing the beating—on a bender, or hungover, or if the kid just turned up at the wrong time. Fathers spanked them or used their belts. And the mothers, as a rule, interceded.

Venya Volkov was beaten by his mother, but always on the cheeks, with the flat of her hand, so it didn't hurt. His cheeks just burned afterward. She never did it because she was drunk or angry. She didn't drink at all. She was always sober, even-tempered, and calm. His father didn't intercede. He was very quiet and unremarkable, as if he weren't there at all. He worked as an engineer in a bread factory, where he spent days on end, and sometimes even nights. His mother never beat Venya in front of his father, not because she was afraid, it was just that his father was so rarely at home. And Venya didn't tell his father anything.

He never told anyone anything.

His entire paternal upbringing came down to one line, repeated endlessly, like a mantra: "Your mama is the purest, most principled person in the world. She's a saint. Everything she does is for your good. You should be proud of your mother and obey her in everything."

His mother was the Communist Party secretary at the same bread factory. She was always elected deputy to the City Council, and her photograph was displayed in the central square, on the "City's Best" honor board.

He obeyed her but he wasn't proud of her. Someone who gets his cheeks slapped at least twice a week is hardly going to be proud of anything or anyone. Now, sitting in his small, smoke-filled office,

Veniamin Volkov, head of the Culture Department of the Tobolsk Young Communists Committee, a tall, blond, and skinny twenty-six-year-old, was gazing at the papers spread out on his desk, and, for the umpteenth time, replaying one of the most painful scenes of his childhood.

. . . It was an icy Siberian February with penetrating, stinging winds. Venya had forgotten his gym uniform and was running home for it between classes.

Venya flew through the blizzard. He was afraid of being late for gym because his teacher would be sure to note it on his record.

His father was home with the flu. Thinking he must be asleep, Venya quietly opened the door with his key. He froze on the threshold.

Strange sounds were coming from his parents' room—the rhythmic creaking of box springs and soft, muffled groans, a man's and a woman's.

Venya tiptoed up and peeked through the cracked door. Two naked bodies were writhing on his parents' bed. One belonged to his father, the other to their young neighbor, Larochka, a twenty-year-old library student. Venya had heard she was home with the flu, too.

This Larochka from the apartment across the way, a small, pudgy little brunette with a turned-up nose and merry dimples, had long provoked a strange feeling in Venya that he couldn't make sense of or define. He ran into her every day. Once as they were leaving the building, he for high school, she for library school, she patted the boy affectionately on the cheek in passing as she ran lightly down the creaking wooden stairs.

She smelled of sweet, cheap perfume, and her round, brightly lipsticked little mouth was always a little bit open, as if ready to spread into a delighted smile. Her large snow-white teeth shone wetly, and her two front teeth were a little bigger than the others, which made her round little face seem funny and touching.

Venya stood there looking at the two bodies bouncing rhythmically on the bed. He saw their faces and the agonizing bliss written on them, saw their closed eyes and slightly bared teeth.

He didn't immediately realize what they were doing. At first the rhythmic bouncing reminded him of another memory, of two stray dogs copulating near the garbage cans behind the school. Only later did he realize that his father and his pretty neighbor were doing the same thing.

All the obscenities, all the mysterious, burning, forbidden conversations in the school toilets, all the anatomical drawings on walls were about this. This was why his pudgy neighbor used bright lipstick and sweet perfume, why millions of women on earth did the same, and why there were films, books, and even music about it. Heroes suffered for their love, schemed, shot themselves, went crazy. For the sake of what? For the sake of this ugly rhythmic twitching? For the sake of this filth?

And this and only this was where children came from.

But the worst was the sudden tension in his groin. A searing, almost tingling pain filled his lower belly, and Venya went as taut as a string. A minute later he felt something wet and sticky in his underpants.

He came to his senses out of revulsion for himself. The two on the bed were busy with what they were doing and didn't notice him. It all lasted no more than five minutes, but to Venya it seemed an eternity.

Trying not to breathe, he dashed for his room, changed clothes quickly and silently, neatly folded his soiled trousers and underpants, and stuffed them under his pillow.

Fifteen minutes later he was in the locker room. He hadn't forgotten his uniform and was just a little late—the bell hadn't rung yet but his classmates had already changed for gym class.

The head of the Culture Department of the Tobolsk Young Communists Committee tore his light, transparent eyes from the papers spread on his desk and looked out the window. The day was clear and sunny. Birch leaves tinged with bright yellow grazed the window, trembling ever so slightly in the warm wind. The birch grew right under his window. It was very old. Its thick, rough trunk had blackened as if charred.

There were lots of trees in Tobolsk, most of the buildings were wooden, and the fences were made of thick, unhewn timber. They didn't spare the forest—there was taiga all around. The city park, almost as dense as the taiga, began at the banks of the Tobol and receded into the distance, becoming utterly primeval. In the daytime there wasn't a soul; in the evening, not a single light.

"Veniamin, are you going to dinner?" Galya Malysheva, the instructor from the next department, asked as she glanced into his office. She was young but quite stout, with a bad wheeze.

He startled, as if caught red-handed.

"Huh? Dinner? No, I'll go later."

"Always working. You're our businesslike one." Galya grinned. "Watch out, you'll get so skinny no one will marry you." Laughing at her own joke, she closed his office door and Venya listened as her heavy steps receded down the hallway.

I really should go have dinner, he thought, and he tried to remember the last time he ate. Yesterday morning probably. He could barely force a bite down at the time. He knew that in the next few days, if he did force himself to swallow any food, it would take colossal effort. But he had to eat something, otherwise he'd pass out from hunger. And insomnia.

The fits had been getting more frequent. They used to come once a year and last no more than a couple of days. Now they happened every three months and lasted nearly a week. He knew it was only going to get worse.

First, a dull, hopeless sorrow would come over him. He tried to fight it, coming up with all kinds of things to do and ways to entertain himself—he read, he went to the movies. It was all useless. Sorrow grew into despair, and an acute self-pity came to the throat of the obedient little boy no one loved.

Previously, he had blocked his despair with a few vivid pictures from the past. He knew the root of his illness was there, in his dark, icy adolescence. So was his medicine.

Fifteen-year-old Venya never told anyone about what he'd seen at home on his parents' bed. But after that blizzardy February day, he started looking differently at his parents and at himself. Now he knew for sure that everyone was lying.

He'd never had much to do with his father before, and he was used to viewing him merely as a gratuitous and pointless attachment to his strong, powerful, and respected mother. Now this justification of her maternal cruelty dissipated.

He'd often heard his father say, "Mama knows best. Your mama loves you very much and does everything for your good." Venya himself would repeat it like a spell: "This is for my good, so I'll grow up strong."

Never once did his mother pity her son, even when he was sick or when he scraped his elbows or knees. "Pity belittles a man!" Never once in her life did she kiss him or pat his head. She wanted her son, the grandson of the legendary Red commander, to grow up strong, without any sloppy endearments. Now Venya knew, though, that she simply didn't love him.

He realized that the only reason his mother slapped him, arranged weeklong boycotts, and said such mean things in her calm, icy voice was because she liked being in charge, she liked humiliating and torturing someone who was weak and defenseless.

Now, though, he knew an important adult secret that concerned his mother, not as a Party leader or the perfect Communist but as an ordinary woman who was neither very young nor very attractive. No Party committee or public opinion could help. Here she was defenseless.

He could hurt her whenever he chose. That finding out about her husband and young neighbor would hurt her, Venya had no doubt.

But he said nothing. He carried this shameful adult secret inside himself with care and a pounding heart. He observed with particular vindictive satisfaction each time his sweet little neighbor respectfully greeted his esteemed mama, and as his mama, out of Party habit, shook the soft little hand of her pudgy rival, not even suspecting she was a rival.

The secret tried to come out, but he realized it was a single-use weapon. Tell it, and it's not a secret anymore. But he was dying to tell, if not his mother, then one of the three most closely bound to the secret. He was dying for the fun of someone else's fear, a grown-up's fear.

One day, he couldn't help himself. Meeting his neighbor on the staircase he said softly and distinctly, straight to her face, "I know everything. I saw you and my father."

"What do you know, Venya?" The neighbor raised her narrow eyebrows.

"I saw you in the bed when you were . . ." He wanted to say the well-known obscenity but couldn't bring himself to.

Her gentle little face fell a little, but it wasn't the effect Venya had been expecting. Sure, she was frightened, but not very.

"I'll tell my mother everything," he added.

"Don't, Venya," the girl pleaded quietly. "That won't make it easier for anyone."

In her round brown eyes he was suddenly amazed to discover pity. She was looking at him with sympathy. This was so unexpected that Venya lost it. She didn't fear him, she pitied him.

"You know what?" the girl offered. "Let's you and me talk this all over calmly. I'll try to explain it to you. It's hard, but I'll try."

"Fine. Try."

"Only not here, on the stairs," she said, suddenly realizing. "If you want, we can go for a little walk, as far as the park. Look what nice weather."

The weather really was marvelous, a warm May twilight.

"You see, Venya," she said while they were walking toward the park, "your father is a very good person. So is your mother. But she's too strong, too harsh for him. Every man wants to be strong, so you shouldn't judge him. You're smart, Venya. Life is full of surprises. If you're afraid I'm going to wreck your family, that's not my intention. I just love your father very much."

She spoke and Venya listened in silence. He couldn't figure out what was going on inside himself now. His head was spinning from her sweet perfume. A small blue vein was pulsing on Larochka's milky white neck.

"If you tell your mother, she won't forgive him. Or me. She just doesn't know how to forgive, that's why being with her is so hard for your father. But you have to learn how to forgive, Venya. There's no living without it. I understand, at your age it's very hard."

There wasn't a soul around. Larochka was so carried away, she wasn't looking where she was going. Thick roots of old trees poked up out of the ground. The girl tripped and went sprawling on the grass. Her checked wool skirt hiked up, exposing the edge of her nylon stockings, her pink garters, and her soft, creamy white skin.

Venya collapsed on her with all his whole strong, greedy fifteen-year-old flesh. He started doing to her what his classmates had talked about in such juicy detail, what he'd seen his father do to her that blizzardy February day on his parents' bed.

Larochka cried out, but he managed to cover her mouth and nose with his hand. She kicked and writhed under him and started to choke. Not letting her breathe, let alone cry out, he managed to turn her over onto her back and hold her trembling, clenched thighs down with his knee.

She resisted as hard as she could, but Venya was large, a head taller than his pudgy little victim. Not for nothing did he get top grades in gym; not for nothing was he the school gymnastics champion. He could do fifty chin-ups in a row and had already passed his army physical.

He was actually surprised at how easily and quickly he managed it all. After he got up and buttoned his fly, he glanced at the sprawled, practically trampled body on the grass. In the thickening twilight he could see the red traces of his fingers on her gentle little round face. For a fraction of a second he thought that she might have died. But right then, as if in response, he heard her weak, pathetic moan.

"You'd better not tell anyone," Venya said calmly. "That won't make it easier for anyone. You have to learn how to forgive, Larochka. There's no living without it."

He turned on his heel and strode off quickly for home.

Before going to bed he washed everything he was wearing—his trousers, flannel checked shirt, warm knit jersey, even his underpants. His things seemed permeated with the smell of sweet, cheap perfume.

A few days later he heard that Larochka had dropped out and signed up for the Virgin Lands Program. Soon after, her elderly parents, their neighbors in the apartment across the way, vanished as well. People said they'd moved to another town, maybe even Tselinograd. But Venya ignored the talk. He didn't care.

CHAPTER 3

Moscow, March 1996

Katya Sinitsyna was woken up by the long and persistent doorbell. She discovered she was lying on the rug in the living room, wearing a raggedy robe thrown over her naked body.

"Mitya!" she called out loudly. "Have you gone deaf or something? Can't you open the door?"

She stood up and staggered into the front hall. The bell kept ringing. Without turning on the light or asking who it was, Katya opened the front door wide. It was unlocked.

"Why all the racket? Can't you see it's open?" Katya, displeased, asked the man standing on the threshold.

Entering and shutting the door behind him, the man flicked the light switch, took Katya's face into his hands, and looked carefully into her eyes.

"Katya, child, you shouldn't be alone right now," he said gently. "Go get washed and dressed and come to our place."

Only then did Katya wholly wake up, stare at her unexpected visitor, recognize her father-in-law, Mitya's father, Mikhail Filippovich Sinitsyn, and burst into tears.

"Yes, child, you cry." He stroked her cropped reddish hair. "That will help. Olga can't cry at all, neither can his mama or grandmother, and I still can't. My insides are burning up, they're on fire, but the tears just won't come."

"Just a minute." Katya freed herself from his hands, sniffed, and wiped her tears with her fist. "If you'll wait here, I'll go get dressed." She pointed to the low bench in the front hall, slipped into her room, and slammed the door behind her, right under Mikhail Filippovich's nose.

He wasn't offended. The front hall was fine with him. How could he expect civility from this poor little girl after what she'd been through? You could see she was in a dreadful state. Everyone was in a dreadful state. Did those niceties amount to anything?

Mikhail Filippovich tried as hard as he could not to think about his son. What had happened seemed like an absurd, impossible nightmare. He still hadn't seen his son's body. He drove the image of it from his mind. The brief sentence, "Mitya hanged himself," seemed like a prank, someone's evil joke.

He'd gone to get Katya because he didn't know what to do with himself, didn't know how to be, how to fill the time until the funeral. More than that, he truly felt very sorry for the girl. She was practically an orphan, a fragile, defenseless creature. There wasn't anyone to think about her, to care for her. Olga had taken on all the details of the cremation. His wife and mother-in-law were wandering around the house like shadows, cleaning, since they'd decided to hold the wake at their place rather than here, in Vykhino. His grandsons were at school all day.

A cremation, a wake—who was it all for? Not for his Mitya, his handsome, talented, kind little boy. They couldn't even have a church funeral. No priest would read the service for a suicide.

His Mitya was gone. He'd killed himself. But why? Why had he done this to himself and all of them? How had they wronged him—his parents, his sister, his wife Katya?

Mikhail Filippovich believed he knew his son and had a fairly good sense of him. Since early childhood, Mitya had been an open and sincere boy. He'd had none of those emotional black holes that might help explain this inconceivable act.

Pulling on jeans and a sweater, Katya wondered whether she should shoot up now, beforehand, or if it would be better to bring a few pills to take later. Lately, the pills had had practically no effect. No high, but coming down was easier. On pills she could hold out, make it through to the next needle. At this moment, she didn't care; she could shoot up there, too, without even hiding in the bathroom. What difference did it make now? Sooner or later, they were going to find out. The cops or someone else would tell them. Not Olga, of course. But what was the point in hiding it now? If Mitya was gone, did it matter that his wife was an addict? Katya didn't even notice she was thinking about herself in the past tense, as if she too were gone.

She remembered six months ago when her husband's sister had turned up without warning. Mitya had gone somewhere for a few days. Katya no longer cared where he went. He'd told her, of course, but she forgot instantly. He's gone. Fine.

Naturally, the apartment was a disaster: dirt, bottles lying on the floor, cigarette butts floating in the sink, music blaring. And Katya staggered around in the same raggedy, soiled robe, high.

There were only two bottles, Privet and Absolut, but both were empty. Katya had decided to have a one-woman party. She hadn't stepped foot out of the house for three days, shooting up and drinking, drinking and shooting up. When Mitya was around, she wouldn't let herself unwind like that. It wasn't until later that she stopped caring altogether, but then she had still kept up appearances around him, trying to let him hold on to the hope that she wasn't entirely on the needle, just partly so, as if that were even possible. But the minute he left, she was off on a bender.

And now—holy shit! Olga the businesswoman, as large as life, the Fury in a business suit was in her home. She dragged Katya into the bathroom, put her under the shower, and, sadist that she was, turned on the icy-cold water. Then she forced her to drink two cups of strong coffee.

"How long has this been going on?"

"A year," Katya admitted.

"What are you shooting up?"

"Whatever I can get."

"Show me what you have."

Katya showed her the ampoules, but only the empty, used ones. There wasn't anything written on them, but Olga wrapped them up neatly in a plastic bag, and then a handkerchief, and put them in her purse.

"You buy it from whoever you can, yes? On the Arbat and in the subway at Pushkin Square? Any debts?"

"No," Katya said with something like pride.

"Of course." Olga nodded. "I give Mitya money, and you take it from him. It turns out I'm working for your drugs. Any pills?"

Katya went into the bedroom and returned with an empty Haldol pack. Olga put it straight into her purse.

"Tomorrow I'm taking you to a doctor. You'll check into the hospital. Don't be afraid, it's a good hospital, not like the one before. You'll stay as long as it takes, until you're completely well."

"There's no such thing as completely well," Katya noted cautiously. "That doesn't happen."

"Yes, it does. So far you're still doing this alone, you're not on the streets, you haven't picked up AIDS. Or have you?"

"Olga, stop it!"

"Well, let's just say you've been going in that direction for a long time. Anyway, this isn't about you, it's about Mitya."

"Olga, I do love him very much."

"I know you love him. Lord, if I'd found you here with a guy, this would be much easier for me, I can promise you!"

"No, I'm not cheating on him!" Katya was offended. "I don't need anyone but him. Mitya's all I think about, all the time. I feel like garbage and I'm so ashamed for you to see me like this. You have to forgive me, Olga!"

"We'll talk about forgiveness another time. For now, remember this. My parents, to say nothing of my grandmother and my sons, can't know anything about this. You're going to the hospital for female troubles." Olga grinned bitterly. "We'll tell them this is the last hope for curing your infertility. Don't worry, I'll take responsibility for the lying. Right now, you're going to put this pigpen in order so that you're ready tomorrow. I'll come by and take you to the hospital myself. Understand?"

Katya understood everything, and she stayed in the hospital for nearly two months. It really was a nice hospital. She had a private room with a television. The doctors and nurses were polite and attentive. But they were using the same treatment methods Katya had tried so many times before. Just as she'd expected, they were just as torturous and ineffective as she remembered.

Katya fell off the wagon less than two weeks after checking out. It just happened.

For some reason, six months later, she recalled that conversation with Olga more distinctly now than she did the events of last night and early this dark morning.

The day had fallen apart into loose, cloudy pieces that flashed before her eyes like snippets from an old film: Mitya's bare feet on the kitchen floor, his still-warm, big, heavy but pliable body, the dull scissors that couldn't cut his thick leather belt. And the cold. The cold was what had woken her. Her blanket had slipped off and the window was wide open. And the night was very cold.

Katya wasn't the least bit surprised that the latch on the window frame in the bedroom had broken, since it had been hanging by a single screw for a long time. Mitya hadn't gotten around to fixing it, which wasn't good when you lived on the first floor and the window didn't shut properly. Actually, Katya didn't give a damn. They didn't have anything worth stealing anyway.

Early in the morning the window thudded and opened wide from a sharp gust of wind. Katya woke up and closed the window. Only when she returned to bed did she discover that Mitya wasn't next to her. She called out to him. Her teeth chattering from the cold, she went into the front hall and saw in the kitchen doorway . . . No, better not to remember.

For some reason the phone wasn't working. Her sleepy, frightened neighbor in curlers and nightgown couldn't understand right away what was wrong or why Katya was asking permission to use her phone at five in the morning.

Then there were the police, and the doctors, and the questions that were so hard to answer. She was ashamed and frightened. Her thoughts kept getting scrambled and her tongue wouldn't work. The cops weren't in the mood to go to much trouble. It was suicide, plain and simple. The ambulance doctor turned back the sleeve of Katya's robe and snickered. She tried to explain that Mitya had never used drugs, but they wouldn't listen or understand.

And Mikhail Filippovich was still waiting in the front hall. Why wouldn't she let him into the room? Her instinct had taken over, her fear of Olga: *"My parents can't know anything."*

Katya came out of the room in relatively decent condition. She hadn't shot up, but she'd brought her pills and tossed a couple of ampoules and a needle into her purse.

Of course, she should also have washed up, combed her hair, and brushed her teeth. Never mind. It didn't matter now.

Interior Ministry Colonel Sergei Krotov's beige Zhiguli had been stuck in a hopeless traffic jam on the Garden Ring Road for nearly forty minutes. The wet snow that had been falling lazily since early evening had turned into a real blizzard. There weren't that many cars at that hour, but there'd been an accident somewhere up ahead, near the Mayakovsky subway station, and there was nowhere to turn off anywhere nearby, and now the whole herd of cars was honking impatiently, waiting for the traffic cops to sort out the mess.

The warmth in the car and the rhythmic movement of the wipers across the windshield were lulling. He could barely keep his eyes open. For the past few days, Sergei had gotten very little sleep. In two days he was supposed to go to England. Scotland Yard had invited a group of Interior Ministry associates for a three-week exchange. Before leaving he had to get through a mountain of cases so high it made his head spin.

The morning of the day before yesterday, he'd handed materials in to the Prosecutor's Office on the preliminary investigation into a shoot-out at the Vityaz restaurant in a Moscow suburb. It was the usual gangland fracas, but of the seven dead, two turned out to have worked for the Interior Ministry. That was why the case had been dumped on domestic counterintelligence and the department Krotov ran.

Ten days ago, there'd been a fancy banquet at the Vityaz. A famous criminal, Pavel Drozdov, otherwise known as Thrush, had been celebrating his forty-fifth birthday. The restaurant had shut down two days before the banquet in honor of the occasion, and Thrush's men had checked every nook and cranny of the dining and banquet halls, bar, kitchen, sheds, toilets, and director's office. A security specialist placed men around and inside the building, an over-the-top cottage with gingerbread trim.

The guests assembled, but before they could eat the cold appetizers, thugs armed with submachine guns burst into the banquet hall. The painstakingly and professionally placed guards didn't help. Not all the guests had time to pull out their guns, and five were taken out right there. First to be killed was Thrush himself, followed by the two men from the Interior Ministry.

What made this so troubling for the authorities was that those Ministry men, a major and first lieutenant, were attending the party as invited guests, and the nature of their friendship with a criminal like Thrush was revealed only after their untimely end.

Another important detail: a witness to the slaughter. He'd been invited to the restaurant to provide entertainment. Friends had once seen Thrush weep as he listened to a recording of one of Azarov's smash hits, "Farewell, My Faithless Love!" and they'd decided to give him this touching performance as a gift.

At the moment the young thugs burst into the hall with their submachine guns, Yuri Azarov was standing on the small stage with a guitar singing the second verse of Thrush's favorite ballad:

Hush, my sorrow, my last sorrow, sleep tight!
Farewell, Svetlana, my green-eyed love.
It's jail for me, and lonely prison nights,
The stars of Magadan are twinkling up above.

He managed to jump off the stage and, using his guitar as a shield, roll under a table and lie there, holding his breath through the entire attack.

The pop star had performed for an audience of criminals on more than one occasion, but this was his first time witnessing this kind of slaughter. He considered it a miracle he'd survived. He was trembling from horror, and it was almost impossible to get a coherent statement from him. The audience favorite demanded protection, demanded to be put in a bunker, and insisted that Parliament immediately pass the kind of witness protection laws that all normal countries had.

The case was solved quickly, though, and two days later Krotov handed all his materials to the prosecutor. Three of the five surviving thugs were in jail. When the story of the dead police officers' involvement was teased out, it turned out to be all too banal. Thrush had kept them loyal to him not through blackmail or fear but simply with money.

This morning it had become clear that the singer's fears were justified after he was found dead in the apartment of his lover, twenty-year-old model Veronika Rogovets.

At nine in the morning, Veronika went to take her Irish setter, Willy, for a walk. At the time, Azarov was sleeping in Veronika's bed. The model usually combined the dog's morning walk with her mandatory half-hour run through Victory Park.

Returning home at 9:35, she found her apartment door unlocked and Yuri lying crosswise on the entry floor with a terry-cloth robe over his naked body. The singer had been shot clean through his skull, and the Walther pistol that produced the deadly shot was lying right next to his corpse. No fingerprints other than Veronika's and the dead man's were found anywhere in the apartment. The neighbors had heard a mild thud but thought nothing of it at the time, and couldn't even say exactly when it happened.

For now just one thing was clear: the murderer had been able to enter Ms. Rogovets's apartment quietly and unnoticed. It seemed likely that he had keys to the front door and possibly to her door as well. The lock on the door was Italian, the latest model, and virtually impossible to pick. And no pick had touched the lock.

That is, either Azarov himself opened the door for his killer, or else the killer had a key to the apartment. The former scenario was more likely because at that time of day Azarov was usually sound asleep, and if the killer had opened the door with his own key, Azarov would have been shot in bed. But instead he was lying in the entry by the front door, which evidently meant he'd been woken by the bell, thrown on his robe, and gone to open the door.

Naturally, the sensible and simple thought that came to Krotov's mind was that Azarov was finished off by friends of the thugs he'd given testimony against. Thus part two began in the successfully completed preliminary investigation into the Vityaz shoot-out. Krotov's superiors said he needed to look for leads in the banquet slaughter.

Misha Sichkin, the senior investigator, had a different opinion. He and Krotov knew from experience that these kinds of obvious theories led nowhere. The singer's murder may easily have had nothing at all to do with the Vityaz massacre.

Krotov felt guilty that he was going to be strolling through London while Misha Sichkin had to conduct this complicated and nasty investigation. Their work involved very few simple or pleasant cases.

The traffic jam on the Ring Road gradually eased up, but the blizzard was in full swing. Finally turning on to Krasin Street, it occurred to Sergei that it was probably real spring in London right now. For the first time in his life he was going abroad—and not just anywhere, but to England.

As he drove up to his apartment building and parked his car, he caught himself thinking that he already missed his family, even though he hadn't left yet.

He'd been married a little more than two years. Sometimes these twenty-five months of family life seemed like one long happy day, and sometimes he felt like he'd known his wife, Lena, a very long time. No one in the world was closer or dearer to him than she was.

Sergei was forty-two now, Lena thirty-six. At their ages it was hard to feel like newlyweds, but they had—for more than two years.

Before they met, they had each had a taste of both family life and of loneliness. Lena had been married twice; Sergei once, for twelve years with his first wife, Larisa.

He had no children from his first marriage, which was probably for the best. His life with Larisa had been so difficult and dreary that even their rare holidays had become like onerous, dismal obligations for Sergei. All those years, the feeling never left him that when he walked across his own threshold and saw Larisa's face and heard her voice, he instantly detached—on purpose and in advance, so as not to react to his wife's constant complaints, big and small, and her frequent and long hysterics.

For many years Sergei racked his brain trying to figure out why it was so hard for him with Larisa. After all, she had lots of good qualities. Larisa was an excellent housewife, and their apartment sparkled with an almost sterile cleanliness. Though she kept herself on a strict diet because she was a professional ballerina, if guests came to their house, she went all out and made kulebiaka, julienne salad, suckling pig in sour cream, and sweet yeasted cakes. More than just a great housewife and hostess, she was practical, smart, and attractive.

Sergei convinced himself their problems weren't about him or Larisa, but about family life as such. By its very nature, he reasoned, a married life couldn't be a happy life. He sincerely believed that everything would be just the same with any other woman, so he didn't divorce Larisa until things became utterly intolerable, until the terrible mutual hostility was strangling them both. Sergei decided on divorce. Larisa raised a fuss for a while but eventually agreed.

Only much later did he realize that it wasn't about family life as such at all, but about the simple fact that he didn't love Larisa. And she didn't love him. Each expressed this in a different way. Larisa would become irrationally jealous, aggressive, and confrontational, and Sergei would maintain a gloomy silence and stay late at work even when there was no need to.

A year after the divorce, he met Lena Polyanskaya. He'd thought he'd never remarry and would live the rest of his life a bachelor. Lena had no intention of marrying, either. She'd had plenty of bitter experience from two marriages. She was pregnant by her second husband, whom she'd only recently divorced. She intended to raise the child alone. When Sergei and Lena met, though, all their plans for a future of proud solitude dissipated like smoke. The two mature, sensible, life-battered people fell head over heels in love. They met and married almost immediately, without giving it too much thought or questioning, as if they were trying to make up for the lost time with each other.

No one but the two of them knew that two-year-old Elizaveta Sergeyevna Krotova was not Sergei's biological daughter. But that didn't matter to either of them. Neither Lena nor Sergei was surprised that the child resembled her father much more than her mother. Not the father who sired her, but her real father, Sergei Krotov.

They themselves didn't notice the resemblance right away, though those close to them did. In the maternity home, when Krotov came to take Lena and his daughter home, the nurse who handed him the baby said, "A chip off the old block!" Later their friends and neighbors would repeat the same thing, and so would the mamas who took their children for walks at Patriarch Ponds, and the doctors at the pediatric clinic. Sometimes some well-wisher might start playing with Liza and say, "Why do you have blond hair, little girl, when your mother's hair is so dark? Why, you don't look at all like Mama."

Lena had dark brown, almost chestnut hair and dark, smoky-gray eyes with dark eyebrows and lashes. But Liza had come out blond and blue-eyed, the spitting image of Krotov, only without his trademark mustache.

Now, nearly two, it was clear that her personality, even her facial expressions, were like Krotov's.

"When I met you I didn't immediately see where it was going," Lena once admitted. "I was still overthinking, doubting. But Liza was sitting in my belly, and it was all perfectly clear to her about you and me. I worried, why hadn't I met you sooner? But Liza just went and got born looking like you. We got a little Krotov."

"Curious." Sergei shrugged. "Who else is our child supposed to look like?"

"At least a little like me," Lena sighed.

"That's all right, our next child will look like you," Sergei consoled her.

⚜

As soon as it became clear that Sergei was going to London, Lena forced him to study English every day for at least half an hour. At one time Sergei had known English at a high school level, but by age forty-two he'd managed to forget it all. Lena knew the language perfectly. She made flash cards for him, put them in all his pockets, and demanded that he practice them every free minute he had. But he had way too few free minutes, and his head was filled with very different things.

Only now, walking into his building, did Sergei remember that he hadn't so much as looked at a single card all day and hadn't memorized his ten assigned words. He was already preparing himself to go to bed an hour later. Lena worked like a dog all day, too, but she forced herself to memorize her daily quota—ten new words—by midnight.

"You can't imagine how awful it is to be in a foreign country without the language," she said. "The interpreter won't be leading you by the hand from morning till night. He's there for the whole group, after all. What if you just feel like walking around the city, stopping at a café or a store, and you can't say anything besides 'how do you do'? No one expects Oxford pronunciation, and you don't have to know a gerund from a modal verb. But you have to have the conversational minimum."

In the mailbox, besides a couple of ads for rowing machines and cosmetics, Sergei found a thick, long envelope addressed to *Mrs. Elena Polyanskaya, Russia, Moscow* . . . with a New York return address.

Lena got letters from America fairly often. In the past six years she'd gone there four times to give lectures at Columbia, or Brooklyn College, or the Kennan Institute. She had friends and business acquaintances in New York, Washington, and Boston.

When Sergei gave Lena the letter, she tossed it on the refrigerator distractedly without even opening it. And she didn't ask to quiz him on his English. She was pale, very tired, and untalkative. Sergei immediately sensed that something was wrong.

What he feared most was Liza getting sick. That was the only thing he truly feared.

"Lena, darling, did something happen?" he asked, putting his arms around his wife.

"Not to us," she answered quietly. "Liza's healthy and so am I. Don't worry. Have something to eat and relax. I'll tell you all about it later."

While Lena was heating up his supper, Sergei tiptoed into the nursery. Liza was asleep, curled up cozily. He kissed the warm brow under the blond bangs oh so lightly and straightened her blanket.

"Papa's here . . ." Liza said loudly in her sleep, and she sighed and turned over.

There was a meal of steaming cabbage soup, sauerkraut, and pickles on the kitchen table—everything he loved.

Lena was reading, perched on the little kitchen sofa. Sergei was surprised to discover that a forensic medicine textbook lay open on the table in front of her. He knew she was translating some article about serial killers for *Smart*, but he was still surprised.

"Lena, darling, why are you working so late?"

"Please, help me," she asked, preoccupied. "Can you tell for certain from the strangulation mark whether it was made when the victim was alive or if the person was first killed and then hanged? They list lots of signs here, but it doesn't say how accurate they are."

"At first glance, of course, no," Sergei replied, starting in on the soup. "But if you're looking for it, you can tell. You need a specific analysis of the skin in the area of the mark."

"Do suicides ever get investigated for possibly being staged?" was Lena's next question.

"Maybe you can tell me what happened so I can better help you?"

"All right." Lena slammed the textbook shut. "Remember about a month ago when Olga Sinitsyna's brother Mitya came to see us? You came home from work early and he was sitting here in the kitchen."

"Yes." Sergei nodded. "A real deadbeat. He talked so long I lost my pulse. He even left a cassette of his songs."

"He hanged himself last night," Lena said softly. "The police and the ambulance doctor say it's a clear suicide, but Olga doesn't believe it. There really is something very odd about it."

"Well, suicide is always a very odd thing. And relatives always want to think the person didn't do it himself. It used to be the prosecutor came out for each and every body, but now there aren't enough of them. But if there were something to it . . ."

"Seryozha, I'm not attacking the honor of the uniform or saying your colleagues are hacks, but I would like you to hear me out."

"Fine. I'm listening." Sergei finished his soup and lit a cigarette.

"First of all, for some reason Mitya's telephone was out for days. Olga had been calling him since yesterday morning and put her phone on auto redial. Then she clarified that there was nothing wrong with the line; something had happened to the phone itself. His neighbor fixed it in five minutes and said that some contact had been broken. This hadn't happened in three years, and then it did, at just this time."

Lena recounted every detail of what she'd learned from Olga.

"Lena, darling, I understand," Sergei said gently after hearing her out. "Sinitsyna is your good friend, and it's very hard for her right now, and you're worried about her. But believe me, in five cases out of ten, suicide comes as a total surprise, especially for the relatives. He might have been shooting up, like his wife, only no one knew it, or he might just have gotten drunk out of grief."

"What grief?" Lena grinned sadly. "That his wife was an addict? That grief was a year and a half old. And people don't hang themselves over that. And he was not shooting up, that's for sure. He loved Katya very much. He worshipped her. They were a terrific couple. They'd been together five years, though they couldn't have kids because Katya had some medical problem. And then the drugs started. He fought for her the best he could. His parents didn't know anything, only Olga. She put Katya in the hospital, but it didn't work. But Mitya wouldn't give in. He was constantly looking for addiction specialists, hypnotists, psychotherapists. He was proactive, he had no intention of giving up. Suicide would be admitting defeat, it would be giving up. No, he couldn't have hanged himself over Katya being an addict. And there was no other reason, either."

"Lena, how would you know why a person would hang himself? Sometimes someone loses everything in life, loses himself. One outcast exiled to Siberia who doesn't even have the right to touch a doorknob gets kicked every day, fucked in every orifice, and forced to lick spit, yet he lives, he clings to life with every fiber of his being. Another is doing just fine—great family, job, friends, respect, money coming in—and bam! He kills himself. You know yourself that the countries with the highest standard of living have the highest suicide rates: Sweden, Denmark, Holland. But where there's famine, war, and real hardships, people rarely kill themselves. Well-fed Roman patricians slit their veins. Here in Russia, at the end of the last century and the beginning of this one, suicide was positively a fad. Putting a bullet in your head was considered a handsome, noble deed. You think they were all idiots, madmen? That some tragedy had befallen them?"

Lena shook her head. "No, I don't. Although . . . there's a certain inner pathology to it. And Mitya had no pathology. He was a healthy young guy. Talented and loved by all as well."

"Fine." Sergei sighed. "Let's say he didn't do it. Let's say someone even had a motive to kill him. Think about it, though. Big bankers, political party leaders, and other powerful men of this world are being shot out in the open these days, without a second thought, shot on the streets and in the lobbies of big hotels. And who was Mitya Sinitsyn? Who would go to those lengths to kill *him*? Do you know how much a hitman costs? And afterward a professional would have finished off the wife, too. What did they need a witness for?"

"What if that's exactly why they didn't finish her off? Maybe that's just what the killer was thinking. After all, he had to be very smart to set it all up so well. If she was an addict, then she didn't see or hear anything. I understand it's a dead end. I understand that intellectually, but I can't believe it. Something's off."

"Lena, when a healthy young man kills himself, something's always off. It's fundamentally wrong. I'll gladly believe he wasn't drinking or shooting up, wasn't on the books at the psych clinic, and was an altogether remarkable person. And I'm very sorry for your Olga. If she wants, she can write a statement to the Prosecutor's Office."

"She will." Lena nodded. "But what's the point? They already gave her the predictable explanation for it. They can't even hold his funeral in a church. There are his parents, and his old grandmother, and each of them is wondering why he did it. Each is trying to find a reason and are blaming themselves. Mitya was the youngest, the baby. They loved him and spoiled him. Can you imagine what they're all going through right now? Olga's not about to look for the murderer, of course, but still, she needs to know for certain whether he did it or not."

"She can hire a private detective. She can afford it, after all."

"She might," Lena said pensively.

CHAPTER 4

"Veniamin Borisovich, the Butterfly duo is still waiting for you," his elderly secretary, dressed in a pink wool suit, told him.

"No." He shook his head. "Tell them to come the day after tomorrow. Even better, Monday at eleven."

"Veniamin Borisovich, you've been putting them off for more than a month. Just take a look at them. They're pretty girls, I promise."

Butterfly—the two eighteen-year-old singers Ira and Lera—had in fact been coming for more than a month to audition, but he never had the time or energy for them.

In forty days they'd managed to give his secretary, Inna Evgenievna, everything from big boxes of Mozart chocolates to the latest Chanel perfume. The secretary accepted these offerings with casual benevolence, as if she were doing them a favor. It all vanished immediately into her desk drawers, where it was instantly forgotten.

Only today did it occur to the blonde, Ira, who was sharper and more practical, just to slip three bills—US hundred-dollar bills—in a white envelope into Inna Evgenievna's jacket pocket.

"Veniamin Borisovich, you do know I have a practiced eye," his secretary persisted. "They're unusual girls. Just take a look at them. There's demand for their type."

"All right." He sighed. "Bring me coffee. Have them come in. Only directly to the stage, and warn them there won't be any lip-syncing."

"Veniamin Borisovich! What lip-syncing?" Inna Evgenievna took offense on the duo's behalf. "So far they haven't done anything but live shows."

"Age?"

"Eighteen. Both."

"Where from?"

"Moscow."

"Fine, call them in. Only get me that coffee quick, and make it strong."

Auditioning novice performers was the hardest and most thankless part of his job. Every time, sitting in the small auditorium of the district's former House of Pioneers, he felt like a tired and grubby prospector stubbornly panning ore in search of the smallest flecks of gold. When those rare flecks did come his way, though, they paid him back with interest for the exhaustion and the bad voices and the tired and tiresome tunes.

He'd bought this late eighteenth-century, two-story private home in the very center of Moscow three years ago. He hadn't scrimped on renovating and furnishing the wooden, almost rotten merchant's home that had miraculously survived the 1812 fire. Now he had his office, sound studio, and editing room here. Even music video producers sometimes worked here.

The house's insides were entirely new, and the walls had been rebuilt altogether. Inside, everything gleamed the way the studio and office of a billionaire's production company should. But there was one room Veniamin Volkov wouldn't let anyone touch.

In the last two centuries, the largest room in the house had served as a drawing room for the former owners, the Kalashnikovs, Moscow merchants who traded in textiles. In the 1930s, the house became the district House of Pioneers, and the former drawing room had served as its auditorium. Drama and dance clubs had used it right up until the early 1990s.

A varnished, time-dimmed barre ran along the walls, which were bedecked with bugles, banners, and other Pioneer symbols. Two little steps, smoothed over the years by thousands of children's feet, led to the small plank wall. Behind the stage there was a tiny, windowless room that still contained parts of plywood stage sets.

He wouldn't allow anything in that room touched. It was here that he did his hardest, most exhausting work.

Once upon a time, a very long time ago, in another life, fifth-grader and Pioneer Venya Volkov got up on the same kind of wooden stage and sang the Civil War–era song "Far Away, Across the River" to the accompaniment of an aged, out-of-tune piano. That was in the Tobolsk House of Pioneers, not the Moscow one, in a similar old merchant's home, in an auditorium with bugles and banners covering the oil-painted walls.

For the seven minutes the song lasted, thirty boys and girls in the small hall were listening just to him, looking just at him, plain, skinny, towheaded little Venya.

He was singing for just one little girl, fifth-grader Tanya Kostylyova. He put his heart and soul into that song as he looked at Tanya's gentle, slightly elongated face, at her slender, defenseless little neck wound round with a red silk tie. At the time, he didn't understand what those feelings were or what the dense, unbearable fever that filled his whole body would later lead to.

He sang the intensely sad melody perfectly, not garbling a single note. At the time, thirty years ago, he didn't understand anything about himself, but now he suddenly thought that it would have been better if back then, right on that creaking wooden stage, he'd been struck dead, instantly and painlessly, without finishing the pretty little song. Yes, that would have been better for him and for the slender-necked fifth-grader in the silk tie—and for many, many others.

"Veniamin Borisovich!" his secretary's voice called sweetly.

She deftly rolled in a tall mahogany serving cart with a big, heavy ceramic mug on it. Venya couldn't stand small, delicate teacups. He drank his coffee strong and sweet with lots of heavy cream. He liked his coffee and his mug substantial.

Two pretty young things in tight blue jeans were already on the stage. Butterfly. He hadn't even noticed them come into the room. For a few seconds he scrutinized them silently. They really were no more than eighteen. One was a cropped blonde, a little plump, with soft, heavy breasts under a thin sweater. The other was a skinny brunette with straight, shoulder-length hair. The blonde was definitely sexier, but in a conventional way. The brunette was more interesting. There was something unusual about her, her high forehead, the arrogant slant of her eyes, her slender hands. Yes, you could sense the thoroughbred in her. Inna may have been right. The combination could be interesting—a standard and overt sexuality alongside something else entirely, an unexpected novelty, a thoroughbred.

Frames of possible videos automatically flashed through his head. *Have I really lucked out?* he thought with cautious excitement, and said, nodding kindly, "Begin, girls. There won't be any accompaniment or mic. For now. Sing your first song standing still. Just sing. Is that clear?"

They waited silently. This was exactly how he always started an audition. What he cared most about were their faces and their voices. You could always add choreography later. Without dances, accompaniment, or a mic, it was terribly hard to perform the pop junk these boys and girls usually brought him. He knew that alone with the empty, meaningless words, a performer was basically naked and defenseless. You could see all of him.

None of his colleagues, his former competitors, bothered with anything this tedious. They made money not on people who could sing but on people who were anxious to see themselves or their wives, children, or lovers in a professionally produced music video. There were plenty of takers for that. Success didn't come from the performer but from the money behind him. You could turn a telegraph pole into a household name—given the right amount of money.

Veniamin Volkov had never succumbed to the temptation of fast, easy money. Everyone else did business for the present, with no thought for the future. For everyone else, the decision was easy: better a thousand right now than a million next week. When it's all dirty money, there's no guarantee you'll live to the end of the week anyway.

Consequently, Veniamin Productions was the only entertainment company that created genuine stars. To make a star, you have to have quality raw material. Other producers turned shit into candy, sickly-sweet lemon drops that made even the Russian consumer's teeth crumble and his belly ache. Veniamin Volkov spared neither time nor effort in creating his stars—and he wasn't afraid of taking risks. He understood that if there were nothing but butts flashing across the television screen, the public would eventually want to see the occasional face.

Standing onstage, arms at their sides, the girls sang some typical garbage, most likely of their own composition, in thin but pleasant voices. He wasn't really listening. He examined their faces and tried to tell whether he could sense the delicate aura of success.

Success in his business was an unpredictable thing. The public's taste can't be calculated using logic, but it can be divined. It just took a special talent. Which Veniamin Volkov liked to think he had. He'd worked long and hard to get to this point, through blood, mud, and mob shoot-outs. He'd stepped over others so many times, he could relax now and enjoy his success.

Smoking, sipping his thick, sweet, creamy coffee, he was annoyed to realize that these girls were just the latest fluff. There wasn't a whiff of success about them. He might get a decent video out of it if he played on the contrast of types, but to do that he'd have to train them for a long time. They weren't worth the effort.

"Thanks, that will do," he interrupted the song, clapping softly.

They broke off in the middle of the beat.

"Veniamin Borisovich, can we sing you one more song?" the blonde suddenly suggested loudly.

"No, that's enough. I know what I need to know. You can go, girls."

"Just one verse, please," the blonde insisted. "Two minutes."

"All right, go ahead." He couldn't be bothered to drive them away, and they clearly weren't going to leave without singing their verse.

Never leave me, springtime . . .

The skinny brunette's voice was lower and deeper. She started, and then the blonde came in. The ballad by Kim from some 1970s movie was beautiful and sad. But that wasn't important now.

Golden days, if only you would last . . .

He lowered his eyelids. It was very pleasant. Something came to him from far away. A campfire on a steep bank, a June morning, the dawn's delicate fog hanging over the river like torn lace, the dense city park, and a melody:

Never leave me, hope!

His heart beat harder. His hands got hot, burning hot. Blood pulsed hotly in his temples.

Two young women, a vivid, plump blonde and a skinny, thorough-bred brunette. A sex kitten and a stray dog.

When nightingales and streams
Sing so joyously, so gently . . .

Soon they would notice how hard he was shaking. Pretty soon he would get up, walk toward the stage, and go up the stairs. His right hand instinctively squeezed his Parker pen with the sharp gold nib. The cap was already off, and the pen lay on his open planner. A very sharp nib.

The girls were carried away with their singing and didn't notice how red in the face he was, how his right hand was shaking the pen it clutched. Fourteen years ago, to the sounds of this very song, he had forced himself to stand up and quickly escape into the swelling darkness of the city park that transitioned smoothly into taiga.

He stabbed the pad of his thumb on the sharp nib. It pierced his skin deeply, but he felt no pain. His blood mixed with the black ink.

"That's enough," he said in a muffled voice, trying to stop his teeth from chattering. "You can go. Leave!"

When they'd left, he walked quickly to the tiny room behind the stage where the dusty, broken-down stage sets from the Pioneer drama club's shows were stored. Without turning on the light, he locked the door from the inside and stayed there in the dusty darkness, which smelled of old paint, for nearly half an hour.

His secretary glanced cautiously into the empty auditorium, saw the door to the room shut, and tiptoed away. Her boss had quite a few eccentricities.

In the funeral chapel at the Archangel Nicholas Mortuary, there were loud, heartrending sobs. Katya Sinitsyna rushed toward the open casket and kissed her husband's icy-cold hands.

"Mitya! Dear Mitya! Forgive me!" she cried.

"Hurry it up, please. We have another funeral in this room after this one." The mortuary employee, a striking redhead in a flawless black suit and white blouse, frowning in irritation, whispered to Olga, who was standing nearby.

A Bach organ fugue poured out of hidden speakers. Olga walked over to Katya, took her by the shoulders, whispered something in her ear, and tried to lead her away from the casket. Two young men, Mitya's friends, approached to help, but Katya wouldn't let her husband's dead fingers go and continued sobbing loudly.

Lena Polyanskaya was standing nearby with Mitya's eighty-year-old grandmother, Zinaida Lukinichna. Up until that moment the old woman had put on a brave face. But Katya's sobs were the final blow, and she began sinking, slowly and heavily. Lena barely managed to catch her.

"Zinaida Lukinichna," she asked her softly. "What is it? Your heart?"

"No, child," the old woman whispered in reply. "I'm just dizzy."

Olga had asked Lena to come to the funeral specifically for her grandmother's sake.

"I'll be with my parents," she had explained. "And his wife is probably going to break down. And it's up to me to organize everything. Please forgive me. I know your Seryozha is leaving for England, but I can't entrust my grandmother to anyone but you. I'm afraid for her, given her age. And you've always had a calming effect on her. She's always had a soft spot for you."

"Dear relatives," the funeral home employee said loudly, glancing at her watch. "Anyone who wishes to say good-bye to the deceased, please do so now."

Members of the next funeral party were peeking impatiently through the room's half-open door. Behind them would be others, and others, and so on, from morning till night. A conveyor belt of death.

Lena thought that you have to have a special emotional profile to work with death, with daily, even hourly, grief. She imagined this red-headed woman drinking her morning tea or coffee, putting on makeup, setting out for work, and returning home in the evening. She wondered whether she discussed her day with her family, her husband and children. Did she share her feelings? Did she even have any feelings about her work anymore?

What am I going on about? Lena pulled herself up irritably. *A job's a job. Someone has to do it. There are lots of professions that bring you in constant contact with death and grief. Over and over, my own husband has to go look at dead bodies. Then there are the medical examiners, the ambulance doctors, the paramedics, the gravediggers, and the people who work here, behind the mortuary's black curtains. What makes this elegant woman any different from an ordinary person, other than the fact that each workday she has to pretend, to depict grief with her face and voice, and to utter perfunctory words of sympathy?*

The investigator investigates murders, the medical examiner examines dead bodies, the ambulance doctors and the paramedics try to save the injured and dying, the gravedigger digs the grave, and the people behind the curtains mind the oven. But the redheaded woman just stands from morning to night, feigning sorrow, hurrying some along, inviting others in.

"Lena, child, help me go to him," Zinaida Lukinichna asked her.

Supporting the old woman by the elbow, Lena carefully led her to the casket. Zinaida Lukinichna stroked her dead grandson's blond curls with her wrinkled hand, kissed his lifeless brow, and made the sign of the cross over him.

"Citizens, it's time!" the redhead's voice announced from the back of the room.

"A little longer, please." Olga quickly slipped another bill into her hand.

"What can I do?" the lady said, more softly now. "There are people waiting."

Lena had never seen a suicide's face before. She was surprised that Mitya's face was calm and untroubled, as if he'd just fallen asleep.

"Lord, forgive him. Lord!" Zinaida Lukinichna whispered. "He knew not what he did . . . My grandson, my Mitya, my baby. I'll try to pray away your sin, my child, my grandson . . . My dearest Mitya . . ."

Lena put her arm around the old woman's trembling shoulders.

Lord, I'm not made of iron, either, she thought.

Right then, her eye fell on Mitya's large, strong hands, with the fingers of a professional guitarist. She noticed a few fine scratches on his right arm. It looked like Mitya had been hurt right before he died. What could he have scratched himself on? Something fine and sharp. A needle!

Looking more closely, Lena noticed several fine wounds between his fingers and on his wrist. Yes, they were definitely needle marks. The policemen and doctors had noticed them and had immediately told Olga, "Your brother was an addict." But why were the needle marks on his right hand? There wasn't anything on his left. Mitya wasn't left-handed. That Lena knew for sure.

"Lena dear, will you come by our house now, at least for an hour?" Zinaida Lukinichna asked once the casket slid behind the black curtains.

No! Lena wanted to say. *I can't. My husband's leaving tonight, I haven't seen my daughter since early this morning, I have piles of work, and all this is hard for me. I want to get home as fast as I can.*

"Of course, Zinaida Lukinichna," she said.

There were lots of people at the Sinitsyns'. Relatives had taken care of the funeral table. As the guests took their seats, they tried to move the chairs as quietly as they could and spoke in low voices.

Katya had another loud breakdown.

"Lena, take her out to the stairs, I beg of you," Olga whispered. "Go out with her and smoke. Let her shoot up quietly there. I can't take this."

Lena was shocked by Olga's suggestion to let Katya shoot up. Ultimately, Katya had lost a husband, a partner she'd spent eight years with, and it was Katya herself who'd had to pull him out of the noose. You couldn't ascribe her emotional breakdown to drug withdrawal alone.

"Here's her purse." Olga handed her the worn leather bag. "It's all there. Do it quickly! Gleb's already picked up on something."

It was true. Thirteen-year-old Gleb, Olga's older son, was already standing in the doorway and listening closely to their conversation.

"Ma, Katya's doing really bad. Maybe we should call a doctor?"

"We'll manage without a doctor." Olga cut him off. "Now go to your room and don't hover."

Two minutes later Lena was leading a sobbing Katya by the arm out onto the stairs. When the front door closed behind them, Lena took out a pack of cigarettes. It's not the easiest thing to tell a woman you barely know that it would be acceptable for her to shoot herself up with heroin.

Katya took a greedy drag—and only then noticed her own purse hanging from Lena's elbow. Her eyes dried up and flashed.

"Katya," Lena said gently, "could you hold off a little longer?"

The question sounded silly. This was neither the time nor the place to get Katya off drugs, but she still couldn't bring herself to actually suggest that someone shoot up.

"If you don't like looking, you can turn away," Katya said and nervously licked her lips. "Don't worry. I'll be quick."

"Fine." Lena sighed. "Only let's go up and stand between floors, at the windowsill, otherwise the elevator will come up and someone might see."

"If you like, you can stand here and I'll go up," Katya offered.

"Yes, that's better." Lena didn't have the slightest desire to watch her shoot up.

It was only a few minutes before Katya came back down the stairs with a calm, almost placid face. Some color had even returned to her cheeks.

"Can I have another cigarette?" she asked.

Lena held out the pack and noticed a few fine, light scratches on Katya's birdlike hand. There were dots on her swollen, blue veins . . . Only it was her left hand.

"Katya, tell me, please, when did Mitya manage to scratch his arm?"

"His arm?" Katya blinked, not understanding. "Which arm?"

"I don't remember which one," Lena lied. "I just noticed he had scratches on his wrist."

"You think he was shooting up like me?" Katya asked with a perfectly calm voice and released a stream of smoke in the direction of the elevator.

"I don't think anything. I'm just asking. It doesn't matter anyway."

"No." Katya shook her cropped head. "It does. Mitya didn't shoot up. Ever. Not once in his life. He detested drugs. It's all my fault he's dead, but there was nothing I could do. I couldn't give him a child, I kept asking for money, and he put up with it because he loved me."

Lena got scared that she was about to break down again, despite the drugs she had only recently shot up. *It's time for me to go home,* she thought sadly. *Seryozha will be back from work soon, he'll pick up Liza from Vera Fyodorovna's, and they'll be waiting for me.*

"Katya, why do you shoot up in your wrist instead of your elbow?" she asked, and then immediately wondered why she'd asked. *What difference does it make? Why should I care?*

Katya silently rolled up her sweater sleeve and showed Lena the bend in her elbow, which was dominated by a large, puffy black bruise speckled with brown scabs. Lena suddenly felt pity for this skinny little girl, now utterly alone, who no one in the world cared about.

Katya's parents lived somewhere in the Far East, Khabarovsk maybe. They had long since divorced, her father was a drunk, and her mother had a new family and no time for Katya. Lena remembered Mitya telling her all this once, in some long-ago conversation. At the time she was happy for him. He absolutely beamed talking about his dear Katya. He really did love her very much.

Now no one cared about this unfortunate addict. Olga wasn't going to have anything more to do with her. She'd only done so for Mitya's sake.

"How did it start for you?" Lena asked quietly.

"After my third miscarriage," Katya told her calmly. "Before that, I didn't even drink or smoke. Mitya and I wanted a baby so badly, but it didn't work out. After the third miscarriage they told me that was it, it would never happen. That's when I got into junk. Someone I knew felt sorry for me and suggested I give it a try—to stop the pain and forget everything. I thought I'd do it once and that would be it. Just to forget."

"Did you?" Lena asked.

"We've had our little talk. That's enough. I don't give a damn about any of it. I'm nobody to you and you're nobody to me. What business do you have prying? I'm scum, a user. You're a decent woman. You have a husband and child. What? You thought you'd take pity on me? Sympathize? I'd prefer money. Olga won't give me any now. After the funeral I'm out on my ass. I'll be lucky if they don't kick me out of the apartment. In her place I would. She was the one who bought us the apartment."

I can't take any more! Lena thought. *This is straight out of Dostoyevsky, in the worst way. That's all I need, Smerdyakov with a syringe!*

"Fine, let's go back in," she said, and she rang the bell.

Olga's younger son, blond, blue-eyed Gosha, eleven and a half years old, opened the door.

Late that night, in her quiet, empty apartment in Vykhino, Katya Sinitsyna stood under a hot shower in panties and a T-shirt. Tears streamed from her eyes, mixing with the hot water. She was so tired from crying, but she couldn't stop. Only now, back from the funeral, did it hit her what had happened.

Mitya was gone. Who cared about her now? Her stash was going to run out very soon, and she wasn't going to be able to get any money for more. If Olga didn't drive her out of the apartment, she might try renting one room or selling the apartment and buying a smaller one. No, it would never work. The apartment was registered in Mitya's name, and Olga had probably done something to make sure Katya couldn't sell it without her consent. She was nobody now. She didn't even have anyone to call since all her friends were Mitya's.

For some reason she was dying to call someone, anyone, to hear her own name through the phone. There was only the noose for her now. But that was too scary. Scarier even than her loneliness. This way at least her soul remained. Here you suffer, but afterward your soul can rest.

Who'd she been talking to recently about her immortal soul? Someone nice, kind, good . . . of course! Regina Valentinovna! Why hadn't she thought of her sooner?

Katya turned off the water, pulled off her wet clothes, wrapped a big towel around herself, slapped her bare wet feet to the kitchen, sat down at the table, lit a cigarette, and picked up the phone.

For a second her gaze rested on the thick gas pipe that passed over the kitchen doorway, and once again Mitya appeared before her, dead. Her heart hurt. It boomed. Shaking her head, Katya drove away the vision and dialed the number.

"Regina Valentinovna, forgive me for calling so late."

"That's fine, Katya. I wasn't asleep. You've had a very hard day. I was expecting your call."

"Really?" Katya rejoiced. "Maybe we can do a little work right now?"

"Certainly, child. We should!"

Closing her eyes, Katya began speaking into the receiver in a strange monotone.

"Mitya's gone. I didn't realize it until now, when I came back from the funeral and was totally alone. Being alone scares me. Olga might throw me out of the apartment. I have no money. I have nothing. I even asked Olga's friend for money today. We went out onto the stairs to smoke. Olga realized I needed to shoot up, so she sent this Lena out on the stairs with me.

"Lena started feeling sorry for me and asking questions. She even asked whether Mitya had shot up. How could she think that about him?

She saw some scratches on his arm. He was lying in the casket, and she noticed the scratches."

"Lena Polyanskaya?" the voice in the receiver asked cautiously.

"I think it's Polyanskaya. I don't remember exactly."

"Was it unpleasant for you talking with her?"

"Yes. I said that if she was so good and wanted to pity me, I'd prefer she give me money. Now I'm ashamed. I have the feeling I'm going to start asking everyone for money soon. I've got some ampoules left, but they won't last me long. I'm afraid I won't be able to take it."

"Yes you will, child." The voice in the receiver was calm and kind. "Go on, please."

"Then there was a meal. It's all pretty foggy. I don't even remember who brought me home. I just have this bad taste in my mouth from having asked a stranger for money. Mostly I'm afraid I'll start asking others. And also, it hurts when people think badly of Mitya. I know, I know for sure he wasn't shooting up. But that woman saw the scratches on his arm.

"She was with their grandmother the whole time at the funeral. That old woman is a rock. She didn't shed a tear. They're all rocks. No one was crying over Mitya but me. Olga thought I was hysterical because I needed a fix. She doesn't even understand how someone can cry over losing someone. All she cares about is that her precious children don't notice anything, that no one knows I shoot up.

"It's always like that with them. As long as everything is proper on the outside, they couldn't care less what's really going on. I'm a human being, after all. No one felt sorry for me. And now no one loves me.

"They have everything, and I have nothing. My father and mother don't need me, and Mitya abandoned me. He really did abandon me, and in a horrible way. He got sick and tired of dealing with me. My addiction ate up his energy. But he couldn't leave or divorce me. That wasn't his way. Lord, what am I saying?" As if coming to her senses, Katya opened her eyes and took a drag on a cigarette.

"Don't get upset, child. Whatever gets said gets said. Remember our method: you have to wrap everything bad in words, like garbage in a newspaper, and throw it out. Only then will your soul be cleansed." The voice in the receiver was soft and reassuring. "Katya, dear, you have to unburden yourself of every last detail. You mustn't forget a thing."

"Maybe I should go to church?" Katya asked suddenly. "Maybe a convent? That's better than the noose."

"Try not to get sidetracked, child. If you do, you won't be able to sleep tonight. And you need to get some sleep. That's what you need most right now, a good night's sleep. Please, continue, Katya. Polyanskaya hurt you. She noticed scratches on Mitya's arm. What else did the two of you talk about?"

"Nothing. She realized the conversation was upsetting me. She was in a hurry to get home. Her husband's flying to England tonight, and her little daughter . . . She didn't even join us at the table. She just stopped into their grandmother's room to say good-bye. The old woman had already gone to her room to lie down. I don't remember anything after that."

"Did Olga see the scratches on Mitya's arm?"

"I don't know. Olga didn't talk to me. She can barely stand my presence. It seems to me all she thinks about is why it happened to Mitya and not to me. She wishes it was me dangling in the noose. That would have been better for everyone, including me. And Olga doesn't believe Mitya did it himself. Neither does Polyanskaya, I don't think. They think someone helped him."

"Did they tell you that? Did they ask about anything?"

"Olga asked me in detail how we'd spent the day, minute by minute. But that was a long time ago, not today. I don't remember exactly when. I just got the feeling she was torturing me with her endless questions."

"And Polyanskaya?"

"Polyanskaya only asked about the scratches."

"Then why do you think she doesn't believe Mitya committed suicide?"

"I just have a feeling. It's as if they all think I'm to blame."

"Have you heard any talk? Where did you get this idea?"

"Does it really matter who thinks what?" Katya shouted into the receiver. "Let them think what they want about me and about Mitya. What's does any of it matter now?"

"All right, child. Don't get upset. I can see you're already feeling better. Now you're going to hang up and go to bed. You'll sleep soundly and sweetly. You'll fall asleep right away. You'll shoot up one last time and then sleep for a very long time. You'll sleep long and hard. You're already feeling very sleepy. Your legs are heavy and warm. You feel calm. You're going to put down the phone, give yourself a shot, and go to sleep. Sleep. A shot and sleep."

Katya walked to the front hall on limp legs and found her purse lying on the floor. Right now all she could think about was that she had a needle and ampoule in that bag. There was one there, another two in the desk drawer, and three more on the bookshelf, in the case from Mitya's old electric shaver. The case was on the bookshelf, and there were three more ampoules there. Katya remembered that precisely, but nothing more.

She was very sleepy, and her eyes kept shutting, like a doll placed on its back. The needle wouldn't go in where it should, and she scratched her skin, but it didn't hurt at all.

CHAPTER 5

Tobolsk, October 1981

On the dusty stage at the city's Pioneer Palace, a dance ensemble was finishing its number, "Russian Quadrille." Boys in yellow silk Russian shirts and girls in boots and blue sarafans dashed gaily across the stage, arms akimbo, stamping loudly to the recorded music.

Fat Galya Malysheva, the propaganda instructor, couldn't keep from tapping her foot to the beat and, in a whisper, joining in with the rollicking song about how much fun and what important work they were doing in the factory and on the collective farm.

"Galya, quit it!" Volodya Tochilin, the arts instructor, elbowed her. "We are the official city commission, after all. Behave accordingly, like Veniamin over there."

Veniamin Volkov was sitting and looking at the stage with a stony face, as befits a member of an official city commission who's come to watch the rehearsal for the holiday concert celebrating the anniversary of the October Revolution.

"You have a terrific ensemble!" Galya whispered loudly, slapping her broad knee. "You should send them to Moscow! Abroad, even, to Karlovy Vary. Hey, Comrade Culture Chief, you should encourage young talents!" She winked gaily at Volkov.

He didn't respond. He didn't even turn his head. He couldn't tear his eyes from the stage.

The soloist's nimble feet were flying across the stage. Her narrow feet, in soft dance boots, barely touched the floor. Several of the girls in the ensemble had artificial braids pinned on that were a slightly different color from their own hair. But the soloist's braid was the same color as her own thick, shiny, and ash-blond hair. The bodice of her blue sarafan tightly swathed her delicate waist, and her wide skirt fanned over her long, slender legs.

Venya saw before him a flushed, slightly elongated, pretty little face with merry, bright blue eyes. The girl was about sixteen.

"No, you absolutely must send them to Moscow for some competition!" Malysheva couldn't restrain herself from exclaiming. "Talents like this are wasted in this backwater!"

"Yes, our Tanya Kostylyova is a diamond in the rough," the Pioneer Palace director sitting next to her said, nodding proudly.

The music ended. For a second, the children onstage froze in their final, triumphant poses. There weren't more than ten people sitting in the auditorium. Everyone started applauding. Everyone but the Culture Department chief, Veniamin Volkov. He sat without stirring, intent on the blue-eyed soloist. Her name thundered in his ears: *Tanya Kostylyova. Tanya Kostylyova.*

"You're some kind of savage, Volkov." Galya shrugged her pudgy shoulders. "You could at least put your hands together once!"

"Russian Quadrille" was the concert's last number. Now the Young Communist Commission was supposed to go to the Pioneer Palace director's office to drink tea and discuss the concert program.

"Well, what do you say?" the director asked as he sat at the head of a table generously spread for tea. "Help yourselves, comrades. The tea's hot. Veniamin Borisovich, how do you like your tea? Strong?"

The dead don't rise up, Venya thought, nodding mechanically at the director. *I haven't lost my mind. It's all very simple. Tanya Kostylyova had a brother. I think his name was Sergei. That Sergei could very well have a daughter that age. He could very well have named her in honor of his dead sister Tatyana. There's nothing surprising in the girl looking so much like that Tanya. Nothing surprising at all.*

"Veniamin, are you unwell?" the elderly director of the dance ensemble asked quietly. "You're very pale."

"Huh?" he caught himself. "No, no. I'm quite all right."

You can't do that. You have to get a grip, he thought, smiling hard. *Or it could end badly.*

"A marvelous concert," he said loudly. "And the dance ensemble was especially fine. Galya's right. We have to take them to the provincial competitions, maybe even to Moscow. The chorus isn't bad at all, but I think that in addition to the revolutionary and Pioneer songs, they could add a cheerful children's song, especially when the younger group performs. As for the poetry reciters, their outfits should be fancier. You've got them too stiff. It is a holiday concert, after all. Those are all my notes."

After tea, the director accompanied the commission through all five floors of the palace. The director showed them the holiday preparations and the concert posters.

A deafening wave of rock and roll struck them as they passed by the auditorium door, which was ajar. Glancing in, they saw Tanya Kostylyova onstage. Wearing her brown school uniform, without the black pinafore, she was dancing a wild dance to an Elvis Presley song. Her partner, a tall, slender boy in navy school trousers and a checked shirt, was spinning her and tossing her around. Her loose, ash-blond hair flew straight out to the sides and fell on her slender, flushed face. The girl stuck out her vivid lips and mechanically blew the hair from her forehead.

"I hope you're not planning to include that in the concert program," Volkov said to the Pioneer Palace director, grinning.

That other Tanya, the soloist's aunt, had been a great dancer, too. She had had bright blue eyes and long, thick, ash-blond hair. She'd been considered the prettiest girl in their class. And Venya Volkov had been an ugly duckling until the tenth grade, when all that changed.

He grew three inches in one summer. His shoulders broadened and his voice dropped. He started shaving. He was amazed to discover that girls were giving him the eye.

Among his classmates, it was the worst students who had that kind of success. They were colorful, manly, brave. They smoked, drank port, spat, swore nonstop, and feared nothing and no one.

The best students and goody-goodies were despised. And Venya Volkov was both. But he was very strong physically and he could push back at anyone who tried to bully him. By tenth grade, no one dared challenge Venya. He fought too well.

Vovka the Dove had lost Tanya in a card game. Not a school boy, Vovka the Dove was an honest-to-God crook just out of prison. He'd been lying in wait for the girl one evening in a dark side street. Venya Volkov just happened to be nearby.

At that point, nothing had happened. Tanya and the Dove were standing and talking. Venya immediately recognized the slender silhouette and long braid.

Whenever he looked at Tanya, his mouth dried up and his hands instinctively balled up into fists. At twelve he hadn't been able to explain it, but now, at sixteen, he was sure he understood his own feelings perfectly well.

Had anyone told him, "Volkov, you're in love with her!" he would have laughed in the idiot's face. There are no such feelings. They don't exist. There's instinct, attraction between the sexes, like in all the rest of the animal world. It's like hunger, only stronger.

"Venya! Venya Volkov!" Tanya's voice sounded scared and pleading.

He took a step in their direction. The Dove's huge paw lay on Tanya's shoulder. Before he could even think, Venya had already thrown that paw off her skinny shoulder, and a minute later the two were locked in a cruel and silent fight.

The Dove fought desperately but was physically weaker than Volkov, and less agile and evasive. Rather quickly, Venya had laid the crook out flat on his back.

Now he and Tanya Kostylyova were "steadies," which at their school consisted of strolling through the streets, going to the one ice cream parlor in town, sitting in the last row of the movie house, and making out, though never daring to go over the limit, which was defined quite specifically as doing anything below the waist.

Venya understood that the "fast girls" that his classmates drooled over in the vacant lot behind the school with their port and cigarettes were nothing but the fantasies of sick young minds. When some pimply lady-killer reported on his latest conquest in a mysterious whisper, Venya could barely restrain a contemptuous laugh.

Actually, he thought about the enthusiastic storyteller, *you're as innocent as a newborn lamb. First of all, you don't have anywhere you can do that. You live in a communal apartment with plywood walls. There are five of you there in one room, and your nasty grandmother is always home. Secondly, your face is covered in pimples, and you've got bad breath. And thirdly, you're telling it all wrong. I would know.*

After his story with plump Larochka, Venya thought he knew everything.

Although he didn't live in a communal apartment or have a nasty old grandmother, he and Tanya Kostylyova had lots of problems. She had no desire to go home with him and didn't invite him over, either.

"You see, Venya," she would say, "I like you a lot. But there's a time for everything. First we need to get to know each other properly. Better we just go for walks and talks for now. And what if your mama comes home from work unexpectedly? Don't be mad, but I'm a little afraid of her. She's so strict, so proper."

Winter wasn't a great time for walks through a Siberian town, though. Sometimes they warmed up at the movies, sometimes in entryways. Every time he was alone with her, Venya greedily sunk his mouth into her soft, salty lips and tried to get his hot hands—hot even in bitter cold—under her rabbit-fur coat and thick knitted sweater. She resisted, but only for show.

"Stop it, Venya. Come on, stop," she would say, pressing her entire body to him and raising her lips for a kiss.

Sometimes he hated it. She was lying, pretending she didn't want to be touched. She purposely aroused him, tortured him, made him gasp and pant. He started hating her in those moments, and he wanted to hurt her, so she would kick and squirm in his hands, the way pudgy Larochka had. He often dreamed of falling on Tanya, pressing her to the ground, and ripping her clothes.

Sometimes he was horrified even in his sleep. He was burning inside from a hard, animal hunger. He felt that if he didn't satisfy it, if he didn't hurt Tanya Kostylyova, hurt her badly, he'd burn up inside, and he'd die.

Everyone around them thought it was love between him and Tanya. So did she. Only Venya knew that in fact he hated his girlfriend.

He was waiting for spring and warm days when they could go for walks in the evenings in the park above the Tobol River. The more trusting and tender Tanya was with him, the more powerfully he hated her. If someone had asked him why, he wouldn't have been able to say. And he had no intention of answering this sensible question for himself. His hunger was more important than the answers to any questions.

He was waiting like an animal before it leaps, patiently enduring Tanya's blind acceptance of social ritual and her belief in the stupid fairy tales about true love and till death do us part. Intuitively, he was afraid of spooking this silly, romantic girl.

"Venya, do you love me?" she would ask in a whisper.

"Yes, Tanya, I love you very much," he would say with a sigh in her pink little ear.

"Venya, you're the best, the strongest, and I love you so much." Her blond head buried itself in his shoulder, and her hand gently squeezed his hot fingers.

Spring came late to Tobolsk, but was always stormy and swift. The ice broke on the Tobol and the Irtysh majestically. On clear days, sunlight fractured the large, slow-moving ice floes, which splintered in the heavy, dark water, and sometimes a vivid rainbow would shimmer at the cracks.

Then came the high waters. The two Siberian rivers, which flowed together in the old town, would leave their banks and, together with the first real May rains, wash away the last remnants of snow. But in the taiga, there could be snow in low-lying areas as late as June.

Right up until their graduation night in late June, Tanya Kostylyova continued to play games with Venya. She refused to go for long walks with him to the park above the Tobol.

"You're so worked up, Venya," she would say, lowering her bright blue eyes. "We won't be able to stop ourselves. And what if I get pregnant? It's too soon for that. We're still children. We have to continue our studies."

There was a lot of vodka at the graduation party. Hiding from their vigilant teachers, the students took turns drinking, shutting themselves up in the chemistry office. The girls drank less, sipped at the glass as it went around the circle, made a face, and quickly took a bite of black bread.

"Is that any way to drink?" Volkov laughed, giving Tanya back the full glass she'd barely even touched. "Take a normal swallow. Graduation only happens once. Come on, drink to my health. You're not a little girl anymore."

Tanya gave in. She'd never drunk vodka before. She was happy, her exams were behind her, and she'd aced them all. It was a time to celebrate, so she should have a drink.

She screwed up her face and knocked back half the glass. Her throat was squeezed by a stinging spasm. The vodka wouldn't go any farther.

Tanya started coughing. Venya stuck a piece of bread and pickle in her mouth. Chewing helped right away.

"Well, did that go down well?" Venya smiled, took the glass out of her hands, and finished the remaining half.

They danced a little more in the auditorium and then quietly ran off to the park. The night was warm and clear. In the mysterious summer silence, the mosquitoes were buzzing, and the old cedars' thick trunks creaking. Using Venya's arm for support, Tanya took off her fancy patent leather shoes and walked barefoot through the nighttime dew.

They kept walking farther along the banks of the Tobol under a full moon. A wide, layered column of moonlight swayed gently on the calm river water. There wasn't a soul around.

"Venya, I'm really drunk," Tanya said gaily. "My head's spinning. Why did you make me drink that horrible vodka? I'm never going to drink again."

"How about a swim?" he suggested. "You'll sober up in a flash."

"But I don't have a bathing suit."

"What do you need a bathing suit for? It's a high—skinny-dipping."

She laughed. "But the water's cold."

He pulled her close and started feeling around for the zipper on her graduation dress.

"Have you lost your mind? Let me go!" She tried to slip out of his arms.

The zipper jammed; a lock of her hair from her long braid got stuck in it. He pulled as hard as he could.

"That hurts! Venya, what are you doing?" Tanya did manage to break away, but only for a second.

He immediately put his arms around her and threw her down onto the wet grass.

"Venya, Venya dear, stop . . ."

Quickly and deftly he pulled off her dress and just as he did with Larochka, he put his hand over her mouth and nose. She started moaning and jerked her head. He felt the warm breath from her nostrils under his hand.

He pressed his hand harder to her face. She kissed his hand and then pushed it off her face.

"Venya, stop, I can't breathe like that. Kiss me," she whispered.

He started greedily kissing her long neck and delicate collarbone. Her skin smelled not of cheap perfume but of lily of the valley and slightly bitter pine needles. Venya's heart started pounding, and he could feel how fast and hard her heart was pounding, too.

It's going to be just like it is for everybody else. My hunger will pass—these thoughts raced through his head. *She's very pretty and she loves me . . . I'm a normal boy, and it's all going to be just like it is for everybody else.*

But a black film fell over his eyes. His body wouldn't obey his will. His hands were living their own, independent life, and he didn't understand what they were doing.

"Quit it. That hurts!" Tanya cried out suddenly.

His hands couldn't stop. They squeezed her small, firm breasts, and his nails dug into her delicate skin.

"Venya, quit it! That hurts a lot!"

She was shouting too loudly. Her shout grated on his ears.

"Easy, easy . . . It's supposed to hurt," he said quickly. "It always hurts."

"No, I don't want it this way. We shouldn't. You're crazy." She attempted to break away. He didn't even notice his hands crushing her delicate neck. She tried to break away from his hands, tried to knee him. It was like combat between two enraged beasts fighting not for life but for death.

With the tiniest corner of his receding human consciousness, Venya understood that this was exactly what he'd wanted, exactly what he'd been expecting.

Tanya Kostylyova was stronger than Larochka. He had to wind her graduation dress, which was lying nearby, around her head. The dress was made of a thick white Crimplene that didn't let air through.

The body beneath him jerked and fought back. A wave of acute, wild pleasure washed over him. It felt as though some new, blinding, invincible power was rushing through him.

A massive shudder ran through the girl's body, piercing him through like a flash of lightning. He felt himself getting stronger now with every movement and every sigh. He felt almost immortal as he satisfied his fierce, animal hunger.

He didn't know how much time had passed. Satiated, he came to his senses, rolled up the white Crimplene dress, and in the light of the moon saw two frozen, vividly blue eyes looking straight at him.

That scared him. Was this really what he'd wanted? Was this the only way he could feed the insatiable beast in his soul? Tanya wasn't breathing, but the satisfied beast could at last take a deep breath.

The blinding strength pouring into him now was the life of Tanya Kostylyova. This and only this was how he could satisfy his hunger. There was no other option. It was her own fault. She'd teased and tortured him for so long. She'd ignited the hatred in him, played her vile, hypocritical, romantic games with him.

He felt hot, bitter tears running down his cheeks. He cried out of compassion—not for the girl he had murdered, but for himself, the obedient little boy who no one loved and everyone lied to. The tears made him feel better. His head cleared.

Quickly looking around, he pulled up the panties on her still-warm body and fixed her bra. He mechanically noted that her underwear wasn't ripped, and he had left no bruises—at least, none he could see in the moonlight.

He neatly hung Tanya's white dress on the trunk of a fallen birch and set her patent leather shoes nearby. Undressing and leaving his own things on the trunk of the tree, he dragged her body to the river, pushed it in the water, jumped in himself, and swam leisurely to the middle of the river, where it was deep, pulling the body behind him.

Lots of people drowned in the Tobol, especially the good swimmers. Usually they had to search a very long time for drowning victims because the current carried them toward the broad Irtysh and there was solid taiga stretching along the banks. Sometimes they were never found.

When he finally climbed out onto shore, his teeth were chattering from the cold. Without dressing, in just his underpants, he started toward the park exit. He walked very quickly and then started to run.

A wet and trembling Veniamin Volkov—graduate of School No. 5, top student, the quietest and most obedient boy in his class—ran into the police station. He had only his underpants on, tears were rolling down his cheeks.

"Help!" he yelled. "Please, help! Tanya's drowned! We were swimming together, and it was dark, and we were talking, and then she wasn't. I looked over and she wasn't next to me. I dove and searched . . ."

He couldn't go on.

They found Tanya Kostylyova's body two weeks later, far from the city, in the Irtysh.

The Young Communist Culture Department chief remembered he'd left his cigarettes in the office of the Pioneer Palace director. Returning, he heard music coming from the auditorium. It was a song from an old American movie. Tanya Kostylyova was doing a leisurely Russian step dance on the stage. Her slender partner was assiduously repeating every step after her.

"No, try it again! Wrong again!" she said. Her light feet in their black gymnastics shoes seemed to fly over the wooden floor by themselves, without any effort, lightly and gaily.

The dead don't rise up, Volkov thought. He softly shut the auditorium door and strode down the corridor toward the office of the Pioneer Palace director for his forgotten cigarettes.

CHAPTER 6

Moscow, March 1996

Lena packed her husband's things in a large gym bag. A van was supposed to come for him from Petrovka, as his workplace was called, in two hours. In the next room, Seryozha was attempting to put Liza to bed and was reading her the first chapter of *Winnie-the-Pooh* for the fifth time. For some reason, Liza didn't want to read any farther, and as the chapter was coming to an end, she would demand it be read all over again. She had no intention of going to sleep, even though it was already past eleven.

"Papa, Papa, Papa!" she said, sighing sadly.

No one had told her her papa was going away. She'd figured it out herself.

"I'll be back very soon," Sergei reassured her. "What should I bring you, Liza?"

"Pooh! Bring Liza Pooh!"

"You want Winnie-the-Pooh? A teddy bear?"

"Yes." Liza nodded gravely.

"A big one or a small one?"

"A big one," Liza informed him in her lowest voice and spread her arms expressively, showing him the size of the bear she wanted. "And a little one," she added after a moment's thought.

"And are you planning to go to sleep tonight?" Sergei asked cautiously.

"Papa, Papa, Papa!" Liza's lower lip jutted out, corners down. That meant she was just about to belt out a magnificent howl. The only way to avert that was to pick her up and walk her around the room. The moment Sergei carried Liza to the window and started showing her the pretty lights shining in the dark, Lena looked into the room.

"So that's how we go to sleep?" She shook her head.

"Oh, we have no intention of sleeping at all," Sergei informed her hopelessly. "Our parents are bad. They have no discipline."

"Fine, then go see how your papa's bag is packed." Lena sighed. "What if your bad mama forgot to put in something important for your bad papa?"

They checked his bag and drank tea, but Liza still had no intention of sleeping.

"Tell me, please," Lena asked pensively, "if someone—a righty—would ever inject drugs into his right arm, especially his hand?"

"Well, if there was nowhere left in either elbow bend, and if the veins on the left wrist and hand were used up, then he might try. Why?"

"There weren't any marks on his left hand, just his right. I didn't see his elbows, but I doubt there was nowhere left there."

"Is this about Mitya again?" Sergei sighed.

"Yes, Seryozha, it's about him again. For some reason I can't stop thinking about it. I noticed the scratches on his right arm and those needle marks, but later his wife assured me he'd never shot up and couldn't stand drugs. Now it's done. Mitya's been cremated. But there are the autopsy results. Olga found a way get them to do an autopsy without waiting in line. I guess she gave them a bribe."

"And?"

"And the same thing. A high concentration of something in the blood. Of what I don't remember, but it was some kind of powerful narcotic. And there were ampoules and needles all over the room."

"Do you know how many unsolved murders there are in Moscow right now?" Sergei put Liza more comfortably in his lap; she was, at last, dozing off.

"Well, I have a rough idea."

"You and I have discussed this. There's no point going over it again, especially before I leave."

"You're right," Lena agreed. "But, those scratches on his right arm trouble me."

Sergei carried Liza, now fully asleep, to her little bed. He came back to the kitchen, put his arms around Lena, and pressing his lips to her temple, whispered, "We still have half an hour left, my dear Miss Marple."

Senior Investigator Misha Sichkin decided to call in Veronika Rogovets, the model who'd been the main witness to the murder of the singer Yuri Azarov, to his office on Petrovka for more questioning.

The first two interrogations had been conducted at her home, where for some reason she insisted on walking around in a see-through negligee with nothing underneath, not even panties. *Basic Instinct*, which had been such a hit, must have made a very strong impression on her, because during questioning she behaved exactly like the thriller's main heroine, carelessly crossing and uncrossing her legs and delivering a seemingly endless stream of clumsy double entendres. When Sichkin asked her how she had spent the night of the murder, she shrugged prettily, jutted out her plump lower lip, and said, "You want to know what we were doing? Making love! I can give you details if it will help the investigation."

Misha, who'd seen all kinds of things in his day and was hard to surprise, was still a little baffled at why the young woman wasn't reacting even a tiny bit to her lover's murder—in her own apartment. She didn't care about anything other than the impression her beauty made on the people around her. She was so wrapped up in herself that she didn't even notice that her charms weren't making an impression on the gloomy investigator.

"Who besides you and Azarov had keys to your apartment?" Misha asked wearily.

"The key to a model's apartment is more valuable than the key to an apartment filled with money," Veronika spoke in a low, chesty voice and focused her languid green eyes on the investigator, waiting to see what impression her joke would make.

"Veronika Ivanovna, let's try to focus on who else might have had keys. He might well be the killer." Misha sighed heavily and lit a cigarette.

"But he already killed Yuri, so what difference does it make now?" The witness slowly batted her eyelashes.

After his conversation with the model, Misha Sichkin was dripping sweat, as if he'd been unloading train cars in one-hundred-degree heat. In summoning the witness to Petrovka, he'd hoped that the official location and the impossibility of wearing only a negligee would have a slightly sobering effect on the model.

She'd shown up half an hour late. She was wearing scarlet leather shorts, black lace stockings, and a see-through black gauze blouse unbuttoned to her navel with nothing underneath. After reading her the official warning about the consequences of giving false testimony and having her sign a document to that effect, Misha started all over again.

"How did you spend the afternoon and evening immediately before the murder?"

"I already told you. We were fucking." Veronika raised her eyebrows. "I already told you everything."

"Fine. That evening you made love with the dead man."

"Wait a minute!" The beauty raised her hand in protest. "How can you make love with a dead man? That's necrophilia! You're confused, Mr. Investigator."

"Veronika Ivanovna, I'm getting the impression that you're refusing to give evidence."

"Really?" She flashed a blinding smile. "I am answering all your questions."

"You have yet to answer a single one of my questions," Misha reminded her gently.

"What do you mean?" The model's little hands flapped in fright. "Then what have we been doing all this time?"

"What have we been doing? I've been trying to question you as a witness to a murder, and you've been staging a farce. I don't think the official investigation into the murder of your lover—in your apartment, I might add—is the appropriate setting for a demonstration of your feminine charms. It's like this, Veronika Ivanovna: either you answer all my questions, or you can write an official refusal to give evidence."

"Are you threatening me?" In the model's beautiful green eyes, Sichkin noted an icy hatred so fierce that it shook him a little. All of a sudden he realized that she was behaving like this because he wasn't reacting to her beauty. She had no control over this. For her, all the people in the world fell into two groups: those who were taken in by her beauty and those who weren't. For her, the latter were enemies, no matter the situation. That was how she was wired, and he couldn't blame her for it. But he, Investigator Misha Sichkin, was an idiot because he hadn't figured it out right away.

"Veronika Ivanovna"—Misha sighed and shook his head—"you don't seem to want to understand one simple thing. The sooner we find and arrest Azarov's killer, the sooner you, above all, can breathe easy. You're young and pretty, and you have your whole life ahead of you. But there's a killer out there who's been in your home. How do we know he won't show up one more time—to pay you a visit personally?"

"Whatever for?"

"Whatever for is a completely different question." Misha smiled enigmatically. "I'm afraid for you, Veronika Ivanovna. Here I am, looking at you and thinking there really are wonders in this world, dazzling, stunning women like you. It's offensive that nearby, somewhere very close, there's scum about, a killer capable of destroying that beauty in one stroke."

You're a poet, Misha! Sichkin congratulated himself. *Now we'll see whether she really is the idiot she appears to be or if she's just faking it. It would be better for her to be an idiot. Otherwise, she either knows the killer and has been doing everything in her power since the very beginning to keep him from getting found out, or else . . . but that can't be possible; she has a solid alibi. Several people, regular runners and dog walkers, saw her in Victory Park. And she has no motive.*

"But I really don't remember who might have the key! I'm such a scatterbrain, so forgetful. I've lost it a hundred times." Veronika smiled disarmingly.

Her icy demeanor had been melted a little by his crude flattery, but she still had no intention of answering his questions.

Fine, Misha decided. *I'll try one last angle, and if that doesn't work, I'll put a tail on her. Her refusal to answer his questions was moving her from the witness column to the suspect column. I wonder whether she understands what she's doing?*

"I understand that we're both sick to death of the subject of keys," Misha said gently, "so let's wind it up. Try to remember when you lost your keys and whether you changed the lock after that."

"I think I did. But maybe not." Veronika wrinkled her low brow, trying hard to remember. "You see, I haven't been able to focus on all those everyday trifles since I was a child. Even in school I was always forgetting everything—my notebook, my textbook. I even developed a complex and nearly went nuts. I kept being afraid I'd forgotten some shit or the other. But then I started working with a good psychotherapist, and I learned how to fight the complex. My memory didn't improve, though. I still forget everything, but now I don't give a shit."

"And what psychotherapist are you working with?" Misha smiled and leaned back in his chair.

"Oh, she's a marvelous doctor. She treats all kinds of complicated psychological complexes. She cures schizos without medicine. You know, all those psychotropic medicines, they're so dangerous, even more than narcotics. But I'm afraid she would be too expensive for you." She smiled slyly. "You were asking for yourself, weren't you?"

"You're a smart woman. You don't miss a trick. I really was asking for myself. In my work, a good psychotherapist is essential. Watch out or you'll lose your marbles. Will you give me her phone?"

"No." Veronika shook her head. "It's too expensive for you, and I doubt she's taking new patients. She's got enough work as it is."

"Oh well." Misha sighed. "I'll have to get through my poverty and misery without a psychotherapist."

You slipped, honey, he noted gaily to himself, *and now you're trying to sweep away your trail with your tail, like that fox in the story.*

"Was Yuri Azarov also seeing the good doctor?" Misha inquired casually.

"Yuri was as normal as a stump." Veronika sighed. "He could have used a little crazy, a few strong emotions, some foolish acts of heroism."

Both of them! I'm chipping away now! Misha thought. *For sure, that psychotherapist needs a good vetting before she's questioned. There's something shady about this doctor. Was she the one who prepped this doll so well for her interrogation? This could be very interesting.*

"So you like reckless acts of heroism, then?" he asked.

"Of course! Life's so boring without it. I love the broad gesture, so that sparks fly. But Yuri was a skinflint, pardon the expression."

"So maybe they killed him over debts?" Misha suggested, and he thought if she latched on to that now, then he definitely had to consider her a suspect.

"What else?" Veronika grinned. "I personally have no doubt of it."

"So why did you need him, Veronika Ivanovna, if all he had was debts? With your beauty, surely you could find someone better."

"Why did I need him?" She thought about that and touched her lips with a sharp nail. Her nail polish and lipstick were the same color— bright red. "Probably for variety," she spoke dreamily and nipped her nail.

Leaving Petrovka and sitting behind the wheel of her nice new red Zhiguli, Veronika Rogovets replayed the entire conversation with that idiot of an investigator and was pleased with herself. Regina Valentinovna had been right when she had said they were all fools in the scheme of things, and no man could resist Veronika's charms. Even that stupid cop, no matter how hard he tried to resist her, eventually succumbed to her charms and swallowed the whole yarn she spun.

The only slipup was when she'd blabbed about Regina. But she'd caught herself in time and shifted the conversation to a different topic. Regina had asked her not to mention her at all; she didn't name names and she didn't give him her phone number. It was as if Regina had a crystal ball; Sichkin had picked right up on her importance. He had a pretty good eye. It was all right, though, she'd given him the slip.

She did wonder who had offed Yuri, though. These stupid cops weren't going to find him, whoever he was. You couldn't do anything on that kind of salary. All they did was loaf and take bribes. Obviously no one had bought this Sichkin yet.

Veronika Rogovets had disliked the police since she was a kid. She hadn't had any run-ins with them lately, but she knew from experience that they were all bastards and mercenaries. The only people who became cops were newcomers from the provinces and morons. Maybe they were even the ones who had offed Yuri. After all, he'd sung at Thrush's birthday party, and there'd been two cops there. Maybe to keep Yuri from ratting them out, they offed him.

She'd done well zeroing in on the debts. That Sichkin had been happy to swallow it hook, line, and sinker. He'd be looking for Yuri's creditors now. Well, let him look!

In fact, Azarov had had no debts. He never borrowed or lent. He really was a skinflint. Veronika didn't figure that out until after their seventh date, when she asked for a diamond ring like the one Irina Moskvina had. Naturally, she could have bought herself the ring; it only cost fifteen hundred dollars. But buying yourself diamonds was a bad omen. You had to be given them or else inherit them, otherwise they brought bad luck.

Veronika knew everything about stones. At home she had an entire shelf of books about the mystic and healing properties of stones. The fact that a diamond had to be given by a lover was a fairly basic and well-known fact. Veronika had told Azarov this when she parked her car by the Princess Dream jewelry store on Tverskaya Street. You could buy on credit there, and Azarov had three cards in his wallet. But he didn't buy Veronika the ring. He didn't even go into the store with her; he stayed in the car and wasn't the teeniest drop embarrassed. Veronika wanted it so badly she had to buy it for herself.

She reminded Azarov of the incident often and bore a grudge. She nearly told him to go to hell, but at the time she couldn't. She was in his third video, and that was good money, so it wasn't worth arguing with him.

She'd even discussed the problem with Regina.

"It's easy to twist a hero's arm," Regina had said. "And boring. But you need to learn to twist Azarov's. It's excellent training that will stand you in good stead later. If Azarov doesn't start spending money on you, you'll only have to crook your little finger at others. Don't be in such a hurry to break with him."

Veronika was a fine pupil. She didn't break it off with Azarov. But the diamond had brought bad luck, only not for Veronika, but for Azarov, who had been too cheap to buy it for her. They killed Yuri. His karma had been bad—cheap, low-quality karma. But she wasn't going to explain that to the idiot cop at the Petrovka. He didn't even know words like that.

Veronika had very high-quality karma—not just high but super-high. And if something wasn't right, Regina Valentinovna would correct it right away. She could sense these things. Even over the phone, she could adjust Veronika's aura if need be.

CHAPTER 7

The dark blue Volvo with the tinted glass sailed smoothly toward the gates of the old mansion in the middle of Moscow. The gates parted without a sound, let the car through, and then closed right behind it.

"Good evening, Regina Valentinovna!" The armed guard opened the front door of her car and held out his arm to the tall, thin woman sitting at the wheel. The woman cautiously placed one suede high-heeled boot on the ground and, leaning on the guard's arm, climbed out of the car.

"Hello, Gena. Don't take it to the garage. I won't be long."

Entering the house, Regina Valentinovna dropped her light mink coat into the arms of the maid who had run up. In the big mirror in the black antique wooden frame, Regina Valentinovna saw an elegant forty-year-old lady in a severe silk suit with a long-legged, tapered figure and a perfectly regular face. Her thick, straight hair the color of ripe wheat had been cut in a simple, severe bob without bangs and barely covered her sleek, slender neck.

Behind her in the mirror there appeared a very pale male face, slightly puffy around the eyes. The man was disheveled, and yesterday's blond stubble gleamed on his sunken cheeks. His pale blue eyes gazed into Regina Valentinovna's calm brown eyes dully and senselessly. She looked around abruptly and noticed that the man's hands were shaking and his right thumb had an ugly black slash from a new scab that looked fresh.

"You should shave, Venya," she said quietly and, walking up to the man, ran her hand over his cheek. She was wearing pale, flesh-colored matte polish.

"Regina, I'm dying. I can't do this," Veniamin Volkov cried out in a loud whisper. "Do something, please. I can't do this."

Quickly looking around to make sure that there was no maid, secretary, or guard in the vicinity, Regina gave him a good slap on the face and said quietly, "Silence, beast!"

Venya's hands stopped trembling. His eyes acquired an intelligent but frightened expression.

"You see? You have to do something," he said in a perfectly calm, matter-of-fact voice. "Any more of this and I'll explode."

"Well, you're a long way from an explosion, I think," Regina responded in the same calm, matter-of-fact voice. She and Volkov had identical intonations.

"No." He shook his head despairingly. "It nearly happened today."

"But it didn't. You were able to control yourself. You've been healthy for fourteen years. That's quite a long time, Venya."

Volkov showed her his injured right thumb. After a careful glance at the ink- and blood-stained pad of his thumb, Regina shrugged.

"You could have gotten along without the pain. You were just tired. What did you use? A pen?"

"My Parker."

"Too bad, it was a nice Parker." Regina sighed. "All right, let's go."

"Only in your car!" He smiled weakly. "The air in it's better."

"The air in the Volvo is better than the Lincoln?" Regina laughed cheerfully. "Yes, Venya, you're definitely tired."

A little over an hour later, Regina Valentinovna Gradskaya parked the dark blue Volvo next to an old two-story dacha in Peredelkino, just outside Moscow. The house was surrounded by a high metal fence, and there was a guard booth just inside the gates.

"Asleep on the job again," Regina remarked good-naturedly, getting the remote out of the glove compartment and opening the tall gates with a press of the button.

The guard's sleepy face appeared in the booth, after which he leapt out into the light of day as if he'd been scalded and out of habit respectfully saluted his bosses.

"Good morning, Retired Captain!" his boss greeted him sarcastically. "How's the sleeping going this evening?"

"My apologies, Regina Valentinovna!" the guard reported. "Honest to God, I didn't even notice I'd fallen asleep!"

"Thank you for not doing it on the living room couch." Regina snickered amiably. "All right, you can go to the kitchen and let Lyudmila feed you. And drink some coffee. It's no good sleeping at your post, Comrade Retired Captain. Watch out or I'll have to fire you." Regina turned to a silent Venya. "He's afraid of losing his job, but he's too tired to stay awake, the rascal."

Venya followed her into the house.

The dacha had once belonged to a famous Soviet writer, a Stalin Prize winner. His heirs had sold it to Volkov for a hefty price, but neither he nor Regina regretted the cost. Regina had long had her eye on this particular place in the small, elite writers' colony. She liked the fact that it was on the corner, well down the road, with one side adjoining a picturesque birch grove and the other, a small pond where, in the summer, bright lemon-yellow buttercups bloomed.

"Think up something for supper for us, Lyudmila," Regina said to the plump, pink-cheeked young woman who met them on the threshold. "Only make it something light, like fish or a small salad."

"I understand, Regina Valentinovna. Should I bake the sturgeon or grill it?"

"Venya, are you asleep or something?" Regina touched his shoulder. "How do you want your sturgeon, baked with mushrooms or grilled?"

"I'm not hungry."

"Fine. Lyudmila, do it on the grill the way I like it, no salt or sauce, just a spritz of lemon. Some new potatoes for him, too, just a few, four or so, boil them and sprinkle them with dill. And for me, asparagus. Plain."

When the cook had gone, Regina cast a cold, assessing look at Volkov and asked, "Well, my unhappy man, will you let me have a smoke, or should we work for the half hour until supper?"

"You can see for yourself."

She saw a fine white film dusting his lips and his hands trembling again.

"Fine, let's go."

In the writer's former study, there was a small eighteenth-century lady's writing table, and the bookshelves were filled with *The Great Medical Encyclopedia*, books on psychiatry in four languages—Russian, English, German, and French—and also works by Nietzsche, Freud, and Roerich. Only philosophical, psychological, and mystical literature livened the three walls covered floor to ceiling with bookshelves.

Pulling off her suede boots, Regina sat on the low, wide couch and tucked her slender legs underneath her. Volkov sat directly on the floor, opposite her, and fell still, looking steadily into her brown eyes, which flickered strangely in the light of the table lamp.

"They came to see me today," he began. "They came from the past. They even sang the same song as back then, on the Tobol."

"Don't tense up. We haven't even started yet," Regina interrupted him. "Who came?"

"Two girls, for an audition. A blonde and a brunette, each eighteen. At first I didn't notice anything, but when they started singing the ballad, I suddenly saw them."

"You realize it wasn't them?" Regina asked quickly.

"Yes. But I'm afraid how everything is coming together like this. First that fellow who had to be done away with. Now these girls. I could barely contain myself, and you know how I've contained myself all these years. But when that fellow showed up . . ."

"He's gone now," Regina reminded him.

"How did you do it? Why don't you want to say?"

"I didn't do it. He did it himself."

"But you were there?" Venya squeezed his fists so hard his sharp knuckles turned white.

"You know very well I was with you."

"Who did you send?"

"I told you, he did it himself! If you don't believe me, at least believe the police report." She laughed out loud. "The investigators were there, and they did an autopsy. Suicide."

"And the singer?"

"The singer was offed by the same thugs who attacked Thrush at his birthday party. Stop it, Venya. You really aren't your best. Watch out or pretty soon you'll be sleeping on the job, like our retired captain. Okay, then, let's begin . . ."

Volkov closed his eyes and began rocking slowly, seated cross-legged on the carpet. Regina began in a low monotone that came from somewhere in her belly.

"Your legs are soft, heavy, and warm; your muscles are slowly relaxing; your arms are dropping, growing heavy; you are warm but not hot, your skin is smoothing out like the surface of the sea, soft and cool. Not a single wave and no breeze, you hear and smell nothing, you feel warm and good. There is nothing but my voice. The rest is silence, peace, nonbeing. My voice is the way out of nonbeing, you're on it, like a moonbeam path, moving toward the light . . ."

Regina's voice grew quieter and quieter. Volkov rocked to the rhythm of her words. He was breathing deeply, slowly, and infrequently.

"Venya, can you hear me?" she asked at last.

"Yes."

"Now try to remember. Feel your way. Don't hurry and don't be afraid. It wasn't you. You weren't there at all, and you have nothing to be afraid of."

"There are three of them on the banks of the Tobol, in the city park," Volkov mumbled almost inaudibly. "And I'm the fourth. Two girls, a blonde and a brunette. The blonde is very striking, with blue eyes, a little plump. Like the girls who used to come out in folk head-dresses offering bread and salt to greet visiting Party bigwigs. The brunette's pretty, too, but in a different way. You sense the breeding in her. People like her were shot in '18 just for their faces, for the curve of their eyebrows and the expression in their eyes. My grand-dad could immediately recognize bourgeois or noble bones from their hands. Noble bones are slender but firm. My granddad chopped them with his sword . . . he could take a swing and chop them in two."

"Venya, don't get distracted. Leave your granddad in peace," Regina intervened cautiously.

"Arrogant eyes," Venya jerked his head back slightly. "Mocking, dark gray . . . slender hands, a long neck. If she were to . . . I couldn't do anything. I stood up and walked deep into the park. A tipsy girl in a sparkly blouse broke off from her friends. The blouse had gold threads, prickly and shiny. A crude, pimply face, the smell of vodka and sweat . . . Afterward I wanted to jump into the Tobol, fully clothed, I had blood on me and I stank of someone else's sweat. The bank was too steep and I heard their voices very close by. The first one to reach me was Mitya. He saw the blood. And he saw my face. My soul was still back there, deep in the park, and he could tell it from my face. It was getting very light, and the dawn was so bright the mosquitoes were buzzing.

"I hadn't had time to wash the blood from my clothes. I'd wanted them to think I'd been so drunk I'd fallen in the water. All four of us were kind of drunk. By the time the girls came up, I had a grip on myself and they didn't notice a thing. I said I'd had a nosebleed and they got excited and started fussing over me."

Regina knew the first part of his memories by heart. Her husband was consistent in his revelations. It had been years since this story, uttered in a state of deep hypnotic sleep, had had a single detail added. Only quite recently had a few substantive details appeared.

"He saw my face and he understood everything. Not right away, but after." Volkov's voice was a hoarse monotone. "Eventually he figured it out. It was fourteen years later when he came to see me. He came for me from there and there were the two others behind him, and that meant they'd never let me forget."

"He's gone now," Regina reminded him gently. "And the girls didn't notice anything then and won't be able to remember now. It's been fourteen years. They're different people now. They're gone, too, essentially."

"They're gone . . ."

Naturally, it would be better if they really were out of the picture, literally, not figuratively, Regina thought, *but that involves a lot of effort, and I have to weigh the risks.*

"Clean, clear water is shining all around you. It's light and warm and tickles your skin in a pleasant way," she said in her well-modulated voice.

"She's red from the blood," Venya whispered, swallowing with difficulty. "It's dark red and thick. It's boiling and bubbling, and I'm choking and covered in blisters." He started breathing hard and fast, gulping air with an open mouth, throwing his head back, pounding his chest with his fists.

"Regina Valentinovna!" The cook's voice came up from downstairs. "Supper's ready!"

Regina didn't answer. She knew Lyudmila wouldn't call a second time because that was the rule: if the mistress didn't come right away or respond, that meant she was very busy and not to be disturbed.

Volkov's face turned scarlet. Fat blue veins bulged on his forehead. He was breathing raspily, beating the air with his fists, and muttering something unintelligible. Anyone walking in on this scene would have thought the billionaire producer was having an epileptic fit, or in his death throes while his wife observed the scene calmly. He could die here and now and she wouldn't bat an eye.

When it seemed as though Volkov was just about to give up the ghost, Regina clapped lightly and said one word in English: "Enough!"

Volkov fell still, first tensely, in an unnatural pose, his head drawn back, his mouth wide open and his arms flung up and back, and then he started to relax, slowly, like a balloon having its air let out. His breathing became calmer and slower, and his face turned abruptly white before taking on a normal, healthy color.

He opened his eyes and sat calmly on the rug. Even in the low light of the table lamp he looked not just good but excellent, as if he'd just been on vacation at an expensive resort—only without the tan.

"Thank you, Regina dear," he said in a low, velvety voice, kissing his wife's cool hand. He sprang up lightly from the rug and, wiping his damp palms, asked, "How are we doing on supper?"

CHAPTER 8

Ever since she was a little girl, Katya Sinitsyna had considered herself both deeply unfortunate and deeply unlucky. Even in kindergarten she got blamed for other children's misdeeds. All the way through school, there'd been no end to her troubles.

Katya was a good student and especially liked math and physics. Her classmates copied her homework and tests. Katya sincerely believed she was doing a good deed by letting them copy the answers to a few physics or math problems. She obligingly put her homework notebook on the windowsill in the school toilet so during the long break, a good five or six people could take advantage of it—that is, as many girls as fit with their notebooks on the wide windowsill of the girls' bathroom.

At tests, Katya managed to write down the answers using carbon paper and pass them on to her suffering neighbors. The first time she was caught was in eighth grade. The bald little physics teacher in his dark blue lab coat pushed her out of the classroom, erased the test from the board, and quickly wrote a new one.

Katya was taken to the principal, her parents were called in, and she was punished as harshly as the rules allowed. She was lucky she wasn't expelled. Katya thought her classmates should have appreciated her heroism and given her her due for her self-sacrifice, but the reaction was nil. Just as no one had been her friend before, no one had any plans to be her friend now.

The school Katya went to was the best in Khabarovsk. It was a special English school with a concentration in mathematics. Only children of the Communist Party and military elite could get in. Katya's mother was a dentist at the elite's military clinic, so her family's connection wasn't exactly direct. They'd accepted Katya at the school because her mother treated the principal and the head teacher.

Children of the elite lived by special rules. For them, people were divided into two categories. First and most important was the small handful of the select. For all the rest they used the contemptuous word "populace." The word, even the very concept, had been borrowed from their parents.

Everything was different for the populace—their way of life, their morals, even their sausage, which was like cardboard, inedible and nasty. The sausage situation had always been bad in Khabarovsk, and the populace stood in long lines to buy it. An elite child looking at that kind of line through the window of his papa's Volga was only reinforced in his contempt for those who hadn't had the good fortune to belong to the close and cozy little world of the select.

Starting in first grade, Katya had felt that she would be an outsider to her classmates forever. Her mama, the dentist, was staff, so to speak. The children of the first and second secretaries of the Provincial and City Party Committees, the offspring of prominent trade union officials and military leaders on a provincial level, would never consider some dentist's daughter their equal.

Still, she stubbornly believed that if she was nice and good, people would like her and want to be her friend. Who cared who her parents were? A dentist wasn't the lowest rung on the ladder, either. After all, everyone was friends with the son of the director of the city's principal food store, and he was a lousy student who liked to pick fights.

In the younger grades, Katya would bring in her favorite toys and give them away. She liked to give presents, but most importantly, she wanted everyone to understand that she was a nice, good, generous little girl and to want to be her friend.

A few of her presents were condescendingly accepted, but the majority of the secondhand plastic dolls and shabby plush animals were rejected with disdain. What did elite children care about the tacky, boring toys put out by the local toy factory for the populace? Elite children had German dolls with real hair you could shampoo and Czech stuffed animals with expressive little faces.

Katya's mama had taught her it wasn't the present but the thought that counted. But it turned out that Katya's thought didn't count to her classmates, none of whom found her interesting, no matter how hard she tried.

Katya wanted so much for everyone to like her. Well, maybe not everyone, but at least a few. She thought she could earn her classmates' love by explaining what they didn't understand in physics and math and letting them copy off of her. She was waiting for them to finally understand how kindhearted she was. But no one did. All her kindnesses were treated as part of the natural order of things, as something that was to be expected. Katya's mama fixed their teeth, and Katya solved their problems.

Another child in Katya's place might have said to hell with her arrogant classmates and stopped dragging toys from home and letting the other students copy from her tests. Another child might get mad and develop a fierce hatred not only for the elite kids but for all humanity for their stubborn refusal to like or accept her. The older Katya got, though, the deeper she was convinced of her own—and only her own—inferiority.

When she tried to share her accumulated insult with her mama, her mama would cut her off.

"Look inside you for the reason! Why is it no one wants to be your friend? Surely you don't believe that everyone else is bad and you're good."

Katya didn't believe that. She believed more and more deeply that she was the bad one.

There was a terrible rainstorm on the evening of her graduation, leaving the streets extremely muddy. Katya left home in a flimsy white dress she'd sewn herself for her first real dance. When she ran across the school yard barefoot, holding an umbrella in one hand and her white patent sandals wrapped up in the other, a black Volga from the City Party Committee rushed past her at full speed.

Its wheels sent up a fountain of mud that drenched Katya from head to toe. Not only was her white graduation dress covered in mud but so was her carefully made-up face and her short, reddish hair. Two of Katya's classmates were in that Volga.

The son of the City Party Committee's second secretary had pestered his father for permission to drive to graduation night in his official car and to let his best friend accompany him in the passenger seat. It had been for the sake of that very same boy, for the sake of the manly, broad-shouldered Party secretary's son, that Katya had made such an effort, spending nights sewing the white dress and applying makeup in front of the mirror for three hours.

They hadn't doused her with mud on purpose. She didn't go to the graduation dance. She didn't even wash the dress. She just threw it out and tried to forget all about the elite school and the boys and girls who hadn't wanted to be her friend.

With the highest grades, Katya headed for Moscow, where she had been accepted into MAI—the Moscow Aviation Institute. Now she was surrounded not by the children of the select, but by children of the populace. However, her experience in the elite school in Khabarovsk had taken its toll. Katya didn't know how to behave normally with people. Before they ever even met, she suspected each one of them of despising and disliking her. She couldn't even say the simplest things to her dorm mates. She apologized forty times a day, wouldn't look anyone in the eye, and earned a reputation as being "a little odd." Once again no one was her friend—not because she was a dentist's daughter, but because of her impenetrable reticence.

She didn't get along with the boys at MAI, either. She didn't go to the parties, and no one noticed her at the institute. She roamed the halls like a shadow, ducked her short ginger head, didn't talk to anyone, and when someone said something to her, she turned red and looked away, as if she were guilty of something. If Katya did like some boy, she would try her hardest to hide it and not to come into his field of vision.

When Mitya Sinitsyn came into her life, he arrived like lightning out of a clear sky. Katya was in her third year. The student club at MAI had a songwriters' concert just before New Year's. After the concert, a cheerful group of students invited a few of the performers to the dorm.

Katya was lying on her bed, alone in her empty dorm room, reading Dostoyevsky's *Diary of a Writer*. She heard them singing and having fun in the next room, but she didn't care. All of a sudden the door opened, and there stood a tall boy wearing a black sweater and black jeans. His curly blond hair was cut short, and his bright blue eyes were full of kindness.

"Good evening," he said in a low voice. "You don't happen to have a little bread, do you? My apologies for barging in. They sent me because I'm the only sober one left."

Without waiting for her answer, he crossed the room and sat right down on Katya's bed.

"Yes, I think we do." Katya tried to jump up from the bed, but he held her by the arm.

"You're reading *Diary of a Writer*? Everyone's drinking and you're here quietly communing with Dostoyevsky? Why didn't I see you at the concert?"

"I didn't go." Katya freed herself, jumped away, and slid her feet into her slippers. "What kind of bread do you want? White or black?"

"Why didn't you go to the concert? Don't you like songwriters?" He seemed to have forgotten all about the bread.

"Why do you say that? I do. It's just . . . I wanted to be alone and read."

Katya was standing in the middle of the room in oversized, worn-out slippers, thin stockings, and a long, loose sweater.

"Do you always look so frightened?" he asked. He got up from the bed, walked over to her, and took her hand. "And are your hands always so cold? My name's Mitya."

"Katya." She could feel herself blushing.

"Pleased to meet you! Could I take them the bread and come back and sit with you a little?"

The suggestion was such a surprise that Katya didn't answer, she just pulled her head down into her shoulders, freed her hand from his warm grip, slipped over to the shared refrigerator, and pulled out half of a white baguette.

"I'm sorry. I guess there isn't any black," she mumbled, holding out the bread.

He returned five minutes later, carrying his guitar.

"Since you weren't at the concert, I want to sing for you. There"—he nodded at the wall, on the other side of which they heard laughing and cheerful whoops—"everyone is drunk and crazy. You and I may be the only sober people in this whole building."

He sat down on a chair, tuned the guitar, and started singing for her. Katya listened as if enchanted. She couldn't tell whether the songs were good. She didn't understand a word of them. She just looked into his kind, bright blue eyes and was afraid to breathe.

After he was finished singing, Mitya moved to the creaking bed, set aside the guitar, took Katya's face in his hands, and pressed his mouth to her tense, clamped lips.

At age twenty, Katya was kissing for the first time in her life. Naturally, what happened after that was for the first time, too. It was something she'd only read about and seen in movies. Before that night, it was like she hadn't been living at all but just looking at a movie about an alien life. Everything had seemed bright and significant for other people. But for her, the nondescript, browbeaten Khabarovsk girl, nothing of significance could ever happen. She'd long made her peace with the idea that she would grow old, unnoticed and unloved, and die an old maid in dreary solitude.

A stranger, strong and handsome, had kissed her slowly and tenderly. Knowledgeably. Mitya Sinitsyn had plenty of experience with women. True, he'd never liked a woman like Katya before. He liked mature women who were uninhibited and sophisticated. He'd been attracted by the kind of women about whom he would say, "Woman exists according to a formula: legs—breasts—lips. If the legs are long, the breasts heavy and firm, and the lips full, the rest doesn't matter."

What he'd felt when he saw the skinny ginger sparrow on the dorm bed could have been called pity. This touching little girl was sitting reading Dostoyevsky against the backdrop of the drunken laughter coming from the next room. Her huge eyes, frightened, were also intelligent.

He felt like staying with her, singing for her—without any ulterior motive. She held her breath listening, and her eyes were full of so much admiration, gratitude, and love. Mitya felt big, strong, and good.

At first he wanted just to put his arms around those sharp little shoulders, stroke that short, tousled hair, and console the defenseless, skinny being on the bed. And the moment he touched his lips to her pursed lips, he suddenly discovered with amazement that he felt a sharp urge he'd never felt before.

Katya's head was spinning. She'd forgotten the world outside her room—her arrogant classmates in Khabarovsk, her stern and cold mother. It turned out that she was alive, tender, and sensitive, that she could be loved and admired, too; she could have words whispered in her ear by hot lips that made shivers run over her skin.

"You're still a virgin?" she heard his hot, questioning whisper, which to her sounded like magical, unearthly music.

⁓

This discovery that he would be her first frightened him, but it also excited Mitya. He'd had many women in his life, but up until this moment he had not been the first for any of them.

Mitya had no problem spending the night in Katya's dorm room. Katya's roommates tactfully didn't show up until morning. And in the morning, they woke to a completely different Katya. In the morning she could see that she actually was very pretty and feminine. From that morning on, she stopped pulling her head into her shoulders. She walked tall and wasn't afraid to look people in the eyes and smile—and live.

Mitya Sinitsyn asked her to marry him just two days later, on the last day of December, when the clock struck midnight, ringing in 1991. Katya had no doubt they would never be parted. It was as if they'd been created for each other.

The Sinitsyn family welcomed Katya good-naturedly. They could tell right away that this quiet, intelligent girl from Khabarovsk was no provincial angling for a Moscow residence permit. She looked at Mitya with such adoration, she was so modest and well-bred, that neither Mitya's mother nor his sister had any suspicions about her motives for marrying Mitya.

Everything was going so well for them. At first they rented a room in a communal apartment, but soon after, Mitya's sister helped them get an apartment. True, the apartment was on the outskirts of town, in Vykhino, and on the first floor, but it had two rooms and its own kitchen and bath.

Katya graduated with honors and got a job at a machine-building institute as a junior research associate, but she realized very quickly that this wasn't a job, but a waste of her time. She wasn't especially concerned about building a career. The main thing in her life was family, that is, Mitya. More than anything in the world, she wanted to give him a child. Her entire being was focused on having a child. She couldn't think or talk about anything else. But three pregnancies ended in miscarriages, and the doctors eventually gave her a diagnosis as hopeless as death: infertility.

Mitya tried to console her. He said there were many families without children, and maybe one day they could adopt a baby from the orphanage; there were so many abandoned children nowadays. But all his consolations were useless. Katya's inferiority complex, a feeling instilled in her since childhood, blazed up stronger than ever. She started to feel she was ruining Mitya's life, that it was only out of pity that he wasn't abandoning her—infertile and useless as she was.

She was so repulsed by herself that she didn't want to go on living. That was when a lab tech from her institute who'd found her crying in a secluded corner of the empty smoking room suggested she shoot up.

"Shoot up. You'll feel better," he said so gently and sympathetically that Katya, without giving real thought to what his words meant, offered her arm to the needle.

"Well, how is it? Are you getting off?" the lab tech asked, looking in her eyes.

"What?" Katya didn't understand.

"Well, the high . . ."

"The high? I don't know. I guess it's a little better," Katya answered uncertainly.

As the drug spread through her body, she was delighted and surprised to discover that the desperate sadness that had been crushing her soul lately was evaporating. For the first time in as long as she could remember, she felt light and cheerful.

"What was that?" she asked tech boy.

"Morphine," he answered matter-of-factly. "If you want more, I can get you as much as you need."

Katya did want more. As soon as the shot's effects dissipated, she felt terrible again, worse than before. At first she had enough money, but before too long she had to get it from Mitya by lying to him.

Soon, she was an addict, though she didn't think of herself that way. Her life with Mitya became a constant struggle. He dragged her to different doctors, drug experts, and hypnotherapists to try to cure her, though to her it felt as though he just wanted to take away the only joy in her life.

Despite the depth of her addiction, Katya realized how important it was not to make friends in the complicated and dangerous drug world. She believed her morphine use was a temporary distraction, that she could quit at any time. Tomorrow, next week, next month—her stash would run out and she'd quit. Just not right now, not this minute. How could she refuse herself a hit when it was right there in front of her and all she had to do was slip a slender needle into her vein?

Later—tomorrow or next month—she would definitely quit. The main thing was to be sensible and cautious, to leave herself a way out, not to forget that the more druggies you have around you, the harder it is to quit. And anyway, a morphine high is such a subtle and intimate thing, it's better to experience it alone.

Katya quit her job. She'd stopped wanting to be around people. She bought her drugs in places she knew and from people she trusted: on the Old Arbat, from a few pharmacies scattered across Moscow, sometimes at hotels and bars. She tried to buy in a different place each time so as not to come across the same dealers too often. Dealers were always trying to get to know you, to solidify the contact. They could tell at a glance that Katya was hooked, and they had an interest in making her a steady customer. But Katya held firmly to her principle and made no connections.

Mitya made his last attempt to drag his wife out of her addiction just six weeks before his death. He introduced Katya to a well-respected and expensive psychotherapist, Regina Valentinovna Gradskaya.

"You have a very serious addiction, and it's going to be very hard for you to quit cold turkey. You have to act cautiously and gradually, lowering the dose a little at a time," Regina Valentinovna told Katya.

Other people said that the most important thing was to make a firm decision, that it was better to quit cold turkey. It would be horrible at first, but then it would get better.

Only Gradskaya didn't demand drastic action. She was subtler and more attentive than the others Mitya had sent her to. She, the famous psychotherapist, treated Katya entirely for free. The others hadn't understood Katya. They'd wanted to doom her to the savage agonies of withdrawal, to the torture of abstinence. Who could she trust if not Regina Valentinovna?

CHAPTER 9

John Condy usually held onto his future victim for several days. It was as if he was trying to get at the person's essence. He said he was like a sponge, soaking up another living being's energy. In solitary confinement at Goldsworthy Prison in Indiana, Condy spoke at length and with pleasure about his sensations—before, during, and after a murder. He is credited with a well-known sentence in forensic psychiatry literature: "I conquered death by killing."

Condy saw himself as something of a murderer-philosopher, capable not only of thinking abstractly but also of articulately expressing his thoughts. John Condy was motivated to kill not by a surge of passion or hatred or by sexual desire.

"From early childhood I was oppressed by death's inevitability. Usually children don't give death much thought, but I was the unlucky exception. When I looked at the world around me, I didn't see people, I saw puppets. Some cruel and mocking being had carved them out of clay, filled them with passions, and given some of them talent, others wealth, and made others unlucky and ugly. Each one of these puppets was destined to decay and turn into mud. This remote and all-powerful someone was just having fun, but people bowed down before that someone and called that someone God. My mother was a proper Protestant, and she dragged me to church every week, but from early childhood all I felt there was cold and death.

"Death was the most irrevocable, powerful, and concrete thing in the universe, the sole reality, and it attracted me, drew me to it. I wanted to come in contact with it again and again. For me, killing was an act of love for, and horror in, the face of death. A greedy killer is boring. It's like love for money or the love of a prostitute. Death is so important in and of itself that one should only kill for the sake of death itself."

Lena Polyanskaya was translating the last section of David Crowell's article "Cruelty and the Victim" and wondering whether she should cut some of the more gruesome bits. She knew full well that readers loved those kinds of details and that many would read the article for the pathology, not the psychology. But those details made Lena a little queasy. The author had obviously gotten carried away with that very thing, aware that this was what turned a scientific article into literature.

Lena realized he was right to do so. No successful general-interest magazine would publish an article consisting of nothing but psychological observations, no matter how interesting, fresh, and lively they may be. It was foolish to expect that kind of pure psychology to appeal to *Smart*'s readers. If she cut even half of the horrific details, the editor in chief was going to ask, "What happened to the good parts? You're insulting the reader, Elena." And he'd be right. The reader grew bored without a little blood.

Liza woke up in the next room and called out loudly, "Mama!"

Lena was happy to be pulled away from her work and to take a break from the philosophizing of a serial killer.

While she was feeding Liza a chicken cutlet and mashed potatoes, the doorbell rang.

At the door, Lena looked out the peephole and saw an older woman, a stranger. Her unbuttoned coat was thrown over a white lab coat and she had a stethoscope hanging around her neck.

"Hello, I'm from the Filatov Hospital," said the voice on the other side of the door. "We're conducting a week of wellness checks for children under the age of three before the next immunization campaign."

The Filatov Hospital's clinic was their neighborhood clinic, where all forms got filled out and wellness checks were done rather frequently, so Lena opened the door.

"We're up-to-date on our shots," Lena told her, helping the woman off with her coat.

"We're planning to introduce an additional flu shot soon." The woman smiled. "Not for nursing infants, of course. Is your card at home or at the registry?"

"The registry. I'm sorry, we're having dinner now."

"That's all right. Take your time and finish. I'll wait." The woman followed Lena into the kitchen.

"Hello, Liza dear," she said. "What are you eating?"

"Potatoes and chicken," Liza told her seriously from her high chair at the table.

"That's wonderful how well she speaks. Perfectly splendid for her age. She's not two yet, am I right?"

"She turned two five days ago. Please have a seat. Some tea perhaps?"

"Thank you. I won't say no. Only a little later. You finish eating now, then I'll examine Liza, and then I'll have some tea."

Liza finished very quickly. As they walked down the hall to the nursery, the doctor noticed the computer screen glowing through the doorway and asked, "How do you manage to find the time to work with such a young child?"

"I have no choice."

"Money problems?"

"More like professional."

"I understand. You work for a private company without maternity or unpaid leave." The doctor shook her head. "What can you do? As the saying goes, you get what you ask for. I'll bet you don't get enough sleep, either."

"Sometimes." Lena smiled.

As she examined Liza, listened to her, and looked at her throat, the doctor kept asking Lena casual questions about her job and personal life. She made them sound perfectly tactful and unobtrusive.

"What firm do you work for, if I may ask?"

"I head up a department at *Smart*."

"Oh, I know that magazine. So, how many teeth do we have?" She counted Liza's little teeth, recorded something in her notebook, and then went back to asking Lena questions about her job.

"Which department?"

"Literature and art. You know, Doctor, sometimes she gets constipated, and I can't figure out why."

"Soak a few prunes in cold boiled water for twenty-four hours, and give her a spoonful of the fruit and juice three times a day before meals. But if you're really worried, we can test her intestinal bacteria levels. She has a bit of a rash. Nothing terrible, but not to be neglected."

"Thank you so much."

Lena noticed that the pediatrician had long, sharp nails and wore pale, flesh-colored polish. That seemed a little odd. Ordinarily doctors and nurses who deal with small children cut their nails short to keep from scratching children accidentally.

After examining Liza, the doctor smiled politely and guiltily reminded Lena about her earlier offer of tea.

"Would you like coffee instead?" Lena suggested.

She was so happy to have the chance to talk at length and at leisure with an intelligent pediatrician. She didn't take Liza to the clinic very often and called a doctor to the house even less.

Svetlana Igorevna, the district pediatrician, was a very sweet person and a well-educated doctor, but she was always in a hurry. She always politely refused Lena's offers of tea or coffee, and Lena felt bad about detaining her with additional questions and conversation. Her head was spinning already from the ten to fifteen house calls she made each day. And there was always a long line to see her at the clinic.

"I'm sorry, I forgot to ask you your name." Lena poured strong coffee for the doctor and herself.

"Valentina Yurievna," the doctor introduced herself. "You make excellent coffee. Tell me, who do you leave Liza with when you go to your office?"

"My neighbor. We're very lucky. She's a lonely older woman, and she watches the child for very modest pay."

"Yes," Valentina Yurievna agreed. "That's great luck. It's very hard to find a reliable and affordable nanny these days. And I'm not even talking about day care, of course. The children are constantly sick there. You stay at home with a healthy child, and the moment you put her in day care, you have to stay at home with a sick one. If you can do it, it's far better to keep your child at home until she is old enough for school. Unfortunately, not everyone has that option." The doctor smiled sadly and sipped her coffee. "Do you have to go to the office often?"

"I have two office days a week, but mostly I work at home. The magazine has been accommodating. Tell me, Valentina Yurievna, what should I do when my child takes a long time to fall asleep?"

"Your Liza is a very calm child. Does she really have a problem with that?"

"Occasionally. We spoil her and sometimes let her stay up late with us."

"Don't make too much of it. A child will always get what she needs. If she doesn't eat or sleep today, she'll make up for it tomorrow. As for spoiling her, when can we spoil them if not at this age? Soon enough comes school and lessons and responsibilities. Tell me, Lena, do you write anything for the magazine yourself?"

"Once in a while. Mostly I work with the authors and translate."

This kind of curiosity on the part of a stranger, a pediatrician, surprised Lena, but didn't put her on her guard. *Smart* was a well-known and popular magazine. If a middle-aged woman had looked at a few issues, naturally she'd find it interesting to chat with the head of a department over a cup of coffee.

It was a little odd that, unlike her colleagues, she was in no hurry to get on with her house visits. There were lots of small children and never enough doctors and nurses, even at the prestigious Filatov Clinic.

"What are you working on now, if I may ask?"

"Right now I'm translating an article by a trendy American psychologist."

"How wonderful! To be honest, I'm very interested in psychology, especially the modern American school. Who are you translating?"

"David Crowell. It's an article on the psychology of serial killers."

"How interesting!" For some reason the doctor laughed, though her face then immediately became serious. "I have to tell you, I became interested in the psychology of suicides recently. There was a terrible case. A young woman, the mother of two children, killed herself, just like that, out of the blue. Everything in her life seemed to be great. Her husband doted on her, healthy children, plenty of money, and yet she hanged herself."

Lena started feeling uncomfortable. All this time she couldn't get Mitya Sinitsyn out of her mind. He, too, had hanged himself out of the blue.

"Yes, life is full of surprises," she said quickly. "More coffee?"

Liza ran into the kitchen crying.

"Mama, my doll's head broke and the blue ball is hiding," she reported tragically. Lena went to the nursery.

She expected the doctor to take this opportunity to leave, but instead she followed Lena and helped fix the beheaded rubber doll and search for the ball, which had rolled under the sofa. Then she went back to the kitchen, and drank two more cups of coffee with Lena. More surprisingly, she returned to the psychology of suicides.

Lena had come to regret her hospitality. The doctor ended up staying an hour and a half, finally remembering suddenly that she had to run out and continue her rounds.

After she'd gone, Lena was left with an odd, unsettling feeling. She couldn't figure out what was wrong, but she felt dreary inside, she was all thumbs, and her head even started to hurt.

Liza played calmly, telling stories to her toys. Lena could well have gone back to her translating and worked another forty minutes or so, but when she sat down at her computer, she discovered her thoughts were tangling and slipping off in all directions. Even the simplest words escaped her, the tiny letters on the screen danced before her eyes. She shut down the computer, washed the dishes, and managed to break her favorite coffee cup in the process.

What's wrong with me? she thought irritably. *Maybe I just need some sleep. I'm probably overestimating my capabilities. I can't sleep so little. It takes a toll eventually. My head hurts, I'm breaking cups, and kind doctors are making me think ill of them. That's wrong. I should take Liza for a walk right now and try to get to bed earlier tonight. Forget about work and finally get a good night's sleep.*

She got Liza dressed and decided to go all the way to Patriarch Ponds, where there was the illusion of fresh air and the paths were relatively clear. It wasn't all that far, but she'd have to carry the stroller up and down the stairs at the underground crossing at the Ring Road. Lena was used to that, though, and sometimes someone helped.

"That was a mean lady," Liza suddenly pronounced as Lena heroically lifted the stroller and carried it down the stairs, which were slippery with the evening frost.

"Why mean, Liza?" she asked after safely navigating the slippery stairs and putting the stroller wheels on the smooth floor of the underground passage.

"Bad," Liza said gloomily. "A mean lady." A boy of twelve or so was walking toward them, leading a big black dog in a muzzle on a leash. Liza bounced up and down in her stroller and cried joyfully, "What a dog! Oh, what a big dog! Why does she have a boot on her face?"

"That's a muzzle," Lena explained. "They put it on big dogs just in case the dog suddenly didn't like something and wanted to bite."

"It doesn't hurt her?" Liza asked, concerned.

Liza loved dogs. Their old dachshund, Pinya, had died just two months ago, and she remembered him still, though children that young usually have short memories. Of course, she didn't understand what "dead" meant. They told her Pinya had gone to a fairy-tale dogland.

Now all the brown dachshunds they met on the street were Pinya for her, but she reacted passionately to big dogs. A dog in a muzzle was more interesting than a "mean lady." The dog was here and now and the lady had gone, and Liza quickly forgot her. Lena was happy not to revisit the subject.

Going up with the stroller wasn't as dangerous as going down. There was less chance of slipping on frozen stairs, although it was much heavier. Lena was lucky, though, as an older man helped her get it up the stairs.

"Why, if it isn't Liza Krotova!" Lena heard behind her.

The stroller was already at the top, and an older woman popped up next to the man. Lena recognized the district doctor, Svetlana Igorevna. The man who'd helped with the stroller was her husband.

They lived not far from Patriarch Ponds, so Lena walked them home.

"We had a visit today from the clinic. You're doing some kind of wellness checkups," Lena told her.

"We are? Checkups?" Svetlana Igorevna was surprised. "What do you mean? We're not doing anything of the kind. Who was it who came to see you? Did you ask her name?"

Lena felt a nasty chill in her belly. She recounted the visit briefly, hoping it might have something to do with the clinic after all.

"What did you say the woman's name was? Valentina Yurievna?" Svetlana Igorevna asked, concerned.

Lena nodded.

"And she spent nearly two hours with you? Did you make sure nothing was missing?"

"To be honest, it didn't occur to me," Lena admitted in dismay. "She was wearing a white coat and a stethoscope, and she examined the child quite professionally."

"You can't be so trusting these days." Svetlana Igorevna's husband shook his head. "There are so many apartment break-ins nowadays. She could have been there to case the apartment. You hadn't called for a doctor; you let a complete stranger into your home!"

The chill in her belly wouldn't pass, and then her knees started shaking. On the way home, Lena recalled all the details of her conversation with the "doctor," and her head constructed a bizarre chain that led from the stranger to suicide, and from suicide to Mitya Sinitsyn.

If Seryozha had been home, it wouldn't have been so frightening, but he was in London and wasn't going to be back any time soon. Lena tried to convince herself that there couldn't possibly be a connection between the fake doctor and Mitya's suicide. The doctor had just been casing her place. She had to make sure nothing had gone missing. She'd call Misha Sichkin for advice on how to protect herself.

But this was a bizarre way to case an apartment—spending so much time, professionally examining Liza, giving sensible advice, and then discussing the psychology of suicides. *Although how would I know how people act when they're casing a place?*

She was especially creeped out that she'd let this strange woman touch her child.

CHAPTER 10

"You have to know how to enjoy life, sunshine. The first snow. The smell of the grass in spring," Regina's mama used to tell her.

Her mama was quiet, intelligent, and unattractive. A lonely librarian, already an old maid at forty-one, she'd let the tipsy electrician Kiril, a broken-down thirty-year-old just back from the front, have his way with her.

He'd come to the library one freezing January evening to fix the wiring. Outside it was forty below. The stove was going full blast, spreading a languid heat through the reading room. Everyone had gone home to their families. But Valya Gradskaya was in no hurry to get anywhere. They asked her to wait for the delayed electrician.

That pitiful little former soldier with the bulbous nose, crooked chin, and crass sneer became the father to Regina Valentinovna Gradskaya.

It was quick and dirty, on the worn prerevolutionary sofa in the reading room, under large portraits of classic Russian writers.

"Why did you tell me this?" Regina asked her mama when she turned eighteen. "Couldn't you have come up with a romantic story about a heroic Arctic explorer who perished on the ice, or a broad-shouldered soldier covered in medals? Why do I have to know that my father was an ugly bastard named Kiril?"

"He did fight," her mama replied with a guilty smile.

"He's a bastard!" Regina shouted. "He's a monster! Men like that shouldn't be fathers!"

"It was January of '46, Regina. What heroic Arctic explorers? There was one man for every ten women. I was forty-one. I was alone in the world and I very much wanted a child. It was my last chance."

"You should have lied to me."

"I can't mislead you, you know that."

Regina did. And she quietly despised her mother's pathological honesty.

"Natasha Rostova was no beauty," Valya would tell her daughter officiously. "Just look at how Tolstoy describes his beloved heroine." And she would shut her eyes and recite from memory long passages from *War and Peace*. "And Princess Maria? That portrait is a hymn to spiritual beauty. Just listen!" And another excerpt from the classic novel would follow. "Pushkin's Tatyana wasn't noted for her beauty, either." Long excerpts from *Eugene Onegin* followed. "You see, Regina, it's foolish and tedious to beat yourself up over the fact that your features aren't particularly attractive. Nothing in life depends on your appearance. The main thing is inner beauty, goodness, and intelligence."

At twelve, Regina already knew that was a crock. A beauty, even if she was sickeningly dumb, would still have an easier time of it in this world than an ugly woman with a brain. No amount of inner beauty and goodness and intelligence could help an ugly girl. The older Regina got, the more deeply she came to believe that.

All her life, she'd been at the mercy of her appearance. Regina Gradskaya was convinced that an unattractive woman could be neither successful nor happy. All it took was one look in any mirror to be unhappy, for any victory to go up in a puff of smoke. Unattractive girls didn't have victories, anyway.

She was fourteen when her mama, frightened by the crashing and banging, ran into her room from the kitchen and found her daughter trampling on the shards of a large, broken mirror, repeating quietly and with concentration, "I hate you! I hate you!" Her clenched fists were covered in blood.

"Regina, darling! What's the matter?"

"Go away! I hate you! This nose, these eyes, these teeth. I hate you!"

The next day her mama dragged her to a psychiatrist.

"It's a transitional age," the psychiatrist said, and she prescribed tranquilizing drops. "Believe me, child, appearance isn't the main thing in life. At fourteen, everyone thinks they're ugly ducklings. By sixteen you'll blossom. You'll see."

By sixteen I'll have lost my mind, Regina thought.

Regina had always been a good student. That came easily to her. In school she taught herself three languages, English, German, and French, using old high school textbooks she found in the stacks of the municipal library. She got into Moscow Medical Institute on the first try, without any pull.

In the first anatomy classes, lots of her classmates went white and even fainted beside the zinc tables where the cadavers lay. Regina Gradskaya calmly picked up her scalpel. She felt neither horror nor disdain—only a cold curiosity.

All medical students get used to anatomy, but it takes time. Regina Gradskaya didn't have to get used to it.

The composure of the taciturn, hopelessly unattractive first-year student from Tobolsk stunned her teachers. To say nothing of her schoolmates. The girls she shared a room with in the dorm were wary of her. They might even have been a little afraid of her. No one once borrowed sugar, tea, or a piece of bread from her.

Five girls lived in the room, and they shared nearly everything. If one of them was going on an important date, the whole room fitted her out—someone gave her shoes, someone else a skirt. Regina never lent anything of her own or borrowed anything from anyone else. She didn't go out on dates. She was neat and thrifty in her daily life, and she managed to save from her miserly stipend. She kept a strict account of everything, even her notebook pages and the ink in her fountain pen.

She got top marks in all her courses. In six years of study, she was never once sick and never missed a single class. She slept four hours a day and read virtually everything there was in the institute's library. She was especially enthralled by books on psychiatry.

More than anything, Regina Gradskaya was afraid of losing her mind. She realized that her obsession with her own appearance bordered on pathology, and that that border was so unstable that her deep inferiority complex could cross over into pathology at any moment.

The deeper Regina delved into psychiatry, the more clearly she realized that there was no precise boundary between normality and pathology. Strict and specific as official medicine's dogmas were, no one really knew how to treat or cure mental illness. They hadn't developed anything new besides aminazine and haloperidol, whose effects on the human organism were much worse than any straitjacket, padded cell, or round of electroshock treatment.

Psychiatry's essence had remained unchanged for over a hundred, even two hundred years. Doctors considered their objective to be making mentally ill people safe and helpless rather than curing them.

Regina was convinced that the human soul should be treated with something completely different from drugs. She began to study psychic practices and hypnosis and read everything there was to be read on these subjects. She learned to treat people with her voice, hands, and gaze. Sometimes it felt as though she were penetrating a person's mind and soul and seeing the essence of his or her emotional pain.

The patients at the Serbsky Forensic Psychiatry Institute, where she landed as a young resident, were unusual. Regina had murderers, rapists, and sadists pass through her office. By working with these people and cautiously testing her psychic and hypnotic abilities on them, Regina discovered that there were some strong and gifted personalities among them—such as one doesn't find among normal people.

What interested her most were the serial killers, the seemingly sane ones with a higher education and a very high IQ, who were fully aware of and admitted to their actions. They killed disinterestedly, not for the sake of material benefit, but to resolve their own profound inner problems. There were very few of them among the ordinary killers. To Regina, they seemed like geniuses of villainy—the living refutation of Pushkin's famous aphorism: "Genius and villainy are incompatible."

These men aroused neither fear nor revulsion in her. She found them more interesting than all the others. She dug around in the black depths of their subconsciouses as calmly as she'd dissected cadavers in her first year of medical training. It was as if she were searching for answers to the questions that inflamed her soul.

Later, when her colleagues found out about her experiments, she was forced to resign from the institute. Regina was unperturbed. She knew she'd be fine.

By age thirty, Dr. Regina Valentinovna Gradskaya owned a two-room apartment in downtown Moscow, a very good car, a closet full of expensive dresses, and more jewelry than she could wear. Her patients included famous actors, writers, singers, Party officials, and their children and wives. She treated them for alcoholism, drug addiction, impotence, depression, and psychoses. Her patients were guaranteed full anonymity, but most important, her treatment was gentle and effective. No Antabuse or abstinence, no destructive psychotropic medicines of any kind. Just her voice and her hands.

Veniamin Volkov showed up at her apartment one cold November evening in 1982. A high-level Young Communist official she knew had called and asked her to take on a new patient, "a good guy, from your part of the world, Tobolsk."

Broad-shouldered and blue-eyed, Volkov perched timidly on the edge of his chair and began quietly telling her about his difficult childhood and how he was now having difficulty with intimacy.

Regina learned the truth very quickly. Under hypnosis he told her all the details of how he had raped and killed seven women.

"I'm afraid," he said. "I'm scared that sooner or later they'll catch me. I don't want to kill, but the urge to kill is stronger than I am. I get insatiably needy, and that need becomes my essence, my soul, and my soul is above my psyche, above my reason. Only it's come crashing down."

Regina often had to deal with male and female sexual problems. Under hypnosis, her patients shared the most intimate details of their lives. There was nothing mysterious for Regina in that complex sphere of the human psyche. She listened to her patients' most intimate sexual experiences with the cold curiosity of a researcher.

At thirty-six she was still a virgin and had long since realized that she was frigid. Unlike her patients, though, this didn't bother her. Given her appearance, frigidity bordering on asexuality was a blessing. She couldn't imagine a man capable of taking an interest in her not out of pity.

Listening to the revelations of this serial rapist and murderer, looking at his broad shoulders and strong, handsome hands, Regina was suddenly surprised to discover that this was exactly the kind of man she'd been waiting for all her life. This discovery didn't scare her. She already knew she could harness Venya Volkov's ferocious need, could guide his powerful energy in a completely different direction.

Without bringing him out from under hypnosis, she went over to him, ran her hand over his bristly cheek, cautiously removed his jacket, and slowly began unbuttoning the shirt on his muscular, hairless chest.

"You won't kill anymore," she said, touching her lips to his hot skin.

For the first time in her life, Regina felt a keen, animal desire, but even at that moment her cold curiosity didn't leave her.

Venya was totally under her control. She did everything she wanted the way she wanted. She penetrated the depths of his subconscious, and this made her pleasure all the more acute.

At a certain point his hands closed lightly around her throat. But she was prepared for that. With a powerful effort of will, she ordered him to remove his hands from her neck.

He obeyed.

She brought him out from under her hypnosis fifteen minutes after it was over. He was sitting buck naked on the fluffy rug in the middle of the room, and he looked around in fright. She threw her robe over him. He remembered and understood nothing, but she knew that everything that had just happened was etched deeply in his soul and he would never forget it. She sat down beside him on the rug.

"There, you see? It's all over. I'm alive. Being with you was very good. Now you'll remember everything, carefully and calmly."

He looked at the unattractive stranger sitting beside him who was wearing his shirt over her naked body.

"You risked your life," he said barely audibly.

"So did you," she smiled in response.

Afterward they had tea in Regina's large, cozy kitchen. Venya spent the night. It was all repeated that night—but without hypnosis. Once again, at the critical moment, his hands closed around her throat. But right then he felt a sharp pain under his left shoulder blade and heard a calm voice: "You won't, Venya."

The pain brought him back to reality. He unclenched his hands.

Regina never let go of the handle of the small, razor-sharp kitchen knife she had pressed into Venya's back. Only later, when it was all over, did the knife fall with a gentle thud onto the rug next to the bed.

"Forgive me," Venya said while she cleaned the cut on his back with hydrogen peroxide and put iodine on it. "You must understand, it's not my fault. It happens reflexively."

"It will pass." She kissed him gently on the shoulder. "My, I hadn't expected the cut to be so deep. Does it sting?"

"A little."

She blew on the wound. Neither his mother nor his father had ever consoled him when he was hurt. No one had blown affectionately and cautiously so that the iodine wouldn't sting.

He felt like a little boy who was loved and pitied. As if he had admitted an awful, disgusting act, but no one had yelled at him, or put him in the corner, or slapped his cheeks—he had been petted and consoled.

He wished this woman would take him by the hand and lead him through life—wherever she thought best. He would have followed her with eyes shut, trusting blindly. She knew everything about him—and didn't turn away in horror. She was pulling him out of the icy abyss of loneliness, stroking his head, warming him, consoling him. He didn't notice her unattractiveness. He didn't care what she looked like.

Regina had big plans. She knew she couldn't manage alone. She needed someone just like Venya Volkov—strong, merciless, devoid of sympathy for others, yet at the same time devoted and submissive to her. The fact that she was also passionate about him was just a nice bonus, nothing more. Or so she told herself.

Fourteen years had passed since then. Regina's calculations had been correct. The fierce need that had seared Venya Volkov's soul had come to live an independent life, embodied in a powerful, relentless machine— Veniamin Productions.

Volkov hadn't killed another person. Several times he'd had to hire hitmen and set up rivals and competitors, but this was less a murderous act than a necessary move in the complex and cruel game of show business.

Now all that remained of the Regina who had hated her own face was her voice and hands. Also her hair and figure. All the rest—the shape of her nose, temples, and lips, the cut of her eyes, her large white teeth—was the result of painstaking work by plastic surgeons.

Today it didn't matter that the real Regina Gradskaya was fifty or that her natural, God-given face had been ugly. As far as she knew, not one old photograph remained. Even from her early childhood, even from her infancy. They had all been destroyed, burned. That Regina with the bulbous nose and small, close-set eyes, crooked chin, and buck teeth had died. The death of the old Regina and the birth of the new Regina—the cold, ideal beauty with the aquiline nose, oval face, and even, pearl-like teeth.

The operations, which had cost tens of thousands of dollars, had been done in stages at a Swiss clinic in the Alps, considered the best in the world, where a day's stay cost fifteen hundred dollars—and that didn't include the operations or procedures. And Regina had spent forty days there.

When the doctors said she could go out, she went to the small village nearby. On the very clean streets, welcoming Alpine doormen greeted the tall, thin lady—in German, French, and English. She would respond, exchanging a few polite words with passersby about the weather, the marvelous Alpine air, and the picturesque mountain landscape that surrounded them.

Neither the passersby nor the owners of the sweet little shops and cafés paid any attention to the fact that the lady's face was covered by a solid veil. For the local inhabitants, ladies like this, the famous clinic's rich patients, were familiar and desired visitors. They provided the little village with additional revenue.

On her first walk, Regina wandered into a lovely, toy-like Lutheran church and ordered a funeral service for herself, for the unhappy and ugly woman who had died here, in the Alps, under the plastic surgeon's delicate scalpel.

A chorus of pretty Alpine children sang the requiem so tenderly and sorrowfully that Regina, standing in the half-empty church, nearly started crying under her thick veil. She stopped herself. Until her scars healed, she couldn't allow herself to cry.

But now she could cry, and she could laugh. She didn't look a day over forty, and that age suited her just fine. She would be the same age for another ten or fifteen years, and then she could go back to the Swiss Alps.

Every time she stopped in front a mirror to fix her hair or retouch her light makeup, Regina saw the little Alpine church and the clean faces of the Swiss children and heard the sweet polyphony of the requiem and the stern, cool sounds of the organ. Sometimes she felt like crying again—and she did, without reserve—provided the situation was sufficiently intimate for those strange, unexpected tears.

CHAPTER 11

Katya didn't hold up well in the cold, and lately she was always freezing. She hadn't left home since she'd gotten back from Mitya's funeral. And no one had stopped by or called. They'd forgotten about her as if she'd died along with Mitya. Katya tried not to think about the fact that there wasn't a kopek in the house, the ampoules were running out, and she couldn't buy more. She'd be getting feverish soon.

She would try to hold out another day on pills. Wouldn't it be better to shoot up all the ampoules, swallow all the remaining pills, and wash them down with two hundred grams of pure alcohol? There should be a bottle in the sideboard. It would be an easy and pleasant death, much more pleasant than what Mitya did to himself.

Why didn't he do that if he'd decided to kill himself? There's plenty of medicine in the apartment. It's much simpler and more pleasant to wash a handful of tabs down with pure alcohol, fall asleep, and not wake up.

All of a sudden it occurred to her that Mitya hated drugs so much that he preferred the noose. This was followed by another thought: why did the cops and doctors keep telling her that he was high? And the scratches on his arm . . . They really were there, the scratches and needle marks. It was just that up until this minute, Katya hadn't wanted to think about it. Every thought of Mitya caused her physical pain; it was like withdrawal. Everything in her head was confused and she was starting to feel nauseated. Her ears were ringing and she wished she could just shoot up and forget everything. But she had to make the ampoules last.

Glancing at the clock, she discovered it was already evening and remembered she hadn't eaten anything since yesterday. She had to get up and at least have some tea. She didn't feel like crawling out from under the blanket, but hunger was clawing at her. Throwing Mitya's jean jacket over her robe, she headed for the kitchen.

All there was in the refrigerator was a dried-up piece of cheese and half a can of corn. In the cabinets, there was stale bread, tea, and sugar. Katya had barely eaten in the past few days. While the kettle was heating, she sat immobile on the stool and looked through the doorway. Again she saw Mitya's bare feet, large body, and strangely calm, almost indifferent face.

Slipping her hand into the pocket of his jean jacket, Katya felt a pack of cigarettes, which she pulled out. Kents. Mitya had smoked half the pack. A crumpled slip of paper fell out of the pocket. Katya picked it up and smoothed it flat.

It was a page from a notebook, crumpled-up and torn in two places. A few lines written in Mitya's fleet handwriting were crossed out. That was how he sketched and crossed out drafts of his poems. But these weren't poems.

Katya smoothed the page out with her open hand on the kitchen table, lit a cigarette, and started to read:

1. Find out what happened to that investigator (maybe from Polyanskaya?).
2. Newspapers (local?).
3. Psychiatry.
You were crazy to do that. Hello! They're sure to finish you off quietly!
But don't take this to the Prosecutor's Office. 14 years!

117

The kettle was whistling desperately. Katya turned off the gas, mechanically poured herself some tea in Mitya's favorite mug, stirred in the sugar, took a big swallow, crushed out her cigarette and lit another.

"Mitya could have been killed, after all," she said out loud, evenly. "He was up to something. He was all worked up and kind of nervous. This page was torn out of his notebook. He was going to throw it out but forgot and dropped it into his jacket pocket. He'd been wearing this jacket lately. He'd put his leather jacket on over it."

Katya quickly rummaged through the jacket's other pockets and found a handkerchief, a few subway and telephone tokens, and three thousand rubles. Nothing else.

I have to find that notebook! Katya thought. *He tore this page out of his diary.*

Mitya used to write potential lyrics that came to mind in his diary, as well as telephone numbers, plans, and upcoming events.

Katya rummaged through Mitya's bag and was surprised to find, amid the sheet music, a forensic psychiatry textbook. But no notebook.

She rummaged through his desk drawers, looked under his dresser, and went through the bookshelves. The small but fat little book that Olga had given Mitya six months ago, a fancy diary bound in black leatherette with embossed gold lettering spelling out *Kokusai Koeki Company, Ltd.* in roman and Cyrillic letters, wouldn't just go missing. There wasn't much in the way of furniture and things in the apartment, and his diary was usually either in his bag or his jacket pocket.

Katya was so worked up she actually forgot about shooting up. Her head hurt. Another half an hour and the pain would be too much for her to think. But if she shot up, she wouldn't be able to think clearly or remember anything. And she had to remember.

Polyanskaya is that Lena who took me out on the stairs to shoot up. But what does she have to do with this? What investigator did Mitya want to ask her about? Her thoughts started getting confused and slipping away from her. *What if I call her? Just call and tell her about this strange*

piece of paper? I think her husband works in the police. Yes, Mitya did say
something about that. He went to visit her. At the time I think he said Lena
Polyanskaya wasn't anything like a police officer's wife.

In addition to her headache, Katya had a bad chill that sent her
into a cold sweat. But instead of shooting up, Katya took some aspirin,
washed them down with cold tea, and ate a piece of bread and cheese
and a spoonful of cold corn straight from the can. That didn't make it
better, but Katya had firmly decided not to shoot up until she found
Polyanskaya's phone number and called her. Right then she remembered
she hadn't seen Mitya's address book once since his death, either. It was
the same brand as his diary, only very small and flat.

That's gone missing, too! The window was open and the telephone wasn't
working. Someone could have easily broken into the apartment, shot Mitya
up with narcotics, and . . . He and I had gone to bed together, we'd been
so, so sleepy. He was tired. He'd been on his feet all day since eight in the
morning, and I'd shot up and taken two sleeping pills. I don't remember. I
don't remember much of anything. Lord, it hurts so much. I need to shoot
up. Right now, this minute.

There'd been just four ampoules left. And now there were three. She
felt relieved and good after shooting up. Katya suddenly understood
perfectly that her husband hadn't killed himself.

"He'd gotten himself into some mess with his producers," Katya
said out loud, calmly and almost joyfully. "All those producers have ties
to criminals. Mitya's no suicide. He doesn't have that sin on him. And
I don't, either. I didn't drive him to the noose."

Her sudden joy was replaced by sobs. Crying made her feel better,
like when you're a child and you cry your heart out and suddenly the
world seems new and bright, as if cleansed by your tears. Katya decided
she had to call Mitya's parents immediately and tell them not to agonize.
Then she had to go to the church and order prayers for the dead. Olga
would give her some money for that. Or she could order them herself.
After all, it didn't matter who did it.

Her mother-in-law came to the phone.

"Nina Andreyevna!" Katya blurted out emotionally without even saying hello. "Mitya didn't do it. He was killed. You have to understand, he didn't commit suicide. Do you hear me? I know now for sure that someone broke in through a window that night."

Tense silence in the receiver. Finally Nina Andreyevna spoke, barely audibly.

"Don't. Katya. Please, don't talk about it."

"Why not? This is very important—"

Katya didn't get a chance to finish. Olga picked up the extension.

"Please, don't bother Mama right now," she asked calmly.

Katya flew into a rage. "I'm not bothering anyone! Am I supposed to apologize to everyone for not dying instead of Mitya? I'm sorry. It's not my fault I'm still alive. But you all have to know that Mitya didn't do this. He was killed. You can go to church tomorrow morning."

"You just shot up and this happy thought has occurred to you?" Olga asked coldly.

"Lord, how sick I am of all of you!" Katya exclaimed. "You only hear and see yourselves. For you, everyone else is a scoundrel and an idiot unworthy of your attention. You come down off your high horse and understand this: your brother was killed. He didn't hang himself!"

"Fine." Olga sighed. "Can you try to calm down and explain to me why this suddenly occurred to you?"

"No, I won't! I won't calm down, and I won't tell you anything. I don't want to talk to you." There were tears in Katya's voice, and she blurted out with a sniff, "Give me Polyanskaya's telephone number!"

"What for?"

"She promised to find me a good addiction specialist," Katya lied.

"You want to try again?" Suddenly Olga felt uncomfortable. *It's true, I'm too hard on her. That's wrong. She's a human being, too, and she's having a very bad time of it now, much worse than me. She's completely alone.*

"I do." Katya sniffed again.

"Fine. Maybe it will work this time." Olga recited Lena's number from memory, and Katya wrote it down with a pencil stub on the same sheet of paper she'd found in Mitya's jacket pocket.

"You don't have any money, though," Olga said gently. "Would you like me to come bring you some food?"

"Thank you, but I'll get by," Katya proudly refused.

Polyanskaya's line was busy when she dialed it a few minutes later. Katya was moaning from impatience. She needed to talk to someone right away, someone who would listen sympathetically. And who else could she talk to? Regina Valentinovna, of course! While Polyanskaya's line was busy, she could dial the other number.

As always, Regina Valentinovna picked up the phone immediately.

"I'm sorry," Katya said softly. "I don't have anyone else to talk to about this."

"Have you run out of drugs?" This time Regina's voice sounded cold and irritable.

"I've got three ampoules left. I'll be out pretty soon. I don't know what to do."

"Do you want me to give you some money?"

"No." Katya was embarrassed. "Have I ever asked you for that? I just wanted to ask your advice. Maybe I could try to go to the hospital for treatment again?"

"Sure. Give it a try," Regina replied indifferently.

"It's very hard. Even in the expensive hospital Olga put me in, they didn't do anything to make withdrawal easier. Now she won't have anything to do with me, and I can only get treated for free in those awful psych clinics. I won't last there. I wanted to ask you, there are all kinds of charitable societies and centers where they help people like me. You must know them. Only it has to happen quickly. I can't be alone. I can't take care of myself. I have no idea what I'm supposed to do, what to do with myself, or how to go on living."

"You've really decided to quit?"

"I decided a long time ago, only it just doesn't work. You were the one who told me I was weak willed."

"And why do you think your will is stronger now?"

"Oh, I don't. But now I know I have to do it. For Mitya's sake. He's gone, of course, but I'm certain his soul will rest easier if I stop shooting up. I also wanted to tell you one thing. I only just realized it tonight. It's very important." Katya's voice was triumphant. "Someone broke in through the window that night."

"And who might that have been?" Regina asked.

"The murderer," Katya whispered.

"I wonder what kind of murderer this was."

"I don't know yet. But I do know for sure that he came in through the window."

"You've decided to play Holmes?"

"You don't believe me either!" Katya exclaimed in despair.

"Who else doesn't?"

"Olga and all of them."

"To believe you, we need facts. Do you have any?" Regina asked quickly.

"Yes! But very few for now, and I'm afraid they'll seem silly to you."

"Why would they? First tell me, and then we can put our heads together."

"Okay. First of all, two things have gone missing, Mitya's diary and his address book. Secondly, I found a crumpled-up piece of paper in his jacket pocket." Katya read into the receiver what he'd written. "And thirdly, I remembered that that night the wind blew the window open, so it wasn't locked. Someone broke the latch, climbed into the apartment, and then, after killing Mitya and making it look as if he'd hanged himself, climbed out."

"Have you told anyone other than me about this?" Regina asked gently.

"No. No one wants to listen to me."

"All right, then, Katya dear. In no case are you to tell anyone anything. If someone did kill Mitya, then it was someone very close to him. If you start sharing your suspicions, you might share them with the murderer without even knowing. To be perfectly honest, what you've told me really isn't enough. Don't be mad, but this seems a little like gibberish. You don't want them to stick you back in the nuthouse, do you? It's better to keep quiet. I promise I'll help you sort this out. Do you understand me?"

"Yes," Katya whispered, distraught. "I won't tell anyone anything."

After hearing Lena's story about the fake doctor's visit, Misha Sichkin sighed heavily into the receiver and said, "Lena, do you miss life on the wild side? Was it too much for you to ask her name and call the clinic before opening the door and letting her in?"

"Yes, it was," Lena admitted. "And awkward. I can't keep a person waiting on the stairs all the time I'm trying to get through on the phone. Do you know what it's like to try to get through to a pediatric clinic?"

"I know you're capable of opening the door without even asking who's there or looking through the peephole! How am I supposed to get even the most elementary rules of safety into your head?"

"Misha, I get it. You're two hundred percent right. It's my own fault. But tell me who this woman might be. And why she would do it. Could she really have been casing our place?"

"Did you call the clinic?"

"Of course. This morning."

"Naturally, they confirmed that there are no wellness checks going on now."

"Right. And no one had any plans to give flu shots."

"Maybe it was a doctor from another clinic? And there was a mix-up with addresses?" Misha suggested.

"Oh, how I wish I could believe that!" Lena sighed.

"If only you'd asked her her name. Listen, Lena, can you repeat the part about the suicide?"

Lena briefly retold Mitya's story and mentioned her conversation with her husband on the subject.

"Things are never boring with you, Lena." Misha smiled into the receiver. "You like to complicate everything. I agree with Seryozha. I don't see anything criminal in the Sinitsyn story, either. Whereas this doctor . . . It's not like she was casing your place, though you never know. The only consolation is that you and Seryozha don't have anything in particular to steal. Your apartment's hardly going to interest serious housebreakers."

"You mean only serious ones have places cased?"

"As a rule, yes. Listen, Lena, I'll send someone over and he'll set up a security alarm at your apartment. If anything happens, we'll have a team there in five minutes. Only don't forget to turn it on, okay? My man will give you detailed instructions. Lock all the doors. And don't let any strangers in."

"Misha, thank you, and forgive me."

"I can't!" Misha grumbled angrily. "When Seryozha comes back, I'm going to tell him I gave you a good tongue-lashing."

"All right, Misha, I get it. Don't make things worse than they already are. You know, the moment she left, for some reason I felt like a squeezed lemon. I got a headache, my knees got all wobbly, and I got sick to my stomach for no reason at all. At the time, I didn't even suspect she wasn't a doctor from the Filatov. I thought I'd been talking to a sweet, normal person, and then there was the feeling, you know, as if she'd x-rayed me or hypnotized me. Just tell me honestly what you really think. Could there be any connection between Sinitsyn's suicide and the doctor's visit?"

"Just think about it. What kind of connection could there be?"

⚜

Regina always took a dislike to beautiful women, especially if they were also smart. But unlike other women, she was honest about it. She could admit to herself that another woman was prettier, smarter, and better—and hate her for it. Regina's hatred had no consequences, provided the woman didn't get in her way.

Everything about Polyanskaya irritated her. Her fresh, regular features, her long, graceful neck, her dark brown hair casually pulled back in a heavy knot, her short, slender figure, even her little diamond earrings. But she especially didn't like the woman's hands—the delicate, fragile wrists, the long, slender fingers, and the shortly cut nails.

How much time and effort Regina had devoted to her own hands with their stubby fingers, broad palms, and fat, plebeian wrists! Even the surgeons at the Swiss clinic couldn't do their magic on her hands.

Of course, Regina had taken a risk when she cooked up the Filatov doctor scheme. But she believed that she should always meet and talk to whomever she was going to be dealing with. She wanted to know them up close, insofar as that was possible. After that, she could decide whether or not her opponent was dangerous and what to expect from him.

She'd prepared painstakingly for the meeting. She'd put a lot of serious thought into altering her appearance, so that the image of the bedraggled but sweet and attentive pediatrician from the Filatov Hospital was 100 percent authentic.

She may have made one mistake: she stayed too long. It was a forgivable mistake, though. Anyone can just be tired and relax over a cup of good coffee. It's perfectly normal.

Not that she could have left earlier. She had to finish the conversation. If Polyanskaya had kept up the topic of suicide and told her Sinitsyn's story, she could have been reassured, at least for a while.

But Polyanskaya didn't say a word about her friend's brother, though she couldn't not have been thinking of him. Another woman in her place would definitely have laid out the story. In the situation Regina had deftly set up, Sinitsyn's suicide just begged to be brought up.

But Polyanskaya didn't say a word about it. That meant, first of all, that she'd taken her friend's brother's suicide to heart and was thinking about it intently. Secondly, it meant that subconsciously she didn't believe it was a suicide. And thirdly, it showed that she wasn't indiscreet.

Am I taking this too far? Regina asked herself. *Why would Polyanskaya get involved in all this? Sinitsyn wasn't family. He was barely anyone to her.* And she immediately answered her own question: *No. Not too far!*

Olga Sinitsyna, the dead man's sister, wouldn't dig deeply. First of all, she didn't have much information to work with, and, secondly, she was inattentive to detail. She hadn't even noticed the scratches on her dead brother's arm. But most important, she had a completely different mindset. She was a tactician where Polyanskaya was a strategist. She thought concretely; Polyanskaya, abstractly. Polyanskaya knew how to generalize and analyze unobtrusive, inchoate facts. The analyst in her would think and act until she had dug all the way to the truth. No matter how dangerous it got for her.

Not only that—the graver the danger, the more decisively she would act.

What if I just got rid of her? Regina thought. *It can't be a suicide this time, obviously. Perhaps an accident would work. But that's dangerous, too.*

As she sat in this stranger's cozy kitchen drinking strong coffee, Regina's spine tingled, sensing the danger presented by her generous host. And now the Crowell article, which Regina herself had just read.

She came across the cassette with Mitya's new songs by accident. For some reason it was in the nursery, at the bottom of Liza's toy box. Lena set everything aside and slipped it into the tape player. A pure, low voice began,

> Going back to nowhere,
> To the distant long ago,
> Where the water rocks, black as sleep,

Lena listened to song after song. Mitya was talented, of course. But it was hardly worth his time to go looking for producers. His songs had a keen sense of time, but a time irrevocably in the past. They sounded great at a songwriters' conference and in nightclubs. But to be successful these days, you had to write and sing differently than he did.

"The Tobolsk rain runs down my collar," the tape player sang.

Yes, of course, we were talking about our trip through Tyumen Province, Lena remembered. *Lord, that was all we talked about that evening. Why? It's been fourteen years, after all. Why was Mitya so adamant about revisiting that subject?*

> The match's flame, how high it blazes,
> In your palms' translucent tent.
> Still alive, as the wind moans in Tobolsk.
> Still alive, and not a soul around.

The song ended and so did the tape—nearly. Lena was about to take it out and turn it over when suddenly she heard light coughing and Mitya's voice.

"I may be acting foolishly and improperly. It would be simpler to go to the prosecutor. Simpler and more honest. But I don't trust our justice system. In a year, the statute of limitations will run out. It might not even apply to you. Your crimes don't have a statute of limitations. Actually, the law isn't my strong point, and I have no intention of hiring a lawyer to explain to me the best way to blackmail you. I might not do anything at all."

More coughing. Then a nervous laugh.

The tape ended. Lena quickly turned the cassette over and listened to the other side from beginning to end, but it was all songs. While they were playing, Lena took down the latest edition of the Criminal Code and searched the index for "statute of limitations."

The tape player sang,

> He thought, I know, I'll do it,
> I'll do just that!
> A cabbage butterfly landed
> On his clenched red fist,

Lena listened to the songs and read the Criminal Code. *Fifteen years after a felony is committed . . . The question of applying the statute of limitations to an individual who has committed a capital crime . . . shall be decided by the court. If the court does not deem it possible to release said individual from criminal responsibility in connection with the statute of limitations, then the death penalty and life imprisonment are not applicable.*

"Fifteen years," Lena murmured thoughtfully. "Mitya said the statute of limitations would run out in a year. That means it was fourteen years ago. Fourteen years ago the three of us, Olga, Mitya, and I, were traveling through Tyumen Province. That's exactly what Mitya was talking about two weeks ago. Lord, what nonsense is this? Who was he trying to blackmail? And what with? What do Tobolsk and the statute of limitations have to do with anything?"

> Everything soon begins and ends,
> Only to perish in blood and smoke,
> But that's the last thing I'd ever want,

The last thing I'd want for him.
He's just one of multitudes,
But a legion stands behind him.

"He was hinting at some similarity, something about some law . . ."

Lena gave a start when the phone rang. *Who could that be so late?* she thought, looking at her watch. It was 12:30.

"Lena, hello," an unfamiliar woman's voice said softly, with a touch of hysteria. "I'm sorry. I probably woke you. Don't you recognize me?"

"No."

"It's Katya Sinitsyna."

CHAPTER 12

Tyumen, June 1982

Every summer, the major magazines, especially the ones aimed at young people, sent out groups of employees to all the ends of the vast Soviet homeland to perform for the laborers of the towns and villages, thus winning over potential subscribers. Subscribers and circulation numbers were a matter of prestige, not commerce. Neither salaries nor author fees depended on circulation numbers. On the other hand, high numbers allowed an editor in chief to shove the circulation numbers of his "leftish" publication in the face of his ideological bosses and say, "See, the people read us, so our policy must be correct!"

Naturally, the Party and Young Communist leadership and the editors in chief all knew perfectly well that the people were irrelevant, but no one had the nerve to violate this sacred ritual, which was strictly observed by the people's servants, even among themselves.

Everyone knew the people were irrelevant, but no one would say that out loud, especially the people themselves. Everyone knew and understood everything—but tacitly.

Department heads and editorial staff preferred to promote subscriptions in southern and coastal regions. Freelancers, and especially student interns, were sent to Siberia, the Far East, and other nonresort spots. Actually, the freelancers and interns didn't mind.

The Soviet homeland was great and multifaceted. There were lots of interesting things in Siberia and the Far East, especially if you were a twenty-something magazine salesperson traveling for free, with all your expenses paid by the state. The per diem of two rubles and sixty kopeks was more than enough for them to eat three times a day, and as representatives of the foremost nationwide youth magazine, the organ of the Young Communists' Central Committee, they were officials—so they were met, housed, fed, and driven around.

Lena Polyanskaya and Olga and Mitya Sinitsyn sat on a bench at the Tyumen airport, smoking and letting the hot Siberian sun bathe their faces. They were discussing whether they should wait for their ride or catch a bus to the Young Communist Committee office.

The Committee's promised car hadn't met them. They took a gloomy look at the long line at the bus stop.

"How can they not meet us?" Mitya asked anxiously.

"Don't panic," Lena reassured him. "The main secretary called me in Tyumen to say that three of her colleagues were on their way, but didn't give me any more information than that."

"How are they going to put us up?" Mitya wouldn't let it go. "It's fine for you. You're interns here on official business. I'm just tagging along, hoping to play a few songs. They'll probably put me in a room with some stranger who'll turn out to be an alcoholic or some kind of maniac."

"You are such a pest, Brer Rabbit." Olga sighed.

"No, I'm not a pest. I'm a well-grounded human being. I like to know everything in advance. You probably didn't even bring an immersion heater or tea or sugar, while I took the trouble to bring two cans of condensed milk and a can of beef stew."

"Well, they've definitely got stew here," Lena grinned.

"Care to bet?" Mitya sulked.

"Bet what?"

"Well," Mitya paused. "A can of condensed milk."

"He's betting you a can of condensed milk." Olga grinned.

"You can tease me all you like, Sis." Mitya shook his head. "All right, I'm prepared to bet a can that they don't have beef stew here. At most, they have 'tourist breakfasts'—fish balls made of ground-up fish bones and rice that looks like mealworms. If I lose, the condensed milk's yours. But if I win, what can you give me?"

"Two packs of Rhodopes or some ground coffee."

"What do I care about your Rhodopes when I've got my own cigarettes?" Mitya snorted. "And you're not going to be drinking any coffee without my sugar and immersion heater anyway!"

"All right, boys and girls. That's enough silliness. We're all going to eat, drink, and smoke together in any case. Look, I think the Young Communists are here!"

A khaki-colored car stopped on the square and out of it jumped a young man wearing a formal charcoal-gray suit, despite the heat, and a shiny Young Communist lapel pin. The young man headed decisively for the terminal looking from side to side.

"Let him look for us. He's the one who's late," Mitya gloated. "When did our flight come in? An hour and a half ago! He can wait for us now."

A few minutes later, a voice boomed over the airport loudspeaker: "Attention journalists from Moscow! They're waiting for you at the information desk. I repeat . . ."

Snatching up all their things and throwing his guitar strap over his shoulder, Mitya headed for the information desk with Olga and Lena behind him.

"You're brother really is a gentleman," Lena remarked.

"I'm educating him." Olga shrugged.

"It's been decided to send you first to Tobolsk and then to Khanty-Mansiysk," the Committee's second secretary told them.

"We'll try to sort out the hotel issue," he said as he handed back their travel vouchers, after the secretary took note of them. "Go for a walk and take a look at the city. You can leave your things in my office. Come by in a couple of hours. We should have your hotel sorted by then. We have a conference of reindeer herders going on and rooms are tight."

"I'm sorry, Volodya, but what do you mean by 'sort out'?" Lena asked the Young Communist in a formal tone. "As I understand it, we have a television appearance today and an event with vocational school students. Moreover, the television event is in an hour, and we need to rest and take a shower beforehand."

"Hey, what's with the bourgeois manners?" Volodya frowned. "What shower? Lower your expectations. Remember, you're not going to have a room with a shower anyway. Tyumen hasn't had hot water for a year, and you're not even the editor in chief."

Olga stepped in. She was good at dealing with these kinds of Young Communist louts.

"Let's put it this way, Volodya," she said softly and gently. "Either you pick your fat ass up off that chair right now and don't 'try to sort out' but *actually* sort out the question of a decent hotel or else we're going to the Party committee and telling them you can't cope with your ideological obligations. If that's not enough, we'll call our offices in Moscow and have our editor in chief get in touch with the Young Communist Central Committee immediately. Do you want the hotel issue decided on that level? If you do, I'm happy to make that happen."

Fifteen minutes later they were taken to the Hotel East.

"Curious," Lena said pensively as she examined the double room. "Why isn't there a single Hotel West in this country? There's the Hotel North, the Hotel South, and the Hotel East, but not a single Hotel West. As if there were no such part of the world."

Tyumen had indeed done away with hot water as a class enemy. But in the intense heat, you could splash yourself perfectly well with cold. They'd been given a room with a shower after all. Mitya did have to share a room with someone, but he was a quiet, educated old man, a supplier from Barnaul. Not an alcoholic and not a maniac, at least not at first glance.

The local TV people were much nicer than the Young Communists. Although, before the taping, the director asked Mitya to sing her the songs he was planning to perform.

"At least give me the lyrics," she said, embarrassed. "And you, Olga, if you can, would you show me the poems you're going to recite?"

"But it's not live television. If something goes wrong, you can cut it afterward."

"If something goes wrong, they'll rip my head off," the plump and weary middle-aged woman said. "Before I have the chance to cut it."

They had their typewritten texts with them.

"Mitya, please, this song here, don't sing 'the train station stank of whores and prison,'" she commented, not taking her eyes off the page. "The rest is fine. And you, Olga, this poem about the migrant worker, 'I'm a migrant, a black seed'—it's very nice, but please don't read it."

Here the ideological censorship ended. There was none at their next stop, the vocational school. The song about the train station and the poem about the migrant worker received loud applause from the students. After the performance, they were invited to stay for a dance, but they refused. They were tired and wanted only to eat and sleep.

They walked back to the hotel. The stores were already closed, as were the cafés and cafeterias.

"My thrifty brother, you could at least have thought to buy a little bread," Olga said. "I'd rather starve than eat your beef stew without bread."

"So starve." Mitya gave his permission. "All the more for me and Lena."

"No one's going to starve," Lena told them happily. "The dumpling shop over there is open!"

"I love Siberian dumplings." Mitya actually moaned. "Love, love, love."

But there weren't any dumplings left. The menu listed ten varieties—dumplings filled with venison, bear meat, salmon. "We're out . . . Out . . . Out of that, too," the waitress replied sleepily.

"What do you have?" Olga asked sadly.

"Northern Lights mutton soup from the day before yesterday, Tenderness veal cutlet, and Romance and Friendship sandwiches," the waitress told them reluctantly.

"Bring it all! We'll have Tenderness and Romance and Friendship under the Northern Lights," Mitya rejoiced. "Three portions of each!"

"I don't advise the Lights," the waitress commented. "It's starting to smell."

"Okay. Bring the rest. And lots of bread!" The Tenderness veal was an enormous lump of dough, burned on the outside and completely raw inside. In the very middle, a tiny piece of dark gray ground veal hid shamefully. It came with limp macaroni seasoned with lard.

Romance was a cooked smoked sausage that oozed yellow grease and was inedible. Only the dried-up but familiar melted Friendship cheese on a piece of bread met their expectations.

They raked all the bread off the table and into a bag and headed for the hotel, still hungry. Along the way they came across an ice cream stand.

"The ice cream's melting," the vendor warned them.

"How's that?" Lena didn't understand.

"Just what I said. The freezer broke down."

"Fine, fill a cup," Mitya said.

The vendor scooped out the white muck and poured it into a cardboard cup.

"Nine kopeks."

Tyumen's June nights were long and bright.

Communist slogans hung on the five-story prefab apartment buildings: **"ONWARD, TO THE VICTORY OF COMMUNISM!" "LONG LIVE THE INDESTRUCTIBLE BROTHERHOOD OF THE GREAT SOVIET PEOPLE!" "THE PEOPLE AND PARTY ARE ONE!"**

Giant, square-muscled men and women workers on posters three meters tall raised their huge fists over the quiet, dirty streets of the sleepy Siberian city.

"If I were a director," Mitya said, "I'd definitely shoot a film of those red-fisted monsters coming to life at night, climbing down from the posters, and marching between the prefab buildings in terrible, silent formation, sweeping everything from their path. It would be a horror film."

"There is no such genre in Soviet cinema, and there never will be." Olga chuckled.

❧

His hands were shaking badly. He thought that dance was never going to end. He peeked cautiously through the doorway and sought her out, his girl. She was shaking and twisting to a two-year-old hit.

> I beg you, at this rosy hour,
> Sing to me oh so softly,
> How dear the land of birches
> In the raspberry-colored dawn.

The girl was wearing a short raspberry-colored skirt that hugged her strong, curvy hips, and a bright pink, short-sleeved blouse. She had full lips thickly smeared with raspberry lipstick and a slight smile. A cheap pendant—nickel silver and enamel, a small heart, and inside, a raspberry rose with a green leaf—swung and hopped on her perfect, milk-white neck.

He absolutely had to see what color her eyes were. Gray-blue shadows on her trembling eyelids rolled up tight under eyebrows plucked to nothing. Straight, peroxided hair in a bowl cut. It was a hairstyle that had become fashionable after the French singer Mireille Mathieu visited the country and gave a series of concerts.

This was the third dance she'd danced with the same guy, a skinny, long-haired macaque. He hunched clumsily, shook his narrow, sloping shoulders, and danced low over his partner as if he were trying to lie down on top of her. He stuck out his scrawny ass in his baggy Soviet "Texas" trousers and shuffled his feet incoherently to the up-tempo music.

If he decides to see her home, I'll have to put it off until tomorrow, he thought. *Or choose someone who's going home alone. But I don't know the other girls' routes, and this one has to cross the vacant lot behind the construction site. She has no other choice. It would be too bad if this long-haired Jap decides to see my girl home.*

He felt the pleasant weight of the small tourist knife in the inside pocket of his track jacket and looked from the dark twilight into the brightly lit school auditorium, where sixteen-year-old Natasha Koloskova was wriggling passionately and rhythmically. Natasha was the only daughter of Klavdia Andreyevna Koloskova, a forty-year-old single mother who had sewn both the short skirt and the blouse of pink crepe de chine Natasha wore. The girl had to have something to shine in at dances. She so loved to dance.

When they announced that the next dance would be the last, an indignant howl went up. Then Alla Pugacheva's song about the crane started:

Take me with you . . .

I want to see the sky.

The couples swayed slowly, embracing.

"Natasha, can I walk you home?" Long-haired, narrow-shouldered Petya Sidorkin whispered into his partner's ear.

"We'll see." She shrugged vaguely and peeked at the couple next to them.

She wanted handsome, broad-shouldered Seryozha Rusov to walk her home. But Seryozha was tenderly embracing the slender waist of Marina Zaslavskaya.

"Uh-uh, Natasha." Petya shook his loose curls, noticing her look. "He hasn't come up to you once. He and Marina have been going steady since the winter."

"Why are you sticking your nose where it doesn't belong?" Natasha cried in a whisper. "I can manage without you."

She disengaged Petya's hands from her waist and quickly cut through the dancing couples toward the exit.

"Natasha!" Petya ran after her. "Natasha, wait!"

"Go away! I'm sick of you!" she said loudly, and she slipped into the gathering dusk.

She walked through the deserted streets, swallowing her tears. Ever since that first year, that first day, she'd liked Seryozha Rusov so bad it hurt. But he would never look her way. She had nothing on Marina! Marina looked like Mireille Mathieu. She was the prettiest girl at the school.

Natasha had had such high hopes that at today's dance Seryozha would finally notice her and ask her for at least one dance. Her mama had made her this great skirt and blouse. Her mama's friend had given her a pretty heart pendant for her birthday, and it looked so stylish with her pink blouse. She had gotten her hair cut like Mireille's, and everyone said it suited her and made her face slimmer and more interesting. But Seryozha only had eyes for Marina.

Natasha felt so sad that she didn't notice anything around her, didn't hear the cautious steps that had been following her since she had left the school, never once looked around to see the tall, broad-shouldered figure of the young man in the dark, loose, waterproof nylon jacket.

All of a sudden an iron hand was covering her mouth and nose. They were on the edge of the vacant lot, near the deserted construction site, and there wasn't a soul around. Natasha didn't even have time to cry out.

"That's enough sleep, lazybones!" Mitya threw open the door to their room, carrying a large package, from which he took out a tin of sugar, an immersion heater, and pieces of yesterday's bread.

"You could have knocked." Lena sat up in bed, yawning sweetly, and stretched. "What time is it?"

"Eight thirty. They're picking us up at nine fifteen. Get out your coffee and we'll have breakfast."

"Hey, where's your famous condensed milk?" Olga slipped out from under the blanket and shuffled barefoot to the bathroom.

"You'll get your condensed milk. Only not right now. Tonight we're leaving for Tobolsk, and how am I supposed to pack an open can?"

"You're a cheapskate, Brer Rabbit," Olga told him from the bathroom, with a toothbrush in her mouth. "So go to the buffet and buy us something. Man cannot breakfast on bread alone."

"All right. But you'd both better be washed and dressed and have the coffee made when I get back." Mitya put his one-liter metal mug out on the table.

"Yes sir, Herr General!" Lena saluted.

"Down the rabbit hole, Brer Rabbit!" Olga mumbled from the bathroom with a mouth full of toothpaste.

There were very few people in the hotel's second-floor buffet. While the server was weighing the sausage she'd cut and wrapping the hard-boiled eggs in paper, Mitya looked out the window.

The window looked out on the small square in front of the hotel. There was a police van and an ambulance right at the entrance. Mitya saw two medics carrying out a stretcher with someone covered in a sheet up to her chin.

"Did something happen?" he asked the server. "The police and an ambulance are here."

"Yes." The server heaved a deep sigh. Mitya noticed she had red tear-stained eyes and rivulets of dried tears on her cheeks.

"They found the body of the daughter of one of our maids early this morning in a vacant lot," the server said, sobbing softly. "The girl was raped and murdered. The police came for her mother to take her away to make the identification, and her heart couldn't take it. They called the ambulance and now they're taking her away."

"Lord," Mitya whispered.

"The girl, Natasha, only just turned sixteen. She'd been given an enameled pendant, a heart with a rose, and she was so happy. Her mama, Klava, and I have been friends since school. She raised Natasha alone." Another sob escaped the server. She wiped her puffy, teary eyes with the sleeve of her white coat. "A year ago something similar happened. Only the girl was from the teachers college, eighteen years old. And the police aren't exactly itching to solve it. They couldn't care less if all our kids get killed off."

"Hey, Tamara Vasilievna, quit running your mouth," an authoritative male voice came from the buffet room.

Mitya looked around. A fat man wearing a white shirt and tie sat at a table drinking tea.

"I have nothing to fear!" Tamara put her arms akimbo. "I'm telling the truth. There's a maniac in town killing our children. There was a similar case in the spring. They could at least write in the newspapers and tell people over the radio not to let their children out of their sight! But no, they don't say anything. It's as if nothing were happening. You have two daughters, don't you, Petrovich?"

"And they're right not to say anything," Petrovich said authoritatively. "The last thing we need is to start a panic. The police know their business. They'll catch the killer."

"Sure!" the server snickered. "They'll catch him! But not before he murders more of our children."

"You've got a son. What are you so worked up about?" Petrovich slurped his tea and wiped his sweaty bald spot with his handkerchief.

"You're an idiot, I swear!" The server shook her head. "You may be a Party instructor, but you're an idiot! There've been two cases in Tobolsk where some monster raped the girls and killed them"—she turned to Mitya—"and no one gives a damn."

"You mean there have been four murders in the province altogether?" Mitya asked softly.

"Four now. Natasha Koloskova's the fourth. She never came back from the dance they had at her school yesterday. Klava, her mama, waited up until two in the morning and then got worried. She ran to her neighbor's, whose son is Natasha's classmate. As soon as she found out the dance had ended at eleven thirty, she went straight to the police. But they wouldn't even take her statement. They said two hours was too soon. 'Your daughter's gone out with her boyfriend.' Workers on the construction site discovered her body this morning."

"What's got you so down?" Olga asked when Mitya came back from the buffet with a sack of food. "Coffee's ready. Sit down and have your breakfast."

"There's a nightmare going on here," Mitya said softly, and he took a cigarette from the pack on the table and lit up.

"Smoking on an empty stomach!" Olga exclaimed, and she clipped her brother on the back of his head, took the cigarette out of his mouth, and snuffed it out. "So what is this nightmare?"

Mitya told them everything he'd just learned.

Before he could finish, there was a knock at the door. Standing on the threshold was Volodya, wearing the same gray suit with the lapel pin.

"Good morning, Volodya," Olga greeted him politely. "Would you like coffee?"

"Thank you, I won't say no. Only we have to be quick. The car's waiting."

Sipping hot coffee from a thin hotel glass, he gave Lena and Olga a critical look, shook his head, and asked, "Can you wear something different?"

"Why?" Lena was surprised. "What don't you like about our clothes?"

"You're showing too much leg, and Olga—excuse me, of course—is showing a lot on top," he informed them without embarrassment.

Lena and Olga exchanged indignant looks, and right then Mitya stepped in. "Listen, my Young Communist Pierre Cardin. Don't you think it's up to them how they dress? They're dressed perfectly decently. Not only that, in this oven, not everyone can go around in formal suits!"

"You Muscovites are so thin-skinned!" Volodya shrugged. "I'm just giving you advice. I'm not the one performing at the prison today, you are."

"Where?" the three asked in chorus.

"The prison. If I were you, I wouldn't be parading my legs and breasts in front of the inmates. Dress more soberly, girls. Please."

Olga was indignant. "I wonder whose big idea it was to send us to a prison?"

"The head of the prison put in a request. Last year a group came from *Youth* magazine and performed for them. Singers, lecturers, everyone performs. Inmates are people, too."

"Fine, Young Communist. You convinced me." Lena gave up. "You and Mitya step out for a minute and we'll change."

Olga and Lena headed out to perform for the inmates wearing long skirts and long-sleeved blouses. When they got to the prison, they realized the Young Communist was right. An outfit that in summertime Moscow had looked perfectly ordinary and proper looked completely different here in Tyumen—especially in a prison.

Lena was struck by the peculiar, heavy smell. Standing onstage in front of the microphone, she surveyed the audience with dismay. Every last one of them had a shaved head and was wearing a navy peacoat. Lena thought it was probably best to start the performance with one of Mitya's songs.

"Hi!" She smiled at the audience. "I have no doubt you all know and like our magazine. We get a lot of letters at our office. You ask questions and send in your poems and stories. Today we have an opportunity to interact face-to-face instead of through the mail. Right now a famous Moscow singer-songwriter, Mitya Sinitsyn, is going to perform for you."

The audience was grateful and responsive. Mitya's songs, Olga's poems, and Lena's stories about the magazine, about the work of its departments, and various amusing epistolary incidents provoked shouts and applause. They wouldn't let them leave the stage. They kept shouting out questions and sending up handwritten notes.

Can I come onstage and recite a poem I wrote myself?
Unfairly convicted. Blindboy.

After reading this note, Lena picked up the microphone.

"Someone who calls himself Blindboy wants to recite his poem from the stage," she told the hall. The hall roared and chuckled.

"You don't want to hear your comrade's poem?" Olga asked into the microphone. "If that's what he wants, he should read."

The hall burst into guffaws.

"Let the fag have his dance!" said a powerful, gold-toothed inmate sitting in the first row—spread over two chairs, spitting juicily. He wore a gold cross aound his neck, and on his right and left sat two goons a little younger, flashing their steel teeth.

Silence hovered in the hall. It was clear that the gold cross was the top gun.

"Hey, go on, shake your ass, Marusya," someone's hoarse falsetto rang out in the silence.

A strange scuffling started in the back rows, and the guard standing nearby was about to take a step in that direction but thought better of interfering, gave up, and turned away, spitting through his teeth exactly like an inmate.

A minute later they dragged a scrawny, round-shouldered kid of twenty or so onto the stage. His face was covered in scars from teen-age pimples. All of a sudden Lena realized why they'd nicknamed him Blindboy. His eyes were tiny and deep set. You could barely see them under his overhanging, eyebrow-less brows. When he got onstage, you could tell his eyes were some odd, very light color, and his pupils were pinpoints. White eyes. Blindboy.

"Hello." Lena gave him the friendliest smile she could. "For starters, let's introduce ourselves. What's your name?"

The small head covered in blond stubble dropped very low.

"Vasily Slepak," he mumbled. So the nickname wasn't just about his eyes. "Slepak" has the same root as *slepoy*—blind.

"Very nice to meet you," Lena said loudly into the microphone. "Now our poet Vasily Slepak will recite a poem."

She stuck the microphone into his shaking hands and clapped softly. Olga and Mitya clapped, too.

The audience didn't. Lena felt the tension of that silence on her skin. It was a nasty, explosive silence. Vasily squeezed the microphone in his sweaty hand. All of a sudden a voice strangely low for such a frail complexion rang out in the silence:

I know you don't love me,
Won't see or caress me,
You've married another,
A bad man, a crook . . .

The audience burst out laughing. But the low voice at the microphone outshouted their laughter and recited one line after another.

So don't mock me
With your unbearable truth,
I'm paying a harsh price
For the right to call you my love . . .

Quickly, Vasily walked over to Lena, handed her the microphone, hopped off the stage, and ran through the whistling, laughing hall. Someone stuck out a foot and he tripped and went sprawling.

"Vasily!" Lena said into the microphone. "Your poem was wonderful! I'll try to get it published in our magazine."

"Are you crazy?" She heard Olga's whisper from behind. "Why are you promising him? It's the usual graphomania!"

"Vasily!" Lena went on, watching the skinny, round-shouldered figure get up from the spit-covered floor. "You keep writing and send your poems to the office, to the Literature Department! Just don't give up. Write your poems. You're a talented man."

The laughter and whistling died down and the hall started buzzing in amazement.

"I should write to you instead." The hulk in the first row flashed his gold teeth. "Let's you and me get to know each other. We can be pen pals. How about giving me your home address?"

Lena didn't even look in his direction and calmly spoke into the microphone.

"Comrades, this is where our gathering ends. All the best. Thank you for your attention."

"Hey, Gray Eyes!" The voice from the first row rang out in the deathly hush. "I asked you a question. Give me your home address?"

"The address of our offices is printed in every issue of the magazine."

"Fuck your offices," Gold Teeth spat.

Lena set the microphone aside. She was afraid to look down at the first row. She noticed one of the guards saying something quickly to another, who went out, and a minute later several soldiers with submachine guns streamed through both doors of the auditorium.

"Answer when someone asks you a question!" one of Gold Teeth's buddies added.

"I just want to be friends. Be my friend, Gray Eyes! Right now. I know a good spot. Don't worry, we can be alone here, too."

The two goons rose lazily, as if reluctantly, and took a step toward the stage. Simultaneously, Mitya and Olga flanked Lena on either side. There was no passage behind the stage; the only way out was by descending into the auditorium.

A minute later the three of them were surrounded by soldiers, and only in that way, in a solid ring, did they exit the auditorium.

In the prison warden's office, Lena gulped down a glass of water from a pitcher and lit a cigarette. Only then did she stop shaking.

"Can you explain to me what I did wrong?" she quietly asked the warden, an elderly colonel.

"Actually, you didn't do anything wrong. They have their own laws here, and you're not expected to know them. It's just that Vasily's a prison bitch. The most despised individual there can be. Gritsenko, the guy in the first row, is the boss. You defied him by praising someone you can only mock. You broke their law. Don't worry, though. Last year, one writer who came with *Youth* magazine had the bright idea of reading a story with an explicit sex scene. Very explicit."

"What happened?" Mitya asked.

"They rushed the stage, and there were two women there, one middle-aged, the department chief, the other, a young reporter. We had to intervene. It was a real mess, and today was nothing compared to that."

"If it's so dangerous, why do you invite people to perform?" Olga wondered.

"Well, there's no particular danger." The colonel grinned. "There's an armed guard and everything's under control. Prison's prison, but there are human beings here, too."

"What's Slepak in here for?" Lena asked.

"Article 161a. He and a buddy robbed a shop."

They were supposed to go to Tobolsk that night. They only had an hour to rest up and pack after their performances. Not that they had much to pack.

They were having tea in their room when Volodya walked in. Next to him was a tall, broad-shouldered blond of twenty-five or so with a pleasant, intelligent face and green-blue eyes. He had a small red Young Communist pin on the pocket of his dark blue windbreaker.

"Meet Veniamin Volkov, Culture Department head for the Tobolsk Young Communists Committee," Volodya introduced him. "He flew in on business this morning and he'll be your escort to Tobolsk today."

"Pleased to meet you," the Tobolsk Young Communist introduced himself, shaking everyone's hand.

He had a guileless, rather enchanting smile and a soft, gentle baritone. He was a lot nicer than Volodya.

CHAPTER 13

Moscow, March 1996

"I'm probably wrong to call. But I thought you . . . Basically, I thought you thought Mitya didn't kill himself, either. Or am I wrong? Don't you care, either?" The hysterical notes in Katya Sinitsyna's voice were gone. She spoke in an indifferent monotone.

"Katya. I do care," Lena said gently. "And you were right to call. I wanted to talk to you myself. I'm sorry, I think I offended you on the stairs."

"What do you mean? No, you didn't offend me at all. Sometimes I behave badly . . . You know, I found a piece of paper in Mitya's jacket pocket. I already shared it with someone, but she said I was crazy. She's a good person, a doctor, and she wants to help me. But I have to talk to someone who isn't going to say it's crazy. I'll read you what it says. Your name's on it."

Lena listened to the strange text that Katya read into the receiver very slowly, syllable by syllable almost, and thought, *A doctor . . . a woman doctor . . . That fake doctor examined Liza very professionally and answered my questions like a real physician. A smart and experienced doctor. And at the same time she persisted in leading the conversation around to suicide, as if she were feeling me out, waiting for me to keep the subject going, to say, you know, "Recently my friend's brother . . ."*

"Katya," Lena nearly shouted when she'd finished reading it. "What's the name of the doctor you shared your suspicions with?"

"I can't tell you," Katya said quietly, embarrassed. "I'm sorry, I can't. She's helping me. She's trying to cure me. But from the very beginning, she asked me not to tell anyone her name. She's a very well-known psychotherapist. People are dying to get in to see her. That's why from the very start she asks those she decides to help not to say her name or talk about her. I'm sorry. I also forgot to tell you that Mitya's diary's gone missing, the one the page was torn out of, and I found a forensic psychiatry textbook in his bag, and also . . . Oh, wait a minute. I think that's my doorbell. I'll be right back."

Katya set down the receiver. Lena heard her steps receding and then a very distant voice.

"Oh, hello." She said a name, but Lena couldn't make it out. Inna? Galina? It was too far from the phone.

A few minutes later she heard someone pick up the receiver and breathe lightly into it.

"Hello, Katya . . . ?" Lena asked cautiously.

Silence. Then a dial tone.

Lena was surprised to discover her hands were shaking. To calm down and collect her thoughts, she had to brew herself a cup of sweet, strong coffee and smoke a cigarette. But first she had to write down exactly what Katya had read to her over the phone. This was very important. She had to write it down before it slipped her mind. Where? On a scrap of paper? No. Best to enter it into the computer.

While the kettle was boiling, Lena switched on her laptop, opened a new file, and called it "Rabbit." That was what Olga had called Mitya since they were kids: Brer Rabbit. Not a very flattering nickname for a boy, but in their family it took on a warm and affectionate tone.

Quickly typing what Katya had told her from memory, Lena slipped Mitya's cassette into the tape player, wound the tape to the spot where the strange words started after the last song, and added that to the document as well. Then she took out a blank disk and copied the file onto it.

The kettle boiled. Katya didn't call back. After pouring boiling water over the ground coffee in the little cezve, Lena started looking for her own notebook. She came across a letter from New York she still hadn't opened, though it had come a long time ago. It was from Michael Barron, a professor at Columbia University. She had to call Katya back. Maybe they just got disconnected. Who could have come to see her so late? A girlfriend? Olga had said Mitya's wife didn't have any friends. Katya's line was busy. Lena dialed her number over and over.

She managed to brew and drink her coffee, smoke her cigarette, and open the letter.

Dear Lena, she read. *First of all, congratulations on your daughter's birth. I'm a little late with the congratulations, of course, since the child's already two, but what can I do? I'm lazy and don't like to write a letter without a practical reason. But now I have one.*

I've started work on a history of Russian Siberia. It's ridiculous, of course, for someone who doesn't know a word of Russian to be studying the country's history. But if it's ridiculous it can't be sad.

I need your help. I'm planning to visit Russia in the near future and travel through several Siberian cities. Above all, I'm interested in Tobolsk and its famed wooden citadel.

I remember your stories about Siberia, especially that city. As you likely realize, I'll need an interpreter on my trip. I know you have a small child, but I would be very grateful if you could accompany me on my trip as interpreter and consultant. I'd rather not hire a stranger.

The trip won't take more than ten days. I can pay you two hundred dollars a day and cover all your travel expenses, hotels, and food.

If necessary, I can even pay a babysitter for your daughter for the days you will be gone. My arrival depends only on your decision. I've bought a ticket to Moscow with open travel dates. I can fly out as soon as you say. I'll be waiting for your call.

A big hello to your husband and daughter. Sincerely yours, Michael.

Then his telephone number.

Katya's was still busy. Lena looked at the clock: 1:50. She had to call New York in any case. She had to say yes or no. And why say no?

She could leave Liza with Vera Fyodorovna. She could even buy them a package trip to a good vacation spot outside Moscow for those days. Lena had wanted to do that for a long time. Two thousand dollars for ten days wasn't bad money at all.

Right then she heard the long ring that meant a long-distance call.

There! Lena had time to think as she picked up the receiver. *It must be Michael. This is a little awkward.*

"Lena! Darling! Who have you been talking to for the last hour and a half?" She heard her husband's voice.

"Seryozha!"

She could hear him so well, it was as if he were calling from the next apartment instead of London.

"I miss you so much. I'm counting the days until I get back. How are things? How's my Liza?"

"All's well here. Liza's healthy but misses you a lot. Every day she asks me ten times when her papa is coming home."

"What about you? Miss me?"

"Of course I do, Seryozha. I miss you terribly. Tell me, how are things there?"

"I won't tell you over the phone. When I get there I'll tell you all the details. Basically, things are fine."

"Seryozha, I need to discuss something with you. I just read a letter from New York only a minute before you called."

"The one I took out of the mailbox? You've only just read it? You've got to be kidding!"

"That's the one. I just didn't get to it." Lena related the letter's contents to her husband.

"So what's the problem?" he asked after she finished. "You don't know whether or not you should agree?"

"That's the problem," Lena admitted.

"Do you want to go?"

"I don't know. On the one hand, yes. You don't often see two thousand dollars lying around. On the other hand, I've never been away from Liza that long and she's still so little."

"Ten days isn't long at all. And you could use a change of scenery, a distraction. At least there you won't be sitting in front of your laptop every night."

"So you think I should agree?"

"Yes. I do. I only have one question. This Michael, is he going to be hitting on you?"

"Of course he will!" Lena burst out laughing. "But he'll do it gently and politely, like a gentleman."

"Don't start anything with that man. If you can promise me you won't have an affair with him, I'll let you go."

"He's fat and bald, and he's got a lumpy nose. He likes to lecture me at length on the dangers of smoking and after a meal he digs around in his teeth with a toothpick in front of everyone."

"Some gentleman." Seryozha snickered. "Well, I'm reassured that you aren't going to have an affair with him."

"You know, I'd like to send Liza and Vera Fyodorovna to a good vacation spot outside Moscow for those ten days, so they can breathe fresh air and Vera Fyodorovna doesn't have to deal with waiting in line at the stores and cooking Liza's meals on top of everything else. Michael's offering to pay for a babysitter, so let him pay."

"A fine idea. Only let me know exactly when you send them off. I'll probably be back before you. Here, write down my number at the hotel. As soon as you know your exact plans, be sure to call me."

After talking with her husband, Lena felt reassured. This was a good time to call New York and accept the offer. But before that, to clear her conscience, she dialed Katya Sinitsyna's number one more time. It was still busy.

⁕

"Well, how are you?" Regina Valentinovna patted Katya on the cheek and passed quickly to the kitchen in her fur coat, boots, and thin suede gloves.

Katya was delayed at the front door when her slipper caught on the leg of a stool. When she got to the kitchen, she saw her guest hanging up her phone.

"I'd been trying to call you back," Regina explained. "But your line was busy. It turns out you forgot to hang up the phone."

"No, I didn't. I was just talking to someone," Katya said, flustered. "I should call back. I feel awkward."

"Who were you talking to, if I may ask?" Regina's suede-gloved hand was still on the receiver. Katya didn't notice that hand shift the receiver ever so slightly. It was no longer pressing down on the lever. Anyone calling Katya's number would get a busy signal.

Regina Valentinovna smelled of fine, slightly acrid French perfume. Katya loved that smell, mysterious and slightly disturbing.

"Why not? I was calling Olga's friend Polyanskaya. Remember I told you about her?"

Regina nodded silently.

"Well then," Katya went on. "I just thought I should tell her about the piece of paper I found. Her name is on it, after all. And her husband works for the police. What if he's able to find something out? You know, through his own channels. Local cops are one thing, but a colonel from Petrovka is very different. They find murderers. Not always, but sometimes they do."

"Katya, Katya," Regina Valentinovna sighed sadly. "I've explained this to you. You shouldn't tell people what you found yet. Loose lips sink ships. What did Polyanskaya say?"

"No, I . . ." Katya was flustered. "You think I shouldn't have called her?"

"You're a grown-up. I can't think for you. So how about Polyanskaya? How did she react to what you told her?"

"She . . ." Katya suddenly blushed, remembering she'd nearly violated Regina's condition by mentioning her in a conversation with an outsider. She didn't name names, but still . . .

"Come on, why are you blushing like a tomato?" Regina asked, smiling. "Did you blab about me? Fess up. I won't hurt you."

"No, I didn't say anything about you! I just read her the text and asked whether she believed the same as everyone else, that Mitya did it himself."

"And? Does she?"

"I don't know. But I don't think she thinks my suspicions are crazy, as if I'd dreamed them up while I was high. She didn't really have time to say anything specific, because before she could say anything, I heard the doorbell and went to open the door for you."

The conversation suddenly made Katya uncomfortable. Why so many questions? Was it all that interesting who said what? First Polyanskaya had asked her about Regina Valentinovna, and now it was the other way around. This was silly. It was as if they were trying to get something out of her, first one and then the other. They should be talking about Mitya and only Mitya. What could be more important than his death? After all, so little time had passed and so much was unclear.

"That's actually why I came," Regina said, as if suddenly remembering something. "I got some new medicine for you. I've actually had it for a week, but I got tied up, there was so much going on. But when you called, I remembered. It's a new American drug developed especially for people like you. It makes you feel approximately the same way morphine does, but it's weaker, naturally. Most important, it's not addictive. It replaces morphine without the withdrawal you're so afraid of. The medicine will let you reduce the dose gradually, until you're entirely cured."

"Have they really come up with a medicine like that?" Katya got very excited. "Can I really quit without the suffering?"

"With money, anything is possible." Regina smiled slyly.

"Oh! It must be terribly expensive."

"Don't be silly, child. That's not why I said that about money. I know your situation. You haven't the means to pay. I'm doing this for myself as much as for you. If I've accepted a patient, I have to see their case through to the end. Otherwise I feel defeated. And I don't like that."

"Thank you so, so much, Regina Valentinovna. I don't even know how to thank you."

"Please, stop!" Regina waved her suede-gloved hand and hitched up her sleeve a little to look at her watch. "It's very late now. You should inject yourself the first time with me here. I have to see how you react so I can adjust the dosage. Here's your first dose."

Regina took a small, dark brown vial, unlabeled, out of her purse.

"How many doses are here?" Katya asked, looking at the vial as if bewitched.

"There's one here. A trial. I'll see how it goes and leave you as much as you need. You have to understand, the medicine is very expensive. And you're not the only patient I have. So I have to dole it all out precisely. You have a needle, I hope?"

"Yes . . . Oh, I'm sorry, I didn't even offer you any tea. Shall we have some tea first?"

"Child, who drinks tea at two in the morning? Come on, don't drag this out. Let's just go into the bedroom. It will be better if you lie down after the injection."

Sitting on her rumpled, unmade bed holding a syringe filled with the translucent liquid, Katya was about to insert the needle in her arm. She searched for a good spot on her well-poked skin, but Regina stopped her.

"Wait. Don't you even rub it with alcohol before the shot? What good is that? You'll get an abscess. Do you have alcohol?"

"Yes, of course. Just a minute."

Carefully setting aside the syringe, Katya ran to the kitchen, got a large bottle of pure alcohol, and in the medicine cabinet right there by the refrigerator found her last cotton ball.

"Well then, I'm ready," she said as she sat back down on the bed.

Regina stood over her and watched silently as the fine needle entered her skin. She watched the blue vein swell up as it filled with the liquid from the syringe.

Katya didn't have time to understand or feel anything. Her ears started ringing. The noise mounted quickly and became deafening, as if a jet plane had flown directly into her brain. Everything started spinning in front of her. Regina's face, then Mitya's face, then other faces, some strange, some vaguely familiar. Gradually they all merged into one dense, opaque blackness.

Regina carefully wrapped Katya's immobile body in the blanket and generously poured the alcohol from the bottle over it. She quickly went into the kitchen, took a cigarette from the nearly empty pack of Kents and went back to the room. She lit it and, after taking a few drags, threw the long, burning ash onto the alcohol-soaked blanket. After another second's thought, she flicked her disposable lighter and lit the corner of the floral duvet cover.

Then she left the apartment quietly, closing the front door firmly behind her. She did all this without once removing her suede gloves.

All this fuss with loose witnesses had pissed Regina off and left her with almost no time or energy for Venya, and he was doing poorly. Worse than ever. He could explode at any moment.

She had to do everything herself. She couldn't turn to anyone for help. When you make a request, you're sharing information and creating a dependence. Given their connections and money, they could hire any killer, the best. But a good killer is cautious. Before carrying out a contract, he might well start asking questions about the individual standing in the way of Veniamin Productions.

There had been instances when the killer had called the person he was supposed to kill and offered him a deal: "They've hired me. If you pay more, I won't kill you." There'd been other cases when the killer had found out that the reason for the contract wasn't revenge, or debts, or territory but information dangerous to the client. Before carrying out the contract, he would try to dig out that information. Information people kill for can come in handy. If it's used intelligently, it can mean sums that make the killer's fee look like a joke.

Regina had to account for every eventuality, even the least likely. That was exactly why she couldn't hire someone good to solve her mounting problems. She had to do everything herself.

CHAPTER 14

Senior Investigator Mikhail Sichkin pondered the two photographs on his desk. One was of a beautiful—Hollywood-beautiful—woman of around forty with refined features and hair the color of ripe wheat. The other was of a young woman whose face was so hopelessly ugly he could only sigh out of pity.

On closer look, though, his pity evaporated. There was something sharklike in that face: the splayed chin, the large flat nose, the small, icy eyes.

The beauty in the other photo had the same eyes, only her expression was slightly different.

"A hungry shark and a full one," Misha muttered. "That's the only difference."

He checked himself. *What am I saying? What if this Regina Gradskaya is the sweetest of women, the kindest of souls? I haven't looked into her eyes and I've already called her a shark. So someone has a few plastic surgeries and changes her appearance to the point of being unrecognizable. The question is, what woman wouldn't like to change her appearance?*

Sichkin's interest was piqued almost immediately by the good doctor that Veronika Rogovets, the model, had casually mentioned. He couldn't let go of this business of motive. Why did Regina Gradskaya groom Veronika Rogovets so painstakingly for her interview with the investigator?

Yes, the doctor had greatly piqued Misha Sichkin's interest. He decided to prepare properly for their meeting and took the time to find out everything he could about her.

The fact that Regina Gradskaya had so completely changed her appearance only intrigued Misha more. He found lots of photographs of present-day Gradskaya, including on the pages of popular magazines, where she was pictured alongside her famous husband, the megaproducer Veniamin Volkov. But the old presurgery photo had been hard to find. All it took was one look at this woman's original face for Sichkin to realize why she'd gone to such lengths to destroy all her old photographs.

As of the time of their meeting, Misha knew only that Regina Gradskaya had been born in Tobolsk, Tyumen Province, in 1946. In 1963 she had entered the First Moscow Medical College and graduated with honors. Then a residency and a specialization in psychiatry. She had worked at the Serbsky Institute, where she defended her dissertation on "The Characteristics of the Emotional Sphere and Volitional Processes in the Formation of Delusional Motivations and Their Correlation to the Nosological and Syndromal Characteristics of Psychiatric Illnesses." During her residency, Gradskaya had worked almost exclusively with psychopathic killers, studying their intellectual comprehension of their crimes.

To be as prepared as possible for the meeting, Misha paid a visit to someone he knew from the Serbsky Institute, an old professor of forensic psychiatry. Luckily for Misha, the professor loved to reminisce, and he remembered Regina Gradskaya very, very well.

"You know, I always felt sorry for the smart, homely girls. A woman doesn't have to be smart," the professor said. "But Regina was an extreme case. Terribly smart and terribly unattractive. At the time I was certain she'd go very far in the field. There was no real hope of a personal life or a family for her. And she might have gone far if she hadn't gotten distracted by quasi-scientific stunts, ESP, and all that other rubbish. It was over that that she ended up clashing with the institute's directors. She could do all kinds of things with her hands and eyes and voice. Scientific psychiatry has no place for that kind of sleight of hand. And then they found out she was practicing out of her home, for money. They let her get her doctorate, of course, but they made it clear she had to leave the institute."

After she resigned from the Serbsky, Gradskaya got a job at the district psychiatric clinic. Back in the early seventies, when it wasn't fashionable, when it was looked on as hocus-pocus, Dr. Gradskaya was actively practicing ESP in her free time. Regina Valentinovna saw patients in her home, treating famous celebrities for big money and working with all kinds of sexual disorders and severe depressions.

The old professor was wrong in his prognosis about ugly Regina's personal life. In 1986, she married Veniamin Volkov. Today every schoolchild knew that name. But at the time, almost no one did.

Regina Valentinovna was ten years older than her husband. Not only that, he was an attractive man, whereas she, at the time, before the plastic surgeries, was ugly.

The marriage had been quite fruitful. The couple hadn't had any children, but they had given birth to and raised a very powerful and famous entertainment empire, Veniamin Productions. The murdered singer had been closely tied to that business, as was his lover. Some of their videos together had been shot at that studio, and Azarov's last tour had been organized by one of Volkov's people. It wouldn't be a bad idea to meet with Veniamin Borisovich as well—if he could find more serious grounds for doing so than the mere fact that Volkov had worked with the deceased. Whether Misha would come up with those grounds was an open question.

Regina Valentinovna spoke quite graciously to Misha over the phone and said she was prepared to meet with him at any time, wherever it was convenient for him.

Misha considered it convenient to call Gradskaya into Petrovka. Now he was expecting her any moment. Glancing at his watch, he neatly closed the file and put the two photos and a few papers concerning the witness into his desk drawer.

He heard a knock at the door.

In person, Regina Valentinovna Gradskaya looked even younger and more elegant than she did in the photograph. She was wearing a gray pencil skirt and a soft pink pullover. Everything about her image was thought through down to the smallest detail. Her boots and small purse were made of the same smoky-gray suede, and her nail polish and lipstick were a gentle matte pink, like her pullover.

His office filled with the subtle fragrance of expensive perfume, and her unnaturally white teeth sparkled as she gave him a warm smile. Gradskaya was the epitome of graciousness and charm. Her soft brown eyes looked at Sichkin with good will and honesty. Written in them was a readiness to answer any question he might ask and to tell him everything she knew about the tragic death of Yuri Azarov.

"Veronika Rogovets underwent rehabilitative therapy with me. She suffered from depressions connected to certain childhood traumas. She's a very vulnerable young woman."

"To be honest, I didn't notice that." Misha smiled. "Rarely have I had occasion to meet anyone so"—he coughed—"so confident."

"That's all just an act." Gradskaya shook her head. "Believe me, the girl is torn up over Yuri's death."

"Has she come to you for help in the last few days?"

"Yes, she came to see me. Literally the same day as the murder. That very evening, in fact."

"And did you help her?"

"Yes, in a way. I gave her support. She was in a terrible state. She was afraid whoever killed Yuri might kill her. She was afraid of being suspected of the murder. That's what she said to me, that they always suspect the people closest to the victim. There was no one closer to Yuri. They were practically never apart. She was worried she'd be pulled in for questioning."

"Did she consult with you about how best to behave during questioning?"

"Yes, she asked me how best to handle the conversation so that they would 'leave me the fuck alone'—forgive the expression."

"Well, that's almost a legal consultation." Misha grinned. "And what did you advise her, if I may ask?"

"What do you think?" Gradskaya smiled cunningly.

"Well, I think you gave her some practical advice. Judging from her behavior."

"I'll bet she flirted with you the whole time." Regina laughed gaily. "I suspect you misread her and she misread me."

"A bad game of telephone," Misha commented, smiling in response to Regina's gay laughter.

"Tell me, do you seriously think I instructed Veronika Rogovets in how to conduct herself during questioning?" she asked after she'd finished laughing.

"You just told me so yourself."

"And do you believe she followed my instructions? Are you ruling out the possibility that Veronika conducted herself with you the same way she conducts herself with everyone else? Do you think I set her on a specific course and she followed that course like a windup toy?"

"Naturally, Rogovets isn't a toy. However, you do have a definite influence on her. Otherwise she wouldn't have turned to you for help."

"If she had followed my advice, she would have told you the truth and only the truth," Regina said quietly and seriously.

"Tell me, Regina Valentinovna, did you know Yuri Azarov well?"

"Not very." Gradskaya shrugged. "I didn't treat him."

"From what you do know of him, could he have had serious debts?"

"What difference does it make what I think about that? Those are things you have to know definitively. I can only say one thing definitively: he never once borrowed money from me or my husband."

When she'd gone, Misha's head started pounding. The interview had left a nasty aftertaste. He had a hard time thinking and was all thumbs. Someone had recently told of him something similar. Very recently. Someone he knew had felt the exact same thing, a terrible weariness and a headache, after speaking with someone.

Misha tried to remember. Something was telling him that this was important. But his head was splitting and he couldn't focus. "Did she hypnotize me, this Gradskaya?" he thought irritably.

After taking two aspirin, Misha made himself a cup of strong sweet tea. The headache abated a little, but it was still hard to think.

That night his wife made him take his temperature. It was high—101.3. No wonder.

Lena had had an insane day. She'd prepared and turned in all her department's materials for the next issue—that is, she'd finished the work meant for the next ten days. She'd managed to order and purchase travel vouchers for that holiday house outside Moscow for Liza and Vera Fyodorovna, and had taken care of so many things, large and small, that even she was amazed.

Her one subordinate, Gosha Galitsyn, kept dialing the same number as he typed up the final paragraph of his article on some trendy rock group. Lena was waiting for him to finish. He'd promised to drive her home in his Volga. She cursed herself for the umpteenth time for failing to get a license.

"That's it, let's go!" Gosha sighed as he turned off his computer and dialed some number yet again.

"Who is it you're trying to get through to?" Lena asked.

"Volkov!"

"Who's that?"

"You've got to be joking, boss!" Gosha actually snorted. "Do you watch TV?"

"Rarely," Lena admitted.

"And you've never heard of Veniamin Productions?"

"I probably have heard something."

"Lena, you have to know these things. Veniamin Volkov is the number-one producer, the godfather of one in three pop stars."

"Veniamin Volkov? Wait, I think I do know him."

"Meaning what? You mean you *know* him? Personally?"

"There was a Young Communist by that name in Tobolsk, a very long time ago, fourteen years ago."

Gosha grabbed a glitzy music magazine from the stack of papers on his desk, nervously leafed through it, and stuck a huge color centerfold under Lena's nose.

A man and a woman were smiling from the page. The man was a balding blond with pale blue eyes and a narrow face. The woman was a forty-year-old brown-eyed beauty with hair the color of ripe wheat.

"Well? Is that him?" Gosha asked, holding his breath.

"Yes, that's Venya Volkov. Only older and balder," Lena replied distractedly.

She couldn't take her eyes off the woman's face. There was something vaguely familiar in the sleek, symmetrical face. Something vaguely and unpleasantly familiar.

"And who's this woman?"

"His wife and business partner, Regina Gradskaya. Listen, Lena, does this mean you knew Volkov personally when he was still living in Tobolsk?"

"Gosha, I met lots of people all across the former Soviet Union. I went on one business trip after another. You don't happen to know what his wife does, do you? Who is she?"

"I told you, she's the co-owner of Veniamin Productions. Why should she do anything else? I think she's a doctor or someone with ESP, like Kashpirovsky. What's the difference? You mean you know her, too?"

"No. I don't know her. I thought I'd seen her somewhere. Her smile's familiar."

"Listen, can you tell me about Volkov? All the details about what he was like then and what you guys talked about?"

"I'll try, though I don't understand why you're so interested."

"You can't imagine how I could kill with that information! It's an exclusive! Do you think he remembers you?"

"Unlikely." Lena shrugged. "It's been so many years. It was 1982. Late June."

Regina couldn't get a few sentences that Venya had uttered in a hypnotic state out of her head.

"She might have saved me. If she hadn't rejected me then, I would have followed her anywhere. I could have conquered any desire. I felt something completely different for her, something new and strange for me, but probably normal for other people. I felt tenderness. I was afraid for her. I loved her. And I can't forget her. But she didn't care for me."

"Who? Who are you talking about?" Regina asked in surprise.

"Polyanskaya," he replied quietly.

"But you only knew her a week. It was so long ago. What makes her better than the others?"

"I don't know . . . I could have been a normal man with her."

"Why?"

"She didn't lie or pretend. There was nothing flirtatious about her. I loved her like a man, not like an animal."

"But did the first girl, Tanya Kostylyova, did she lie and pretend?" Regina asked cautiously.

"No. Now I know she didn't. But I was a young fool. Back then I didn't believe anything but my own hunger."

"I taught you how to conquer that hunger," Regina quietly reminded him.

"Yes. But she could have saved me, too. Before. And differently than the way you did."

"You would have killed her eventually, just like the others. Only I taught you how to satisfy your hunger without killing."

"Yes . . . Only you."

Then he had the fit that usually signaled the end of their session.

Regina didn't remind him of what he'd said under hypnosis. But she herself couldn't forget it.

Throughout their life together, there had been lots of beautiful women around: print models, runway models, singers. But Regina trusted her husband. He didn't sleep around. She convinced Venya that he might kill anyone he slept with. And he feared that more than anything in the world.

She had no grounds for jealousy because Venya was addicted to hypnosis. Their sessions were his drug. He couldn't exist without them, which meant he depended wholly on Regina.

And now it turned out that he had once known ordinary human love in his life. It was such an acute and powerful idea that he could have rid himself of his psychological malady without Regina's help. Of course, no normal woman would ever agree to live with him had she known what he had done. That arrogant Polyanskaya would have turned him over to the first cop she met. Had she known the truth, she would have felt only horror and revulsion for him.

She was pathetically normal. She didn't contemplate life outside the framework of the commonly accepted morality. But it was to her, this banal, insipid doll, that the only healthy male emotion in Venya's life had been directed.

Regina, who had invested her whole self in making him into what he was, had not won Venya's first and last love. This bitch had.

For the first time in many years, real jealousy, deep and dark, awoke in her. But she dealt with that foolish, unnecessary emotion. She was sure she had. The problem wasn't that Venya had once been in love with Polyanskaya and now suddenly, for no apparent reason, had remembered it. The problem was that this love was a dangerous and active witness to his first great crime. Every step she took was fraught with grave consequences for Venya, for Regina, and for their business.

CHAPTER 15

It took Liza a long time to get to sleep. Lena kept telling her how she and Nanny Vera were going to the country, to a holiday house. They were going to take walks in the woods, breathe the fresh air, and watch the coming of spring.

"What's a holidouse?" Liza asked.

"It's a house in the woods in a very pretty place. People go there for vacation," Lena explained.

"Are you coming with us?"

"We're all going together. We're driving with Aunt Olga. And then Papa will pick you up."

"I want you to stay with us at the holidouse."

"Liza, sweetie, you and Nanny Vera won't be there long without me. And I'll be working."

"Why?"

"So that we have enough money to go to the sea this summer."

"I don't want to go to the sea, I want to be with you and Papa. Is Papa coming back soon?"

"Yes, little one, Papa's coming back soon. Have you already decided which toys you're taking with you to the holiday house?"

Liza was out of her little bed in a flash. She ran to her toy box and started pulling out one toy after another very seriously, saying, "I'll take you, little elephant, and you, little dog. And I'll take all my blocks. And this big car, and my dolly stroller. Don't cry, dolly, I'll take you with me to the holidouse."

It was eleven thirty by the time Liza closed her eyes. But even in her sleep she kept murmuring, "Mama, Mama, I want to be with you and Papa . . . Let's all go to the holidouse together, please . . ."

Highway Patrol was starting on channel six. Lena turned on the kettle, pulled her legs underneath her on the kitchen sofa, lit a cigarette, and without looking at the screen, listened distractedly to the offscreen announcer's voice and thought about what she had to do tomorrow. Stores and cleaning in the afternoon, and Michael was arriving in the evening. He'd asked whether he could spend the couple of nights before their flight to Tyumen at Lena's so he wouldn't have to pay for a hotel.

"There are no hotels anywhere in the world more expensive than in Moscow," he'd said, apologizing.

She'd probably have to cook something and organize a dinner in honor of his visit.

"One person has been reported dead in a fire on Zaslavsky Street," the offscreen voice said. "At about three in the morning, residents of the first and second floors were awakened by the strong smell of smoke coming from an apartment on the building's first floor.

"Arriving firefighters discovered the body of a young woman in the apartment. The deceased, Ekaterina Sinitsyna, had lived there alone as of very recently. According to neighbors, she kept to herself and did not abuse alcohol."

Lena shuddered and stared at the screen. "According to preliminary reports, the fire was caused by smoking in bed."

The screen changed and a report on road accidents followed. Lena turned off the television and dialed Olga's number.

"Yes, I know." Olga sighed. "We should have expected this. She injected a huge quantity of morphine, a fatal dose, and fell asleep with a cigarette."

"The fire started at about two?"

"Yes, by three everything was in flames."

"I spoke to her just after one. Some woman had come to see her. Katya apologized and set the receiver down to go open the door. When I tried to call her back, the line was busy. Olga, they killed her. The same people who killed Mitya. It's all so smooth and logical again. A failed singer indulges in drugs with his addict wife and then hangs himself. A few days later, his wife dies as a result of an accident completely typical of drunks and addicts. It's all too logical, too neat."

Lena fell silent. She could hear Olga sobbing softly into the phone.

"Olga, sweetheart, I beg of you, please, listen to me. You didn't want to listen to Katya last night. Listen to what she read out to me."

Lena took the phone into the bedroom, turned on the computer, and opened the "Rabbit" file.

"The text was on a crumpled piece of paper that was in Mitya's jacket pocket. And this second one, it was on a cassette of songs that Mitya left with me."

"Was Mitya trying to blackmail someone?" Olga asked hoarsely after she'd heard the whole thing.

"At the least, he was thinking about whether or not he would. I think he decided not to. It made him sick. Try to remember all your last conversations. Look around your house. Maybe there's something still there. Could he have left his diary and address book with you?"

"Fine." Olga sobbed. "I'll try. But we definitely don't have his diary or notebook. You know what our apartment is like; there isn't anything just lying around. Everything is in its place."

After talking to Olga, Lena immediately dialed Misha Sichkin. But no one answered. Listening to the long beeps, Lena remembered that Misha's wife, Ksenya, often turned the phone off after midnight. And it was almost twenty to one.

Who else in Seryozha's department could she call at this hour? No one, probably. She had to wait until tomorrow, when she could call

Misha at work. At least she wouldn't have to start at the beginning. He already knew about Mitya and the fake doctor.

Now Lena had virtually no doubt that the mysterious Valentina Yurievna had not been casing her apartment. It was no accident that after her visit Lena had been left feeling as though her visitor had x-rayed her. That woman was connected to the people who did away with Mitya and Katya. She was just feeling Lena out. They wanted to know what she knew and how dangerous she was.

But in that case, why hadn't anyone shown up at Olga's for the same purpose? Olga was his sister, after all.

But that wasn't what was most important. She needed to understand why all this was happening. Who benefited and why.

For now she could draw just one cautious and highly vague conclusion: it had something to do with their Siberian trip long ago. Those memories were why Mitya had come to see her the month before. He'd been trying to clarify something with her, but at the time she hadn't attached any importance to it. She'd thought he was just feeling nostalgic for his youth.

Lena had a pretty decent memory, but the events of fourteen years ago had settled somewhere very deep down. Over the intervening years so many significant things had been layered over them. Fourteen years felt like a lifetime.

Maybe photographs would help. She doubted there were any from the trip. They hadn't had a camera with them, but there had to be lots of university photos from 1982. Maybe if she looked through them, some unexpected yet important detail would come to mind.

She only had one photo album. Seryozha had bought it especially for photos of Liza. Lena had never kept albums. She kept her old photographs at the bottom of her great-grandmother's antique trunk in the entryway.

As she rummaged through the old trunk, Lena found a large, light gray sweater. It was very old. It had belonged to her father, but Lena had shamelessly taken it from him. She liked to go around in her papa's big sweaters. They felt especially warm and cozy. She had taken this very sweater with her to Siberia in the summer of 1982.

Her papa had died five years ago, but to this day, the most trivial thing—a random object or a turn of phrase—would bring memories of him flooding in, drowning out everything else. It especially hurt that her papa had never seen Liza. He'd wanted a grandchild so badly, but Lena had had too complicated a personal life and too interesting a job. She'd thought she had plenty of time for that.

Her papa was never sick. When they got the terrible diagnosis of stomach cancer at the cancer center on Kashirka and the doctors told Lena there was nothing to be done—that Nikolai Polyansky had no more than two months to live—she didn't believe it. To the very end she didn't believe it. She kept hoping the doctors were wrong, that a miracle would happen.

Lena had no one in the world but her papa. He'd raised her alone. Her mama, a hiker and master sportswoman, had fallen off a cliff on Mount Elbrus when Lena was barely two.

I was the same age as my Liza now, Lena suddenly thought. *I'm not climbing mountains like my mama, but there is something serious and dangerous in my life right now.*

Lena shook free from the flood of memories and discovered she was sitting on the floor of the entryway, her face buried in her papa's old sweater.

This was the sweater she'd been wearing fourteen years ago, standing on the step in the train car door. The train was going from Tyumen to Tobolsk. It was a bright but foggy night. The sense of solitude and the endless taiga racing past had etched itself firmly in her memory. She'd had a bizarre and unpleasant conversation with the Tobolsk Young

Communist on that train. With Volkov . . . the very same Veniamin Volkov.

He was now a famous producer and businessman. Gosha Galitsyn had gotten the shivers when Lena told him she knew "Volkov himself."

Suddenly her heart started pounding madly. *Mitya had talked about some famous producer but hadn't named him. No. It couldn't be.*

Finally finding the torn, stuffed folder of old photographs and going through them quickly, Lena was surprised to come across one she'd completely forgotten about.

It was a large black-and-white photo. A few people, young men and women in construction brigade outfits, were standing against some kind of trailer. And in the middle were Mitya, Olga, Lena, and Veniamin Volkov.

Mitya was smiling straight at the lens. Olga was smiling, too, but looking down. Lena's face in the photograph was tense and distraught. Looking more closely, she realized why. Tall, broad-shouldered Volkov was standing next to her and looking at her. He was looking at her and not at the camera, and Lena looked uneasy under his gaze.

On the back of the photo it said *Tobolsk, June 1982, the Hope construction brigade.*

They'd performed for the brigade. That was one of their best performances. Later they'd had tea in the construction trailer, the same one that was in the photo. The men from the brigade had sent it to the youth magazine where Lena and Olga were spending their internship, accompanied by an amusing letter. The letter was long since lost—but the photograph had survived.

CHAPTER 16

Tyumen and Tobolsk, June 1982

The train slowly crossed the taiga. It was a bright night, almost white. No one felt like sleeping. The four were drinking tea in their compartment to the soothing knocking of the wheels.

"The more northerly we get, the brighter the nights. In Khanty, they're completely white." Venya Volkov was cutting a stick of dry-cured sausage into thin, perfectly even slices with a razor-sharp tourist knife.

"This sausage," Olga said dreamily. "The last time I ate sausage like this was during the 1980 Summer Olympics."

"Don't play poverty, sister dear." Mitya sent two thin sausage circles into his mouth. "Just two weeks ago at the Russia Cinema, you bought eight sandwiches at sixty kopeks apiece. You threw out the bread and ate the sausage. And washed it down with a milkshake." One more slice disappeared into Mitya's mouth.

"Yes, that's true. Only that sausage wasn't nearly as good. And the film afterward was so lousy, all my sausage impressions evaporated while I was watching it."

"Sausage impressions always evaporate quickly." Venya smiled. "Leaving only heartburn. I wonder why, as soon as people get on a train, they immediately start eating and talking about food?"

"Out of boredom." Mitya shrugged.

"Right, I can see how bored you are," Olga commented. "That's the tenth piece you've scarfed down."

"Venya, what's that hut we just passed?" Lena asked, looking out the window at the endless, silent taiga. "Does someone really live there?"

"Not now," Volkov replied. "In the old days, Old Believers, schismatics, lived here. They hid from the Soviet government until 1932."

"What happened in 1932?"

"They burned themselves alive. Nine adults and three children. An NKVD detachment had come for them. But someone managed to warn them. So they locked themselves up in one of the hermitages and set fire to it. The detachment stood there, watching them burn."

"Wasn't there anything they could do?"

"No. And why should they? Who would risk his life for their sake? They'd been sent to arrest them anyway. All right, let's have a drink." He took a bottle of five-star Armenian brandy out of his bag.

"Tobolsk Young Communists live well," Mitya remarked.

"We're not complaining." Volkov pulled out the cork and poured brandy into the empty tea glasses.

The brandy made them sleepy. They had five hours to go until Tobolsk. There weren't any sheets on this train. Everyone lay down to sleep fully dressed.

When Volkov climbed onto his upper berth, a small object fell out of his pocket. Lena picked up the cheap enameled pendant on the short, thick, plain metal chain. A white heart with a red rose in the middle.

"Venya, is this yours?" she asked, holding out the pendant. "Your chain broke."

"Yes, it's mine. Thanks."

Sleepy Mitya raised his head on his upper berth, glanced at the cheap decoration, which immediately disappeared into Volkov's jeans pocket, and murmured, "So that's what Young Communists wear instead of crosses!"

Lena just couldn't get to sleep. She was cold and uncomfortable lying there in her jeans and flannel shirt on the bare mattress, under a damp flannelette blanket, which smelled of chlorine. A distinct, awful picture rose up before her eyes of a burning hut in the taiga near the railroad. There were soldiers around it, their rifles tilted forward.

Why do you keep getting bogged down in these horrors? she argued with herself. *Now you're going to imagine the three children dying in the fire.*

Quietly, she got up, put on her sneakers, pulled her warm sweater out of her bag, grabbed her cigarettes and matches, and slipped out of the sleeping compartment.

The platform at the end of the car was stuffy and stank of cigarettes. The mysterious white light came through the filthy, smoky windows of the train car doors.

Lena carefully pulled on the handle. The door yielded with a creak. She smelled fog and fresh pine needles. A cool evening wind struck her in the face and ruffled her hair. The taiga sailed by very close. Lena sat on the step in the door well, the rails directly beneath her feet.

All of a sudden she felt alone in the vast, limitless taiga, which swayed around her like the ocean, living its own complicated and mysterious life. Tree trunks were creaking, nuts were ripening in cedar cones, sleepless wolves and bears were roving, and swamp bubbles were bursting with a heavy screech.

Some solitary person in the taiga I am, she thought. *I can go back to my compartment at any time. For me, this solitude is just a game. If you do end up there, among the thick, creaking trunks, you must feel terribly lonely and defenseless.*

She lit a cigarette.

"Lena, aren't you afraid of falling?" She heard a quiet voice very close behind her.

Lena startled and nearly did fall. Volkov held out his hand, pulled her up, and immediately closed the outside door.

"You shouldn't sit like that," he said, lighting up. "It's dangerous."

"Venya, you scared me. I didn't hear you come up."

"I'm sorry. I was frightened for you. Your husband probably didn't want to let you go on this trip."

"I'm not married."

"I'm glad." He smiled gently. "You and I barely know each other, but the thought of you is keeping me awake. I'm not married, either. It's hard for me to interact with women. I feel like an idiot."

"I'd never say that, looking at you."

"You mean, I look complex free?"

"I don't know. Everyone has complexes."

"What about you?"

"Me, too, probably."

"I think you have the same thing I do, a loneliness complex. You tire quickly of people and of socializing, especially when there's no point. You'd rather go off on your own. But you're afraid to offend anyone and that bothers you. Even now, you'd like to go. This stranger is pestering you with his confessions. You're afraid of offending me, but you don't like the conversation, either. You want to be alone so badly, and now here I am pestering you with my chatter. Am I right?"

"Why? Strangers often share confessions on the train. It's nice to bare your soul to some random person you'll never see again. It doesn't obligate anyone to anything. And everyone likes talking about himself."

"Does it ever turn into more?" Venya asked quietly.

"Meaning what?"

"Well, could random people become close as a result of a railroad confession?"

"Life is full of surprises."

"But could you?"

His face was very close. Suddenly she noticed a heavy, ferocious longing in his handsome blue eyes and she felt uneasy. He was looking at her as if something vitally important hinged on her answer. No one had ever looked at her that way before.

"I don't know," she said quietly, trying to avoid his strange, imploring look.

He moved even closer.

"Lena, forgive me," he whispered quickly and hotly. "I don't understand what's happening to me. I don't know how to make a woman like me. It's all so simple for other people. But not for me. I am so scared of frightening you off. Help me."

Lena felt his hot fingers grab her hand.

"Venya, have you ever gone into the taiga alone?" she asked, gently freeing her hand.

"Yes, for bear," he replied after a brief pause.

Whatever had flamed up in his eyes was immediately extinguished. They became totally pale and dull.

"And did you kill one?"

"Of course. I've got the skin on my floor at home. When we get to Tobolsk, I'll invite you over and show you the bearskin."

"It's hard to believe."

"Why?"

"You don't look like someone who could kill a bear alone."

"Lena, how do you know what a man capable of killing looks like?" he asked quietly.

"Killing a bear?"

"Killing at all. Taking the life of a living being."

"No, those are completely different things. To be honest, I don't quite understand you, Venya."

"You know, the Khanty believe that the bear is man's equal. They don't hunt them with rifles, just with bear spears, to keep the playing field even. Shooting a bear is considered murder."

"There's probably a certain logic to that."

"Forget the bear for a moment. What do you think? Is there a difference between a murderer and an ordinary person? I mean outwardly. Could you pick out a murderer in a crowd of ordinary people?"

"I don't think so. Just yesterday we were performing at the prison, in front of criminals. Some of them were probably killers. I couldn't tell from looking at their faces. Though some people think you can. You've probably heard of the Italian psychiatrist Cesare Lombroso. He said that killers have a different skull structure, a low forehead, a flattened nose, and an unusual ear shape."

"Interesting. And do people take his theory seriously? Can a low forehead and the shape of a man's ears be entered as evidence in court?"

"I don't know about court, but in journalism and literature, including Russian, there have been serious debates about it. The theory gave Dostoyevsky no rest. And Bunin has a story, *Loopy Ears*. Then there was some other theory about handwriting and the shape of a person's hands. You know, man is always drawn to certainty. He wants to know everything in advance, to have it all sorted. It would be convenient for a criminal to be different from a normal, law-abiding citizen in some specific, outward way, for him to have a special sinister nose or something. There's a good reason they used to brand convicts."

"There, you see? You're contradicting yourself." Volkov smiled sadly. "You were so sure when you said I don't look like someone who could kill. And now you're saying you can't judge by appearances."

"You can't. But I'm not judging, either. I'm just saying I don't think—"

"Could you kill a bear?" he asked.

"No."

"What if it attacked you?"

"I don't know." Lena shook her head. "I don't know—and I don't want to know."

"Why so categorical?"

"I have no desire whatsoever to try to imagine what would happen if a bear attacked me. I very much hope nothing of the kind ever happens."

"And a man?" Venya asked very quietly. "What if a man attacked you? Could you kill him? That's more realistic than a bear, after all. Imagine this. You're attacked by a robber, or a rapist, or a maniac. You're terrified. He's going to kill you. Unless you kill him first. You save your own life, but you become a murderer. You aren't imprisoned, of course. After all, he attacked you. But, still, deep down, you've crossed the line that separates a killer from an ordinary person. What I mean is, you never know. Life holds all kinds of surprises. Anyone can be a murderer."

Volkov's face was very close. He leaned his palms on the wall, and Lena's head ended up between his arms. He stared anxiously into her eyes.

"Venya, you aren't planning to attack me, are you?" Lena smiled, dove under his arm, and opened the door to the corridor. "I need some sleep. I'm tired."

She walked quickly to her compartment without a backward glance. The train jerked hard, and Lena was swaying as she walked, and right then Volkov took a firm grip of her elbow.

"Forgive me, Lena," he breathed into her ear. "That was an idiotic thing to say."

"Venya," she said, freeing her elbow. "I don't like people breathing in my ear."

❦

In Tobolsk, Volkov didn't leave their sides for a minute. He went to all their performances, took them around town, and arranged a visit to the famed wooden citadel.

The days were so full that by evening, all three were dead on their feet and just crawled to their beds and crashed.

Volkov had arranged the best rooms for them in an old-fashioned commercial hotel. This time Mitya had his own room. Lena and Olga had a two-room suite with a refrigerator, a television, and a huge bathroom. Not that there was any hot water. But Volkov took them to a real Russian bathhouse.

"It's a kind of elite club for the Party and Young Communists," he explained. "Your bosses in Moscow go to saunas, but here in Siberia, we prefer a good Russian steam."

"I've never seen a naked Party elite," Olga snickered. "In Moscow or Siberia."

"I don't think you've missed much, Sis." Mitya shrugged.

"I have to warn you that there's just one steam room there, for men and women. One dressing room, too," Volkov told them. "But don't worry. You can take turns going in."

"We aren't worrying." Olga shrugged. "We have no doubt you won't take us anywhere improper, Veniamin. We trust you entirely. Right, Lena? We trust him?"

"Naturally." Lena smiled weakly.

"Do your elite Party women and men take turns going into the steam room, or do they go together?" Mitya wondered.

"They take turns, of course." Volkov laughed.

In a quiet, secluded spot on the bank of the Yenisei, there was a large, five-walled structure. Steam poured out of the chimney. The door was opened by a plump woman wearing a white robe.

"Good afternoon, Veniamin Borisovich. Welcome. Everything's ready."

The inside walls were timbered. In the middle, there was a low oaken table surrounded by big, deep armchairs. The broad benches along the walls were covered with starched sheets.

"Veniamin Borisovich, let me know when to bring the samovar. Girls," the bathhouse attendant said to Olga and Lena, "you can change in my room. The men can do it here."

She led them into a cozy little room where a radio was playing softly and a large electric samovar was boiling on a stool.

"Tell me, Zina. Why can't they build separate bathhouses for men and women?" Lena wondered.

"This is a Party bathhouse, not a public one," Zina explained authoritatively. "It's the bosses here, not the ordinary people."

"You mean your bosses are sexless?" Olga giggled.

"Usually, it's only men who come here." The baffled attendant shrugged her pudgy shoulders. "If they bring girls, they're the kind who don't get embarrassed."

Olga whistled. "You mean they have orgies here or something?"

"Why orgies? Respectable people come here. Party people. Municipal leaders. And provincial ones, if they're here on an inspection or some kind of commission, they always visit. How can a Russian get along without a bathhouse?"

Wrapped in sheets, Olga and Lena slipped through the dressing room and into the steam room.

"Don't be too long!" Mitya shouted after them.

"What an odd man that Volkov is," Lena said as she lashed Olga with the fragrant birch broom. "He's treating us like we're Party bigwigs and doesn't leave our side even for a minute, like he's our babysitter or something."

"What's so bad about that? We should thank him. Would we be steaming in a bathhouse like this at home?"

"I'm grateful to him, of course, but he's still odd. You know, that night on the train when I went out to the platform to smoke, he came on to me."

"He likes you. He's positively drooling over you. All these provincial Young Communists are suckers for Moscow girls."

"He'll get over it." Lena grinned.

Olga got up from the bench and stretched sweetly so that her spine cracked. "Now let me lash you properly with the broom. I'll show you how it's done."

When all four of them were sitting in the dressing room, steamed and wrapped in sheets, drinking strong tea infused with herbs, Mitya suddenly asked, "Lena, do you remember when we were on the train and Veniamin dropped that locket with the rose?"

"Yes." Lena nodded in surprise.

"There!" Mitya rejoiced. "You were wearing it around your neck. I didn't imagine it!"

"Mitya, leave Venya alone!" Olga said. "Why do you keep going on about that locket? Maybe it's a present from a girl he likes."

"I don't care who wears what around his neck, I just want Lena to confirm that I didn't imagine it, that I'm not crazy, that my brain's not malfunctioning yet. Veniamin says I just thought I saw it."

"Mitya, stop!" Olga said sternly, and looking at Volkov's pale, petrified face, she added, "Forgive him, Venya. He's a dreadful pest."

After the bathhouse, on the way to the hotel, Volkov invited them over to his place.

"You and Mitya should go," Lena whispered into Olga's ear. "I don't feel up to it."

"Are you crazy? You're the reason he's inviting us!" Olga answered in a loud whisper.

"Where did you get that idea?"

Volkov was walking behind them, but closer than they thought.

"Lena, Olga's right. I want to show you the skin of the bear I killed. Otherwise you'll think I'm all talk."

They looked back over their shoulders. He looked at them with a guilty smile.

"Young Communist, did you really shoot a bear yourself?" Mitya asked.

"Yes." Volkov nodded.

Venya lived alone in a two-room apartment. The five-story building for the Young Communist and Party elite was newly built. The apartment smelled of paint and wallpaper paste. There was almost no furniture, just a large desk and a few chairs. Books were stacked in the corners of the main room. In the other room there was just a low, wide couch neatly made up with a checked blanket and an antique wardrobe. On the floor in front of the couch lay the thick, rough skin of a brown bear.

"Wow!" Olga shook her head. "Venya, doesn't it scare you? It's like the bear is looking at you and saying, 'Why did you kill me, Young Communist?'"

"To be honest, sometimes I do get a little uneasy." And again that lost, guilty smile.

"Venya! I'll be your friend!" Mitya's shout came from the next room. "You have nearly the entire Poet's Library series!" He walked in holding two dark blue volumes. "Will you let me borrow it until we leave? Just the Mandelstam and Akhmatova? I'll answer with my head."

"Sorry. I can't. I don't even take these books out of the building, and I don't lend them to anyone. You can read them here. You can come again. You can stay here if you like, but I won't let you take them with you."

"I get it." Mitya sighed. "I wouldn't, either."

"I don't have a big dining table yet," Venya told them. "We won't all fit in the kitchen. I suggest two options. I can spread a tablecloth on the desk or we can sit on the floor, on the bearskin."

"You're the host. You know best." Lena shrugged.

"On the bearskin! Of course!" Olga declared.

"I have vodka and champagne," he told them.

Everyone except Lena chose vodka. Volkov went to the kitchen. Mitya and Olga rummaged through his bibliographic treasures. Lena had the same titles at home—the Poet's Library, Bulgakov, Platonov—and lots more besides. She went into the front hall, which had the only mirror in the whole apartment, and started combing her hair, which was damp from the bathhouse.

All of a sudden Volkov's reflection appeared next to hers in the mirror. He approached her from behind, came very close, and nuzzled his face in her damp hair. She shuddered and pushed him away, but he squeezed her shoulders and she felt his hot, firm lips on her neck.

"Venya, something's burning in the kitchen," she said quietly, trying to slip out of his grip.

But he turned her toward him abruptly and started greedily kissing her face, eyes, and lips.

"Don't be afraid of me," he whispered, as if delirious. "Don't be afraid. I love you. I won't hurt you. I'd rather die than hurt you. No one in the world loves me. Stay with me. Save me."

Lena already understood that this odd young man burned with a passion for her. She admitted to herself he didn't repulse her. She found him attractive and even interesting in a certain way. There was a deep peculiarity, a terrible but exciting mystery about him.

I'm free. I don't have anyone. I'm only twenty-one. Nothing need come of it. Lots of people have these kinds of flings when they're traveling. He's handsome, smart, charming, and utterly alone. Why not?

"I love you. Save me."

He smelled of good tobacco and expensive cologne. He held her even harder against his body, his lips sank into her mouth, and his hot hand slipped under her sweater.

Oh my God! I'm making out with him! I'm making out with a boy I barely know! Olga and Mitya are going to see and I'll be so embarrassed.

"Lena, dearest Lena. Be mine, all mine," he whispered, pulling his lips away for a second.

"Venya, where are you?" They could hear Olga's voice from the kitchen. "The bread we were toasting in the skillet burned."

Lena pushed him away abruptly. They were standing in a corner by the front door. Olga hadn't noticed them when she'd run to the kitchen. There was a bad smell of burning coming from the kitchen. Pieces of charred bread smoked in the skillet.

All evening, Volkov couldn't take his light, transparent eyes off of Lena. They drank vodka and champagne, spread the tablecloth on the floor, and quickly set down plates of cured salmon, sturgeon, Hungarian sausage, and Finnish cheese.

No, she thought. *These intense passions aren't my thing. I don't need adventures. What good are they? It's bizarre and embarrassing to make out with a stranger you feel nothing more for than sympathy. I didn't give him any reason to act that way. This is a passion beyond me. He's charming, complicated, and lonely. Why did he keep saying, "Save me!" and with that melodramatic crack? There must be a lot of women happy to save a complicated and lonely man like him. But it's too much for me.*

When they were getting ready to go, Volkov squeezed her fingers and said quietly, "Lena, can I talk to you for a minute?"

She was grateful that at least he hadn't said anything about what happened between them in front of Olga and Mitya.

Pushing her back, into the bedroom, and shutting the door with his foot, he again sank his lips into hers. Lena immediately pushed away.

"Venya, listen to me."

"You want me. I know it. I can tell. Stay here. Please. I beg you. You don't understand how serious this is for me."

"I can't." Lena shook her head.

"Why? Because of them?" He nodded toward the door, where Olga and Mitya were waiting.

"No. Because of me. I'm not capable of these fiery emotions."

"You'll like it with me. I love you so much. You must feel the same. I've never known anything like this."

"Venya, couldn't you just have made this all up? There are so many other pretty women in the world."

"No!" He exhaled quickly, put his arms around her again, and held her tightly. "No. There is no one but you. Do you understand how badly I need you? Do you understand that I'll die without you?"

"You're scaring me, Venya." She broke away again and opened the door.

Olga and Mitya weren't in the front hall. And, right then, she really was scared.

"Olga!" she shouted. "Mitya! Where are you?"

"There. You see? They understood. They left," Volkov said, grabbing her by the shoulders again.

"No, we didn't leave," Olga's cheerful voice came from the other side of the door. "We just went out on the stairs and the door closed behind us. But we can go. We'll find our way back to the hotel. Okay, Lena? We'll do whatever you say."

"Wait a minute," Lena said, trying to open the lock. "I'm coming with you."

"I'll see you to the hotel." Volkov helped her with the lock.

"I understand," he said softly while they were walking through the nighttime streets to the hotel. "I'm doing something wrong. I want everything at once. I'm terrified you'll leave, and I'll never see you again."

"Venya, I'm no fan of flings. Let's keep things friendly, neutral. It'll be easier that way."

"Lena, this is no fling," he said calmly. "You can't imagine how serious this is for me."

"But a serious relationship should start differently. Not so fast, not so pressured."

"How then? How should it start? Tell me how I should act so you won't be afraid of me and push me away."

"I don't know. I'm sorry. I may have done something wrong, too. We're here. Good night."

The next evening, someone knocked cautiously at the door of the hotel room where Olga and Lena were staying.

"Come in. It's open!" Olga shouted.

Standing in the door was a short, stocky man of about thirty.

"Hello. Forgive me for disturbing you," he said in embarrassment, not coming into the room. "I just found out that a group has come from my favorite magazine in Moscow. I wanted to ask you . . . Oh, forgive me, I didn't introduce myself. Police First Lieutenant Zakharov."

"Hello. Come in. Don't be shy." Lena smiled.

He took a hesitant step into the room and closed the door behind him.

"The thing is, I write stories."

"Oh, Lord," Olga sighed under her breath.

"I sent them to your office and to *Youth*," Zakharov continued quietly. "They told me my work was raw and needed serious editing. And I didn't understand what 'raw' meant."

"'Raw' means badly written," Olga explained.

"Could you just read one of my stories?" he asked, looking at the floor. "This is very important to me. I know lots of manuscripts come to your office and you don't even read them. You just fill out form rejection letters. I'd like to talk with a real person."

"We're pretty tight on time. We're leaving for Khanty-Mansiysk tomorrow evening," Olga said.

"It's a very short story. It won't take up much of your time."

"Okay." Lena nodded. "Let's have your story. Stop by tomorrow morning at nine-ish. I'll read it."

"What are you doing?" Olga jumped on her when the door shut behind the first lieutenant. "You do know that no good deed goes unpunished. Just look!" She opened the file Zakharov had left and started reading loudly:

"The first sticky leaves pecked their way out on the slender, white-trunked birches. A gentle spring breeze fluttered a rosy young woman's golden braids. Her beaming eyes, blue as forget-me-nots, shone with joy and happiness."

Olga shut the file.

"No need to go on. It's all pretty clear. Tomorrow you're going to have to give this shy police officer a long and tedious explanation of why 'sticky leaves' and 'beaming eyes' are awful literary clichés. He won't understand, and he'll be hurt."

"Fine, quit muttering." Lena lay down on the bed with the manuscript.

The story was called "Monster." On twelve typewritten pages, he described in gnarly detail how a rosy young woman with beaming eyes was discovered in the city park, murdered and raped, and how the daring detective quickly found the perpetrator, a vagabond drunk who had no choice but to confess his evil deed.

Veniamin was supposed to stop by for them at two in the morning. He'd invited them for a farewell nighttime picnic with shish kebab on the banks of the Tobol.

It was all Mitya's idea. He loved the idea of greeting the dawn in the taiga on the banks of a Siberian river.

"Well, are you done? Get up, it's ten to two." Olga pulled on her jeans, combed her luxurious fair hair in front of the mirror, and yawned sweetly. "I won't last till dawn. I won't even last for the shish kebab. I'm sleepy."

"Well, you can blame your little brother. He's the one who dreamed all this up." Lena set aside the manuscript and put on her sneakers and her warm sweater. "The mosquitoes are going to eat us alive."

"This isn't my little brother," Olga objected. "This was Veniamin's idea. Mitya just mentioned it, and your Young Communist ran with it."

"Olga, why is he 'mine'?"

"Because all these entertainments—the bathhouse, the excursions, the constant attention—are exclusively for your benefit."

"Olga, that's enough. I'm sick of it." Lena frowned.

"Volkov is crazy about you. Big time. Anyway, he's a handsome guy, with shoulders as broad as an ox! And he's going to go far. From the Municipal Committee to the Provincial Committee and all the way to Moscow. Do you know what kind of pull these Young Communist boys have? Don't miss your chance, Lena."

Olga laughed merrily but immediately fell silent. Volkov was standing in the doorway.

The mosquitoes bit them mercilessly, despite the smoke from the birch cankers Volkov had shaved and tossed on the fire. The night was very bright. Olga dozed on soft pine branches, rousing every so often to slap at the persistent mosquitoes. Mitya plucked lazily on the guitar, and Lena smoked, gazing at the smoldering fire.

The shish kebab was all eaten and the vodka all drunk. A huge, whitish sun rose over the tops of the trees. After a sleepless night, everyone was a little subdued.

"Listen, I want to go back to the hotel," Olga said, raising up on one elbow.

"Just a second." Lena nodded. "Veniamin's coming and then we'll pack up."

"Where'd he go?" Olga wondered. "He was just here."

"He's been wandering around for forty minutes or so," Mitya said, stopping his strumming and glancing at his watch. "He probably went somewhere to relieve his longing. He's miserable because Lena won't give him the time of day."

"Mitya, quit your clowning." Lena frowned.

"Poor Yorick always told the truth." Mitya sighed.

"For which he was beaten without mercy," Olga added.

"Listen, why are you always after me about Veniamin?" Lena tossed her butt into the smoldering fire. "Whether he likes me or not has nothing to do with me. Those are his problems."

"You are a heartless woman." Mitya sighed and rose lazily to his feet. "I'm going to look for our unlucky lover."

"Just make sure you don't get yourself lost," Olga warned.

"I'll call out and you call back." Mitya started down the riverbank. He ran into Volkov about fifteen minutes later.

The Young Communist was stumbling. There were dark spots on his light sweater. His wide eyes were looking straight at Mitya with a crazed, unseeing gaze. He was breathing noisily.

"Venya! What happened to you?" Mitya cried out, and only then did he realize that the spots on the sweater were blood.

A powerful shudder ran through Volkov, and his eyes filled with intelligence again. Mitya heard branches breaking behind him, and a minute later Olga and Lena were standing next to him.

"My God, Venya, you're covered in blood! What happened? Are you all right?" Lena walked up to him and touched his shoulder.

"I had a nosebleed," he rasped.

"You should lean your head back and put something cold on the bridge of your nose." Lena took out a handkerchief from her jeans pocket. "Wait. I'll be right back."

"You stay with him." Mitya took the handkerchief out of her hands. "I'll go down to the river and get it wet. Olga, don't just stand there. Help him sit down. He's as pale as death."

Olga turned away. Since she was a child, she hadn't been able to stand the sight of blood. The sight of it made her sick to her stomach. Lena took Volkov's wrist and felt his pulse.

"Your heart's beating very hard, at least a hundred and twenty," she said. "Do you have heart problems?"

His hot hand caught and squeezed Lena's fingers hard. Lena gasped from the pain. Volkov's breathing was hard and shallow.

"Venya, can you hear me?" Lena asked in fright.

"Yes," he said hoarsely. "Don't worry. I'm fine. I just shouldn't drink."

The first lieutenant didn't come for his story. Olga and Lena slept until two in the afternoon, but after their sleepless night they felt wrecked anyway. They hadn't gotten back to the hotel until eight in the morning and had slept like logs.

At two thirty, a sluggish, puffy Mitya made his way to their room.

"Where's your literary police officer?" Olga remembered when they'd sat down for coffee. "We have to leave in two and a half hours. What are you going to do with his work of art?"

"Maybe he knocked while we were asleep and we didn't hear him."

"You can leave the story downstairs with the administrator. Write a little note. What was his story about?"

"A murder."

"A detective story?"

"Not quite. More like a psychological thriller."

"What are you talking about?" Mitya inquired listlessly.

"Oh, this graphomaniac brought us his story. And Lena, good soul that she is, agreed to read it and talk to him about it."

"I see." Mitya finished his coffee, poured water from the pitcher into a liter mug, and switched on the immersion heater. "I wonder what happened to Volkov last night?" he said thoughtfully, and he lit a cigarette.

"He probably just drank too much." Olga shrugged. "He went to get some air and felt sick."

"Where did the blood on his sweater come from?"

"He said he'd had a nosebleed," Lena reminded them.

When you have a nosebleed, usually you have it on your face, near your nose, and around your mouth. But Volkov's face was clean. All the blood was on his sweater, Mitya thought, but he didn't say this out loud. Why should he? Olga would start teasing him, calling him Sherlock Holmes or worse. It wasn't as though he was ever going to see Volkov again. He'd see them off to Khanty and they'd forget about the odd Young Communist as if he'd never existed.

"Maybe we should go to the police station?" Lena asked, lighting a cigarette. "That Zakharov said he was a police officer. It doesn't feel right leaving the file with the administrator. They change so frequently. They could lose it."

Right then there was a knock at the door.

"Second Lieutenant Nikonenko," the young fellow in the police uniform introduced himself and saluted. "Comrade Zakharov left a file here with you and asked me to pick it up. Here's his address." He held out a piece of notebook paper folded in fourths. "He asked you to be sure to write to him."

"But what happened? Why didn't he come himself?"

"He got held up at the briefing and then went straight to look at the body," the second lieutenant explained.

"He went where?" Mitya asked.

"To look at the body. There was a murder. On the edge of the park, by the Tobol. They found a young woman murdered. I'm sorry, but I have to go." The second lieutenant saluted and left with the story file pressed under his arm.

"Hold on. Where exactly?" Mitya jumped up and ran into the hallway after him. "Lieutenant, hold on," he shouted down the stairwell, leaning over the railing. "Where exactly did they find the young woman?"

Holding his cap, the police officer looked up. "I told you, on the edge of the park, by the Tobol."

"How did she die?" Mitya asked, more softly now.

"A knife wound to the heart. That's all I can tell you, young man. I'm in a hurry." The second lieutenant's boots clattered down the stairs.

As Mitya turned back toward the room, he saw coming toward him, in no particular hurry, a fresh, cheerful, and smiling Volkov.

CHAPTER 17

Moscow, March 1996

Liza was in the habit of waking up at seven, sneaking into bed with her parents, and sleeping another hour or two there. Today she was sleeping so soundly, she didn't even hear the alarm go off. She just gave a grumpy snort and turned over.

It was nine in the morning and drizzling, the first spring rain of the year. Lena slipped out of bed and pulled the blanket up over Liza. Let the child sleep another half an hour. She really didn't feel like taking her with her to the store, but it was risky buying shoes without trying them on first. Not only that, she wanted to give Vera Fyodorovna a chance to pack for her holiday in peace.

Lena took a shower and drank her coffee. By the time she was finished with her last cup, Liza had woken up.

"Are we going to the holidouse today?" she asked, happily scarfing down her oatmeal.

"Tomorrow, Liza darling. Today we're going to buy you new shoes and some new toys, just for your trip."

She polished off her oatmeal and milky tea in five minutes.

"That's all, Mama! Let's get dressed fast!" the child declared delightedly.

Usually getting Liza dressed turned into an ordeal. Liza would race around in one boot, and Lena would try to catch her to put on the other. Then she'd have to catch her again to put on her hat, jacket, and her mittens. That could take twenty minutes, sometimes even forty. This time, though, Liza let herself be dressed without running around, so inspired was she by the idea of buying new toys.

Over the past few days, the last remnants of snow had nearly vanished, though there were still spongy, blackish drifts here and there. It was nice pushing the stroller over smooth asphalt. They reached Children's Wares in half an hour. For the first time, Liza chose her own toys. She was very excited and talked nonstop.

All the fuss of choosing her own toys wore Liza out, so she calmly offered her feet for trying on shoes and didn't whine or fuss while her mama bought her tights, T-shirts, pajamas, and other things for the upcoming trip.

Finally, after dropping an unthinkable amount of money at Children's Wares, Lena put Liza in her stroller and headed for home. She also needed to buy food, but she'd run out of both energy and money. Nothing wore her out so much as shopping trips.

Along the way, there was a large connecting courtyard with a playground.

"Mama. Let's swing on the swings a little," Liza asked. "Just a little. A tiny bit."

Lena parked the stroller near one of the wet benches, lifted Liza out, and carried her over the puddles to the swings.

Killing someone without resorting to using the services of a professional hitman or leaving any traces is very hard.

A healthy young woman who has a small child, doesn't drink, doesn't use drugs, and lives quietly and well is hardly going to hang herself out of the blue in a state of narcotic intoxication or inject a fatal dose of morphine and drop a burning cigarette on her blanket.

If Polyanskaya had the kinds of connections in the criminal world that Azarov did, there'd be something to latch onto to create the appropriate circumstances for a hit. If only. But Polyanskaya wasn't Azarov. She didn't sing for thieves, she hadn't been a witness to a shoot-out, and she hadn't given testimony.

The temptation to hire a professional was great. But employing a professional required going through a middleman. Every decent killer had his own representative, the way a prostitute had a pimp. That meant two more people would know about the contract—the middleman and the killer.

Just because the police very rarely solved contract killings didn't mean who ordered a particular killing was a mystery in the criminal world. This murder had to be a complete mystery to everyone. Even the smallest leak of information could be deadly for Veniamin Productions.

In this case, she had to do it herself, quietly, cautiously, and intelligently. So far she hadn't come up with the right way to pull it off.

An accident would be the ideal option, of course, but only in theory. What could a person accidentally die of in the middle of Moscow in the middle of the day? A car could run her over, but the driver was unlikely to get away unnoticed.

An icicle could fall on her head. There were lots of them now, in March. For that, though, she'd have to climb onto a roof, and not just any roof but a roof that Lena was definitely going to pass under. The personal risk to Regina was great, and the chance of success ridiculously small.

After a lot of thought, Regina settled on two possibilities that she considered viable.

The first option was a small bomb, fifty grams or so of TNT, that could be slipped quietly into a coat pocket, a purse, or a bag of groceries. The explosion wouldn't be terribly powerful and could be set off in a deserted place. No one but Polyanskaya would be hurt. At worst, her child might be hurt as well.

The second option was poison. Having been in Polyanskaya's home, Regina had had a chance to examine the lock on the front door closely. With a good pick, she could break into the apartment when no one was home. She just had to choose the best place to put the poison. The sugar bowl? The teapot? The soup pot?

The first option seemed more reliable and less risky to Regina. She decided to start with that and adjust her plan later, if necessary.

The next day, at nine in the morning, Regina sat in a low-profile green Moskvich with a mud-splattered license plate. Her eyes were glued to the door Polyanskaya might come out of at any minute.

Polyanskaya emerged with the stroller a little after ten.

Since you're with the child, that means you're not going to work and you'll be coming home soon. I might not have enough time to plant the bomb before Polyanskaya returns, Regina thought. She turned the ignition, and, cursing the pathetic tin can of a car, drove out of the courtyard at minimal speed.

Regina knew every gateway in this old Moscow neighborhood. But she didn't know Polyanskaya's route. And it was virtually impossible to tail a pedestrian from a car so that neither the pedestrian nor anyone else noticed.

Judging by how fast Polyanskaya was walking, she wasn't taking her child for a walk.

Where are you headed? Regina thought. *To the store for groceries? But there are several supermarkets nearby, and you've already pushed your stroller past one of them . . . No, you haven't gone out for groceries. Or to the Filatov Clinic.*

Pulling up at the head of a long side street, waiting for Polyanskaya to get halfway down it, Regina started following her again slowly. That kind of driving gets on your nerves. Regina lit a cigarette and cracked her window. She drove a little ways and stopped. So did Polyanskaya.

She started straightening the child's cap—directly across from Regina's open window.

"Mama, are we going to buy doll dishes?" Regina heard the child ask.

"Absolutely, Liza," Polyanskaya replied, tying the strings under her chin.

Right then Regina remembered that twenty minutes from here, on the square by the Metro station, there was a big department store, Children's Wares. That was where they were headed. Regina could relax a little.

Parking near the store, Regina decided to follow Polyanskaya in. If there were a lot of people there, if Polyanskaya got distracted at some counter, Regina might find an opening.

As long as Polyanskaya's daughter was choosing her toys, Regina couldn't get close. There was no one else in the toy department but this mother and child. The sales clerk took down one toy after another for them to examine. This went on for half an hour.

Regina loitered in the cosmetics department across the way. She sniffed perfume and toilet water samples and read the brochures for the endless varieties of creams, shampoos, and hair dyes. She kept casting brief glances at Polyanskaya and thinking there was nothing more annoying and bad for your health than surveillance. She pitied herself and consoled herself with the fact that this was the first and last time in her life she would be engaged in this kind of tedious spying.

What idiocy, Regina thought irritably. *I drive around in that nasty tin can of an automobile, I squeeze into ugly cheap dresses so I can blend in with the crowds on the street, and I hang around a department store sniffing mass-produced perfume. I have to get this done, and soon.*

"Madam, may I help you?" She heard the sales clerk's sleepy voice.

That polite question held so much rude, lazy arrogance that it made Regina squirm. She glanced at the pudgy woman in the violet satin jacket. Under a thick layer of makeup you could see her dirty, porous skin; her thin, insipid hair hadn't been washed in a long time, and her small brown eyes were full of dull ill will.

If you only knew who you were talking to. Regina grinned privately and out loud said with a gentle smile, "No, thank you, young lady."

Looking around yet again, she discovered Polyanskaya wasn't at the counter anymore. Cursing herself, Regina headed deeper into the store.

You can't get distracted for a minute. No, a second! She was seriously worried she had lost her quarry.

There were lots more people at the back of the store near the children's clothing and shoe departments. *Don't tell me she's left!* Regina's mouth went dry with frustration. But then she heaved a sigh of relief. Polyanskaya and her stroller were headed straight toward her. She was coming back from the cashier in the toy department.

A few minutes later she was carrying not only her small purse but a plastic bag, which she hung on one of the stroller handles.

Now that's better, Regina thought tensely. *That's much more convenient.* Her hand slipped into the pocket of her cheap sheepskin jacket and cautiously felt the package, a little smaller than a cigarette pack.

Polyanskaya lifted the child out of the stroller, sat her down on a chair in the shoe department, squatted, and started removing Liza's boots.

The stroller with the bag hanging from the handle was so close, and no one was looking at it. Regina took a step toward it. Her hand, the small package squeezed tightly inside it, was already reaching cautiously for the bag.

All of a sudden a fat lady flew up to the counter, bumped into the stroller, and hollered in a thunderous voice, "Whose stroller is this? Move it this minute! It's blocking the counter!"

Regina abruptly stepped aside and put her hand back in her pocket.

"Forgive me, please." She heard Polyanskaya's calm voice. "It's our stroller. I'll move it right now."

Leaving her child on the chair in the shoe department, she quickly rolled the empty stroller away and put it next to a glass wall away from the counters and aisle. She took the bag with her.

Regina waited a couple of minutes, walked over to the stroller, and examined it carefully from all sides. There had to be some pocket, some hidden hollow where she could slip her small package without being noticed. But there wasn't.

Idiotic construction, Regina thought as she calmly stepped to the side.

Polyanskaya emerged from the store twenty minutes later. Now there were bags hanging from both stroller handles. Regina decided her subject would go back the same way she'd come, taking side streets and connecting courtyards.

Slowly following Polyanskaya in her car, Regina cursed herself for never having had the wit to learn how to shoot. Her job today would have been simplified if she could have used a rifle like a sniper. You never know what skills will end up being useful in life.

Right now she could only count on luck. And Regina did. Her intuition told her that today she would be lucky. She was already starting to get the hang of it—the hunt.

Polyanskaya turned into a big connecting courtyard with a playground, pushed the stroller up to one of the benches, lifted the child out, and carried her over the deep puddles toward the swings. Leaving the bags hanging on the handles. Regina held her breath.

The courtyard was empty. The weather was nasty—a fine drizzle, cold and annoying. The place where Regina parked her car gave her an excellent view of the playground and provided her an excellent escape route. She could easily leave the courtyard and slip down a side street.

Polyanskaya wiped off a wet swing with her glove and sat her child on it. Regina calmly got out of her car, walked up to the bench where the stroller was, dropped her small package into one of the bags, and just as calmly went back to her Moskvich, got in, and turned on the engine.

Polyanskaya was wholly focused on her child and never even glanced at the stroller.

Holding the tiny remote in her hand, Regina began to wait, calmly and patiently, for Polyanskaya to approach the stroller.

⚜

"Mama, swing me a little more," Liza asked. "Just a little."

"Little one, let's go home. It's such awful weather. Look, we're both soaked." Lena tried to take her daughter out of the swing, but Liza protested.

"I want to swing some more. Please!"

There were a few different kinds of swings on the playground, and Liza wanted to try them all.

If Liza gets a good outing now, she'll fall asleep faster after dinner and sleep a little longer, and I'll be able to get at least some of my to-do list for today done, Lena thought as she pushed the swing.

"That's enough, Mama. Now let's go home. I'm hungry. Take me down," Liza said at last.

Lena picked her up. The stroller was about twenty meters away. Stepping cautiously through the wet crusts of ice, trying not to slip, Lena took a few steps.

She heard the squealing of brakes. A new SUV, painted black with zigzags and stars on the sides, drove into the courtyard. The muscle-bound thug sitting behind the wheel was swearing colorfully. Parked right where he usually parked when he visited twice a week was some dirty old pile of Moskvich junk.

Ever since the SUV's owner had rented an apartment in the building for his lover, almost none of the building's occupants with cars had had the nerve to park in his favorite spot in the courtyard lot. The

SUV's owner was used to the spot being free and drove in without even looking. That's why he noticed the worthless piece of shit too late.

"Fuck you!" he said, and he rammed his powerful bumper into its pathetic rear end.

Before she could think, Lena fell to the soft wet grass, covering Liza with her body. Car alarms started howling desperately.

Then there was a very bright flash very close by. Lena was afraid to look. All she could think was that Liza was lying on the wet, cold ground. Her snowsuit would get soaked. And it was a fifteen-minute walk home. Lena saw her child's enormous, frightened eyes quickly fill with tears.

Lena was surprised that Liza was crying without making a sound. Then, gradually, the sound of her desperate, indignant crying started to mount, and Lena realized she'd temporarily lost her hearing from the shock of the blast.

"Mama . . . Mama . . ." Liza kept repeating through her tears, unable to say anything else.

Slowly, as if in a dream, Lena raised her head and then got to her knees. Liza jumped up and clung to Lena's wet coat, still wailing.

She had to get up off her knees, but her legs were like cotton wool. Added to the cascading car alarms was another sound—the wail of a police siren.

A few minutes later the courtyard was sealed off and there were police everywhere.

"Are you and your little girl okay?" An overweight young captain asked as he helped Lena get up off her knees. "Do you need a doctor?"

"I don't know," Lena whispered.

"Is this your stroller?" A plainclothes officer walked over to it.

Feeling an icy emptiness inside, Lena slowly turned her head. In the middle of the courtyard lay the stroller's frame. Scraps of green fabric and foam rubber were burning on the twisted tubes of the metal carcass. Only one of four wheels remained, and it was spinning slowly, helplessly.

"Yes." Lena nodded. "That's our stroller. Only I left it somewhere else, by the bench."

"The explosion carried it away," the captain explained.

"My monkey!" Liza cried, and her sobbing turned to a desperate wail.

"I have to change the child's clothing. I have to go home. We live very nearby, fifteen minutes' walk." Lena couldn't tear her eyes from the twisted frame.

"We'll take you home. Let's go to the car," the overweight captain said. "It's warm there. Let me take the child."

"No!" Liza clutched Lena. "No! I don't want to go to the man! Where's my monkey?"

"Your purse?" The officer picked up Lena's black leather purse.

"Yes, thank you."

It turned out that the small plush monkey was in her purse, not in one of the bags hanging from the stroller. Hugging the toy animal to her wet snowsuit, Liza stopped crying.

The SUV's owner didn't understand what had happened. He'd only given the back of that heap of junk a light tap, but then, for some reason, a baby stroller thirty meters from him had blown up. He didn't have time to be astonished or to think it through any more than that. He knew what would happen after an explosion, and the prospect of giving testimony to the cops who would be arriving shortly did not appeal to him one bit.

Swearing loudly and nervously, he stepped on the gas and shifted into reverse. As he was pulling away from the scene, he noticed a woman shoot out of that heap like a bullet and race off as fast as a sprinter. But that was not his concern. He had to get away, the faster the better.

CHAPTER 18

Regina tried not to run. That courtyard was far behind her. She walked quickly without looking around. The police siren's insistent monotone seemed to follow her. She knew no one was chasing her, but that awful wail still drilled into the back of her head.

Everyone should mind their own business, Regina kept repeating to herself dully as she walked through the first spring rain. *Everyone should . . .*

She came across a trolleybus stop as a half-empty trolleybus was pulling up. Without looking at the number, Regina hopped on and dropped into an empty seat. The doors closed, but the police siren kept after her. Regina realized no one else could hear it; it was all in her head.

The back of her head and her neck hurt badly. When that huge SUV rammed into her pathetic tin can, Regina's head whipped back and the finger she had on the remote's button jerked. And set it off. That it happened a few moments too soon was no one's fault.

She should be glad she hadn't broken her back; even her Swiss doctors couldn't replace vertebrae. Her muscles hurt, but that was nothing. Most important, she hadn't lost consciousness and was able to jump out and run away in time. It might have been much worse. She should be glad.

"Lady, have you gone deaf or something? Show me your ticket!"

Regina had sunk deep into her thoughts and didn't understand immediately what was happening. Looking up, she discovered a young man peering down at her. He was holding a metal badge and poking Regina in the nose with it. That was when she remembered she hadn't taken public transport for at least ten years.

"Pay the fine or we're going to the station!" the inspector threatened.

That's crazy! Regina thought. *The station is all I need now!*

"How much?" she asked the fellow quietly.

"Ten thousand," he told her angrily. "Look, it's all written here in big letters. Come on, lady, shake a leg!"

You animal. You bastard! Regina shouted to herself, but she made a heroic effort and said politely out loud, "I'm sorry, young man. I'll pay the fine right away."

She started rummaging around in the pockets of her Afghan jacket, which was just as disposable as that pathetic Moskvich. But all she had in her pockets was a fake driver's license made out to Galina Vladimirovna Tikhova, a pack of cigarettes, a lighter, and the tiny remote that had set off the bomb.

"Hey, what's going on?" The inspector's coworker came up, a guy a little older but with the same crude face.

"The woman doesn't want to pay the fine," the fellow told him venomously.

"I feel very unwell," Regina said.

"Let's go to the station." The older one tried to pull Regina up by the elbow.

All the passengers' heads turned in their direction.

"Shameless!" An old woman intervened. "Don't you have anything better to do than to hound a person! Can't you see the woman doesn't feel well?"

Regina really did not look her best. That morning she'd been painstaking about her makeup: gray shadows under her eyes, exaggerated folds around her nose and mouth, thin pale lips. She wore a black knit cap, old and falling apart, which gave her face a pitiful, even funereal look. It was exactly how she thought an elderly, well-educated woman driving an old used car ought to look.

In creating this image, Regina had pictured a vocational school teacher or a senior researcher at some lab. Everything good in life was behind her. Today she lived off a miserable check every month, subsisted on bread and potatoes, wore crummy twenty-year-old clothes, and bore her poverty with quiet dignity.

What could a poor, sweet, educated Moscow lady have to do with a bomb in a baby stroller?

Regina had anticipated everything, down to the tiniest detail. Except for this one. She wasn't carrying cash. Not a kopek. She'd forgotten it. In Regina's day-to-day existence, Russian cash was virtually useless. She was used to paying with a credit card, since she only shopped at the best and most expensive stores. Whenever she got stopped by a traffic cop, she gave him a US fifty-dollar bill.

But she wasn't carrying US currency, either. Regina swore at herself. She actually wept from fury. The two inspectors were shouting obscenities and trying to raise her up by the elbow.

"I'm sorry," she said through her tears. "I'm coming back from a funeral. I don't have any money. I don't feel well. I'm sorry."

The situation was getting dangerous. Any minute they would lift her from her seat, drag her off at the next stop, and take her to the police station. She wouldn't even have a chance to toss out the remote. They were holding her by the arms, and very tightly.

"Stop shouting," came a young woman's voice nearby. "Leave her alone. I'll pay the fine."

Sitting across the aisle was a pretty young woman with a boy of about four in her lap. She held out a ten-thousand ruble bill to the inspectors, who fell silent and exchanged stunned looks.

"Really? You're going to pay for her?" the older one asked, incredulous.

"Take the money and write out a receipt," the woman replied calmly.

"Okay, we've got ourselves a good Samaritan," muttered the young one, snatching the tenner and slipping it into his pocket.

"Don't forget the receipt," the woman reminded him.

"Yeah, yeah." The younger one reached into his pocket.

"Thank you so much," Regina murmured, distraught. "I don't know how to thank you."

"My pleasure." The young woman smiled, stood, and picked up her child. "Anyone could find herself in your situation."

What a strange town, Regina thought. *On the one hand, those louts, and on the other hand, good souls like this woman. For someone who takes public transportation, ten thousand is serious money. Why did that young mother waste that money on a woman she doesn't know? Out of compassion? It really is funny.*

The trolleybus pulled up to its next stop and the doors opened. First to hop out were the inspectors. Then the young woman, carrying the child carefully down the steps. Followed by Regina.

Leaping lightly over a black, hardened snowdrift, she scrambled into the street and hailed a ride.

"Volokovsky Lane," she told the driver as she sat in the front seat of the first car to stop.

The young woman with the child looked on in astonishment at the green Opel spiriting away the impoverished old woman who hadn't had the money for a ticket.

⚜

"I saw it! I saw it all!" a skinny, energetic old lady who'd dashed out of the front door in her robe and slippers jabbered. "I was looking out the window. My cat ran away. He needs a kitty in the spring and he goes missing for days. I get so, so worried, I look for him out my window. I can't call out because my window doesn't open. I puttied all the cracks in the fall. You know how drafty it gets here. And they're always turning off the heat. I used to go to the building office and complain! The kind of money we pay for our apartments."

"Hold on. Let's take this slowly." The investigator stopped her. "What floor do you live on?"

"The second. There it is, that's my window."

The officer looked where the old woman was pointing. Indeed, from her window she should have an excellent view of the playground and parking lot.

"At what time did you start looking out the window?"

"Oh, I don't remember." The old woman was huddling from the cold.

"Maybe we can go to your apartment?" the officer suggested.

"I haven't tidied up," she said, embarrassed.

"That's all right, it doesn't matter."

The small apartment smelled strongly of cat. The radio was turned up loud. With a glance at her unmade bed, the embarrassed old woman shut the door to the bedroom and took the officer into the kitchen, where she busied herself clearing crackers off the table.

"Let's start at the beginning," the investigator said when his host had finally calmed down and taken a seat across from him. "Your full name."

"Klavdia Semyonovna Kolesnikova, born 1925."

Despite her advanced years, Klavdia Semyonovna had remarkably sharp vision. She described in detail the young woman who'd come into the courtyard with the stroller and how the child was dressed.

The officer himself had seen that woman and child half an hour before, so he knew that the old woman hadn't missed a single detail.

"Well now," Klavdia Semyonovna continued. "She left the stroller by the bench and went over to the swings. She was carrying the child. The child's big enough to walk, but the puddles are something! And there were two bags hanging off the stroller. I even thought, 'What are you doing, dearie, leaving your bags like that without anyone watching them?' And it's a fine stroller. Imported. Then I see a woman come out from that car over there."

She and the officer went over to the window and she pointed to the small, light green Moskvich.

"See? She got out, that woman. She walked over to the stroller and then straight back to the car, quickly. She got in and sat there."

"Did you notice what she was doing by the stroller?"

"No, I didn't. I couldn't see. It all happened so fast. Now I think the woman dropped a bomb into one of the bags. But at the time I didn't think anything of the kind. She walked up and walked away. Who knows why? Maybe she wanted to take a seat on the bench. But she saw it was wet and changed her mind. And then this one drives in in one of those, oh, I don't know what you call it. A hefty kind of car, black. Mainly black, but with colorful doodles on the sides. I've seen it a lot lately. I don't know if he lives here or he's visiting someone. It's across the way, not our building. I know all of ours. So this black behemoth rams into the green car from behind. I can't tell what's going on. The woman with the child has fallen to the ground, like this, you know, on her elbows. And the little girl's underneath her. She was shielding the child with her body, and then something went off with a bang. My first thought was little boys up to mischief. Lately we've had them misbehaving here a lot, setting off those . . . what do you call them . . . firebangers."

"Firecrackers," the officer corrected her.

"It's all the same. It makes a big bang and the windows rattle. And you, the police, how is it you let this disgrace continue?"

The officer smiled. "Continue, please, Klavdia Semyonovna."

"What's there to continue?" The old woman sighed. "I look and the stroller's flying. Flying through the air. And on fire."

"And the cars?"

"I wasn't looking at the cars. My heart just sank. That's all we need, I thought. How terrible! If it had happened just a little later, that woman would have put her child in that stroller. That's where they were headed, toward the bench. What kind of beast do you have to be to put a bomb in a stroller!"

"Klavdia Semyonovna, please describe in as much detail as you can the woman who got out of the green car."

"Well, she wasn't young." The old woman furrowed her brow in concentration. "But not old, either. Middle-aged. Fifty maybe, or a little less. Tall, but not very."

"Approximately how tall?"

"Stand up, young man," the old woman ordered him.

The officer stood up straight in front of her. He was tall, well over six feet six. The witness eyed him critically.

"Compared with you she was short, of course," she concluded. "But basically tall."

The officer sighed and sat back on the stool. "Taller or shorter than the one with the stroller?"

"A little taller, I'd guess. Or maybe the same." The old woman shrugged.

"Okay. What was she wearing?"

"A jacket, a short brown jacket. With a fur collar. Tanned leather. A shaggy black collar. She had a black knit cap and her hair was tucked under it. A dark skirt. Brown, I think. A simple kind of skirt, not full or narrow. Long, but not very. Boots . . . that I can't remember exactly. Black, I think."

"Was she carrying anything?"

"No. She had her hands in her pockets. She didn't have anything. No purse or bags."

"What about her face? I realize it's hard to make things out from your window, but still . . ."

"It was like she didn't have a face." The witness shrugged.

211

"What do you mean by that?" The investigator was surprised.

"Well, it was unremarkable. The most ordinary face there could be. Like she didn't have one."

The officer stood up, went to the window, and asked the old woman to come over. Below, in the parking area, the crime scene unit from the Federal Security Service was hard at work. The officer pointed to one of them whose face could be seen.

"How would you describe that face?"

"Round, snub-nosed," she answered without hesitation. "A peasant face. Simple. Fat lips. He looks like some actor. There was this wonderful film, about the war. *The Dawns Here Are Quiet.* They showed it again on channel six a little while ago. I always watch our Soviet films. There's an elder in it, such a sincere, simple man. This one here looks like that elder in the face. I mean the actor who played him . . . I'm sorry, I can't remember his name. He's a fine actor, only he wasn't in a lot of films."

The fat-lipped, simple-looking crime scene investigator really did look like Vaskov, the elder from *The Dawns Here Are Quiet.* The officer himself had enjoyed watching it on channel six.

"You should come work for us." The officer smiled. "What about that woman? Maybe she resembled some actress or news announcer, too? After all, when she was walking from her car to the bench, she was facing your window."

"No." The old woman shook her head. "She doesn't look like anyone."

"But if you came across her, could you recognize her?"

Klavdia Semyonovna thought about that and then said slowly, "Depending on what she was wearing."

"Do you think she was dressed richly or poorly?"

"In between . . . Maybe more not rich. So-so."

The officer was very sorry. Old lady pensioners like this one often came forward as witnesses. They look out the window during the light of day and sit on benches by front doors. They notice all kinds of things. Their testimony is usually inconsistent and muddled. The old women don't see or hear well and they love to chatter on about irrelevant topics. It's hard and exhausting to work with witnesses like that. But here he'd struck gold. He envied her vision and powers of observation. But almost nothing substantive had come of it.

He was, however, able to establish fairly quickly that the hefty black car with the "doodles" on the sides was a Jeep Cherokee. The neighbors from the building across the way informed him and his colleagues that about three months ago, a single woman had moved into apartment 170. It was this young and beautiful woman that the owner of the Jeep visited a few times a week.

The woman was home. Natalia Kosenko, born near Moscow, in Podolsk, in 1975, had rented this two-room apartment in November of last year. She was calm and indifferent to the police's arrival.

"Did you hear the explosion in the courtyard?" they asked her.

"I thought I heard a bang about forty minutes ago, but I was in the kitchen, and the window there looks out on the street, not the courtyard. And I had music playing. I didn't pay any attention. We have kids setting off firecrackers here all the time."

"Does anyone you know have a black Jeep Cherokee with colored designs on the doors?"

"Vovka the Dove," she blurted out and immediately clarified that. "Vladimir Bogatykh. Why?"

"Do you know his license plate number, home address, and telephone number?"

"I don't remember the license plate number. It's a new car. I don't know his address, either. He's the one who visits me. He's never once taken me to his place, and I've never written him any letters." She grinned. "But his phone number—that I have."

The Jeep driver's identity was established quickly and easily. By the time he was twenty-eight, Vladimir Bogatykh had managed to be convicted twice, the first time as a minor, getting probation for armed assault. And at eighteen for real, five years, for car theft.

According to police files, for the last six months he'd been a member of the Lyublin criminal organization, which controlled a major goods market and a chain of stores in the Lyublin district. It was a small gang of about twenty that operated under the wing of Garik the Orange, an ethnic Georgian.

To think that this low-level thug would place a homemade bomb, the equivalent of fifty grams of TNT, in a stroller in the courtyard of his lover's building, and use his own car to do so, was the height of idiocy. Moreover, Bogatykh had never had anything to do with hits before. And if he'd been told to off someone, he'd have gone about it completely differently. He certainly wouldn't have arranged to do the hit in the courtyard of his girlfriend's apartment building.

It became obvious to the investigator that the person who'd contracted Lena Polyanskaya's murder had to have followed her first. It was just chance that Polyanskaya had turned into this courtyard on her way home. If that monster of an SUV had been following her, she would have been sure to notice it.

As convenient as it would be to pin the blame for the bombing on Vladimir Bogatykh, who was a known criminal, after all, the case fell apart under even the most cursory examination.

Consequently, when they tracked down Bogatykh and questioned him, he honestly told them everything he could remember: about the crappy tin car and the lady in the short jacket and black cap he noticed as he drove out of the courtyard. The fact that he had cleared out as fast as he could was understandable. Why should they lay eyes on him if they didn't have to?

Meanwhile, the crime scene unit, after painstakingly examining the abandoned Moskvich with the crumpled rear, had come up with nothing of use to the investigation. Not even fingerprints. The woman behind the wheel must have been wearing gloves the whole time. The only trace of the woman who had occupied the vehicle was the faint, barely detectable fragrance of expensive French perfume.

According to the traffic police, the green Moskvich had been reported stolen three years ago. The license plate was fake.

CHAPTER 19

It took Liza a long time to fall asleep. She kept sobbing and hugging her toy monkey. The major waited patiently in the kitchen, smoking, thoughtfully blowing the smoke out a partially opened window. At last, Lena quietly shut the door to the nursery and went into the kitchen.

"Would you like some tea?" she asked.

"I won't say no."

She switched on the electric kettle, sat down on the kitchen sofa, and lit a cigarette.

"How's your little girl doing?" the major inquired sympathetically.

"She doesn't understand any of it, but of course she's still scared out of her wits."

"Elena Nikolaevna, are you comfortable answering my questions now? After all, today had to be quite a shock for you."

"I'm perfectly fine. Ask away." Lena smiled weakly.

She answered all his questions calmly and precisely. In going through her memories of the day, she even recalled that twice on their way to the store, she'd noticed the dirty green Moskvich. She hadn't attached any importance to it at the time.

The major wrote down her statement and suggested that what happened might be connected with her husband's job at the Interior Ministry.

"Will you be calling your husband in London to tell him what happened?" the major asked.

"No," Lena replied firmly. "I'm going to call him, of course. But I won't tell him what happened until I see him."

"Why?"

"You can't talk about things like this over the phone. Why scare him and pull him away from his work? What's going to change if he cuts his trip short and flies home? It will just make him nervous. Everything is okay, after all. We're alive, thank God. You think this was connected with his work?"

The major smiled. "That's what immediately comes to mind."

"I can see that," Lena said thoughtfully, and she stood up to pour the tea. "How do you like your tea? Strong?"

"Yes, please."

"As I said, that makes a lot of sense. It may well be that someone really did try to get their revenge on my husband through me and Liza. But, two other people I know died before this happened. People who are not connected at all with my husband. I knew them, though, even if we weren't all that close."

Lena told the major about the Sinitsyns, Mitya and Katya. She laid out only what she knew for sure, leaving aside her own hypotheses and conjectures.

The major listened silently and tensely. A few times he wrote something in his notebook, but he didn't take detailed notes. He didn't start really writing until Lena told him the story about the strange fake doctor. At that point he started putting everything down, word by word.

"Was it only the doctor you found interesting in this whole story?" Lena asked when she'd finished her story. "I knew it."

"Elena Nikolaevna." The major sighed. "To be perfectly honest with you, I just don't see the connection between what happened to you today and the death of the Sinitsyn couple. It seems like quite a stretch to me."

"If you would just check it out for me. You do have that ability, after all."

"I don't know."

The major lit another cigarette, and Lena took another cigarette out of her own pack.

"I have one request to make of you," she said quietly. "Tomorrow morning I'm sending my daughter away with my neighbor, her nanny, to a holiday house on the Istra Reservoir. Could you get in touch with them, with the security there, so that they—"

"Yes, I understand," the major interrupted. "I'll do everything in my power. And what are your plans?"

"I'm supposed to go to Siberia to serve as a consultant and an interpreter for an American professor." She smiled.

"Will you be gone for long?"

"Ten days. The American's arriving late tonight. And in a day or so we're flying to Tyumen."

"I'll give you my number," the major said. "Be sure to check in occasionally from Siberia. We may have questions for you. Okay?"

"Yes, of course. Only you mustn't pull my husband back from London ahead of schedule. This is his first time abroad. If you need to speak to anyone from his department, you should be in touch with Mikhail Sichkin. Just please don't bother Seryozha. There's no need to alarm him, he's only got a week left."

"All right, Elena Nikolaevna." The major smiled. "I promise we won't bother your husband while he's away. You're right to be sending the child to the holiday house and leaving Moscow yourself."

When the major left, Lena called Misha Sichkin at work.

"He's not here," they told her. "Who's asking?"

"This is Polyanskaya."

"Hello, Elena Nikolaevna. Sichkin's been out sick with the flu for two days."

Lena immediately called Misha at home. He was completely hoarse.

"How are you feeling?" Lena asked.

"Horrible. I'm taking all kinds of aspirins to bring down my temperature."

"Watch out, you'll ruin your stomach. Tell Ksenya to rub you down with vodka."

"I prefer my vodka internally," Misha muttered.

"Sure. It works great with aspirin."

"All right, Madam Doctor, we'll talk about the flu and vodka later. What's happened? Spill."

"Our stroller got blown up today. Someone put a bomb, fifty grams of TNT, into the bag with Liza's new shoes. Some Security Service guys are going to come see you. They think it's connected to Seryozha's work."

"Are you serious?" Misha's voice started to give out, he was so disturbed. "Someone put a bomb in Liza's stroller? Where were you?"

"Fifteen meters away. We hadn't quite got to it when it blew up. We were just thrown to the ground. But Misha, don't be worried. We're totally fine. We're just a little shaken, that's all."

"You have to call Seryozha."

"Not on your life! Don't even dream of telling him before he gets back. You know him. He'll go crazy. You're going to have to deal with these Security Service guys yourself. And I wanted to tell you, the guitarist's wife, she's dead."

"What? When?"

"The night before last. At about two thirty. She injected herself with a fatal dose of morphine. Then she dropped a burning cigarette on her blanket, and her whole apartment went up in flames. But half an hour before that I was talking to her on the phone. We didn't get to finish our conversation. Some woman came to see her and interrupted us. But Katya managed to tell me quite a few interesting things before she died. For instance, she told me about a doctor who was treating her, a doctor so brilliant and famous and popular she wouldn't even tell me her name. It's entirely possible that it was that doctor who visited Katya that night, Misha. The receiver was lying next to the phone when Katya went to open the door. I heard Katya say a woman's name, but it was far away. Inna, or maybe Galina."

"Regina?" Sichkin asked, surprising himself.

"Possibly Regina," Lena agreed. "It was hard to hear. Did that name just come to you? Or do you have something specific in mind?"

"I don't know. Not yet. I need to get well fast and go back to work."

"Misha, what's going on? Please tell me I'm imagining things. Tell me that Katya was a drug addict and her death was accidental. Tell me it was just some young thugs that put that bomb in the stroller for a laugh."

"When do you leave for Siberia, Lena?"

"The day after tomorrow."

"It's good that you and Liza will be out of Moscow for a while."

"Major Ievlev of the Security Services thinks the same."

The guard barely recognized Regina Valentinovna. "Gena," she said as she got out of the green Opel, "pay this man his fare."

"In dollars?" Gena whispered.

"Give him whatever you have." She darted through the office gates.

In the front hall, the maid flew at Regina.

"Hey! Where are you going? How did you get in here?" The maid barred her way.

"Excellent work, Galya." Regina patted her on the cheek. "Keep it up. Only, please never address anyone with 'hey.' It's impolite."

Pulling off the black knit cap, Regina shook out her sleek hair the color of ripe wheat and proceeded calmly to her office.

"Regina Valentinovna, forgive me. I didn't recognize you." The maid's lips quivered.

Locking herself in her office, Regina stripped off her 'everywoman' outfit, under which she wore delicate French lingerie, which she took off in the shower stall with great care. Standing under the hot shower, she washed off all the smells and sounds of the dirty, boorish city.

Regina turned off the water, pulled off her shower cap, and wrapped herself in a fluffy terry-cloth bath sheet. *What now?* she thought. *Poison? But that's doubly dangerous now. Wait it out? Maybe it's better not to do anything at all for now.*

Right then she heard a cautious knock at the door.

"What's the matter?'" she asked angrily.

"Regina Valentinovna." The frightened voice of her secretary Inna came through the door. "Veniamin Borisovich isn't feeling well. Some journalist came to see him. He asked that you stop in at the audition room to see him."

"I'm on my way!" Regina put a plaid kilt and thick white hand-knit sweater over her naked body. Slipping her bare feet into soft suede flat slippers, she glanced in the mirror, ran a brush through her hair, and left her office.

Venya was pale as death. His hands were shaking. He stood in the narrow aisle between the chairs, his mouth open but unable to utter a word.

Sitting right there, by the stage, was a dark-haired fellow of about twenty-five with a pleasant, intelligent face. Regina noted quickly that he looked nothing like a music journalist. He was wearing expensive jeans, a neat, dark blue sweater, and clean, high-quality shoes.

"Hello." He rose to meet Regina and held out his hand. "Georgy Galitsyn of *Smart* magazine."

Regina shook his hand. And immediately saw the small voice recorder he was holding in his left hand.

"Venya, what's wrong?'" She walked right up to her husband.

"I . . . I'm not feeling well," he managed to get out, looking into Regina's eyes with horror.

"We were just talking," Galitsyn began explaining in a gentle, apologetic voice. "Veniamin Borisovich was the one who made the appointment. Maybe we should call a doctor?"

"How many cassettes have you recorded?" Regina asked quickly.

"One."

"Give it to me, please."

"Excuse me?" The journalist was surprised. "It's an ordinary conversation. We were talking about Tobolsk. I can let you listen to it."

"You'll give me the cassette and leave immediately," Regina said with a polite smile.

"Fine!" Galitsyn shrugged. "If you think your husband might have said something he shouldn't have, take it." He pulled the microcassette out of the recorder and held it out to Regina.

"Don't be offended, young man." Her voice softened after she took the cassette from him and slipped it into her skirt pocket. "Veniamin Borisovich is in no condition to give an interview today. I know your magazine. It would be better if you came another time. Veniamin Borisovich will be happy to answer your questions. But not today. Please excuse us."

Galitsyn quickly left the room.

The cassette he'd given Regina was blank.

⚘

"Child, you mustn't. Throwing out a perfectly good stroller just because its wheels came off is wasteful." Vera Fyodorovna sat sedately on the kitchen sofa and shrugged.

"Vera Fyodorovna, would you like some groats and mushrooms?" Lena asked.

"Yes, please. But don't you try to sweet-talk me. Liza, what were you looking at?"

"The stroller's all broken." Liza sighed and sent a spoonful of groats and mushrooms into her mouth. "I'm a big girl now. I can walk myself. Do you want to see my monkey?"

Liza climbed down from her chair and ran to her room.

"You could have it repaired. Why are you giving me so much? I don't like to go to bed full."

"Vera Fyodorovna, Liza really can walk herself now. It will be dry before long. Sooner or later we'd have to get rid of the stroller," Lena said, setting a plate in front of Vera Fyodorovna.

"You want to throw everything out? What if you and Seryozha decide to have another child? You mean you'd buy a new one? It was such an excellent stroller."

"Nanny Vera, look at my monkey!" Liza exclaimed as she ran into the kitchen. "We're taking him with us to the holidouse. He'll sleep and eat with me there."

"Have you decided on a name for him?" Vera Fyodorovna asked as she examined the toy animal.

The doorbell rang. Lena looked through the peephole and saw Gosha Galitsyn.

Liza ran into the front hall as he was taking off his boots.

"Hello!" she said very seriously.

"Hello, little girl. How are you?"

"Good. Our stroller broke today." Liza ran back to the kitchen shouting, "Nanny Vera! I'll name the monkey Gosha!"

"Who is it you're naming in my honor? Show me." Gosha walked into the kitchen, greeted Vera Fyodorovna, and sat down beside her on the sofa. "I have nothing against it at all," he said after looking at the monkey. "A very attractive namesake."

"Gosha, this isn't a snake, it's a monkey," Liza objected seriously. "Gosha the monkey had a little stool and a little bed and little dishes, too. Mama and I bought them, but the stroller broke a lot."

"How's that?" Vera Fyodorovna didn't understand.

"The stroller went like this." Liza took a deep breath and shouted at the top of her lungs: "Ka-boom! Mama and I fell down, and then a fat man wanted to pick me up. But I cried."

"Oh, Liza! I totally forgot!" Gosha went out to the front hall and came back a minute later, carrying a small set of toy dishes in a plastic wrapper. "Look. Just for your monkey."

"Thank you! It's got little spoons and little cups! Open it!"

"Lena, I don't understand," Vera Fyodorovna asked sternly. "What happened to you today?"

"Nothing, Vera Fyodorovna." Lena put a plate of groats in front of Gosha. "I told you. The stroller broke as we were walking. I slipped and fell, and Liza fell with me. It's very slippery right now."

"And what happened to the toys? You did go to the store this morning, didn't you?"

"Everything fell out and drowned in the slush."

"And who was this 'fat man'?"

"A passerby helped us up."

"Oh, you're hiding something, girl." Vera Fyodorovna shook her head. "Fine. Liza and I are going to bed. You have to go meet your American."

"I was at Volkov's today," Gosha said when they got in the car. "You know, it was all very strange. He made an appointment to meet me in his office. He's got a gorgeous place. You can imagine. A fancy office. Maids, guards, and an audition room that was oddly shabby, like some Soviet-era House of Pioneers. I started asking him questions about his childhood and his parents. Then about his youth. Very basic stuff. He was so languid, I decided to change things up and asked whether he remembered steaming in an official bathhouse with a group of journalists from Moscow during his Young Communist days. And if he remembered drinking vodka with them and roasting shish kebabs one night on the banks of the Tobol. And at that moment something happened to him. He turned white, sweat broke out on his forehead, and his hands started shaking. He looked at me with bugged-out eyes and asked, 'Who told you that?'

"I said, 'Elena Polyanskaya, my boss and friend. You must remember her.' And at that he shouted so the whole office could hear: 'No!' His secretary flew in, and then his wife came running and demanded I give back the cassette. I'd just put in a new blank one. That's what I gave her. Do you want to listen to the interview?"

"Yes." Lena nodded.

"Take my bag out of the back seat. The Volkov cassette is in the pocket."

Lena put on the headset and turned on the recorder. "I had a very strict mother. She was the secretary of the bread factory's Party organization. She was very demanding, but she taught me to be strong."

"Is that why you became a Young Communist?" Gosha's mocking voice asked.

"Yes. I had specific ideals. Unlike lots of people, I truly believed in the victory of Communism."

Lord, what rot! Lena thought. *Venya Volkov, the Young Communist who took us to the Party bathhouse, fed us shish kebab and cured sausage. Venya Volkov, who burned with an unearthly love for me. That Venya Volkov believed in the victory of Communism? Why is he making himself out to be an idiot? There was something sensitive and abnormal about him.*

Right then, Gosha asked about the bathhouse and the shish kebab. Volkov's "No!" hit her headset so loudly that Lena shuddered. That cry rang out immediately after Gosha said her name.

"Tell me about Volkov," Lena asked, turning off the recorder and putting it back in Gosha's bag. "How did he become a millionaire?"

"From '85 to '87 he had a chain of nightclubs and sound studios in Tyumen, Tobolsk, and Khanty-Mansiysk. But by that time he had already moved to Moscow and was working for the Young Communist Central Committee. In what capacity, I don't know."

"Hang on, Gosha. In '85 we didn't have private property. How could he own nightclubs and studios?"

"Well, formally the music business was communal, owned by the Young Communists. But in reality, at least in Western Siberia, it was completely controlled by Volkov. Simultaneously, he ran the so-called Central Committee propaganda train. You must have heard of it."

"I even rode it once." Lena smiled. "It was a nightmare. There was a children's chorus from Lipetsk going to New Urengoi. I remember the chorus's conductor warming water in the boiler and washing the children's heads and her own over the only sink. They were afraid of lice. I'll never forget it. Fine, go on about Volkov."

"In '88 he started making stars. First he took a children's dance ensemble from the Tobolsk Pioneer Palace around the country. The kids would tap-dance and dance to rock and roll. He'd squeeze those dancers dry and made crazy money off them—for those days.

"Later he had a serious clash with the ensemble's director, Tatyana Kostylyova. In an interview I read, she had some unflattering things to say about Volkov. She said he was profiting off the children, treating them as slaves, forcing them to work for twelve hours a day, dragging them all over the country. They couldn't even go to school.

"It was a major scandal. Then the parents of one of the boys in the ensemble sued Kostylyova, accusing her of indecent assault against minors. Everyone knew she hadn't done anything improper with any of the boys. But the newspapers had a field day."

"Was there ever a trial?"

"No, it never went to trial. It took quite a toll on her nerves and her family, though. They ended up moving to Canada."

"What happened to the children's ensemble?"

"It fell apart. But Volkov pulled an incredible coup. In '89 the Nightingales group appeared on the music scene. You must remember them, four boys, all eighteen, singing love songs. They had some producer named Granayan, an Armenian millionaire. He made loads of money off those boys and slept with each of them. The group was a sensation. Sold-out halls, girls pissing their pants in ecstasy at their concerts.

"And then something strange happened. Granayan was suddenly hospitalized with a serious case of pneumonia. Tests showed he had AIDS. At the time, hardly anyone knew what that was.

"The boys in the Nightingales panicked. It turned out that two of the four were infected. You know how it all ended? Volkov took the healthy ones under his wing and found replacements for the two sick ones. He created a new group, Bicycle. He didn't even have to promote them. They were even more popular and their shows were sold-out everywhere.

"Then one journalist tracked down a male prostitute, an Algerian studying at Lumumba U. in Moscow. He admitted he'd been paid to entice and infect 'a certain rich Armenian' with AIDS. He didn't know who'd paid him, but it was a lot of money. All he said was that all his dealings had been with a woman who only spoke French with him.

"Soon after that, the prostitute vanished, no one knew where. And the journalist got a bullet in his skull as he was walking his dog one night."

"What happened to the Armenian and the two infected boys?" Lena asked quietly.

"The Armenian died shortly thereafter, in the hospital, but those two—I don't know."

"Do you think this was Volkov's doing?" Lena asked.

"Who else's could it be? Look at his career. Whenever anyone got in his way, there was an accident and that 'someone' was eliminated one way or another. Granayan was just one of those people who got in his way. Then there was Olya Ivushkina. Maybe you remember her? She was huge in the early '90s."

"I did hear something. What, AIDS again?"

"No. The Olya Ivushkina story is much simpler and cruder. Volkov found her in a discotheque. He literally picked her out of the crowd. You know her type: a real cutie-pie, a skinny redhead with freckles on her snub nose, round glasses, and her hair in braids. She sang songs about high school love. Volkov made her a name and fast. He shot a few videos and started making good money off of her. And then all of a sudden, at the height of her fame, she said she had no desire to sing anymore. She was in love with some shah from the Emirates and he'd forbidden her to appear onstage. She wanted to marry him and be a shah's wife, so she had to put an end to her musical career.

"Tour dates had to be canceled. Volkov would have had to kiss his money good-bye, but then they found a dead prostitute in the shah's deluxe suite at the Metropol Hotel. All the clues pointed to the Arab. No amount of money, no attempts at diplomatic intervention could help him. The shah ended up in a special prison for foreigners.

"And Olya Ivushkina is singing to this day. Only she completely changed her image. Now she's a blonde femme fatale with silicone breasts."

Gosha's white Volga drove onto the curving ramp in front of the terminal at Sheremetyevo 2.

"Lena, what really happened with the stroller?" Gosha suddenly asked.

"I'll tell you later. Look, there's a space. Park there."

CHAPTER 20

Late that evening, lying in a warm, lavender-scented bath, Regina started humming a tune, and then remembered the words:

> When your soul has been stripped bare,
> How sweet to drift to sleep, like a baby bird,
> Entrusted to the state's abiding care . . .

Regina had an excellent memory for texts, especially poetry. She'd had occasion to listen to a great many songs with Venya at auditions and sat in occasionally on recording sessions. Often some random snippet would stick in her memory, and she'd find herself singing it, days, even years, later. *What's that? Where is it from? It's not pop. The melody's totally different, and the text . . .*

Swaddled in her soft terry robe, Regina tucked her feet under her in her big leather armchair and lit a cigarette.

> The match's flame, how high it blazes,
> In your palms' translucent tent . . .

That was when she remembered the tall young man on the Pioneer stage where Venya listened to all kinds of street performers. The young man didn't stand like the others; he sat on the edge of the stage. A guitar in his lap. Big hands and strong, agile fingers. A very pleasant voice.

"Sinitsyn!" Regina actually slapped her bare knee. "Of course. It's a snippet of a song by Sinitsyn. Sinitsyn, who started this whole mess."

"Why did you blow him off like that?" she'd asked Venya when the tall young man had left. "I thought he had something."

"And I didn't," Venya replied, irritated. "That kind of music was fine for Moscow kitchens in the early eighties, but it won't work today."

"You know best." Regina shrugged.

That evening, under hypnosis, Venya had told the story of the nighttime picnic on the banks of the Tobol and added new details.

"Venya, you have to keep that fellow under control," Regina said later at dinner. "You shouldn't have blown him off. He could be dangerous. It would have been better to promote him and shoot a couple of videos for him. You know it's just like getting someone on the needle. He'd be tame and quiet. He'd forget everything that happened fourteen years ago—if he even remembers anything at all."

"He remembers. It's hard for me to look at him. I'm afraid."

"Fine." Regina sighed. "I'll take care of it."

It didn't take her very long to determine that Mitya's Sinitsyn's wife Katya was an addict. Regina called them at home.

"Hello, Mitya. This is Regina Gradskaya. Do you remember me?"

"Yes, of course. Hello." She could tell he was thrilled to hear from her. Of course he remembered her. His audition had only been three days before.

"I have to tell you, your songs made a very powerful impression on me. We should meet and talk. What are you doing this evening?"

"I . . . I'm free."

"That's excellent. I can come to your place in an hour, if that's convenient."

"Thank you," he mumbled, embarrassed. "But I live on the outskirts, in Vykhino."

"That's nothing." Regina smiled into the phone. "I have my car. I'll take down the address."

"Sometimes Veniamin Borisovich's taste and mine don't coincide," she said later that evening, sitting on the old couch in the shabby two-room apartment in Vykhino. "He's a practical and harsh man. He didn't see the prospects in your songs, but I haven't been able to forget them.

> I've been happy for so long,
> I scarcely recognize myself,
> I don't recognize me when we meet,
> I don't invite me over."

She sang his song quietly and accurately, with a pensive smile. Sinitsyn blushed with pleasure.

"Did you really memorize it on the spot?" skinny, cropped Katya asked, shifting her eyes from their visitor to her husband.

"I did. I have a good memory for exceptional verse. There's so little of it nowadays, and in the pop music business, none at all. Will you give me a cassette?"

"Yes, certainly. With pleasure," Mitya said.

Katya immediately jumped up and ran into the other room. She came back a minute later holding an entire box of cassettes.

"Babe, why so many?" Sinitsyn was embarrassed.

Regina spent a couple of hours with them, drinking their awful instant coffee and talking about literature and music and about the mysterious nature of talent. She made no promises. She just admired Mitya's songs and complained about the lack of talent in modern pop music and about her husband's cold pragmatism.

"See me to my car, Mitya," she asked when he gave her her coat in the front hall.

They stepped out into the empty, snow-drifted courtyard. It was a starry January night.

"I can see Katya has serious problems." Regina tried to speak as gently and sympathetically as she could.

"Well, she does have a few health complications."

"You don't have to beat around the bush with me, Mitya. I'm a doctor. In fact, I am exactly the kind of doctor your wife needs. Katya's addicted to drugs."

"Is it really that obvious?" he asked in fright.

"To me, yes. But I'm a specialist."

"It's been going on for a year and a half. I've been trying to fight it, but without success. Sometimes I think it's hopeless."

"You're mistaken, Mitya. In my opinion, there is hope. Assuming we don't delay, of course."

"She's already been in the hospital and we've gone to private specialists as well. It's very expensive and it's had no effect."

"You know what?" Regina touched his hand. "I'll try to help. I'll work with Katya. Don't worry about money. I've been treating people for free for a long time. I can always tell whether a person is my patient or not. I only take someone on when the case interests me."

"I don't know how to thank you, Regina Valentinovna."

"Go inside, Mitya. It's cold and you're just wearing a sweater." She smiled as she got behind the wheel of her dark blue Volvo.

In a month's time she made herself indispensable to the Sinitsyns. She visited them often and held hypnosis sessions with Katya. She really might have been able to cure this quiet, broken girl with the deep complexes, which stemmed from childhood.

Katya Sinitsyna was quite suggestible and trusting. She worshipped Regina. But Regina had no intention of curing this child of her addiction. She just eased the symptoms slightly and made very slight improvements in her condition.

Katya was sure she was on the mend. She thought she might reduce her dose. In fact, Regina had been periodically changing out her morphine ampoules for a higher concentration.

Mitya was effusive in his thanks and tried as hard as he could to please their new benefactor. He, too, was trusting and suggestible. He never said a word to her about his songs. Regina Valentinovna had done so much for them as it was, treating Katya for free, out of the goodness of her heart.

One day he said, blushing and embarrassed, "Forgive me, Regina Valentinovna, I'm going to ask you an immodest question. You don't have to answer if you don't want to."

"Ask away, Mitya," she replied condescendingly.

"What connects you to that man?" Regina understood who he was talking about, naturally.

"Veniamin Borisovich is my husband," she replied with a smile. "That says it all."

"But are you sure you know everything about your husband?"

"Mitya." She burst out in cheerful laughter. "Are you trying to suggest that he's sleeping with models and aspiring singers?"

"No," Mitya said, embarrassed. "No, you've misunderstood me. It just seems to me that Volkov is a very cruel and cold person. Whereas you . . . are you ever afraid of him?"

"Explain what you mean by afraid."

"Well, aren't you afraid to live with someone who's capable of anything? Show business is a cruel business, a bloody one even, and closely connected with the criminal world. But you're different. You're sophisticated, intelligent, and noble. I'm sorry, I'm rattling on."

"Why do you say that, Mitya? In your way, you're right. I really am out of place in the foul, dirty world of entertainment. I don't have any friends there. I think that's partly why I've become so attached to your family. But life takes different forms. Fourteen years ago, I met Veniamin Borisovich. Trust me. He was different then."

"Yes." Mitya nodded. "He may have been different then."

"Are you saying you've met him before?" Regina's eyebrows rose up in surprise.

"No, never," Mitya mumbled, not looking her in the eyes.

A few days after this conversation, Sinitsyn sat down with Venya at a small table in the bar at Ostankino.

It was night, and Venya had stopped in for coffee. The bar was nearly empty. Venya was exhausted after taping a popular game show. He wanted to be alone, so he told his bodyguard to wait in the car. Ostankino was like home. A man like Volkov didn't go into it with his bodyguard!

He smoked and thought, sipping coffee from a mug. They'd made it just the way he liked it, with heavy cream.

"Hello, Veniamin Borisovich," Sinitsyn said softly, sitting down across from him.

"Good evening. To what do I owe this pleasure?" Venya glanced at him indifferently.

"Don't you like my songs at all?" Sinitsyn lit a cigarette.

"I do. But I don't see a future in them."

"You told them to let me through for an audition without waiting in line. Did you recognize me?"

The waiter came over. Sinitsyn ordered coffee, cognac, and some roasted nuts.

"And why should I recognize you?" Venya replied when the waiter had moved away.

"Haven't we met before? Young Communist?"

"I don't seem to recall." Venya shrugged.

"The summer of '82, in Tobolsk." Sinitsyn smiled. "You were in charge of the City Committee's Culture Department. You took us around."

"I took a lot of people around. I can't remember them all."

"But I doubt you forgot Lena Polyanskaya, Young Communist. You liked her an awful lot."

"Polyanskaya? Never heard of her."

"Really? And Olga, my sister? You don't remember her, either?"

"No."

The waiter brought Sinitsyn's order.

"Have some nuts, Young Communist. Help yourself." Sinitsyn moved the bowl of hazelnuts to the middle of the table. "You fed us! You treated us to some excellent shish kebab and took us to the Party bathhouse in Tobolsk."

Sinitsyn drank the cognac in one swallow, made a face, and tossed a nut into his mouth.

"You know, I never forgot you all these years. I remember especially clearly that night on the banks of the Tobol. You arranged that farewell picnic for us. You grilled some terrific shish kebab, Young Communist. You got ahold of excellent pork, lean and tender. You'd marinated it in a special wine sauce. Do you remember the recipe for that sauce? No? Of course not. You haven't grilled shish kebab in a long time.

"Sometimes I even dream of that night. You cut the onion with a razor-sharp knife. Then you threaded the thin slices on the skewer. The onion didn't make your eyes water. Ours were all watering like crazy. We were laughing and crying while you were handling that knife with such a serious face. And you kept sneaking peeks at Lena."

"This is all very interesting." Venya tried to smile. "But I don't remember any Lena. Yes, sometimes I did arrange picnics for our guests. A lot of people came—from Moscow and from Leningrad. I would meet them and take them around."

"You mean you don't remember us? And the girl they found in the morning on the riverbank, not far from our campfire? You don't remember her, either? That's impossible! All Tobolsk was talking about that murder. People were even discussing it in Khanty. 'Something's happened to my memory,'" he sang unexpectedly loudly.

The few people sitting at the bar turned around.

"You're drunk, Sinitsyn," Venya said softly. "Go home."

"No, Young Communist. I'm not drunk. I'm no young lady getting tipsy on one cognac. You know, I was prepared to forget this. So many years have passed. I've had so many problems of my own. And then one day I saw you on TV. You were giving an interview about philanthropy. The correspondent was hanging on your every word.

"Later, right after the interview with you, they showed an episode of *Criminal Russia*, the documentary series. This particular episode was about a serial killer who operated in Tyumen Province in the early eighties. He raped and murdered six girls ages fifteen to eighteen. He strangled four. Slit the throats of two. They found him. A vile man, an alcoholic. He got caught at a beer stand selling some cheap jewelry taken off one of his victims. But he never did admit to a single murder. No matter what they did to him, and they worked him over pretty good. Eventually he was executed, but he never did confess. Up until the very last minute, he insisted he hadn't killed anyone. How do you like that story, Young Communist?"

Sinitsyn spoke quietly and quickly. He leaned across the table and breathed cognac and tobacco into Volkov's face. Volkov listened in silence. He could feel sweat soaking through his shirt.

"Here you are sitting in front of me, pale and sweaty, and you don't know what to say." Sinitsyn grinned. "Tell me you remember us coming to Tobolsk. Tell me you remember Lena Polyanskaya and my sister Olga. And you recognized me right away. But you didn't kill the girls. That never happened. Go on, say it, Venya. All I need is your word, and I'll believe you. No one's going to hear us now. You and I are talking about something known only to the two of us—you and me. I confess, at first I wanted to blackmail you. But that made me feel dirty. I don't want your money or to be in one of your videos. Just tell me you didn't kill those six girls. I'll take your word for it."

"You're drunk. Go sleep it off," Volkov said softly and added loudly, "Get out of here. I'm sick of you!"

"If you say so." Sinitsyn shrugged, got up from the table, gulped down the rest of his cold coffee, went over to the counter to pay the waiter, and left the bar slowly.

Volkov wasn't able to tell Regina about the conversation right away. She wasn't in Moscow. She'd flown to Paris for a few days.

She'd returned and gone straight from the airport to the Status Club, where they were releasing Yuri Azarov's new album. She liked turning up like that, straight from an international flight to a party. Actually, there wasn't much of a party at the Status, just a buffet.

After sauntering around the room and schmoozing with everyone they needed to, she and Venya got ready to leave and headed slowly to the door. Azarov was seeing them out.

All of a sudden Sinitsyn materialized out of nowhere. They had no idea how he'd gotten into the private club, and wearing jeans and an old sweater.

He walked straight up to Venya and said quietly, "Listen, Young Communist, that was no nosebleed. You lied. It was that girl's blood. And you took that heart pendant from the girl you killed in Tyumen. You do remember the dance at the vocational school, don't you? Do you know what that girl's name was? Natasha! She was all her mother had. Her mother died of a heart attack. Immediately. After she learned what had happened to her daughter. The drunk they executed was right not to confess. He didn't kill those girls, you did. They executed him in your place, Young Communist."

Sinitsyn's voice was getting louder and louder, but the crowd drowned out what he was saying. Regina was the first to recover.

"Is there security here or not, damn it!" she said calmly. "Get this madman away from us!"

Two broad-shouldered toughs in formal suits dragged Sinitsyn to the exit.

"You're a maniac, Young Communist! A serial killer! Regina Valentinovna, he'll kill you! Be careful!" Mitya cried out as he was carried to the exit.

Looking around, Regina encountered Azarov's cold, attentive eyes.

CHAPTER 21

Michael was a little fatter and had let his beard grow. He was as bald as an egg, and his girth and short stature made him look a bit like a tennis ball. He looked cheerful and rested, despite the long flight.

"I'm starving! The vegetarian meal on the plane was disgusting," he jabbered in his Brooklyn English. "But Lena, you look marvelous. And this, I understand, is Mr. Krotov. Am I right?" He shook Gosha's hand mercilessly.

"No, Michael, Mr. Krotov is in London right now. This is Gosha. We work together."

"Goshua? Wonderful! Do you speak English?"

"Yes, a little," Gosha told him modestly, although he had a degree from the English department of the prestigious Foreign Languages Institute.

"Very pleased to meet you." Michael kept on jabbering. "How are you doing? Now where did you say your husband was? London? Steven said you married a police colonel. Congratulations! And he went to London to help out Scotland Yard? Ha ha ha! You know, Sally got herself a third dog. Another Airedale. There's no end to it. My wife's decided to turn our house into a haven for dogs. By the way, Sally sends a big hello. She sent along some medicines for you."

"Medicines?" Lena said, surprised. "What for?"

"Her friend Judy read in some newspaper that there'd been several aspirin poisonings in Russia. Sally sent high-quality American aspirin for you. Just in case. And something else. You'll see when we get to your apartment. Sally and I spent a very long time picking out a present for your daughter. In the end we decided on Legos. We bought a small set geared to two-year-olds. Our psychologists say that building sets have a very good influence on a child's intellect. It sure is cold here in Moscow! In New York it's full-blown spring. True, they're promising colder temps next week, but Sally doesn't believe the forecasters. Me neither. Everything here's changed so much! You're becoming much more European. I never ever expected it would happen this quickly."

"Lena, does he ever shut up? Do you think you'll last ten days? And with that accent—won't your eardrums get sore?" Gosha whispered in Russian, leaning toward Lena.

"Gosha, stop it. It's not nice."

"Wow!" Michael howled at the top of his lungs. "We're riding in a Volga! A real Russian Volga! It used to be rich Communists riding around in these cars. Now it's rich New Russians? Goshua, are you a New Russian?"

"He's mocking me now!" Gosha whispered, rolling his eyes. "No, Michael," he said in English, smiling graciously and unlocking the car. "New Russians prefer Mercedes and BMWs."

"Oh, right! Not long ago I saw on television . . ."

Michael didn't shut his mouth the entire drive. Lena nodded distractedly in reply, sometimes saying, "Yes, certainly" or "Really? Impossible!" She was thinking about Volkov. Why had her name caused such a stormy reaction in someone she'd only barely known fourteen years ago? According to what Gosha said about him, Veniamin Volkov should have been someone with nerves of steel. But the reaction was hysterical.

It makes no sense. A millionaire, a megaproducer who's up to his elbows in shit and blood, was frightened by the mere mention of my name. He did have a fierce, burning passion for me fourteen years ago. But that's ridiculous to think of now. No, not ridiculous. Dangerous, very dangerous. Old passions have nothing to do with this. Still, there must be some connection to our past.

Everything was shipshape at home. Vera Fyodorovna had even remembered to make up the couch for Michael in the living room.

"It's too late to eat," Michael declared. "I know you Russians like to sit drinking tea in the kitchen at night. But with your permission, I'm going to take a shower and go to bed. Tomorrow morning I want to get to the Tretyakov Gallery."

"Of course, Michael."

Gosha had a quick cup of tea and headed home. Lena was glad to sit in silence. Everyone in the apartment was asleep. It was two thirty, but Lena knew she wouldn't be able to fall asleep.

This terrible day refused to end. She turned on the kettle, trying not to make too much noise, took a small stepladder out of the hall closet, climbed onto it, and took the cardboard vacuum cleaner box she kept her old manuscripts and letters in off the top shelf.

In Soviet times, half the country's population wrote. Mountains of manuscripts were sent to magazine offices. Mostly it was poetry, but there was fiction, too. Those outpourings of the people's creativity had to be read, reviewed, and returned to the author with a detailed, substantive reply.

Every literature department had a regiment of freelance literary consultants performing this dreary but well-compensated labor. For the most part, the consultants were unemployed writers and poets, but sometimes the magazine's own employees did it on the side for extra money. Every twenty-four typewritten pages was worth three rubles. If you grabbed a stack of manuscripts from the office, took them home, and worked at the typewriter for a few hours, you could earn an extra fifty or even a hundred—if you had the energy to read through 240 pages of mediocre prose.

Everybody wrote. Young Pioneers and war vets, tractor drivers and milkmaids, miners and pilots, sailors and housewives. But most of the poetry came from people who'd been sent to prison or to the camps. These were the most patriotic and most ideologically keen opuses.

Burglars and rapists wrote poems about Lenin, the Party, and the victory of Communism. As a rule, they weren't shy about bringing up the articles for which they'd been "unjustly and illegally" convicted.

After university, when she was working as a special correspondent for a popular youth magazine, Lena often patched her financial holes by taking home manuscripts that had come to the literature department. But it wasn't just about the money for her. She liked it when she unexpectedly glimpsed a faint flash of talent in all the verbal garbage.

Sometimes, the submissions were accompanied by long letters in which the person told their life story. This usually turned out to be much more interesting than the works themselves. As a rule, authors were profoundly lonely people, and their few crooked quatrains were just an excuse to express themselves, get a human response, and write more.

In her years of work, about three hundred of these letter-confessions had been sent to the editorial office and addressed to her personally. She'd kept a number of them; she couldn't bring herself to throw them out.

Now, in the dead of night, she searched through the old papers for a few letters once sent to her from Tobolsk and Tyumen. She came across one of them almost right away.

Dear Elena Nikolaevna,
Writing to you is Nadezhda Ivanovna Zakharova. My son Igor Zakharov, a police first lieutenant, gave you his story to read. You were kind to him and sent him

a detailed reply. He sent you another story, and you again replied with a letter. Although you rejected it for publication, you explained to him many things about literature. Now he would like you to read another story of his. He was planning to retype it at work and send it to you, but a great misfortune occurred.

My dear son Igor was killed by a gangster. He was stabbed in the heart. Now I'm sending you his last story. Since my son wanted to send it to you, I'm sending it for him.

Wishing you health and peace and all the best,

Nadezhda Zakharova, Tobolsk, November 12, 1984.

The letter was stapled to a manuscript, "Justice," a strange story set out on ten typewritten pages about an officer who doesn't believe a murder suspect's guilt. This officer, Vyacheslav, has a feeling that someone else is the murderer.

At the base of the plot were general arguments, not facts or clues. In rereading the story, it seemed to Lena that the dead first lieutenant had left out the specifics on purpose. He may have been lightly fictionalizing a real case, and out of a police officer's natural caution, preserved a certain amount of secrecy even in a work of literature. But he couldn't remain silent. This case bothered him so much he decided to write a story.

The story had a happy ending. Justice triumphed. The innocent man was released, his elderly mother sobbed on the noble officer's chest, and the real killer, crafty and cold-blooded, was escorted to prison.

"Zakharov, Zakharov. Could you have been that conscientious and honest officer? And is that why they killed you?" Lena didn't notice she was talking out loud.

Setting aside the manuscript and letter, she started reading through some more of the letters. There was one more letter she remembered—from a prison with a long code. But Lena knew that prison wasn't far from Tyumen.

Dear Lena,

Thank you for publishing my poem in your magazine's "Anthology of One Poem." You really did choose my favorite, and I agree with your small corrections. It really is better that way. Also thank you for sending the magazine to my mother, who sends her deep regards.

My life isn't going well. In fact, it's pretty crappy. They're trying my dad for six murders. They say he killed six young girls. That's ridiculous. He's a drunk and he's willing to sell his soul for a bottle and he gave me and Mama pretty regular thrashings. But he's no killer. He couldn't rape girls and then strangle them or slit their throat.

I'm not writing the details. You know why. I'm just sharing this with you and no one else. Mama's cried her eyes out.

Write me—about anything. Anything you like, just write.

I hope you meet a nice boy and marry him and have kids. Unless you're already married? Write about that, too.

Vasily Slepak. April 6, 1984.

"Vasya," Lena sighed after reading the letter. "Vasya Slepak." Again she'd spoken out loud without noticing.

He hadn't told her the details in his letter because prisoner letters went through the censor. And a letter that discussed a criminal case might not get through for censorship reasons.

Many years ago, Lena had kept her promise. She got Vasily Slepak, the prisoner outcast, published.

It hadn't been easy. Lena pestered her editor in chief and department head for a week and listened to all their heavy sighs, exclamations, and reprimands—and what they had to say about her and her pushiness. But in the end they did publish Vasya Slepak's poem in the "Anthology."

All that was a very long time ago, another lifetime practically. That youth magazine was long defunct, and her department head had retired and was looking after his grandchildren. The editor in chief had jumped into politics, ridden the wave of '91 high, and then quietly and smoothly sank into private entrepreneurship. Soviet poet Studenets turned himself into the founding father of one of the many Nazi-Communist organizations.

The only one Lena knew nothing about was Vasya Slepak.

CHAPTER 22

Venya flew into the room as if he'd been scalded.

"You were prepared to kill a child? A two-year-old? You don't care? Even the lowest thug wouldn't dream of putting a bomb in a stroller!" he shouted.

"What's the matter, my darling?" Regina asked, turning toward him—having covered her face with a green mask.

"I was watching the local news. Do you want to finish off Polyanskaya so badly that you don't give a fuck who else you kill? Do you have any idea what you're doing?"

"Calm down," Regina said through her teeth. "What makes you think they're talking about Polyanskaya? Did they actually name her?"

"Don't play innocent with me!" Venya shouted. "Why did you cook this whole thing up to begin with?"

"I cooked it up? Me? How interesting! Do you have the slightest idea what you're saying? Now you feel sorry for the child! Do you think you're Alyosha Karamazov? I'm living with a softie! And don't yell at me! Sit still and keep quiet. Do you understand? Everything I do, I do for you. I deal with all kinds of undesirables, risk my own skin, and you feel sorry for a child."

"For me? For me you could have stopped at Sinitsyn. He was plenty."

"Uh-huh." Regina nodded. "Sinitsyn, Azarov, and then Katya. And that's it. Stop there. No, my happiness. The machinery's in motion. Polyanskaya's next, with or without the child. You know as well as I do that if anything, even a drop of information about what you did to those girls gets out to our mobster friends, it will be worse than the courts, worse than death. For me, too, naturally. But I'll be able to wiggle out of it. Whereas you . . . I'm doing all this for you. Get a grip and quit sniveling."

"That's what my mother used to say," Venya said quietly.

Regina looked him in the eye for a few seconds without saying a word.

"Fine." She sighed. "I'll wash off this mask and we'll go to work."

"No." He shook his head. "We have to talk. Just talk. No hypnosis."

"Knock yourself out. I'm listening."

"Regina, I don't want you to kill Polyanskaya," Venya said quietly and hoarsely.

"She'll be the last. Everything hinges on her. I'm not going to touch Olga Sinitsyna. She presents no danger. But Polyanskaya is dangerous. Even you must realize that."

"Leave her alone."

"Why?"

"Because"—he swallowed nervously—"because you can't do it neatly. You've followed her too much as it is. You can't pull it off and it's too risky to hire someone else to do it. Can't you get it into your head that her husband is a police colonel? Cases like this are always solved."

"Is that the only reason I shouldn't touch Polyanskaya?" Regina asked quickly.

"Yes."

❧

247

"Lena, child, wake up."

Lena pried her eyes open and looked at Vera Fyodorovna, who was standing over her holding the telephone.

"Yes . . . Good morning. What time is it?" she asked, sitting up on the bed.

"Eight thirty. You have a call from work."

"Thank you." Lena took the receiver from Vera Fyodorovna.

"Get up." She heard the voice of Masha, the editor in chief's secretary, on the line. "They moved the planning meeting to today. You need to be here by eleven. The chief said you had to come."

"Fine, Masha. I'll come. Thanks for waking me up early."

Liza ran into the bedroom in tights and a warm sweater.

"Mama, good morning! Nanny Vera and I already had our breakfast, but you've been sleeping and sleeping. And this man can't talk like us. He's so funny! Look what he brought me!"

Liza ran off to her room and came back holding a box of Legos.

"Vera Fyodorovna, where's Michael?" Lena asked as she climbed out from under the blanket and threw on her robe.

"I think he went for a run. When I woke up, he was standing in the hall in shorts and sneakers. He tried desperately to explain something to me, but I didn't understand. Then he made gestures, and I figured it out. He'll probably be back soon. Maybe I'll take Liza for a walk and give you a chance to get ready for work."

"No need, Vera Fyodorovna. The weather's awful, and I haven't had time to pack Liza's things. I wanted to do that this morning, but it turns out I have a meeting." Lena smiled guiltily. "Everything's been selected, washed, and ironed. You just have to put it in the suitcase."

Lena didn't wake up fully until she'd had a hot shower. *Naturally, if you don't go to bed before four thirty, you're going to feel and look awful in the morning. All right, a little lipstick and powder.* Looking in the mirror, Lena suddenly noticed that her eyes were different, worried, frightened even.

I'm not frightened. I got over that two years ago. I'm not frightened at all, she thought, and she tried to smile at her reflection.

"Nanny Vera made you coffee and an egg!" Liza informed her.

The doorbell rang. Michael was back from his run. He was beaming, his bald head was pink and damp.

"It's raining," he said cheerfully.

"Where did you run?" Lena inquired.

"Around the building. Fifty times. So I wouldn't get lost."

"There's yogurt and orange juice for you in the fridge. I have to go to work for a couple of hours. Then my friend Olga will come and we'll take you to the Tretyakov."

"Sure. Your daughter's going to teach me Russian while you're out!" Michael said, and he headed for the shower.

"Vera Fyodorovna, don't offer Michael salami or sausage. He's a vegetarian," Lena said, as she took her leather jacket out of the closet. "And he doesn't drink coffee. I have a special herbal tea for him there, whole-grain bread, margarine, and jam. Will you be able to find it?"

"Don't worry, child. I'll figure it out."

Kissing Liza and Vera Fyodorovna good-bye, Lena grabbed her purse and ran down the stairs. It was ten thirty. She hated being late.

It really was raining. And quite warm. Spring had arrived overnight.

It wasn't far to Novodmitrovskaya Street, where her office was, but it was very inconvenient to get there on public transport—a transfer on the Metro and then four stops on the trolleybus. Lena decided to hail a car. A minute later a black Mercedes pulled up.

Rarely do owners of foreign cars moonlight as drivers. The Mercedes wasn't a 600 series, it wasn't new, and there was no one in the car but the driver, and Lena felt uneasy very briefly.

I shouldn't have hailed a car. But he's alone, and something could happen in the Metro, on the trolleybus, or on the street, too, she thought, and she glanced at her watch. She had twenty minutes until her meeting.

"Novodmitrovskaya. Past the Savelovsky Train Station. Thirty thousand," Lena said.

"Let's go." The driver nodded. She got into the back seat.

"In a rush?"

"Yes, very much so."

"Going to work?"

"Yes."

They rode in silence for a while.

"Do you mind if I smoke?" the driver asked.

"Please do."

"Would you like one?" Without turning around, he held out an open pack of some unfamiliar and probably very expensive cigarettes and a Ronson lighter.

"Thank you." Lena took a cigarette. She really did want to smoke. She was nervous and in her haste had left her cigarettes at home.

"I'm sorry, you don't happen to work at *Smart* magazine, do you?" the driver asked as he turned onto Novoslobodskaya.

"Yes. How did you know?" Lena said, surprised.

"Your photograph was in the issue before last."

The editor in chief had had the idea of putting a photo montage on the back cover under the heading "Meet Our Staff." It had the photos of nearly everyone. The magazine photographer had raced from department to department with his camera snapping everyone unsuspectingly, so it would be silly and casual.

He got Lena at her computer. She managed to look around and say, "Kolya, don't. I look terrible—" at which point she heard a click. But the photo came out quite well. At least Lena was recognizable.

"You're Elena Polyanskaya," the driver went on. "You're the head of the literature and art department. You're thirty-six years old. You're married and you have a two-year-old daughter named Liza."

Lena's heart started pounding. There'd been nothing under the photographs but their names and titles.

"I'm sorry," she asked as calmly as possible. "Do we know each other?"

"Yes. You and I met a very long time ago and not in Moscow. But you haven't changed at all. It's just amazing."

Stranger things have happened, Lena thought, a little calmer. *It's true I've barely changed in the last ten years. People I knew long ago often recognize me, but I don't recognize lots of them right away.*

"Remind me when and where, please," she asked with a smile.

"In Tobolsk. June of '82," he said quietly.

Volkov? Lena screamed inwardly. *Why did I get in this car? What does he want? Lord, what am I supposed to do? How should I behave?*

Right then, he turned into a quiet side street, stopped, removed his cap and glasses, and turned abruptly to face Lena.

"Hello, Venya," she said calmly. "How very nice to see you. Unfortunately, though, I'm in a hurry right now." She took a quick glance at her watch. Eleven on the dot.

"Lena, are you hurrying to a planning meeting? Don't worry. There isn't one. You weren't summoned to the office."

"Meaning what?" She cautiously pulled at the door handle.

"Don't try to open the door. It's locked. I asked my audio director to call you at home. Her voice resembles Katya's, especially over the phone. I said I wanted to play a trick on a good friend. I'm sorry, I couldn't think of any other way to see you."

"What for?" Lena asked, barely audibly.

"I had to see you. Don't be afraid of me. Would you like coffee?"

"Yes."

He took a thermos out of the glove box and two mugs and poured some for Lena and himself. The coffee was strong and sweet and milky.

Lena felt her teeth clatter against the china mug.

"If you have my phone number and needed to see me, why didn't you just call me at home? Why make it so complicated, Venya?" She tried to smile. "Why have you locked the doors, and why would you think I would be afraid of you?"

"A long time ago I didn't behave my best with you," he said slowly. "I didn't think you'd want to see me."

He was sitting half-facing her. Suddenly his face seemed lost, almost childlike.

"Venya, it's been fourteen years. You and I are adults now. We're not kids anymore. As far as I know, you've made a big success of your life. You're a millionaire, the owner of the mighty Veniamin Productions. The whole country knows you. And you're acting like a little boy."

"Yes, Lena. It has been fourteen years. But it feels like yesterday to me. I still remember how your wet hair smelled after the bathhouse. I remember the taste of your lips and the feel of your skin. If you hadn't pushed me away then, it might all have turned out differently."

He's insane, Lena thought, horrified. *His hands are shaking. His eyes are wild.*

"Did things really turn out so badly for you?" She tried to speak as calmly and kindly as she could. "Venya, don't pretend. You're rich and famous, and you have a beautiful wife."

"I'm alone in the world. She doesn't love me. No one loves me. She's made a puppet out of me, a zombie. Lena, if you hadn't pushed me away then . . ."

"Venya, this is very good coffee. Did you make it yourself?"

"You said then that something was burning in the kitchen. Now you're talking about the coffee."

"I'm sorry. Did you have something important to say to me?"

"Yes. Can you kiss me and stroke my head? Please, just a kiss and a stroke on the head. That's it. That's all I need from you."

He pressed a lever and his seat abruptly dropped back. Lena shuddered. All of a sudden he was very close. He took the mug of coffee out of her hands, leaned over, and put it on the floor.

What am I supposed to do? Lena thought in a panic. *The main thing is not to spook him or put him on his guard, not to let him know how terrified I am.*

She cautiously ran her hand over his balding blond head. He caught her hand and pressed his lips to her palm.

"Lena, don't abandon me. I'm in a very bad way."

"Venya, why me?" she asked quietly. "You have so many women around you, all much prettier and younger than I am. All you have to do is crook your finger and any one of them will come running."

"Yes, they'll come running for my money, my connections, and my power," he echoed.

"But you have a wife! She loves you—and not for your money and connections."

He pressed her palm to his cheeks and looked into her eyes.

"You don't love me, either," he said sadly. "But you could have loved me the way I want, the way I need."

"How do you know? It's entirely possible nothing would have come of it. You just think it would be better with another woman. But romance is one thing and a long life together is totally different. Believe me, you should be glad you have beside you—"

She didn't get a chance to finish. He sunk his lips into her lips so greedily and hard that it hurt.

Some ancient, vague, saving instinct told Lena that she shouldn't break away and resist right away. She didn't respond to the kiss, but focused all her powers on enduring it.

As soon as he tore his lips away from hers, she said calmly and kindly, "Venya, please listen to me. Fourteen years ago it was exactly that kind of pressure, that kind of impetuosity that scared me off. Give me time. Don't repeat old mistakes. You don't want me to get scared of you again, do you? Then don't rush me. I'm not going anywhere. I couldn't forget you all these years, too, but something that's hard at twenty-one is even harder at thirty-six. Give me a chance to get used to you. Do you really want it all to happen for us like this, in the car, in this dirty side street? Is that really what you've been waiting for for the last fourteen years? You and I aren't teenagers. We both have families."

She spoke and cautiously stroked his head like a child. She forced herself to believe what she was saying, afraid he'd be able to sense any hint of falseness, no matter how subtle.

"Now I understand I made a mistake then, fourteen years ago. But we still have time to fix our mistake. You and I are going to be calm and careful, so we don't hurt anyone—not your wife, and not my husband. Okay?"

"Yes," he whispered. "Whatever you say."

"Well then"—she gently kissed his forehead—"I'm not afraid of you. I believe you. I feel good and calm with you. Now we're going to smoke another cigarette and go."

"Where?" His voice was no longer hoarse, and his hands had calmed down.

"After the planning meeting you made up"—she smiled—"I was supposed to stop at the children's store and buy spring shoes for my daughter. Do you have children, Venya?"

"No." He pulled out his pack of cigarettes and they lit up. "My wife doesn't like children. She never wanted them."

"What about you?"

"I don't know. I haven't thought about it. What store do you want to go to for shoes for your Liza? Tell me about her. Who does she look like, you or your husband?"

"Both," Lena replied evasively. "There's a Children's World nearby. Very close."

"And then?"

"Then, Venya, I have to go home. Liza's nanny is with her, and I have to let her go by one thirty."

Lena was hoping he'd wait in the car and wouldn't go into the store with her. But he did go in and didn't leave her side for a minute. She examined one pair after another with such concentration, you'd think there was nothing more important in the world than children's shoes.

When she headed for the cash register, he took out his wallet, but it turned out he only had US dollars and credit cards. Fortunately, the store didn't take credit cards.

"Does your husband make so little?" he asked, taking the light box out of her hands.

"Why?"

"Because you're buying clothing for your child in a store like this," he said calmly.

"It's a normal store." She shrugged. "The ones that take credit cards sell the same things but at five times the price."

While they were walking to the car, he held her arm. This time, she had to sit in the front seat, next to him.

"Why did you marry a police officer?" he asked as they drove.

"What's wrong with a police officer?"

"Nothing," he agreed. "Do you love your husband? Are you happy with him?"

"We have a normal family. Do you love your wife?"

"What do you think?" He grinned.

"What does she do? I mean, what's her specialty?"

"She's a doctor. A psychiatrist."

"What's her name?"

"Regina."

"She must be a very strong and authoritative woman."

"Let's not talk about her right now. Let's talk about you. I want to know what you've been doing for fourteen years. I want to know everything about you."

"Fine, Venya. I'll tell you. But not all at once. Fourteen years is a long time, a lifetime nearly."

They were already pulling up to Lena's building.

"When will we see each other?" he asked, stopping at the front door.

"I'll call you."

He took a business card out of his pocket and underlined two of the five numbers.

"This is my cell and this is my office. Can I call you? What should I say if your husband picks up the phone?"

"Of course you can." She smiled. "If my husband picks up the phone, just say hello and ask him to call me to the phone."

Before letting her out of the car, he kissed her again so greedily it hurt. Lena got scared that one of her neighbors would walk by, look into the car, which he'd parked so boldly by the front door, and recognize her. *Cheating is like stealing,* she thought, kissing Volkov. *It's worse than stealing. Although this doesn't feel like cheating.*

Flying through the front door, she raced up the stairs, ran the several flights, and stopped at a landing between floors to press her forehead into the cold tiled wall. She stood there until she heard the car pulling away. Only then did she take a deep breath and calmly climb the stairs to her own door.

CHAPTER 23

"I'm from Criminal Investigations," Misha Sichkin said, showing the guard his ID.

The guard studied it carefully and silently. Finally, without saying a word, he stepped back and let Misha through the door.

The offices of the men's magazine *Wild Honey* occupied one whole floor of a four-story prefab building on the outskirts of Moscow. Once upon a time there'd been a kindergarten here. There were still swings, slides, and fairy houses in the courtyard.

"Hello. Where might I find Irina Moskvina?" Misha asked a heavily made-up young woman with a shaved head sitting at the computer in the reception area.

"End of the hall on the right," she replied without tearing her eyes from the screen.

"Irina! Watch your face!" A booming bass voice thundered from behind a partly open door at the end of the hall. "Hold your head. Hold it, I said! Smile! I don't mean bare your teeth like a stray dog looking at a cat! Nicer, Irina. Nicer!"

Misha glanced cautiously through the door. In the middle of a large room brightly lit by a bank of lights, a big-breasted blonde was half-lying on a striped mattress, wearing nothing but an unbuttoned lance corporal's tunic with badges and medals and a service cap tipped flirtatiously over one eyebrow.

Hopping around a tripod and camera with his back to the door was a short-legged man in black jeans.

"Who do you need, young man?" the young lady asked.

"Excuse me." Misha coughed. "I'm from Criminal Investigations. I need to speak with Irina Moskvina."

"Show me your documents," the photographer said.

Misha held out his ID.

"I'm Irina Moskvina," the young woman said. Rising lazily from the mattress, she shrugged off the tunic and stretched. The cap fell to the floor, and the model kicked it with her bare foot. Just like that, in her birthday suit, she started walking toward Misha, who had stopped by the door.

"To what do I owe this visit?" she asked in a serious voice.

"Irina Sergeyevna, I have to ask you a few questions," Misha murmured, not knowing where to look.

"Go ahead."

"Where can we go to speak privately?" Misha asked, looking to the side. "And forgive me, but would you mind putting some clothes on?"

"Oh!" the model suddenly remembered. "Pardon me."

She disappeared behind a screen in the corner of the room and appeared a minute later, wearing a floor-length white robe.

"Let's go into the next office," she invited Misha.

"Is this going to take long?" the photographer asked.

"No more than twenty minutes," Misha promised.

The office turned out to be a tiny room filled with equipment. Two armchairs and a coffee table were perched in the corner.

"Irina Sergeyevna," Misha began, seating himself. "Did you know the singer Yuri Azarov?"

"So that's what this is. You're here about that. Yes, I knew Yuri."

"How long and how well?"

"Veronika Rogovets introduced us six months ago."

"Veronika is a friend?"

"Yes."

Irina took a pack of More menthols from her robe pocket. Misha took out his Rothmans, and he flicked his lighter, lighting the lady's cigarette.

"Tell me, had she and Azarov been having any serious problems lately? Any fights?"

"I don't like to meddle into other people's business." Irina shrugged.

Unlike her friend Veronika Rogovets, this young woman behaved perfectly naturally. She didn't care what kind of impression she made on the investigator. She answered his questions politely, without batting her eyelashes or pooching her lower lip. She just sat across from him, smoked, and looked Misha in the eye.

"I see." He nodded. "You yourself said that Veronika is your friend. She must have shared some of her problems with you."

"Yes, Veronika does like to rattle on. She shares all kinds of things."

"Did she tell you about her fights with Azarov?"

"They didn't fight seriously. They'd bicker occasionally over little things. You know, Veronika's like soda water. Lots of fizz, but she settles down fast."

"Does she have problems in her relations with men in general?"

"Veronika?" Irina laughed. "She has no problems with men. Where did you get that idea?"

"I assume a woman who sees a psychotherapist must have some problems," Misha mumbled reflectively.

"Are you talking about Gradskaya?" Irina guessed. "To be honest, I don't understand why Veronika needs her. She's gone batty over all this mystic shit. That's all I hear: 'karma,' 'astral.' She's started reading books."

"Do you know Gradskaya?"

"Only in passing."

"Have you ever had occasion to be around her, to talk with her?"

"Oh, you know, just to say hello. Occasionally we see each other at parties. Sometimes she recognizes me and sometimes she looks right past me. Try to keep in mind who she is and who I am."

"But your friend is fairly tight with Gradskaya," Misha reminded her.

"Veronika's gone to a completely different level." Irina grinned.

"I'm sorry. I don't know much about show business. I may be asking you a silly and tactless question. Going to 'a completely different level,' as you put it, does that depend on personality, luck, what?"

"Stupidity."

"Meaning?"

"You don't understand?" Irina sighed wearily and tapped another cigarette out of the pack. "The higher the level, the shorter the life. Go a couple of steps higher and bang, you're dead. It's good if it's someone close to you and not you. But tomorrow it might be you."

"Tell me, did Veronika take Azarov's death hard?"

"Of course she did. She even cried."

"In her conversations with you, has she expressed any suspicions about who might have done it?"

"Well, you know"—Irina chuckled disdainfully—"Veronika's a little fool, of course, but not to that degree. Those things aren't discussed."

Misha bit his tongue. In that circle there was probably no doubt that Azarov had been offed by friends of the thugs he'd testified against. And that probably ruled out any conversation on the subject. Blab and you won't live to see tomorrow.

All right, Misha decided. *If those things aren't discussed, then we won't discuss them.*

"Irina, you said you've met Gradskaya at parties. Where and when did you see her last? Do you recall?"

"Why are you so interested in Gradskaya?" Irina squinted. "Is she mixed up in this?"

"You know, in order to solve a murder, we have to look at lots of different people, most of whom turn out to be totally irrelevant. So, part of that means going around collecting gossip on people like Gradskaya." Misha smiled wearily and confidingly. "At times, even I'm disgusted by it. But there's nothing I can do. That's the job. So, can you recall when and where you saw her last?"

"What a foul job you have." Irina shook her head sympathetically. "Not that mine's any better. I saw Gradskaya about a month ago at the release party for Yura's album at the Status Club. There was a little scandal there, too."

"What exactly?"

"Oh, it was nonsense. Not really worth mentioning." Irina shrugged it off.

"Nonetheless, I'm interested. What kinds of little scandals are there at release parties? I've never been invited to one, nor am I likely to be."

"Well, some psycho burst in and started badgering Volkov. The guard walked him out two minutes later. That was the sum total of the scandal."

"And who was this psycho? Do you happen to know?"

"Apparently some singer or composer. I don't know exactly. If you're curious, you can ask Veronika."

Misha found Veronika Rogovets at the Fairy Health Club on Kashirka. She was pedaling an exercise bike and was far from thrilled at another visit from the investigator from Petrovka.

"Some jerk barged in," Veronika said through clenched teeth as she kept pushing the pedals, "and started shouting something in Volkov's face."

"Did you see the man yourself?"

"Yes."

"Had you ever met him anywhere?"

"I think I may have seen him somewhere. Maybe he'd come for an audition or something? What's the difference?"

Misha himself didn't really understand why he'd latched onto this scandal. "You mean he wasn't a completely random individual? Not just some drunk off the street?" Misha wouldn't let it go.

"I don't remember!" Veronika snarled, and she pedaled even more furiously. "There are a ton of losers like him circling around Veniamin Productions!"

"You mean this man was a singer or a composer?"

"Well, he wasn't a machinist!" Veronika snorted. "Volkov fired a musician. He got tanked and came to have it out."

"And how did he do that? Was he actually trying to pick a fight?" Misha asked.

"Oh no. He was shouting something."

"Swearing?"

"No, not swearing. He was just calling Volkov a killer, probably in the sense that he'd killed his career."

"Any chance you might remember this musician's name?" Misha asked desperately.

"I don't even remember your name, even though we've met ten times. But hundreds, thousands of people go to Volkov's for auditions. All I'm saying is that I happened to see the guy. We were shooting a video, and Volkov was in the studio. Then the secretary looked in and said that somebody had come . . . I don't remember the name. Volkov stopped the shoot, and told us to take a break. And he went to his audition room. Naturally, we got curious. Who would Volkov interrupt a shoot for? Some of us, me, Yuri, and the cameraman, took turns peeking into the room. I even heard a few of the guy's songs. But his name?" Veronika frowned irritably. "No, I don't remember it."

Irina Moskvina had been right, Misha thought, her friend Veronika really did like to chat and gossip.

"There! See how much you remembered!" Misha smiled delightedly. "It's good for you to remember. You were telling me how much you suffered because of your forgetfulness. And look how great you did! Well, let's try a little more."

"Now, what's your name?" Veronika even stopped pedaling. She must have liked this memory game Misha had her playing.

"Sichkin."

"And he was Sinichkin!"

"Maybe Sinitsyn?" Misha asked, feeling his heart sinking and his head clearing.

"Maybe Sinitsyn," Veronika agreed lightly.

"Veronika, how did Volkov behave while the man was yelling at him?"

"He didn't. He stood there and didn't say a word."

"So, he listened calmly as someone screamed at him?"

"No. Not at all. Yuri said he turned green and started shaking."

"Was Yuri nearby?"

"Yes. Volkov and Regina Valentinovna were getting ready to leave, and Yuri had gone to see them out. That's when all this happened."

"You mean he heard everything Sinitsyn was shouting? Did he tell you about it?"

"No. He just said Volkov turned green and started shaking. That he'd never seen him like that before."

"But you did ask what the fellow said, right? You must have wondered what had rattled Volkov like that."

"What kind of a fool do you think I am? That's not a question you ask."

"So you never brought the subject up again?"

"There was no point." Veronika snorted disdainfully.

"Was this scandal ever discussed among the people you know?"

But this question went unanswered. Veronika became gloomy and shut down. She didn't like the investigator's game anymore.

❧

Lena entered the Tretyakov with Michael and bought him a guidebook in English and a ticket.

"Do you have rubles?" she asked.

"Oh, I forgot to change money!" Michael slapped his bald head.

There was an exchange office, but it was closed.

"All right, here's a hundred thousand for you." Lena handed him a few bills. "You can have a bite to eat in the café. If you decide you want a real meal, go to the restaurant. They take credit cards there."

"Do they have vegetarian food?"

"Someone there is certain to speak English. Explain what you want and they'll understand. When you get tired, go home. Here's the key, and here's the address. Give the taxi driver this piece of paper. From here to my place shouldn't be more than thirty thousand."

"How much is that in dollars?"

"About five. But don't give them dollars. Here, look, three tens. Understand? You won't get lost?"

Lena really was worried about Michael. He was so friendly and scatterbrained. He could stumble into trouble so easily. Not only that, his Russian vocabulary was limited to about ten words, two of which were *vodka* and *perestroika*.

Olga, Liza, and Vera Fyodorovna were waiting in the car. It was a two-hour drive to Istra. Liza fell asleep in Lena's lap on the way.

These last two years I haven't been apart from Liza more than a day, Lena thought. *I'm going to feel empty and terrible without her. I don't want to do anything without her. I'm looking forward to all this being over.*

She forbade herself from thinking about what had happened this morning and tried to drive out the cold, sticky fear that had settled over her. Settled over her when, actually? At what moment did she get truly scared? Yesterday, when the stroller blew up? No, before that. Well before that. The fear showed up after the "doctor's" visit. Volkov's wife's name was Regina. She was a doctor. Misha Sichkin mentioned that name when he was talking about Katya Sinitsyna.

Should she call Misha and tell him about her encounter with Volkov? No, that was too much—sharing a story about an admirer with her husband's subordinate and friend. Should she tell Misha how she and Volkov kissed in the car? And then how they went to buy Liza shoes together?

What could he do to help, anyway? Organize security? He'd already done something major by installing an alarm system in the apartment.

After today's encounter, this whole story had taken on much darker overtones. If before she could lay everything out to Seryozha, now she'd started to have doubts. Could she tell him everything?

She and her husband had lived together a little more than two years, but she had never figured out whether or not he was jealous. There hadn't been the slightest grounds for jealousy. They both trusted each other so implicitly that it had never even come up. Lena tried to imagine herself in Seryozha's place. What if he'd told her that because of work or business or some other reason, he'd had to pretend to be in love, had to kiss another woman. No, he hadn't felt anything, he'd just pretended he did. Nonetheless, that would have been an extremely nasty piece of information for Lena. She would have understood everything and not condemned him, but she would have been jealous. No matter the circumstances, it would have been nasty.

Lena had gone through with the kiss because her instinct for self-preservation had kicked in. She'd been trying to blow smoke at a dangerous and psychologically unbalanced man. She'd felt nothing but fear. Still . . .

No, she thought irritably. *I have to get this whole question of jealousy out of my head. Jealousy has nothing to do with this. The problem isn't that Volkov is smitten with passion for me again, after fourteen years. But why all the complications? If for certain reasons I represent a danger to him, why doesn't he just hire a hitman to take care of me? Given his money and connections, that would have been perfectly logical.*

The main thing now is to understand the reason—if there is one. Well, that's why I'm heading for Siberia and why I've been digging through old letters. I doubt anyone but me would do that.

The Istra holiday house was situated in a handsome pine forest. Lena hadn't been in the countryside for a long time, and when she got out of the car, the fresh air made her head spin. Here it really did smell like spring. The sky had cleared and a gentle blue peeked through the tops of the trees, making her believe that summer would come soon and all would be well.

"Gorgeous!" Olga exclaimed as she climbed out of the car and stretched. "I should send my family here for a week, too. The kids and the old folks. Let them get their fill of fresh air and long walks. Listen, I took the entire day off from work anyway. Let's stay a little longer. I really don't feel like leaving right away."

"And Michael?"

"Lena, he's not a baby. He's a grown man. You gave him the key and he has the address. He'll be fine."

"She's right, Lena, dear. You should relax and take a breath, at least for a few hours," Vera Fyodorovna cut into the conversation. "Look at yourself. Pale, skinny, circles under your eyes."

Lena didn't object. She wanted to spend a little more time with Liza.

There were two dozen guards dressed in camo at the holiday house entrance. They were guarding the gates, too, but more formally. These guards instilled trust. The room where Vera Fyodorovna and Liza were to spend the next ten days turned out to be an excellent two-room suite, with a television and refrigerator.

As they strolled down the cleared paths of the park, Lena told Liza a fairy tale which she composed on the fly. In it, bad robbers were chasing a little girl, but she was constantly triumphing over them because she was smarter and stronger than they were. Time and again the robbers would be fooled, but there was nothing they could do about the smart and strong little girl. The fairy tale was supposed to end well, but she just couldn't find a way to end it.

It started getting dark. Vera Fyodorovna and Liza went off to dinner. Olga and Lena drank coffee in the bar off the dining room. Afterward they walked a little more through the park. It was time to leave.

"Let's all go up to the room together," Vera Fyodorovna whispered in Lena's ear. "While Liza's watching *Nighty Night,* you can leave quietly."

But they couldn't fool Liza. The minute Lena took a few cautious steps toward the door, the child would rush to her with a desperate wail.

"Mama, don't leave! Please!"

Vera Fyodorovna picked her up and tried to distract her, but in vain. Liza wept so bitterly, they had to stay another hour so that Lena could put her to bed. Even asleep, Liza held her mama's hand tightly.

"Enough, girls. Go quietly," Vera Fyodorovna whispered. "It's late. Lena, don't worry. I'll take good care of her."

They didn't get in the car until ten thirty. On the drive back to Moscow, Lena laid everything out for Olga: the doctor, the bomb in her stroller, and the encounter with Volkov. Olga listened silently, only asking the occasional, pertinent question.

"Now try to remember," Lena asked, having finished her story. "Has anyone tried to start a conversation with you about suicide?"

"There's nothing to remember." Olga cut her off. "No one has. And you know why?" She grinned bitterly. "Because no one mentions rope in a hanged man's house. You don't have to be a psychologist to guess what my reaction would be. I'd have told them to go to hell—even if that someone was a potential client. And I'd have the right to do that."

"So it would be impossible for anyone to know who informed you on all this?"

"And there's no need to. What I do or don't know is no threat to anyone. It's only in American action movies that people are so eager to investigate the mysterious circumstances around the death of their close friends and relatives. In real life, that just doesn't happen. I'm not about to go looking for Mitya's killer—if there even is one. If I were to run into him face-to-face, in the heat of the moment I'd probably end his life. Or maybe not. I don't know. What I do know is that it wouldn't make me feel any better. I have to go on living and get used to the idea that he's gone, and get my mama, my papa, and my grandmother used to it, too. That's hard enough, I don't have the strength for all the rest."

"I wonder, why do you think they knew I would take up a private investigation into the murder, but that you, his sister, wouldn't . . ."

"The deaths of Mitya and Katya haven't the slightest thing to do with the stroller bomb. At least I don't see the connection. I think Volkov's wife is trying to get rid of you."

"Volkov's wife?" Lena grinned. "Out of jealousy or something? Do you realize what nonsense that is?"

"Why? Murder out of jealousy is a perfectly real thing. It was no rarity three hundred years ago, and it's no different today," Olga said firmly.

"But the stroller blew up yesterday. And I met with Volkov today. We hadn't seen each other in fourteen years. If we had an affair, if that affair threatened a family's well-being, then jealousy might be the motive."

"Why are you ruling out the idea of the wife deciding to get rid of you in advance? She might have sensed something. You have to understand. Losing a husband like Volkov is very serious business. It might not be just about jealousy but about money."

"Olga, Volkov and I are nothing to each other. I'd completely forgotten he existed."

"But he didn't forget you. Maybe he's been saying your name in his sleep for fourteen years!"

"Even my last name?" Lena chuckled nervously. "In that case, why didn't she lay a finger on me before?"

"People change." Olga sighed. "Men have midlife crises. Venya Volkov was living his life, building his career, making his money. But at some point he got fed up. All of a sudden he realized life was passing him by, that he had no love or kindness in his life. But, at one time he was passionately in love with this beautiful, mysterious, and inaccessible young woman named Lena Polyanskaya. And all these years you remained his warmest and purest memory. Especially since he never got you to bed. And he so wanted to. Even I remember that."

"Uh-huh." Lena nodded. "And that's why his wife, one of the richest women in Russia, decided to plant a bomb in a stroller? Olga, quit playing the fool. They nearly killed me and Liza yesterday."

"And you believe Volkov did it?"

"No . . . I don't know. But I don't think his wife would have done it out of jealousy. Olga, it's ridiculous! He's surrounded by the most beautiful women in Russia. He could have any of them. So why me?"

"He's surrounded by Russia's best tits and asses"—Olga grinned—"as my brother would have put it. But very few real women."

"Fine, let's say Volkov is still in love with me like a sixteen-year-old boy. Why in that case did the mere mention of my name send him into hysterics? He shouted 'No!' on that interview tape."

"That's exactly why. Too many emotions."

"Marvelous." Lena lit a cigarette. "Very logical. And the following morning he arranged that business with the planning meeting because why?"

"Don't look for logic," Olga advised. "This is about passions."

"It is about passion, all right." Lena nodded. "Volkov's fallen in love, his wife came to my home pretending to be a doctor, and then she put a bomb in the stroller. To be honest, I don't trust these Shakespearean passions, but let's say that's what's motivating all this. But, even if that is the case, Volkov's wife could have easily hired a hitman. Her money and means permit that."

"Well, maybe it's not quite that easy. You and I have never hired hitmen, so we don't know how it's done. Sure, it seems like it's just as easy to hire a killer as it is to call a plumber. But what if she's afraid her husband will find out? Or maybe she's a control freak and enjoys doing everything herself. Your problem is that you always discount human passions. The simple idea that a man has fallen in love with you and his jealous wife wants you gone doesn't even enter your mind. It should. If jealousy doesn't seem a sufficient motive on its own, add money to that. Lots and lots of money. The fact that she attempted to get rid of you before a romance could blaze up between you is also perfectly explainable. If something were to happen to you at the height of an affair with Volkov, she would be the prime suspect."

"But why does she think an affair is inevitable? I'm married. And I have no intention of being unfaithful my husband. If she's so smart, why hasn't that thought occurred to her?"

"Because she's not interested in your intentions. She's worried about Volkov. For her, you're a natural disaster that has to be dealt with, and quickly. She understands that the longer you're around, the more his passions will be enflamed. She can tell he won't calm down."

"What is she, some kind of genius?" Lena grinned.

"You don't have to be a genius to know that. All it takes is female instinct."

"So what am I supposed to do now?"

"Nothing. Do as you planned. Fly to Siberia. Maybe she'll back off from her plans after ten days."

"And Volkov?"

"Volkov will find you everywhere." Olga laughed. "And he won't rest until he's dragged you to bed. That I guarantee you. But he's no danger to you. In the sense that he isn't planning to kill you. Quite the opposite."

Lena completely disagreed with her good friend. But she wasn't going to argue. She didn't like arguing in general. What was the point? Everyone has a right to their own point of view.

They reached Moscow in the middle of the night.

"Listen," Olga proposed. "Why don't we go to a club? Honestly, you need to unwind. So do I."

"What club? It's the middle of the night!"

"Tramp? The Stanislavsky Club? It's quiet there."

Lena shook her head. "I'm embarrassed to say I prefer chips and Coke and a McDonald's apple pie to any club."

"I had a friend like you. Once in Paris, in an expensive restaurant, he asked for a hot dog with ketchup."

"An American?"

"A Russian! Fine. If you want chips and a Coke, then we'll go to the American bar on Mayakovsky Square."

"And Michael?"

"There's a pay phone over there. Call and let him know you'll be home late. You can start your consultant-interpreter duties first thing tomorrow."

"What if he's asleep?"

"Then you can really relax."

Lena jumped out of the car at the pay phone and dialed her home number. Michael wasn't asleep. He started right in sharing his impressions of the Tretyakov.

"Don't wait for me," Lena said. "Go to bed. I'll be back late. Lock the lower deadbolt. I have the key."

"I won't be going to bed for a long time," Michael promised. "You have such interesting TV. I don't understand a word, but I can't tear myself away."

Polina Dashkova

"Was it you who took the old Mercedes from the garage?" Regina asked.

"Yes." Volkov nodded.

"It was? And I was about to give the guards a good dressing-down, thinking it was one of them. By the way, where were you this morning? The bank called."

"I had business to attend to," Venya answered calmly, not looking at her.

"Why so gloomy?" Regina smiled. "How do you feel?"

"Okay."

"Good." Regina walked up to him and stroked his cheek. "I saw Veronika Rogovets today."

"Congratulations," he growled and nearly jerked his head back, shaking her hand off his face.

"You shouldn't be so cheerful, Venya. That idiot told the investigator from Petrovka about what happened at Status. She even remembered the name Sinitsyn. I don't remember whether I told you or not, but that investigator is Krotov's direct subordinate."

"So what? Who's Krotov?"

"Venya, Venya." She shook her head sadly. "Police Colonel Sergei Krotov is Polyanskaya's husband. He's in London now, but he'll be back very soon. And he's going to get an earful from his wife when he does. Do you think he won't care?"

"No, Regina, I don't." He sighed and leaned back in his chair. "What do you want from me?"

"Venya, I want you to focus. This is serious. And you've shut down at the critical moment. Tomorrow you're going to go into hysterics when the next journalist shows up. You'll turn green and whisper, 'Regina, I'm dying!' Venya, people are already talking about this. It's being discussed. Tomorrow morning you have a live broadcast on ORT. Can you the guarantee that you won't flip out?"

"I won't," he said calmly and firmly. "You don't have to worry."

"How can you be so sure? Only yesterday . . ."

"Regina, I won't flip out on a live broadcast," he repeated, and he looked her in the eye.

They looked at each other for a second without saying a word, and Regina was surprised to realize that no, he really wasn't going to flip out. Something had happened. Since that day when Sinitsyn showed up for an audition, Regina hadn't once seen her husband this calm and confident.

An hour before, painstakingly rummaging through the old Mercedes, she'd found a single woman's glove. A small, black leather glove that would only fit a very slender hand.

"Venya," Regina whispered, and her lips grazed his. "How I love you when you're so . . ."

"So what?" he asked, moving back a little.

But she didn't answer. She slowly and gently slid her lips down his chest, undoing his shirt buttons, one after another. At first he sat there like a sculpture, his face frozen and resolute. But eventually she managed to arouse him. He closed his eyes and she felt his heart beating faster and his body coming to life.

He'd never been so gentle and unhurried before. Everything happened as if in slow motion. They fell on the thick carpet, right in the living room, forgetting the door wasn't locked and that the cook or maid could walk in at any moment. Regina felt time stand still. She was amazed to catch herself thinking that for the first time in years, she didn't need to control her husband, didn't need to be on her guard, especially toward the climax, when he started breathing fast and hard and his hands could reach for her throat. For the first time she could truly relax. For all these years, even in bed, she'd been the doctor and he the patient—and a dangerous and unpredictable one at that.

And she did relax. She felt better than she ever had. She whispered senseless words to him, and he whispered something back, but she didn't listen . . .

Breathing deeply, feeling nothing but a sweet, soaring weakness, she opened her eyes and saw his face. His eyelids were firmly shut and his mouth half open.

"Lena," he said, softly but distinctly.

⁓

Michael wasn't asleep. He was watching TV. He didn't understand a word of what he was watching, but he was laughing almost to the point of tears. He was especially entertained by Russian commercials that were so different from the American ones he was used to. Chocolate and shampoo were advertised by actors with such repulsive faces and voices, you'd think someone was purposely trying to dissuade you from buying them. It was like anti-advertising.

Russians are in such a hurry to make up for what they missed, the professor thought, *that they're forgetting about good sense. They're rushing headlong after capitalism and democracy, like little kids running and falling and scraping their knees.*

Feeling his eyes closing, he glanced at the clock. One forty-five. Michael turned off the TV, took a shower, and as he headed off for bed remembered he needed to turn the lower lock. He went to the door, reached out, and at that moment he thought there was someone on the other side of the door. He heard a quiet scratching in the upper lock.

"Lena?" he called out loudly. "Is that you?" The scratching stopped. It got very quiet.

"Who's there?" Michael looked through the peephole, but the landing was empty.

In addition to the two locks, there was also a bolt. Michael shot it and then quickly closed the additional lock. Something scratched in the upper keyhole again.

"If you're a burglar, I'm calling the police!" the professor warned loudly.

No response. Michael started feeling uneasy.

The police? he thought. *I don't know the number, and there's not likely to be anyone there who speaks English.*

The person outside the door didn't leave.

"Go away right now! Do you hear?"

If this burglar can hear me, he's hardly likely to understand what I am saying, Michael decided. *He's not likely to know English. I wonder if he's going to stay there all night. I can't go to bed until I'm sure he's gone.*

He heard a dog barking. A lock clicked, and Michael went to the peephole again to see what was happening. A man stepped out of the apartment across the way with a fat boxer on a leash. Then he heard the elevator moving. The dog barked once more and the man said a few words in Russian. The elevator door rumbled, and Michael thought he heard a woman's voice answer the man. Or maybe he didn't. Maybe it was just the owner talking to his dog. He couldn't see the area near the elevator through the peephole.

Anyway, the old professor thought, *if anyone was standing by the door, the neighbor and his dog probably frightened them off.*

Just in case, he looked out the kitchen window, which faced the courtyard. In the bright light of the streetlamp, Michael made out the man with the dog and a tall woman wearing a dark coat. She emerged from the front door with the man but headed in the opposite direction.

When Regina heard English at the door, she grinned nervously. She pictured the confusion if she'd entered the apartment with her gun but had found an American man there instead of Polyanskaya.

A New Yorker, she noted mechanically as she listened to the frightened threats to call the police and cautiously pulled out her picklock. When a man stepped out of the apartment across the way with his boxer, she barely had time to slip the bundle of picklocks into her coat pocket and step toward the elevator.

She rang for the elevator. The boxer tugged at its leash, bared its teeth, and barked. Regina shuddered.

"Harry, stop it!" the owner shouted at the dog. "Don't be afraid. He doesn't bite," he told Regina, politely letting her get in the elevator first.

"Oh, I'm not afraid," she replied, and tried to smile.

I have to get a grip, she thought. *I've failed yet again. The idea wasn't bad—just enter the apartment and shoot her point-blank. Enter and shoot. If only it were that simple! Maybe I was lucky. If that silly American hadn't come to the door at the very moment I was trying to open it, I would have had my cover blown for good. I might have had to kill a total bystander, a foreigner. Enough with trying to play gangster. It's time to bring in a professional. And now I have a perfectly reasonable reason to do so. I can't have my husband carrying a torch for some other woman. Jealousy is a motive for murder any common thug would understand.*

CHAPTER 24

Security Services major Nikolai Ievlev had taken the death of the thief known as Thrush personally. The major had spent nearly two years building a case against the crime boss. He had enough material in his safe to send him to the gallows. But no one knew that besides Ievlev. Nikolai had collected his materials against Thrush with the utmost discretion.

Two years ago, Thrush had put out a contract on the major's brother, Anton Ievlev, a successful businessman. Not for any particularly salacious reason: their interests had just crossed, and Thrush thought it easier to remove his competition than reach an agreement with him. His hitman killed Anton inside the front door of his apartment building.

Thrush was considered uncatchable by most in the Security Services. He'd been convicted of petty crimes in the past, but his convictions always ended with early release. No one had any doubt that the famous thief had done things worthy of the gallows, but there'd never been enough proof. There couldn't be. Thrush had people everywhere—the Prosecutor's Office, the Security Service, the Interior Department, even the State Duma. Major Ievlev knew this full well and had conducted his investigation into the boss's operation quietly and cautiously.

Ievlev was on the verge of presenting all the evidence he had amassed to the State Prosecutor when Thrush was killed at the Vityaz restaurant outside Moscow. Major Ievlev actually did care how Thrush took the bullet he so richly deserved. Ievlev's innate sense of justice demanded that Thrush's execution be legal, authorized by a court's verdict, not as the culmination of some kind of gangland shoot-out.

When Ievlev found out that the investigation into the Vityaz shooting was being run by the department led by Colonel Sergei Krotov, his heart began to pound. Naturally, Senior Investigator Mikhail Sichkin wasn't burning to share Security Service materials on the Azarov murder with the major. He told him as much as the rules of interdepartmental relations required. And not one word more. But what he told him was more than enough.

Ievlev had already guessed that it wasn't a typical gangland shoot-out. A strong hand was behind the murder of Thrush and his men. Now that a remote-controlled bomb had been planted in the stroller of Colonel Krotov's daughter, Ievlev no longer had any doubts that Thrush had been offed on specific orders from above.

Someone was sending Colonel Krotov and his men the message that they shouldn't dig any deeper. That someone had acted crudely but convincingly. Most likely, Krotov had already been warned. But he hadn't heeded the warning. Now he'd been warned again. They doubtless were calculating that his wife would call him in London and that the frightened colonel would cut his trip short, race back to Moscow, and make sure that the investigation into the shoot-out and the singer Azarov's murder never went anywhere.

Ievlev was convinced that the fact that the stroller blew up before the child was in it was no accident. They didn't want to kill the colonel's wife, just give her a scare. But that strange woman, Lena Polyanskaya, scared though she was, hadn't told her husband about the bomb. Maybe they'd try to scare her again. And whoever "they" were was of the greatest interest to Major Ievlev.

He decided that when she was in Tyumen Province, Polyanskaya should be under constant and close surveillance. They might well try to scare her a second time there rather than in Moscow.

ఴ

It was a quarter past two. Michael had forgotten to pull back the bolt, and Lena had to ring the bell for a long time to wake him and bring him to the door. He greeted them in shorts and a jersey. He was rubbing his eyes and yawning.

"Someone tried to open the door," he told her mysteriously and gravely. "I threatened to call the police."

Olga shook her head disapprovingly after hearing his whole story. "You've been watching too much TV about crime in Russia, and now you're seeing criminals everywhere. Maybe someone just tried to put their key in the wrong door?"

"You say you saw a tall woman in a dark coat leave the front entrance?" Lena clarified.

"Yes, the courtyard was fairly brightly lit. But the woman may just have happened to be coming out. I mean, it might not have been her trying to open the door."

Right then the phone rang.

"Oh," Michael remembered. "Some man keeps calling you, but he doesn't speak English. All I could get was that he was asking for Lena."

"Hello," Lena said wearily, picking up the receiver.

"I'm sorry. I miss you," she heard a quiet voice that she immediately recognized, although she'd never spoken to this person over the phone before.

"Venya, it's very late."

"I know. But I can't get to sleep without talking to you. At least for a minute. Tell me, did I just imagine what happened this morning?"

"No, Venya, you didn't imagine it." Pressing the receiver to her ear with her shoulder, Lena took off her boots and got slippers from the closet for Olga and herself.

"You sound tired," Volkov said. "I'm not asking you where you were so late. Am I doing the right thing?"

"Yes, Venya. You're doing the right thing."

Meanwhile, Michael headed off to bed. Olga shut herself up in the bathroom, and Lena took the phone into the kitchen, sat down feet first on the kitchen sofa, and lit a cigarette.

"I love you," Venya said quietly. "I can't live without you. I've never said those words to anyone, and I've never felt anything like this in my life."

"And where's your wife right now?" Lena asked.

"I don't know. Why do you ask?"

"Well, she's hardly going to like hearing what you're telling me now."

"She won't hear it. She's not home."

"What if she finds out? This would hurt her terribly."

"As it will your husband."

"Yes, it will hurt him, too," Lena agreed mechanically.

"What are you doing tomorrow? Can I see you?"

"No. A professor's come to see me from New York. I'll be showing him around Moscow all day tomorrow."

"Is that who picked up the phone?"

"Yes."

"How old is he?"

"Sixty-two. Venya, you don't have to be jealous of Michael."

"I'm jealous of the whole world," he admitted with a heavy sigh. "You know what, let's show the American professor Moscow together. It's much better by car."

Lena gave it some thought. With Michael there, Volkov was hardly going to come on to her. They wouldn't be left alone for a second. In that situation, she would be safe. Or nearly so. Most of all, maybe at least something would become clear at last.

"Fine, Venya," she agreed. "Only I have one request. Michael mustn't have an inkling of the fact that we . . . that there might be something between you and me."

"Yes, of course. I'll act like an old friend. I'll act however you want me to. What time should I pick you up?"

"Noon. We'll be downstairs. Thank you."

This is all too strange, Lena thought after she hung up. *Volkov's wife isn't home. That doesn't mean she was the one trying to open the door. But she isn't home. And Volkov is acting as if he really is in love. He's prepared to drive a man he's never met all over Moscow for the sake of spending a few hours by my side. It makes perfect sense to pretend he's in love, to stay close to me and not take his eyes off me. I am, after all, a danger to him, to his wife, to his empire. On the other hand, he must have the resources to put professional surveillance on me. Why should he do the heavy lifting himself? Is the information I have so dangerous for them that they can't turn to anyone for help? Even with all their money and connections? And if I possess such dangerous information, why am I still alive? If they're acting together, why did she try to get into my apartment today? He was calling all evening and knew I wasn't home. Michael hadn't just dreamed someone had tried to get in, had he? And if it wasn't her, then who was it?*

No, I won't solve this puzzle until I find out what really happened in Tobolsk fourteen years ago. What did we see but not notice? Volkov might have done something, and the three of us were indirect witnesses to his crime. Mitya saw more than we did, Olga might not have noticed anything, and I . . . So now they're checking me out—what I remember, what I saw, whether I link Mitya's death to our time in Tobolsk. Mitya remembered everything. He figured it out and took it to Volkov. Maybe if he'd decided to blackmail him, he would have lived. Or not. In any case, he laid out what he remembered. And they killed him, and not in a straightforward way. They staged it all. Nothing here is simple. Just thinking about it is making my head spin.

All this means none of them, under any circumstance, can know exactly where I'm flying tomorrow night. And I need to keep playing the game Volkov's started.

That this was a game Lena did not doubt for a second. She was very scared, and fear clouded her thinking. She could be doing the wrong thing. She should call Seryozha and ask him to come home. She couldn't cope with this alone. And no one else could help. Who could she seek protection from if not her own husband? But they could kill her even with him around. If they wanted to. Did that mean they hadn't decided to yet? Was there hope? Or maybe Olga was right. Maybe Volkov was burning with passion and his wife was afraid of losing him and all his money and wanted to stop their romance before it could start. But then how could she explain Mitya and Katya's murders? Was she trying to catch the tail of a ghost? And was she chasing the ghost or vice versa?

"Well, you've been smoking up a storm!" Olga whispered, slipping out of the bathroom in Lena's old robe. "Do you have any moisturizer?"

"In my bedroom, on my vanity."

"Listen, quit worrying!" Olga settled on the stool facing Lena and pulled out a cigarette. "Tell Volkov his wife tried to kill you. Ask him to protect you!"

"Yeah, he'll protect me!" Lena grinned. "I know exactly how he'll protect me. Olga, I have a favor to ask you. If someone, under any pretext, tries to find out where I am, please—"

"Polyanskaya," Olga interrupted her indignantly. "Who do you take me for?"

"I'm sorry. Don't be mad. I'm so tired."

"I advise you to tell Volkov everything. At the least you'll see his reaction and, maybe, you can learn something from that. Although, in my opinion, it's all perfectly clear. I still remembered how, fourteen years ago, the poor guy got so worked up, his nose started bleeding. He really suffered over you." Olga grinned. "You know, I still can't stand the sight of blood. If one of my kids scrapes his knees, I feel woozy."

"Yes, he was wearing a light sweater," Lena said slowly. "And it had brown blood stains."

Before going to bed, Lena set the alarm for nine. She had to call her neighbors in the apartment across the way. The owner of Harry the boxer usually left for work at nine thirty.

⤞⤝

To get to question a potential witness in the cardiology department, Misha Sichkin had to spend a long time prevailing upon first the attending physician and then the department chief.

"Galina Sergeyevna cannot be disturbed," the attending physician insisted. "She's in serious condition. She had a heart attack, you know."

"But haven't they moved her out of intensive care?"

"Yes," the doctor said. "But after talking to you she may have to go back. You're going to talk about her son's death, aren't you?"

"I promise the conversation won't take long."

"All it takes is a few words on the subject for the patient's condition to deteriorate. It's not the length of the conversation I am worried about, it is the subject."

"I don't think the fact that his murderer hasn't been caught yet can be helping her condition," Misha noted somberly.

"That's your problem," the doctor snorted.

"I won't take on that kind of responsibility," said the department chief. "It has to be approved by the attending physician. That's the way we do things."

It seemed like there was no way the hospital administrators were going to allow Misha Sichkin to question Yuri Azarov's mother. Misha couldn't drag this out any longer. He decided to take drastic measures. Politely pushing the attending physician aside, he headed decisively for Galina Sergeyevna's room.

"You'll answer for this!" the physician called after him. "I'm going to complain to your superiors!"

But Misha had already gone in.

"I've been waiting for someone from the police to come," a plump, pale woman of about sixty said, rising on one elbow.

"You can at least put on a coat," the attendant demanded, rushing into the room after him.

"Give it to me and I will." Misha smiled. A minute later a nurse appeared with a starched, snow-white coat.

"Did your son visit you often?" Misha asked when they were finally alone in the comfortable, private room.

"He visited me once a week sometimes, every other week sometimes, depending on how busy he was."

"Did he ever bring guests?"

"Rarely. Usually he came alone. He could unwind with me. If he did bring anyone, he always warned me, saying 'Mama, I have a secret meeting.' Usually if he didn't come alone, that meant he wanted to have a quiet talk about something important."

"When was the last time he visited you?"

"Just two days before the shoot-out in the restaurant. You know, he came with some fellow. He even whispered in my ear, 'Mama, I'm having a secret meeting with a secret agent.' He said it like a joke, but he was warning me. Not that I need warning. I never told anyone about his meetings. They have their intrigues in show business. It's a real swamp."

"Galina Sergeyevna," Misha cautiously interrupted her. "Please, if you would, tell me more about that meeting."

"They shut themselves in the room and discussed something for more than an hour. I went in once and brought them tea. I heard a snatch of their conversation, but I didn't understand a thing. The young man was probably connected to music. They were talking about promotion . . . You know, all those professional terms."

"Did Yuri call him by name?"

"Not in front of me."

"What did the young man look like?"

"Tall and blond. Wavy hair cut short. I worked as a hairdresser for many years. Blond hair rarely curls naturally, which is why I remembered it. His face"—she thought about it—"was nice, handsome even. He looked about thirty, maybe a little more. Gray-blue eyes, and his nose . . . No, I can't remember that much detail."

"What was he wearing?"

"A black sweater, I think, a thick one, knit in English rib, and black jeans. He was all in black. Yes, and I remember he was wearing these big, dirty, worn boots. He took them off in the front hall."

"Galina Sergeyevna, could you identify this young man from a photograph?"

"No question. I have a good memory for faces."

"Did it seem to you they were talking calmly?"

"I think so. At least, I didn't sense any hostility between them. Yuri was a good boy. Even as a child he never fought or argued. Everyone liked him."

Misha noticed her voice begin to shake and her breathing get labored. He needed to leave. The attending physician hadn't been trying to be difficult. Azarov's mother really was still in serious condition.

"Thank you very much, Galina Sergeyevna. You can't imagine how important what you just told me is," he said softly. "I won't bother you anymore today, but tomorrow I'll bring a few photographs by for you to look at."

"You can bring them today. I'll ask the doctor to let you in. Just find his killer."

I should bring not just photographs but flowers, too, for her and the attending doctor, he thought as he left the room.

Mitya Sinitsyn's parents were quite surprised when a senior investigator from Petrovka asked them for a few photographs of their dead son.

"Are the reasons for Mitya's death really still being investigated? We got an official reply from the Prosecutor's Office. The police never had any doubt that Mitya killed himself," Mitya Sinitsyn's mother murmured in a breaking voice as she paged through the family album.

"All kinds of things happen in our work," Misha replied vaguely.

"Please, return the photos," the elder Sinitsyn asked. "You do understand."

"Yes, of course. Don't worry, I'll return everything." By nightfall, Misha Sichkin knew for certain that two days before the restaurant shoot-out, Yuri Azarov had met with Mitya Sinitsyn. Apparently, the scandal at the release party had made a powerful impression on the singer, so powerful that he didn't hesitate to seek out the man who had caused it and meet with him secretly, at his mother's rooms, two days later. That likely meant he was more than a little intrigued by Mitya's use of the word "killer." It's unlikely he took the word figuratively, like all the other witnesses. He alone may have realized that Sinitsyn the scandal maker was not referring to the killing of a career.

With both of them gone, no one now could know what those two discussed. But the result of that conversation was death for both—the successful entertainer Yuri Azarov and the failed songwriter Mitya Sinitsyn. Both murders were subtly staged and bore the same cunning signature.

When her alarm went off, Lena felt as if she hadn't slept at all. She'd only just shut her eyes, and now she had to get up.

Olga was having breakfast in the kitchen, already dressed and made-up.

"That's it, I'm off," she told her, jumping up from the table and finishing her coffee as she walked. "Michael went for a run. Listen, why'd you get up so early? You could have slept in. You can barely keep your eyes open. Okay, I'm off." She put on her coat and gave Lena a kiss on the cheek.

When the door closed behind her, Lena dialed her neighbors in the apartment across the hall.

"Yes," the boxer's owner confirmed. "A woman was waiting for the elevator on our landing at around two in the morning. She looked wealthy. I thought she'd been visiting someone on our floor. I didn't see which door she came from. She was standing by the elevator. Why?"

"Oh, nothing. Do you remember exactly what she looked like?"

"Tall and elegant, about forty. Honestly, I didn't look very carefully. What is it, Lena? Did she come to see you?"

"Yes. Only I wasn't home. Thank you very much."

Lena hung up the phone, thought for a second, and dialed one of the numbers Major Ievlev had given her.

"How are you planning to spend your day?" the major asked after hearing her out. "Remember, your plane for Tyumen leaves at one in the morning. Elena Nikolaevna, what are your plans for today?"

"I'm going to take my American friend around Moscow."

"Yourself? In your car?"

"I don't know how to drive. An acquaintance has come to the rescue."

At 12:10, the major got a report from the tails that the subject and an older foreigner had left for downtown in a black Mercedes. Half an hour later, Ievlev was astonished to learn that the car belonged to Veniamin Volkov. It was a name in need of no comment.

That's quite some acquaintance you have, Elena Nikolaevna. The major whistled and ordered the surveillance to continue.

CHAPTER 25

He really did behave like an old acquaintance. His eyes were concealed by dark glasses. Lena put on dark glasses as well; the day was bright and sunny.

"Your political commentators used to like to call New York the city of contrasts," Michael said when they were walking down the disfigured Old Arbat. "But even in Cairo and Bombay I haven't seen contrasts more striking than in Moscow. It's amazing. You had the Arbat, this marvelous, cozy street that had so many names and historic events associated with it. And what did you do to the poor Arbat? It's like a cheap nesting doll, a mockery of the city. Listen," he suddenly caught himself. "Why's your friend so quiet?"

"Veniamin doesn't speak English."

"So you can interpret. I'm curious to talk to someone who drives in a Mercedes. Isn't he one of those 'New Russians'?"

"Venya, are you a New Russian?" Lena asked.

"I don't know. Yes, probably. Depending on what you mean by that."

A few minutes later, lively, sophisticated chatter had sprung up between Michael and Volkov. Mechanically interpreting from English to Russian and back, Lena thought about how, looking at this sweet, not unintelligent, well-bred man, you couldn't possibly imagine him as a gangster, or a thug. Or a lover.

"We still don't have business in the pure sense of the word," Volkov said. "It's so saturated with criminal elements that there's no drawing a line between them."

"You mean to say there's no practical difference here between a businessman and a gangster? What about politicians?"

"Same thing. Our funds, including political funds, are criminal at base."

"What do you think? Is that the result of the Bolshevik regime or some completely new, independent phenomenon?" Michael actually pulled out his small notebook and pen from his jacket pocket as he walked.

"Both. What's happening right now didn't materialize out of thin air. I don't know which regime is better, the Bolsheviks' or the criminals'."

"Don't you think they're related concepts?" Michael squinted. "Lots of Bolsheviks were bandits. And they came to power on the backs of the proletariat and the criminals."

"My grandfather was a commissar, a Bolshevik." Volkov smiled. "And I'm in business. Everything in life is relative and interconnected . . . Are you freezing? Your hands are like ice. I want to hold you and warm you."

Lena was interpreting mechanically and accidentally interpreted those last two sentences. Michael's eyebrows shot up.

"I'm sorry?" The professor didn't understand.

It turned out Volkov was holding her hand, firmly and tenderly, discreetly stroking her palm with his fingertips. And she was so busy with simultaneous interpreting that she hadn't noticed.

"Oh, McDonald's!" Michael exclaimed happily. "I heard there were a lot of them in Moscow, but this is the first time I've seen one. I wouldn't mind a bite to eat."

"Is he hungry?" Volkov asked quietly.

"Yes." Lena nodded. "And so am I."

"Well, we're not going to eat there." Volkov nodded contemptuously at the McDonald's. "Tell him we're going to a private club where he'll see real New Russians in all their splendor."

They returned to the car, and ten minutes later, an iron gate separating a nobleman's old mansion from Herzen Street opened for them. The letter *K*, an intricate, twining monogram, solitarily graced a stone pillar by the gates.

"What an interesting place," Michael chattered while a smooth, broad-shouldered young man in a formal suit helped him off with his jacket. "Is this a real private club? And what does the letter *K* mean? Everything here must be very expensive. Hey, hold on, my scarf, too!" He ran after the young man who was carrying away his light-colored jacket.

"My happiness," Volkov whispered, removing Lena's leather jacket and quickly pressing his lips to her ear. "My joy. I have a live broadcast on ORT today, so I have to get to Ostankino by eight. It won't take long, just an hour. I'll take you and the American home after we eat, and then I'll come for you from Ostankino. I have an apartment not far from here. I can't go on without you. We need to make the most of this precious time while your husband is away on business."

How does he know Seryozha's not in Moscow? Actually, I shouldn't be surprised at anything. But I didn't tell him. Or did I? In any case, he's overplaying this, Lena thought. *Or else he's so into his role that he can't let it go anymore.*

"No, Venya, today won't work. It's inconvenient. Michael is my guest, and not only that—"

You have to tell him we're leaving tonight. He can't catch me in a lie. I can't quietly disappear. How much longer can I lead him by the nose like this? I can say we're flying to Siberia. Siberia's big. The main thing is not to mention Tobolsk. But what if he already knows? All this raced through

Lena's mind while the waiter seated them at a round table covered with a pink cloth and set with silver utensils.

"I don't see any New Russians," Michael commented, surveying the small restaurant.

Indeed, the room was empty. Modern abstract paintings in heavy antique frames hung on the pink walls.

"They'll turn up," Volkov promised. The waiter lit the candles on the table, spread a pink linen napkin on Lena's lap, and handed them enormous leather-bound *cartes de vins* and menus.

"Oh, it's all translated into English," Michael rejoiced. "Lots of vegetarian food. And prices in dollars. I hope they take credit cards here. It would be my pleasure to treat you both."

"Tell him I'm the one doing the treating here," Volkov asked when Lena interpreted. "He can order for himself. The waiters speak English."

"You're feeding everyone again, like that time in Tobolsk," Lena said quietly.

"Do you remember Tobolsk?" he asked, gazing into her eyes.

"Vaguely. It's been many years."

"How have you been all these years? Is the police officer your first husband?"

"The third. But the first two don't count."

"And the colonel does?"

"The same way your wife does." Lena shrugged. "You know, I've never had an affair with a married man. I always thought that having an affair with a married man was worse than stealing. Even now, I'm scared. The day before yesterday, someone put a bomb in a bag hanging from Liza's stroller. It's a miracle we survived. The device went off a few moments early. And last night someone tried to open the door to my apartment. Michael heard a scratching at the lock. And then my neighbor came out with his dog and saw a tall woman in a dark coat. She was waiting for the elevator on our floor at about two in the morning."

"Could it have had something to do with your husband's job?" he asked in a whisper. He sipped his mineral water, put the glass down, and accidentally knocked his fork off the table. "How could he ever leave you alone? If I were him . . . How could he leave in this situation?"

"What situation? This all started after he'd left Moscow."

"Did you call and tell him what happened?"

"No. I didn't want to frighten him for no reason. He may be a police colonel, but he can hardly put Liza and me in a steel-clad bunker. If this does have something to do with his job, then his return will only increase the danger. He'll start searching for the perpetrators, who aren't likely to remain idle. You know, Venya, it's very scary when a stroller that your child is in might have been blown up. I just can't go through that again. I can't live in a constant state of tension and fear." She looked into his eyes. "Are you sure your wife doesn't know anything?"

"Nothing else is going to happen to you or your child," he said firmly, and his hot fingers grazed her hand. "You have nothing to be afraid of."

"How do you know?" Lena grinned bitterly.

"I just do. Take me at my word. That won't happen again."

The waiter appeared, bearing silver trays lined with ice and generously filled with black and red caviar, salmon, enormous tiger shrimp, and other delicacies.

"I don't know whether vegetarians eat caviar," Volkov said with a charming smile. Lena interpreted.

"No, vegetarians don't eat caviar, but I can't bear to refuse," Michael admitted. "I've never seen it in such quantities. It's absolutely fantastic!"

The stroller bombing wasn't news to him. He didn't attempt to feign surprise and horror. He didn't even attempt to conceal the fact that he knows a lot, Lena thought, spreading pressed caviar on a slice of rye toast. *I tossed out the topic of Tobolsk memories. He didn't pick up on it, but he could have. What is all this for? The private club, the mountains of caviar, the hideously expensive brandy?*

Suddenly she became aware that she was lying more to herself than to Volkov. Olga was right. The great and powerful producer Venya Volkov had fallen in love. It wasn't about caviar and brandy, sighs and confessions. It was about a feeling you can't quite put your finger on.

What do I need this for? I don't understand what to do with this, how to act. I could cope with a logical puzzle, but what am I supposed to do with a besotted Volkov? He's probably good for his word. As long as I pretend I'm ready for anything, I'm safe. And so is Liza. But what if he realizes his love is like a bone stuck in my throat? He might even kill me himself. He might. If I say that Michael and I are flying to Siberia tonight, he'll definitely ask to what town. I'll say Tyumen, and that will be the truth. But if this is all just about his jealous and cautious wife, do I really have to go digging around in Tobolsk?

"Lena! Why aren't you interpreting?" She heard Michael's voice. "We're deaf and dumb without you!"

"I'm sorry, it's all so delicious," she smiled guiltily.

"I'm trying to ask Veniamin exactly what kind of business he's in," Michael explained.

Lena tuned back in to the conversation, interpreted, laughed, and joked with her companions. But she couldn't relax. The same desperate question kept pounding in her brain: *What am I supposed to do?*

The combination of vodka, brandy, gin and tonic, and Baileys turned out to be too much for Michael.

"I think your friend is about to fall off his chair," Volkov noted quietly when the waiter brought the coffee. "I'll stop by your place at ten or so, after the broadcast. Your professor's going to sleep through the night. He won't even notice you didn't spend the night at home. And if he does, he's not going to tell your husband."

"That's impossible." Lena shook her head. "Tonight we're flying to Tyumen. Our plane leaves at one thirty. At eleven my coworker is going to pick us up and take us to the airport. And it's already five forty-five."

"You're going to Tyumen?"

His face turned to stone. A strange look flashed in his eyes.

Well, that's it, Lena thought, terrified. *I'm not going anywhere. I may not even make it home. And Michael? What an idiot I am! Volkov's in love. He's lost his mind. I'm the one who's lost her mind! What Gosha told me was enough for me not to believe a single word from Veniamin Volkov's mouth. That alone was enough. And I know much more and I still believed him. But what do I actually know about him? He's playing a complicated game with me. He undoubtedly has serious reasons for not doing away with me immediately.*

"How many days will you be gone?" He sounded like he was talking through cotton wool.

"Ten."

"That's an awful lot." He said in a voice made gloomy by melancholy.

Trying not to look him in the eye, Lena took a cigarette out of her pack. He flicked his lighter, and she noticed the flame trembling in his hand.

"Actually, this Siberia trip was why Michael came to Russia," she said as calmly as she could. "His specialty is Russian history, and he asked me to help him, to work as a consultant and interpreter. It's two hundred dollars a day. Very decent money."

"I won't see you for ten days," he said quietly. "You're only going because of the money?"

"Why else?"

"I can give you all you need."

"Venya, I'm used to earning my money, not taking it."

"But wouldn't you just take it from your husband?"

"My husband and I share our money. Don't you and your wife? Let's drop this subject."

"But I don't want you to leave."

"Venya, you're not a little boy. Ten days will fly by. Before you know it, I'll be back. And, this isn't just about money. I promised Michael, and you understand that promises have to be kept."

"Yes, I understand."

Where did this sense of being helpless and lost come from? These imploring looks. He actually has tears in his eyes! Lena thought, looking at his pale face and trembling hands. *After all he's been through, all the dead bodies he's stepped over, now he's sitting in front of me like a little boy being left at day care for the first time. Either he's a brilliant idiot or I'm an utter fool. I don't understand anything about him. When I'm with him, I feel like I don't understand anything about people at all.*

"Who will your Liza stay with?" he asked, lighting up and calming down a little.

"Her nanny. We have a very good nanny."

"Are you just going to be in Tyumen or will you go somewhere else?"

"I don't know yet. Michael's interested in Siberian villages. Why?"

"I could get away for a couple of days and go to Tyumen. Do you already have a hotel? Do you know where you'll be staying?"

"Venya, I'm not going to have a free moment there. I'm going to be working. Venya, you're not a little boy."

"You don't want me to go there?"

"I'll call you. Now take us home, please. I have to put Michael to bed. And I still need to pack."

The professor was snoring quietly, leaning back in his chair. Volkov took Lena's hand in his and cautiously began kissing her fingers.

"You're slipping away," he whispered. "You don't believe me. It's okay. I don't believe anyone, either. Except you. You can't imagine how I love you. No one has ever loved you like this. I used to think love like this wasn't possible, but when I saw you . . . fourteen years later . . . there's been so much filth, blood, and shit since then . . . before . . . and now. I'll die without you."

He spoke as if delirious. Out of the corner of her eye Lena noticed the waiter poke his head around the door and then immediately retreat. There was no one else in the restaurant besides them. The New Russians Venya had promised Michael would see never did come to the K Club that evening.

CHAPTER 26

Pavel Sevastyanov, or Pasha, a twenty-two-year-old gunman from the Yasenevo gang, was in jail for the first time in his life. They'd put him right next to the latrine bucket in a jam-packed cell. The stink and stuffiness kept him from sleeping. Then there was the itching.

Lying on his bunk at night, staring into the cell's putrid murk, Pavel scratched until he bled and thought how much better it would be if they'd arrested him right away, with everyone else, and not a few days later.

He was the only one who managed to escape and hole up after the shoot-out with Thrush's crew at the Vityaz. He was more surprised than anyone to have gotten away, and he thought he'd keep on being lucky, the fool. But someone in his crew squealed. Only they knew he might be hiding out with Natasha's granny in Koptevo, an old abandoned village outside Tula. Only his own guys. The cops wouldn't have found out about Natasha, let alone her grandmother. Nobody knew about their friendship, or romance, or whatever it was, not even her parents.

Now he saw it would have been better to be picked up right away, with everyone else. The police thought that it was a survivor of the shoot-out who had offed Azarov—which made him, Pasha Sevastyanov, the prime suspect. Azarov was killed in the morning, and Pasha was picked up late that night. He could easily have made it from Koptevo to Moscow and back in time. He had both motive and opportunity. And the fact that Natasha's grandmother honestly told the police that Pasha hadn't gone anywhere that day, that he'd been there all day fixing her roof, that didn't count. She was the only one to have seen him on the roof. And she was blind, deaf, and ninety years old. She could confuse the day and time and even Pasha himself. That kind of witness didn't count for much.

In that crowded cell, as his neighbors snored, moaned, and muttered away in their sleep, Pasha Sevastyanov thought about how happy the cops would be to pin Azarov's murder on him. He didn't have the slightest chance of beating the rap. Which meant the gallows.

Sevastyanov wasn't able to fall asleep until almost dawn, and it was a lousy, unhealthy sleep. He was awakened what felt like minutes later by a wave of familiar sounds: coughs, groans, and the doleful cursing of his neighbors. Someone was pissing at the bucket so that the spray flew straight at Pasha. Metal clanged and mugs of their morning gruel rattled. Pasha rubbed his cloudy eyes with his fists and tried to shake off the remnants of his nightmarish sleep.

"Sevastyanov! To questioning!" he heard through the ringing in his ears and noise in the cell.

They took him to an empty cell. Investigator Sichkin was sitting at a table. Pasha was surprised and pleased. He thought he was going to be questioned by the officer who usually came to see him, an old goat with icy, cutting little eyes. But this investigator was a completely different deal.

"I'd like some tea," Pasha mumbled, casting hunted looks to either side. "And a smoke!"

Sichkin called the duty officer, and they brought tea, hot, sweet, and strong. Pasha's eyes danced with pleasure. The good investigator also put two sausage-and-cheese sandwiches in front of him. Then offered him cigarettes.

"You've got yourself in quite a mess, Pasha." The investigator sighed, lighting a cigarette. "A stinking mess. But I don't have to tell you that."

"I didn't kill him," Sevastyanov said, picking at the loose corner of the table and not looking the investigator in the eye. "When there was the shitshow with Thrush's men, I fired like everyone. That's the truth. But I didn't kill the singer."

"Pasha, you're a smart man. You understand that your only chance of not getting the noose is if we find the real killer. Understand?"

Sevastyanov nodded, greedily smoked the cigarette down to the filter, and immediately lit another.

"Why are you digging around like this when you've already got me set for the gallows? You've done your job."

"If I'd done it, I wouldn't be talking to you. Pasha, understand that you've got a lot riding on this conversation of ours. If you help me, you're helping yourself. You don't have a choice. Your pals already turned you in and they'll do it again, which is why you and I should be talking freely and openly."

"I already told you everything. You and the officer."

"How far did you get in school, Pasha?" Sichkin asked, squinting a clever eye.

"High school."

"Plus two years at the Transportation Engineering Institute, which you didn't finish. Not because you didn't want to, you were just greedy. You wanted easy money. You wanted to have all the things other people had. Fine, I don't intend to lecture you. I say this because you do have those two years, after all. And the army. You did a decent stint there. That comes to fourteen years. So, for the fourteen years of your adult life and the childhood before you went to school, you, Pasha Sevastyanov, were a regular guy. Your mother was a nice, educated woman. You know how to talk like a regular human being, not just hurl obscenities and prison slang. You haven't been part of this crew all that long, just half a year. You haven't even had the time to enjoy the money or the good life, and you're already looking at the noose. But it wasn't your pals who set you up. They don't give a shit about you one way or the other. You were set up by different people, serious, powerful people. I want to find them, those people. And you're going to help me. Pasha, you have to remember how your crew came up with the idea of starting a shoot-out at Thrush's party. Who specifically pointed you to the Vityaz?"

"Well, I can help you there," Sevastyanov was happy to say. "The three of us, Shovel, Claw, and I, we were at the Europa Casino on Voikovskaya. Shovel saw a dame he knew there. She and Shovel had a long conversation, but I wasn't paying attention. I did realize she was setting him up, though. Afterward Shovel says, 'Tomorrow we're going to crush Thrush and his men. No more delays. I've had it with Thrush horning in on our territory.'"

"Had you ever seen that girl before?"

"Don't think so. I don't remember."

"What did she look like?"

"Oh, elegant, about forty, maybe less. Tall and her hair was kind of light, but not blond."

"Eyes?"

"I didn't get a good look. I just remember she was beautiful and elegant, nice clothes, everything just right."

"Did Azarov come up in the conversation?" Sichkin asked quietly.

Pasha thought about that and started digging his nail into the corner of the table.

"I can't remember." He shook his head sadly. "I'm not going to lie. I really don't remember."

"Fine." The investigator nodded. "Let's try this. Was the fact that Azarov was singing at the Vityaz news for you, or did you know about it beforehand? What do you think, did Shovel know?"

"Shovel definitely knew." Pasha nodded. "It was like that dame was asking Shovel about Azarov personally, for us to . . . well, we could deal with Thrush and Azarov, at one go."

"You mean she ordered it?"

"Well, I guess. Afterward I heard Shovel and Claw get into it a little when we were leaving the casino. Claw says, 'Hey, she should pay like for a regular hit,' but Shovel laughed and said, 'What, saving on bullets?' At the time I thought she'd probably either paid Shovel or promised to. And he wasn't cool about sharing. But Claw shut up right away. He knows Shovel. Look at him cross-eyed, and he wouldn't hesitate. That's why he's lasted so long."

Before pulling out the envelope of photos, Misha finished his cooled tea, lit a cigarette, and then fanned out a few color photos of women's faces in front of Pasha.

Pasha recognized the woman Shovel had been talking to immediately. Of the six snapshots, he picked two. Both were of Regina Valentinovna Gradskaya.

⁓⧉⁓

Volkov did not have a breakdown on air. He was charming, witty, and self-assured. Not even a hint of nervousness. Regina thought she could smell the very faint smell of another woman's perfume on her husband's jacket through the television screen.

She knew he'd canceled all his meetings and appointments today. He'd taken the old black Mercedes out of the garage again and left the house at eleven in the morning without a word to her. People called him all day, and she didn't know what to tell them. For the first time in all the years they'd been together, she didn't know where her husband was. Naturally, she lied. She covered for him automatically. Not for his sake, but for the sake of their business. Regina could decide certain questions herself, and she did. But there was a lot, an awful lot, that couldn't be decided without Volkov. He needed to be present, in the flesh—not for Regina but for the business. And there was nothing in the world more important than the business.

The broadcast had been over for a while, and the nine o'clock news was on ORT. Right then Regina noticed she'd been fiddling the whole time with the black leather glove she'd found in the Mercedes. That was where that smell came from, so familiar and alien.

Regina had a good nose for perfume. The perfume a woman uses says a lot about her. Warm, cold, sweet, bitter—perfume smells differently on different skin and can be in-your-face saccharine or create an aura of mystery and inaccessibility. Perfume tells you who a woman wants to be, how she sees herself, how much she loves herself, whether she has complexes about her looks or is confident that she's irresistible.

She knew now that for the rest of her life she'd have an aversion to Miss Dior. A warm, unobtrusive scent with a hint of sandalwood. That's what the glove she was fiddling with smelled like. That scent hovered in the black Mercedes. There was nothing provocative or brazen about it. Today, when her husband came back—if he did come back—his jacket would give off this exact same gentle, unobtrusive fragrance.

"What does that mean, 'if he did'?" she said, loud and clear. "What's become of him? He's gone off the rails, certainly, but not to that extent!"

She turned out to be right—as usual. He came back at ten thirty. She offered him her cheek for a kiss, which he gave indifferently and, refusing dinner, he went directly to his study. His jacket, which he had shed on a chair in the living room, really did smell of Miss Dior.

She waited ten minutes or so and cautiously cracked the door of his study. He was lying on the sofa in his trousers and unbuttoned shirt, looking at the ceiling.

"Tired?" she asked, approaching and perching next to him on the sofa.

"Yes, a little," he said, not looking at her.

"You know, there were lots of calls while you were out." She started telling him about the calls, about business matters, about the problems she'd resolved for and without him.

He replied in monosyllables: "Yes, no, right, I'll have to think about it." And kept looking at the ceiling.

"I saw you on television. That all went excellently. You really are in great form right now. What do you think that has to do with?"

"Why does it have to do with anything?" he asked calmly. "Am I still desperately ill and in need of constant medical intervention to be in good form?"

"No, Venya. You're healthy." She laughed gaily and stroked his bristly cheek. "You're amazing. Lately we've been working so much, you haven't been able to go a day without a session. I get awfully worn out when we work like this, too. That's why I'm so glad I can relax now and not worry so much about you."

"Yes, Regina. You can relax and stop worrying. The furor over the Vityaz scandal is over. I'm totally fine now. You know, I think I'll have some tea."

He got up abruptly from the sofa and headed for the kitchen, followed by Regina.

"Oh, I forgot to tell you." She turned on the electric kettle and put two cups on the table. "Someone left a glove in the Mercedes. It should probably be returned. It's on the magazine table in the living room, black, leather, a small size. Do you remember who you gave a ride to yesterday?"

"Yes, I do. I'll return the glove."

"Polyanskaya has very slender hands," she said.

His light, almost translucent eyes gave her a sudden look, and after a moment's silence he said quietly, "Regina, if so much as a hair falls from that woman's head, I will kill you."

"Oh ho!" she laughed gaily in reply. "Has it come to that?"

"Consider yourself warned." He stood up from the table, got the box of Lipton tea bags from the shelf, opened it without hurrying, put a bag in each cup, and added boiling water.

Regina observed his hands carefully. They weren't shaking. They were calm. She caught herself thinking that she wished his hands would shake so the boiling water would splash on his skin and he would cry out in pain.

"Venya, Venya." She shook her head. "Do you really believe that that cop's wife shares your feelings? She's just afraid of you. I'll bet nothing's happened yet and nothing will. She's leading you on. She has no intention of cheating on her husband. Believe me, I'm speaking now not as your wife but as a psychiatrist with twenty-five years' experience."

He sat there, staring silently into his cup.

"You're silent because you have nothing to counter that with. You know I'm right. You never had a real first love. You and I know why. And now, at forty, you've suddenly remembered that and you've decided life is passing you by. Right now it's as if the whole world's been turned upside down. You've met a woman you were powerfully attracted to once, fourteen years ago. It wasn't your hunger or your illness but a healthy, normal male emotion. Polyanskaya hasn't changed in all these years. She's young and good-looking. Yes, Venya, even I can admit that Polyanskaya is a very beautiful woman. There's something about her that I don't have and neither do all the women we meet in our work. Breeding and nobility. Right now you think that real human warmth can come from this woman and this woman alone. Notice how calmly I'm talking about this. I love you too much to be jealous. I'm not making a scene and I'm not disparaging her. I'm not against your affair. Ultimately, there is no such thing as a faithful husband. But partners should protect each other's monastic faithfulness. Otherwise business suffers. There's not going to be an affair, Venya. Polyanskaya doesn't love you. She's lying to you."

Regina's voice dropped deeper and deeper and she didn't take her eyes off her husband. Her monologue transitioned smoothly into a powerful hypnosis session.

"Polyanskaya is lying. She doesn't care for you. She's laughing at you. You're going to calm down and realize that there's only me. No other woman exists for you. I'm the only one you can trust. She's a stranger to you. She's your enemy. There's only my voice; it is a bridge over the abyss. It is a bright, moonlit road you are walking down, calmly and confidently. I'm the only person you do not have to be afraid with."

He had already closed his eyes. He was rocking slowly in rhythm to her smooth voice. She had time to think that she should carefully move him to the floor; otherwise he'd fall off the chair when he came out of the trance. She took a step toward him—and the phone rang loudly.

Venya shuddered, opened his eyes, and shouted harshly, "Stop it! I didn't ask you to!"

It was Regina's cell. She picked up the phone, said, "I'm listening"—and walked out of the kitchen.

Left alone, Venya took a few swallows of tea and lit a cigarette.

"Venya, do you have cash? I need four hundred dollars," Regina asked when she appeared in the doorway a minute later. "I am going to meet an informant. I've got six hundred but I have to give him a thousand. And the bank's closed."

"I can probably find four hundred. But why the urgency? Can't it wait until tomorrow?"

"No, it can't, Venya. You only think it's all over. In fact, it's only just begun."

"Regina, can you explain to me what this is about?" He stood up and went to the living room. His wallet was in his inside jacket pocket. He found four hundred dollars there.

"I'll be back in an hour and I'll explain then," she promised. "Don't worry, this has nothing to do with your Polyanskaya."

Pretty soon, nothing will have anything to do with Polyanskaya, she thought as she got into her dark blue Volvo and drove through the blackness of the March night. *I'm not jealous at all. It's ridiculous to be jealous of a dead woman whose days are numbered.*

Parking the car not far from near the Pushkin Museum, Regina proceeded on foot to Gogol Boulevard. The street was deserted. The loose springtime slush gleamed in the streetlamps' shaky, trembling light. Stepping carefully, trying not to soil her light-colored suede boots, Regina headed down the boulevard. She saw a man's dark silhouette on one of the benches. The bright light of his cigarette blazed up in the darkness.

Regina sat down beside him silently and lit up. Heavy shuffling could be heard in the darkness. A drunken bum was stumbling down the boulevard. Lurching toward the bench, he rasped, "Treat me to a little cigarette?" Regina silently tapped a cigarette out of her pack and held it out disdainfully, with two fingers.

"Thank you kindly," he rasped. "And a light, too, if it's not a bother."

The man sitting next to Regina flicked his lighter. Lighting up, the bum glanced for a second at their faces, which were illuminated by the flame.

"Thank you kindly again."

He staggered away, muttering under his breath, and disappeared into the boulevard's darkness.

The man waited a minute more and quickly slipped a small, flat package into Regina's hand. A minute later there were ten hundred-dollar bills in his jacket pocket.

"I'll wait for your call at exactly two in the morning," the man said.

Regina nodded, tossed her unfinished cigarette into the puddle under the bench, and, stepping cautiously, returned to her car. Before starting the engine, she pulled out and unwrapped the small package. It was an ordinary cassette tape. Regina immediately slid it into the player and listened to it.

She got home at half past one. Venya was sleeping peacefully, like a child, one hand under his cheek. Regina took off her clothes and stood under a hot shower.

How odd, she thought. *I spent so many years forcing him and myself to live balanced on the brink of serious psychosis. His illness didn't prevent him from doing some excellent thinking and work. On the contrary, he was strong and cautious. He had a keen nose for danger and knew how to avoid it easily. That was what I based all my calculations on at the time. His illness was like a protective capsule, a second skin. He had no doubts or regrets and didn't reflect. The energy of his illness pushed him forward and made him invincible. I didn't think he would ever get well. Yet it was all so simple. Terribly simple. He fell in love. Now he's like a little boy discovering the world all over again. And that's keeping him from thinking clearly and reacting appropriately to what's happening. It's much harder with him healthy than it was with him sick. I'm losing control of him. He relaxed only when I started singing Polyanskaya's praises. I always knew he was crazy, but I never thought he was a fool.*

Half an hour later, sitting in the kitchen in her robe, she dialed a number on her cell phone and said just three words: "Shovel. Claw. Five."

"Apiece?" the unseen person clarified.

"Fine. Eight for both. But it's urgent."

"If it's urgent, then ten."

"Can you do it in the next twenty-four hours?"

"We'll do our best." The unknown man responded and then hung up.

She had to go to bed. Tomorrow morning she'd have to go to the bank and take ten thousand dollars out of the account. "No, better fifteen. Just in case. And not tomorrow. It's already today."

Listening to the recorded conversations that had taken place in the black Mercedes, Major Ievlev thought about how you can't trust women. They'd been able to plant an eavesdropping device while the three-some had been strolling around Poklonnaya Hill. Naturally, the main conversations didn't occur in the car but outside and in the private K Club, where his surveillance team didn't even attempt to go.

Nonetheless, he understood exactly what was going on. The famous producer was wooing the police colonel's wife. And she was open to his advances. That explained why she hadn't phoned her husband in London and asked him to come home. What did she need her husband for when she had a millionaire as a lover? And it was Volkov's wife who'd put the explosive in the stroller. Who else? What normal woman is going to stand idly by while her husband woos another woman? In Polyanskaya, Mrs. Gradskaya detected a serious threat to her familial and financial well-being.

Life is full of surprises, Ievlev thought to himself. When jealous, a woman can be motivated to commit all kinds of abominations. So can a man, of course. But right now he was thinking about one particular woman. Regina Gradskaya. She'd been seen in the courtyard where the stroller blew up. She'd tried to get into Polyanskaya's apartment.

Regina Gradskaya's resources were not inconsiderable. But she probably wanted to solve her personal problems herself without resorting to a contract killer. She was an experienced and intelligent woman, and she had an insider's knowledge of the criminal world. It's only the naive who watch *Highway Patrol* and movies who think you can solve any problem with a hitman without complications. She and her husband probably did have ties to organized crime. What if one of their mutual acquaintances found out about her plans and ratted her out to Veniamin Borisovich?

Not expecting success, the major decided to tail Gradskaya himself and see what she would do next. Sitting in his nondescript car near the elegant nine-story building on Meshchanskaya Street where Volkov and Gradskaya had an apartment, the major was about to doze off when he saw Regina Valentinovna's dark blue Volvo come rolling out of the underground garage. Ievlev woke up, shook himself, and started following her.

In the darkness of Gogol Boulevard, it wasn't at all hard for the major in his tattered jeans and old ski jacket to play the part of an inebriated bum.

Regina Valentinovna was not out for a tryst on Gogol Boulevard. She was there on business. In order to figure out what kind of business, Ievlev focused his attention on the man she was meeting, whose face in the flickering flame of his lighter seemed vaguely familiar. But the man covered his tracks well. When the meeting was over, he dashed down the Arbat side streets and dodged quickly through entryways and connecting courtyards until he arrived at the Arbat Metro station. Ievlev got there in time to see the last train carry a thirtysomething man of average height wearing a brown leather jacket and a military-style crew cut off into the night.

Major Ievlev returned to his car to rack his brain over where he'd seen the guy before.

CHAPTER 27

In Tyumen, spring seemed a long way off. Snow was falling in big, soft flakes on the morning that Lena and Michael arrived in the small Siberian town. Moscow may have been dirty and cold, Lena thought, but at least it was spring there.

For some reason, having to return to winter saddened Lena. Huddling in her leather jacket, which was too light for the freezing temperatures, she tried to flag down a car in front of the Tyumen airport. Michael looked around ecstatically.

"Tell me, has anything changed here in the last ten years?" he asked. "Do you remember the last time you were here? It was still Soviet then, right?"

"Michael, let's first get to the hotel," Lena implored.

There were lots of cars, but their routes were probably strictly determined by the local mafia. Some drivers refused to go to the Tura Hotel for some reason, and others quoted such crazy prices that Lena wouldn't use their services on principle. Tired and chilled as she was, she still couldn't let Michael throw away a hundred dollars on this ride—not even if her teeth were chattering.

"Why did you refuse that car?" the professor asked. "That's the fourth one!"

"There are two people there and they're asking a hundred dollars. It's too dangerous, and it's too expensive."

"Lena, you're blue from the cold. What am I going to do if you get sick?" Michael shook his head. "I don't care if it's a hundred dollars!"

A nondescript Moskvich pulled up. There was no one inside except for the driver, a young, skinny guy in glasses.

"The Tura Hotel," Lena said wearily.

"Hop in." The driver nodded.

Lena and Michael got in the back seat, and only when they'd driven onto the highway to town did Lena ask, "How much?"

"How about fifty?" The driver smiled in the rearview mirror.

"Fifty's good." Lena smiled back.

"From Moscow, are you?" the driver inquired.

"Yes."

"And this guy is a foreigner?" The driver lowered his voice a little and winked in the mirror.

"An American."

"Here on business? Or a private tour?"

"Business. He's a scholar, a historian."

"Yeah, you can tell right off he's a professor. Which makes you his interpreter, right?"

Lena nodded and looked out the window at the blurry, snowy city she hadn't seen in fourteen years. Michael dozed off with his head leaning back on the seat. Cheerful though he was, after the long night flight, he too was exhausted.

The city hadn't changed much. The same gray prefab tenements, only the red Communist posters had been replaced by billboards, just like in Moscow, Saint Petersburg, New York, and the rest of the world. Smiling people urging you to drink Coca-Cola, take soluble aspirin, chew sugarless gum, smoke Marlboros, and buy Salita shoes.

A few shops had popped up here and there, and there was the occasional foreign car on the road. Clusters of somber men from the

Caucasus dressed in sheepskin jackets and saggy, wide trousers circled near the stores, restaurants, and cafés, of which there were many.

"In these parts for long?" the driver asked.

"A few days," Lena answered.

"And then?"

"Then Tobolsk and Khanty-Mansiysk."

"That's quite an itinerary. Will you be flying back from Tyumen?"

"Where else?" Lena shrugged.

"Listen." The driver's voice became more confiding. "You're going to need a car to get around town. Why don't I take you where you need to go and when you get back, I'll take you to the airport. It'll be cheaper than hailing a taxi every time."

Lena took a close, careful look at the narrow, pleasant face reflected in the mirror. Indeed, she hadn't thought about a car. If taxi drivers and freelancers were going to continue to quote her extravagant prices, this trip would bankrupt the professor. And there was nothing immediately off-putting about the fellow. He didn't look like a crook. And he knew the town.

"How much would your driving services cost?"

"Let's see how much we drive." He smiled. "I won't ask a lot. You don't have to worry about your friend's wallet. I have a conscience. What's your name?"

"Lena."

"Pleased to meet you. I'm Sasha. Write down my phone number."

Lena took a notebook and pen out of her purse and he dictated the number.

"What plans do you have for today?"

"We're going to rest up a little at the hotel, eat, and then go for a walk through the historic city center."

"Why don't I drive you around instead? I know the town well. I was born here."

Michael woke up, yawned, and asked what they were talking about. Lena laid out the driver's proposal.

"Excellent!" Michael rejoiced. "He doesn't look like a crook. And I'm curious to talk to a native Siberian. Ask him what his field is."

"I used to work as an engineer at a woodworking factory," Sasha offered readily. "But they held up our pay for months. And I've got a family, a small child. So now I drive and make whatever money God sees fit to grant me."

Michael and Sasha chatted and Lena interpreted the rest of the way.

The Tura Hotel was the best in town. When Lena finally got to her small single room, she dropped her bag on the floor, took off her boots, fell into the armchair, and just sat there for a few minutes looking out the window at the blue-gray northern sky. In a separate pocket in her small black purse, she had the letters from Vasya Slepak and the mother of the deceased First Lieutenant Zakharov. Both had home addresses— one in Tyumen and one in Tobolsk. Should she go to those addresses? Completely different people could be living there, and even if they did still live there, what was she going to say to them?

Where did I get the idea that Zakharov's story has anything to do with Mitya and Katya's deaths, the stroller bomb, and Volkov and his wife? What connection could there be? she asked herself, and rising from the chair, she started unpacking.

Vasya Slepak's father was accused of raping and murdering several girls, she thought as she set her bottle of shampoo, toothpaste, and soap out on the bathroom shelf. *Zakharov's last story talks about someone unjustly suspected of several rapes and murders. Slepak the father was executed. Zakharov was killed. It's just a night's train travel from Tyumen to Tobolsk. And an hour by plane. Volkov was born and lived in Tobolsk. Fourteen years ago, they found a raped and murdered girl in a park above the Tobol. That same night we had lit a campfire, roasted shish kebab, and sang songs there. But meanwhile, someone was raping and killing a girl. Very close by. Venya Volkov was with us the whole time . . .*

Lena turned the handle on the hotel shower and couldn't believe it: hot water came out right away. A lot had changed in this town in fourteen years after all! Quickly undressing, she happily stood under the shower.

No, she thought as she washed off the dirt and weariness of travel. *He did go somewhere that night. He disappeared for a while. And Mitya went off to find him. And then there were the spots of blood on his sweater. Volkov had looked very odd. He'd had this crazy, wandering gaze. He said the blood was from a nosebleed, that he shouldn't drink. But he'd barely had anything to drink that night. Why do I remember it all so well? Could I be confusing things? Fantasizing?*

Swaddling herself in a large hotel towel and slipping her feet into her slippers, Lena took an enameled mug from the bottom of her bag, along with an immersion heater, a tin of ground coffee, sugar, and the small, nickel-silver cup she'd been taking with her on business trips for years.

After the water in the mug boiled, Lena turned off the immersion heater, put four spoonfuls of coffee in the water and three cubes of sugar and plugged the immersion heater back in for exactly two minutes to make it foam ever so slightly.

While the coffee was cooling, Lena got dressed—just in time. No sooner had she zipped up her jeans when she heard a knock at the door.

It was Michael. He, too, had taken a shower and changed his clothes.

"Here's what I keep worrying about," he said, sitting in the arm-chair. "What if there's nothing vegetarian in the local restaurant? What am I going to do then?"

"Let's have some coffee for starters," Lena suggested.

Michael chatted on about the difficulties of finding vegetarian food in some of the places he had visited in his travels, but Lena was only half listening.

There were spots of blood on his sweater, Lena thought. *I don't remember how long Volkov was gone, but . . . When I was packing up the dishes after the picnic, we were missing a knife. I remembered the knife because Volkov had sliced the onion for the shish kebab so deftly, in thin, even circles. It was a young onion, strong, all three of us were tearing up, though we turned away. But he sliced dry-eyed. It was so surprising, I remembered it.*

"It Italy it was like they had never even heard the word 'vegetarian' before! I would tell them I didn't eat meat, and they would just bring me chicken. If I said I didn't eat chicken, they brought me fish!" Michael got up from his chair and started pacing around the small hotel room, gesticulating expressively.

Something happened in Tyumen, too. Lena looked at the enameled blue mug with the immersion heater and suddenly remembered that June morning at the Hotel East. *Mitya had a mug just like this, but twice as big, and the immersion heater . . . He went to the hotel buffet while Olga and I made coffee. When Mitya got back he was white as a sheet. Someone had told him about a girl who'd been raped and murdered. The girl had been a student at the vocational institute where we'd performed the night before. Stop! It doesn't make sense!*

"And what if it is like that here as well? What am I going to do? I have a lot of work to do, and I can't do my work and think clearly if I am not eating. In Italy, I could just eat pasta with tomato sauce at every meal, but this is not Italy. We are in Siberia, of all places!"

Why doesn't it make sense? Lena asked herself. *Just because I'd be so scared if it was Volkov? He was in Tyumen at the time, after all! We traveled to Tobolsk together. That was the night when he and I had that bizarre conversation on the train.*

Her heart started pounding. Lena mechanically tapped a cigarette out of the pack and lit it.

"Lena!" Michael shouted in despair. "I don't think you've been listening to me at all. You've been thinking your own thoughts!"

"Oh, Michael, I'm sorry!" Lena caught herself. "Please forgive me."

"Be honest, are you thinking about your friend, Veniamin, who took us to that fancy club?"

"Why do you think that?" Lena asked in fright.

"Child, I'm an old man. I've seen lots in my life, even though I've been living with the same woman for forty years. I'll tell you another banality, but believe me, sexual intimacy ends very quickly. All you're left with is bitterness and disappointment. You're a young and beautiful woman, and nothing can keep someone from courting you, not even the fact that you are married. But be careful. Don't go too far. Forgive me for meddling, but I know how Steven worries about you, and he and I are close friends. I don't have daughters, but if I did, I'd tell them the same thing. Be careful. Don't go too far."

"I have no intention of going too far," Lena replied quietly. "There is no romantic interest, not on my end anyway."

"Well, that's very good." Michael smiled, delighted. "You know, while I was fretting about food, I managed to get good and hungry. Let's you and I go down to the restaurant and see whether they have any vegetarian food there."

When Lena was already locking the door behind her, the phone rang.

"That's curious," Michael said, surprised. "Who could that be?"

It was Sasha, the driver. He said he was downstairs, at the front desk.

"I thought you would have eaten and be ready to head out for your tour of the city. But that's all right. I can wait."

Lena was mildly surprised at his zeal. But she assumed that the young man was anxious to make some money and maybe he was afraid someone else would poach his rich foreign client.

"Yes, please wait in the lobby. We may have to go somewhere else to eat if this restaurant doesn't have vegetarian food."

"You mean your friend doesn't eat meat?"

"Or fish."

"I sympathize. He's going to have a hard time here. All right, if the hotel restaurant doesn't have anything for him, I'll find somewhere else to take you."

I was very lucky with this Sasha, Lena thought, hanging up the phone. *He probably knows where Malaya Proletarskaya Street is.*

Malaya Proletarskaya was where Raisa Slepak had once lived. She might still.

The hotel restaurant turned out to be just fine. The tablecloths were white and the waitresses polite and smiling, though the vegetarian options were limited to the vegetable appetizer and roast potatoes.

"We also have pancakes with sour cream for Shrovetide," the waitress told them. "Get that for your friend. I recommend them."

She brought such a stack of pancakes that Michael clapped his hands.

"I've read that Russian merchants died of overeating at Shrovetide! If we eat all this, we're guaranteed to wreak havoc on our stomachs. Listen, you said that young man, the driver, is sitting in the lobby. Why don't you go and invite him to join us? He can help us deal with this giant stack."

Sasha was sitting in an armchair, leafing distractedly through one of the magazines fanned out on the table.

"Hello again!" he exclaimed. "Finished eating?"

"No, we've only just started. Michael wanted me to invite you to join us for pancakes."

"Thank you."

Returning to the dining room with Sasha, Lena suddenly felt someone staring at her back. Turning around, she noticed a young, mustached bartender wiping glasses behind the bar. Meeting eyes with Lena, he immediately turned away and started rubbing the fine glass so furiously that the glass shattered in his hands.

CHAPTER 28

Before Masha Kolosova, secretary to *Smart*'s editor in chief, could take off her coat, the outside line rang in the reception area.

"Who on earth could that be so early?" Masha grumbled, lifting the receiver.

"Hello!" a high-pitched female voice said in English. "Is this *Smart*?"

"Yes," Masha replied in English. "How may I help you?"

"I'm calling from New York," the woman on the line said. "Your colleague, Mrs. Polyanskaya, is accompanying my husband as his interpreter. I know he stayed at her home in Moscow and I can't find them. No one's answered for more than a day. I'm so worried, you see. My husband is rather elderly."

"Don't worry, ma'am. All's well. They've gone to Tyumen."

"Oh, yes, of course! Is there some way I can contact them there? Did Mrs. Polyanskaya say which hotel she'd made reservations for?"

"Unfortunately not. But they won't be in Tyumen long, as far as I know. They have an ambitious itinerary—Tobolsk, Khanty-Mansiysk. If Mrs. Polyanskaya calls, I can ask her to—"

"No, thank you, there's no need. I'm reassured. My husband always says I'm an old worrywart. Again, thank you so much. All the best." And there was a dial tone.

Darn it! Masha suddenly remembered as she was hanging up. *Lena asked me not to tell anyone where she was going with her professor! But it was a call from New York, after all.*

The professor's wife had a staccato way of speaking, just like New Yorkers have. Masha knew that distinctive New York accent very well. She often had occasion to deal with New Yorkers, on the telephone, in Moscow, and in New York when she was lucky enough to have the editor in chief take her along.

For a second the thought flashed that it hadn't actually been a long-distance call. It just sounded too crisp in the morning quiet of the empty office. But she discarded the thought. She had a long, busy day ahead of her.

❧

I knew it, Regina thought. *I knew it. Tyumen, Tobolsk, Khanty. Well, now I am free to do whatever I want. She's there without her child, after all. She's got that American professor, but not the child. Blindboy has no principles when it comes to old men. But the timing, the timing. I have to get in touch with Blindboy, and he has to fly there.*

The mere thought of what Polyanskaya might be doing in Tyumen and Tobolsk made Regina's palms sweat. And if she imagined someone helping her there . . . No, she had to stop this right now, this minute. Blindboy would do his job, of course, but that wouldn't be for at least three days. Maybe more. Every step that woman took now could be the last for their company, and that meant the last for Regina.

After thinking just a few seconds, she dialed 8, the code for Tyumen, and then a few more numbers. She had an excellent memory for phone numbers, especially the ones that shouldn't be kept in notebooks.

❧

"They're just spitting in your face, all three of them," Vladimir Trofimov, an investigator in the Prosecutor's Office, said, looking at Misha with pity. "You should have stayed home with the flu, Sichkin. Your bosses would have waited. Now look what you've dumped on me! You've dragged up suicide, and a fire, and an accident. And you've got strollers blowing up. It's hitting the fan, Misha!" he said, loudly slapping his desk with each word as if he were driving in invisible nails.

"Does this mean you don't want to attend the lineup?" Misha asked gloomily.

"I see no reason to. The case is set for trial. Don't you understand that? Sevastyanov's going to point the finger at anyone—his own mother, Pushkin—he'll do anything to send the case back for further investigation."

"He didn't kill Azarov," Misha said brusquely.

"Well, hello." The investigator was at a loss. "He has no alibi and the motive's plain as day. He's a thug, Misha. I hope I don't have to prove to you that Sevastyanov participated in the shoot-out all over again."

"He did participate in the shoot-out, but he didn't kill Azarov."

"You are one stubborn guy, Misha." The investigator sighed. "Think about it. How many careers do you think Volkov has destroyed over the years? How many people do you think are out there wishing evil on him? Does it really matter what some psycho with hurt feelings called him? He could call him a murderer, or a vampire, or the devil himself! What, are Volkov and Gradskaya going to off them all afterward because they have such a heightened sense of their own dignity?

"Misha, do you at least understand who you're going after?" the investigator continued in an agitated whisper. "Have either of them—Volkov or Gradskaya—ever come up as a suspect or defendant even once? Sure, they probably didn't get to where they are in our new free market without some connections to the criminal world and organized crime. There's a gallows waiting for each of them—Gradskaya and

Volkov both. But you can't prove shit. You won't have time. And I'm not your friend in this. I have two children and a grandson who was just born yesterday."

In and of itself, the testimony of the suspect, Pavel Sevastyanov, was worthless. It only took on real weight and meaning if Shovel and Claw not only confirmed the fact of their meeting with Regina Gradskaya but also laid out the substance of their conversation with her.

At first, even Misha thought the idea of a lineup was absurd. But he was fresh out of ideas, so he gave this option very careful thought. He came to the conclusion fairly quickly that there was a chance, albeit a small one, of forcing testimony out of those thugs.

Misha knew from experience that thugs, as a rule, were impressionable and neurotic by nature. Especially after they'd cooled their heels for a few days in jail. Misha was counting on them losing it. Before the lineup, he decided to call Shovel and Claw in for questioning separately. He would tell each a sad story about how a smart and rich woman, Regina Valentinovna, had squealed on them, sold them down the river. She'd stated that she had met two bad guys, real gangsters, once at the casino on Voikovskaya. But the honest woman had no idea she'd been face-to-face with real bad guys.

Out of naïveté, Regina Valentinovna thought she was talking to nice, normal people about trivial things, like the big party being planned at a restaurant outside Moscow where none other than Yuri Azarov would be performing. That was what she told investigators she talked to the two young men about. She didn't know, the good, naive woman, that she was dealing with violent criminals who were just waiting to shoot everyone they could. She couldn't have guessed that those bloodthirsty bad guys were taking advantage of her harmless gossiping.

Sichkin had an extra surprise in reserve for Shovel. In searching his apartment, a substantial sum in US dollars had been found in his mirror bar. Misha was going to tell him that, by the way, the experts said those greenbacks, fifty-three hundred in all, were counterfeit. And he'd ask, "Where did you get those lousy bills, dear friend? Who deceived good-hearted you so cruelly?"

His hopes for success were slim. Shovel would lose his temper and lash out, of course, and so would Claw. But they weren't going to rat out Gradskaya. Neither wanted to die.

CHAPTER 29

Sasha led them on an excursion through the historic center. Talking nonstop, he told them how there was once a Tatar town here, Chingi-Tura, and how in the sixteenth century the great Ermak's Cossacks fought Kuchum Khan and won three Siberian rivers for Russia—the Irtysh, Tobol, and Tura—and how in 1584 Ermak drowned in the Irtysh and in 1586 a valiant commander named Sukov founded Tyumen on the Tura River.

Michael couldn't contain himself. He kept saying, "Boy, did we luck out with Sasha!"

And Lena couldn't have agreed more. They really had lucked out with Sasha.

"You don't happen to know where Malaya Proletarskaya Street is, do you?" Lena asked when he was taking them back to the hotel at seven thirty.

"It just so happens I do." Sasha smiled. "Why?"

"I need to visit some people I know."

"Good ones?"

"Marvelous ones. Very old and fine people."

"Then you can call and let them meet you if they're old and good. There are phones nearly everywhere in that part of town."

"There weren't in '83."

"Yes, that's true. That means you haven't seen your Tyumen friends since '83?"

"Well, we did correspond for a while afterward." Lena shrugged. "Listen, why are you so curious?"

"I'm curious by nature." Sasha laughed. "Why don't I take you to Malaya Proletarskaya? It'll be faster than explaining how to get there."

"Thank you for the kind offer, but your family is probably at home waiting for you."

"My family's visiting my mother-in-law in Tobolsk right now," Sasha said, looking at Lena through his glasses with his clear, honest brown eyes.

"Listen, are you near- or farsighted?" she asked quietly.

"One eye is -3 and the other is -2. Why?"

"Nothing. Usually glasses make eyes either bigger or small. But it looks like yours are plain glass. You might think you wore them for looks. All right, it's late. I have to visit my friends on Malaya Proletarskaya today."

"Let's go. I'll take you there and back."

"Even back? And how much will that cost?"

"A cup of coffee." He smiled broadly. "But if we're being serious, why should I take anything more from you if your professor is already paying me a hundred dollars a day? I'm no bloodsucker."

Lena saw Michael to his room. Sasha waited for her in the car. It took them twenty minutes to drive to Malaya Proletarskaya.

Number fifteen was the only one-story wooden house among the gray prefab tenements. A light burned cozily in the window. The gate was open. Lena walked onto the creaking porch. There was no bell. She knocked.

She heard quick shuffling, and the door opened wide. On the threshold stood a tall, lean old woman wearing a white cotton kerchief.

"Hello," Lena said. "Tell me, please, do the Slepaks live here?"

"Yes." The old woman nodded. "Come in."

Lena was amazed. The old woman hadn't asked who she was before she opened the door. She was letting a stranger into her house.

"Are you Raisa Danilovna?" Lena stepped hesitantly into the dark anteroom, where the floor was spread with clean cloths.

The house smelled of a freshly washed wooden floor, roasted potatoes, and medications.

"I'm her sister," the old woman said. "Take off your boots. I just washed the floors. Go on inside. Raisa!" she called out. "There's a young woman here for you."

Lena unlaced her tall boots and, stepping cautiously over the damp cloths in just her thin stockings, she went through the half-open door into a small, perfectly furnished room hung with old photographs in carved frames. Between the two windows, an icon lamp glowed under the dark icon of Our Lady of Kazan. In the middle of the room, under a wide, orange-fringed shade was an empty round table covered with a snow-white embroidered tablecloth. Sitting at the table was an old woman in the same white kerchief and with the same sharp features as the woman who'd opened the door.

"Hello. Are you Raisa Danilovna?" Lena stopped, at a loss.

"I am." The old woman nodded. "Why are you standing? Come in. Sit down."

Lena sat at the table across from her hostess.

"My name is Lena Polyanskaya. I'm from Moscow," she began, feeling the heavy gaze of the old woman's faded blue eyes on her. "Thirteen years ago I sent you a magazine with a poem by your son Vasily. Do you remember?"

"Yes, I do." The old woman kept looking at her just as heavily and intently.

"And how is Vasily doing?" Lena asked, and she smiled.

Right now, more than anything, she wished she could get up and leave. She felt uneasy under the old woman's heavy, penetrating gaze.

"Do you have business with him or are you simply curious?" A smirk flashed in her faded eyes.

"I . . . You see, I'm a journalist. I'm writing an article about what happened to the self-taught poets who were once published in our magazine." Lena said the first thing that popped into her head.

"You're saying Vasily's a poet?" The old woman burst out in quiet, creaking laughter, but her eyes were still grave.

"Yes." Lena nodded. "He wrote interesting poems."

"Raisa!" a voice was heard from the next room. "Your potato's getting cold."

"Will you have supper with us?" her hostess asked.

"Thank you."

Lena was dismayed. There's no way she could say they were glad she'd come, but they were inviting her to supper. She'd spent time with so many people—hundreds of people of every kind. But never had she felt so awkward with anyone as with this old woman, who seemed to see through everything with her cold, faded blue eyes and knew Lena was lying about the article.

Lena heard shuffling, and the one who'd called herself her sister came in. Silently setting a large enamel bowl covered in a linen towel on the table, she went out and returned a minute later with plates and forks. She set the table silently. Besides the potatoes, there were pickles, bread, and sauerkraut.

"Why aren't you eating?" Raisa Danilovna asked. "Don't be afraid. Eat first, and then I'll tell you everything you need to know."

"Thank you." Lena smiled and started mashing the steaming potato with her fork.

"Have a pickle, they're homemade," the sister's voice chimed in.

"I'm sorry, what's your name?" Lena asked her.

"Zoya Danilovna," she introduced herself and smiled.

It was a warm, lively smile. Lena felt a little more at ease. The pickles were delicious, and the sauerkraut with cranberries crunched delightfully between her teeth. A few minutes later, Lena felt totally comfortable, even cozy, although her hostess hadn't taken her strange eyes off her.

Then they had tea with a little mint and lemon. Only after the second mug did Raisa Danilovna say, "You're looking for the murderer. I knew someone would come sooner or later to look for the real murderer. Not the police, but someone like you. Only you have to know. There was one other person who tried to prove that my dear departed husband Nikita, God rest his soul"—the old woman turned to face the icon and crossed herself three times—"that my Nikita was innocent. Just one person, and they killed him. He was from Tobolsk himself, and he worked for the police. God rest his soul, too"—and she crossed herself three times again.

"First Lieutenant Zakharov," Lena said quietly.

"Correct." The old woman nodded. "Zakharov. There was a whole team working there, from Tobolsk, and Khanty, and here in Tyumen. Ten men in all. They arrested my Nikita trying to sell some jewelry near a shop. He'd found it in the pocket of his quilted vest. It wasn't enough for a bottle, so he went to sell it. That was where they picked him up. That summer he'd found some work in Tobolsk, so he'd gone to stay with his brother-in-law there. The last murder was in Tobolsk."

"In June of '82?" Lena asked.

"Yes, in June, right before Whitsunday."

"Tell me, Raisa Danilovna, besides the jewelry and the fact that your husband was in Tobolsk in June, what other evidence was there?"

"The blood matched."

"The blood type?" Lena clarified. "Your husband's blood type was the same as the murderer's?"

"Yes. And also they found a sweater here behind the stove. Someone else's sweater. It was light colored. There were blood spots on it that had been washed off but not completely. Their analysis showed it was the murdered girl's blood. And there was a knife wrapped up in the sweater, a small one, with a plastic handle. They said it was the murder weapon."

"Raisa Danilovna"—Lena felt a nasty chill in her stomach—"I realize many years have passed. But you wouldn't happen to remember what the sweater looked like, would you?"

"Light-colored wool, but not bleached white. The usual kind of collar, with elastic. And a simple pattern, little diamonds, I think."

"Knit by hand or machine?"

"By hand. The Khakaskas who come from Abakan used to sell sweaters like that at the market."

"Had any strangers, people you didn't know, been in your home before they arrested your husband?" Lena asked.

"A woman came and brought money. She said she was from the Committee of Soviet Women. She was delivering aid for prisoners' mothers for the New Year. Fifty rubles. She gave me a receipt to sign."

"You remember that precisely? It's been so many years," Lena said, surprised.

"That's why I remembered, because there'd never been such a thing. I'd never heard a word about there being any committee like that. I asked my neighbor, Varvara Strogova. Her son Andrei was in prison then, too. But no one came to see her or gave her any money. I thought I was the only one to have such luck—in those days, fifty rubles was a lot. I went to church, too, and lit a candle for that committee and sent Vasily a New Year's package with the money. And the woman was memorable, very scary looking."

"What do you mean, scary looking? Ugly?"

"Ugly is too kind. I even thought how awful it would be for a woman to be born with a face like that. More freak than woman. But well educated and polite and very well dressed. And it was a proper receipt, with a seal."

"Did you tell the investigator about her?"

"What do you think? In great detail! At the time they said, 'Oh, you're lying, Raisa Danilovna.' 'We feel sorry for you,' they said. 'Not only is your only son in prison, but now your husband is, too. But if you're going to lie, you'll go to prison yourself.' No one believed me. One evening later, Zakharov came and started questioning me in detail about the woman. He wrote it all down. A week later he went home to Tobolsk only to get his throat slit there. That's a mother's true grief! He was a fine man."

"Forgive me, Raisa Danilovna, but did your husband drink a lot? Was he enrolled at a rehab clinic for alcoholics and drug addicts?"

"Drug rehab and psych. All kinds. He won't be remembered fondly for the way he drank. He could be brutal. And he was always hungover and angry."

Lena's head started spinning. She forgot about time. Only when Raisa Danilovna had told her everything she could did Lena glance at her watch. Ten forty-five! Sasha had probably gone. She was going to have to find her way back to the hotel herself.

"Since you're here, please give me a hand," Zoya Danilovna asked. "Raya's legs are paralyzed, so I have to move Raya to her bed. Usually I do it myself, but since you're here . . ."

"Yes, of course." Lena stood up.

"Here, take her on the right, like this, under her knees. Raisa, put your arm around her neck. That's the way. And mine with the other hand. All right, lift!"

Even together, moving someone whose legs are paralyzed from chair to bed is very hard.

"How do you manage alone?" Lena quietly asked as Zoya Danilovna saw her to the front door.

"I'm used to it." The old woman shrugged. "Now it's better. At least her arms are working."

"Has this gone on long?"

"Eleven years. When she found out they'd executed . . . that Nikita was gone, she collapsed on the floor. And never got up again."

"Tell me, Zoya Danilovna, how could she know why I'd come?"

"She tells everyone the same thing. Whoever comes—from social security, or the clinic, or the post office, or the savings bank—she focuses her little eyes on them and after a few words asks, 'Are you looking for the real murderer?' Some get scared off, especially the young girls. The doctor says she suffers from mania. And it turns out she was right. Are you truly looking for the murderer? Perhaps you're from the police?"

"No." Lena shook her head. "Not from the police. I really am a journalist."

"Yes, I understand." The old woman pursed her lips. "Don't say if you don't want. I won't try to get it out of you."

Lena had already laced up her boots and put on her jacket.

"Zoya Danilovna, where is Vasily?" she asked. "How is he doing?"

"Not too badly, I guess," the woman began very quietly and brought her dry face closer to Lena. "He sends money regularly, good money. That's what we live on. It's enough for food and medicine. The last time he showed up was a couple of years ago. He was well dressed. He'd grown up and was as strong as an ox. You'd never recognize him! He didn't tell us anything about himself. He spent the night and brought his mother a wheelchair, a collapsible one, so nice and light. He brought a fluffy shawl, too, and two warm dresses, and a coat for me—expensive, with a fur collar. It's a pity to wear it, so it's still hanging up. And he left a lot of money. If Vasya happens to turn up, should I tell him about you?"

"You can tell him"—Lena nodded—"but please, no one else."

"Yes, that's understandable." The old woman pursed her dry lips significantly. "Raisa and I aren't going to blab. Not that we have anyone to blab to. God willing, Vasya will come visit. I don't have children of my own. He's all Raya and I have. One son for two. Are your parents alive?"

"No."

"An orphan then?"

"I have a husband and a two-year-old daughter."

"Who did you leave your daughter with?"

"My neighbor."

"You're like a child yourself, so skinny, and such a slender little face. How old are you?"

"Thirty-six."

"You don't say." Zoya Danilovna shook her head. "I'd never have guessed. You look like a little girl. Isn't it scary looking for a murderer?"

"It is." Lena smiled. "Very scary. But if I don't find him, it will be even scarier."

Am I really looking for a murderer? Lena asked herself as she walked out the gate into the snow-covered yard. *Yes, I am. And I'm scared.*

There were no streetlamps on. The street was deserted. Lena looked around, hoping to see Sasha's car. She didn't even remember which direction to go. She was just about to return to the house and ask Zoya Danilovna the best way back to the city center, when she heard a light honk. Headlights flashed. Sasha was waiting for her, his Moskvich parked in a narrow alley between tenements. Lena rejoiced as if she were seeing a member of her family.

"She went to see Slepak's mother."

"Who?"

"Vasily Slepak's mother. She spent three hours there."

"And then?"

"Then I took her to the hotel."

"What did you talk about on the way?"

"She asked me whether I happened to know where the psychiatric clinic for the Malaya Proletarskaya district was. I promised to drop her off there first thing tomorrow morning."

"Did you ask why?"

"Of course! She had an explanation for everything. She said she'd recently translated an article about serial killers by an American psychologist for her magazine. She'd taken a tremendous interest in the subject. She wanted to write something herself. And here in Tyumen Province, she said, in the early eighties, there was a serial killer who targeted young girls. So she wants to go to the clinic to do some additional background research and collect local color for her article."

"You've given me quite a surprise. Quite. What about tails?"

"Don't think so. But that's all ahead of us. It's going to get dangerous for her if she keeps this up. Curious people aren't very popular here."

"What do you think about it?"

"It's too soon to think anything. You should look through everything there is, not just on Slepak but on his father, too, through your own channels. And I'll work mine. Just in case."

"The older Slepak was that maniac they used to call Stealth Nikita. He was executed eleven years ago."

"That's quite a memory you have!"

"I'm not complaining. But I'll stop by the archives. Just in case. Is that all you have for now?"

"I think so."

"Think or know?"

"You see, Slepak's mother had a heart attack eleven years ago. Her legs are paralyzed and her mind's not all there. There's another old woman there, with her, her sister. But you can't squeeze a word out of her. They say the old woman's not in her right mind. So, here's what I'm wondering: what was your Polyanskaya discussing for three hours with two crazy old ladies? How did she even find the address? She's an interesting woman."

"Yes, more interesting than I'd expected."

"Maybe I should tell her who I am?"

"I wouldn't be surprised if she tells you."

"What now?"

"Keep driving. Don't take your eyes off her."

"So should I tell her or not?"

"Let's see how things fall out. If necessary, you can say hi for me. Until then, watch her closely, and report to me daily."

Major Ievlev hung up and stared at his office wall. This was a turn of events he'd never expected! The night before Polyanskaya's flight out, he'd contacted the Federal Security's Tyumen office and asked them to keep an eye on her and the American, just in case. He was a cautious and conscientious person and couldn't have it on his conscience if suddenly, contrary to expectations, something happened to the Interior Ministry colonel's wife.

Lena Polyanskaya had turned out to be anything but frivolous. This wasn't just about love and jealousy. It was all much more serious. Judging from what his Tyumen tail had reported, Polyanskaya had decided to open her own private investigation. Which could be tangentially connected to Volkov and Gradskaya. Perhaps love and jealousy were just a cover. He wondered which of the three was the lead player. Gradskaya, Volkov, or Polyanskaya? Or were they playing this game—whatever it was—as equals?

Ievlev knew that Veniamin Volkov was born and raised in Tobolsk. His wife, Regina Gradskaya, was born there as well. He also knew that in June 1982, Polyanskaya and her friend Olga Sinitsyna and her brother Mitya, the same one who recently hanged himself, had been there, too. Polyanskaya had told him about Sinitsyn. She'd gently pushed her own theory of why someone had planted a bomb in her stroller, but at the time he'd thought it was ridiculous, that she was making things up, connecting disparate events that didn't have the least relation to each other.

She kept hinting, and he kept not taking the bait. Probably no one else had, either. So she'd taken matters into her own hands.

I have to go there, Ievlev reflected. *I have to look at the older Slepak's file.* He decided to fly to Tyumen the next evening.

CHAPTER 30

Lena opened her hotel room window and lit a cigarette. She was thinking about what she'd say tomorrow morning at the district psychiatric clinic. Would anyone even speak to her? Was there any point in going?

Suppose someone had looked through the patient charts in November and December of 1982. They were sure to indicate blood type. Would the murderer himself have looked at the charts? Hardly. That would be too risky. In any case, he had to have had friends in that clinic or else he knew someone who had official access. Who could have official access? Someone in the police or prosecutor's office, or a psychiatrist from another district or town. They didn't let just anyone in, after all. Of course, an outsider could make something up to get access, but then he risked being remembered and exposed. No, the murderer wouldn't do something like that.

A woman had gone to see the Slepaks. Suppose she was the one who'd stuck the light-colored, hand-knit sweater behind the stove. Then it was perfectly logical that she'd had access to the files. Volkov's wife was a psychiatrist. No, that didn't fit. Raisa Danilovna had said the woman was "scary looking." Regina Gradskaya was beautiful. Had she altered her appearance when she'd visited Raisa Danilovna? Yes, that was a logical possibility. A woman can change a lot about her appearance. But she doesn't make herself so ugly that that would be the main feature to stick in someone's memory.

Fine, let's leave Volkov and Gradskaya out of it for now so we don't get mixed up. Let's say we have an equation with two unknowns. X and Y. A man and a woman. So, woman Y was murderer X's accomplice. She helped him frame the older Slepak and planted evidence. After they arrested Slepak, the murders stopped. Did he stop killing? How? Why? Did she cure him or something?

Lena suddenly remembered that the psychologist had written in his article that some sexual psychopaths could be treated with hypnosis, that those patients were highly suggestible, and instances were known when hypnosis and psychotherapy made them completely well. If the illness wasn't connected with deeper pathologies, like schizophrenia, then there was hope. Hope doesn't help anyone, though. And serial killers don't get treatment. Society gets rid of them. And rightly so, probably.

Lena had a poor grasp of psychiatry and regretted not bringing a copy of the article or at least a printout of her translation. Not that one article covered everything. She needed to talk to a professional. But where was she going to find one? Not at the local clinic! She should at least read a psychiatry textbook of some kind.

It had turned cold. Lena shut the window and put on her jacket. But she was shivering anyway. She remembered that Mitya had been reading a psychiatry textbook. Which meant he had been following the same line of thinking. And how had that ended?

Lena picked up her enamel mug, poured out the coffee dregs, and washed the mug and immersion heater. She needed some tea to warm up. She thought she had packed a Pickwick herbal teabag. She'd put it in at the last moment, not at the bottom with the coffee and sugar, but in a side pocket.

Squatting in front of her bag, Lena discovered that the side pocket was unzipped. She specifically remembered she hadn't gone in there that day. The zipper to the main compartment, on the other hand, she'd left open. And now it was closed.

The Pickwick was where it was supposed to be. Lena opened the bag. Now she had no doubt that someone had been rummaging through her things. Rummaging neatly, tactically even. But whoever had done it had made mistakes: they'd mixed up the zipped and unzipped zippers, they hadn't bothered to put her nightshirt and other underwear back in their separate plastic bag, and they folded her sweater and wool skirt much more neatly than Lena herself had in her haste.

Maybe the maid? But they get fired for that. And the room hasn't been cleaned.

After going through her things, Lena discovered everything intact, and nothing had gone missing. She'd just been searched. What for? This didn't look like a continuation of what had been happening to her in Moscow. This was something new.

Please let it be that sweet, talkative Sasha really is from the Federal Security Service and not something else. What if Misha was more worried than I thought and decided to watch over me while I'm here? No, he would have warned me. And Sasha would have behaved differently. Did Major Ievlev order him to drive me? I hope to God he did.

Misha Sichkin was in mourning. He'd just learned of the untimely death of his two suspects, Andrei Likhanov, born 1967, and Ruslan Kabaretdinov, born 1970. Both had been neatly strangled in the night.

Shovel and Claw had been killed in prison. Naturally, none of their cellmates saw or heard a thing.

That bitch! Misha thought as he paced around his office and puffed at his seventh cigarette of the morning. *She's clever, I'll give her that. She didn't touch Pasha. Someone had to hang for Azarov, so she couldn't get along without Pasha. That was a brilliant move.*

Misha couldn't concentrate. He was angry and nervous. It was beyond his abilities to figure out who could have copied the recording of Sevastyanov's interrogation and gotten it to Gradskaya. But from the very beginning he should have thought of that. Should have, but didn't.

The telephone rang so unexpectedly that Misha startled.

"It's Ievlev," he heard when he picked up the receiver. "We need to talk."

"We do," Misha echoed. "And better in the fresh air."

Half an hour later they were sitting on a bench at the back of the Hermitage garden. It was a clear morning. Sparrows were chirping and hopping around a soggy crust of bread. Young mothers, slowly pushing strollers down the still-wet paths, were raising their faces to the warm sun.

"I'm flying to Tyumen tonight," Ievlev informed him as he watched a mangy crow make off with the crust the dozen sparrows had been arguing over. "Your boss's wife has decided to open her own investigation. I think it's time to let him know. Something might go wrong and your colonel could wind up a widower with a babe in arms."

"You must be joking." Misha shook his head.

"I couldn't be more serious." Ievlev lit a cigarette and leaned back on the bench. "I think it's time we shared information. Honestly and frankly."

"As of this morning, my information isn't worth a brass tack. During the night my two suspects were killed in their cells. Their good neighbors strangled them with their bare hands. And now I'm like a dog. I understand everything, only I can't tell anyone. I know Gradskaya's behind it. All I had left was to put some pressure on those two thugs to get the evidence I need."

"And the motive?" Ievlev asked quickly.

"The motive," Misha repeated pensively. "There are lots of clues, but not even a glimmer of a motive."

"That's what your boss's wife is in Siberia for."

"Are you joking again? Or mocking me?"

"Listen, Major, I understand you're trying to regroup after losing your only good lead." Ievlev put out his cigarette on his boot's rippled sole and threw the butt straight into the bin by the next bench. "But you have to remember, Polyanskaya probably did share her thoughts with you. At first I thought she was dwelling on the Sinitsyns' deaths out of an excess of emotions."

"Did you come here by car?" Misha asked.

"Yes. What of it?"

"Let's go. I'll tell you on the way. Only we have to call first. Do you have a phone in your car?"

"I'm not a Gradskaya or a Volkov." Ievlev stood up and started digging in his pockets. "Here's a token. Call from a payphone like an ordinary Soviet man. So where are we going?"

"First to a Japanese firm, and then to my boss's apartment."

"Got it." Ievlev nodded.

For a long time they didn't want to call Olga Sinitsyna to the phone. The secretary politely explained in a delicate voice that Olga Mikhailovna was in a meeting.

"Tell her it's Sichkin from the Interior Ministry," Misha insisted.

"The Interior Ministry?" The delicate voice sounded astonished. "Couldn't you call back in half an hour?"

"I could and did."

"Well, all right," the secretary conceded. "One minute." He heard a soft melody and a minute later a woman's low voice.

"This is Sinitsyna."

"Olga Mikhailovna, hello. My name is Sichkin. I—"

"Hello. Lena told me you'd be calling," Olga interrupted. "I have a key. When will you be here?"

"Right away."

"Do you know the company address?"

Misha repeated it. Olga explained the best way to get there.

On the way, the two majors continued to share information and learned much from each other that was new and interesting.

"So you were never able to figure out who the guy was that Gradskaya met on the boulevard?" Misha asked when they'd driven up to Kokusai Koeki.

"Ex-military." Ievlev grinned. "I could tell from his bearing."

"That makes sense," said Sichkin. "All the guards at the Butyrka Prison are ex-military."

Olga Sinitsyna bore a striking resemblance to her dead brother. Looking at the tall, beautiful blonde, Misha suddenly pictured Mitya Sinitsyn, just as blond and blue-eyed, with the same broad, joyous smile.

"Go into Windows and you'll find a file called 'Rabbit.' Write it down or will you remember?"

"We'll remember. Rabbit, in English."

As they were walking to the car, the young secretary caught up with them and said in her delicate voice, "Olga Mikhailovna asked if you would water the cacti."

"Yes. Tell Olga Mikhailovna not to worry. We'll be sure to water the cacti."

Entering the empty apartment, Misha first lifted the telephone receiver and dialed the duty officer, to verify whether the alarm he had installed had gone off.

"They never turned it on, Major," the duty officer reported.

"What a muddlehead," Misha cursed Lena.

Besides Mitya's texts, Lena had also entered both letters in the "Rabbit" file—from Slepak and from First Lieutenant Zakharov's mother. Ievlev actually whistled.

"Slepak wrote poetry! Who would have thought!"

Misha turned on Lena's little inkjet printer and printed out everything in the file in triplicate.

"I wish she'd left a note." Misha shook his head. "What does this Zakharov have to do with this? I don't see the connection. Other than time and place. But Slepak lived in Tyumen and they tried him there. And judging from the address, this Zakharov was from Tobolsk."

"They must have had a large combined operation going there," Ievlev said thoughtfully. "There were murders in a few towns. Including Tobolsk. So the team was big. And Zakharov could well have been a part of it. One last thing, where are the cacti?"

It was nearly dawn before Lena fell asleep. She dreamed of Liza and Seryozha. Her dream was so vivid and happy, she didn't want to wake up. Liza was playing with a huge yellow ball on a sun-drenched beach. Seryozha was walking out of the sea, tanned and smiling. He scooped up Liza and sat her on his shoulders. "Papa, my ball!" Liza shouted. The ball was rolling swiftly and ringing so loudly that Lena opened her eyes.

The telephone on the bedside table was about to explode.

"Lena, you took so long to pick up, I got scared." She heard Michael's voice. "Did I wake you?"

"No. All's well. Good morning." She glanced at the clock. It was ten.

"Well, all's not well with me. I was getting ready for my run and I went into my bag for my sneakers only to discover someone had rummaged through my bag."

The remnants of sleep vanished as if by magic. Lena sat up abruptly on the bed.

"Is anything missing?" she asked.

"Nothing but my talcum powder. They must have gone through it yesterday, while we were riding around town. But I didn't check the bag last night. I got out everything I needed in the afternoon. But today I went for my sneakers, which had been on the bottom, and they were right on top. It's a good thing I took my wallet with me yesterday."

"Wait, did you say you're missing your talcum powder?"

"Yes. Lightstar English Talcum. A big tin can, like in the old days. I've been using that brand for years. We have to tell the administrator."

"Absolutely. Someone rummaged through my bag, too. But nothing's missing. Nothing at all. I'll get washed quickly and we'll go downstairs."

"I guess I won't be running today."

Before going downstairs, Lena dialed Sasha's number. He picked up immediately.

"What's missing? A can of talcum powder?" he asked after listening to Lena. "Talcum is that white powder people sprinkle on their feet and armpits, right?"

"Exactly. A fine white powder."

"Got it. Okay, you go down to the administrator and I'll be there in half an hour."

The administrator, a plump young woman in a formal suit, refused to acknowledge their complaints.

"This is the first complaint like this we've ever had," she said. "And nothing's missing. I'd understand if it were money or valuables. But the hotel rules are written out in black and white: the administration bears no responsibility for valuables left in rooms. It's in Russian and English. And a can of talcum isn't much of a valuable. Basically, your things were already unpacked. What grounds do you have for a complaint?"

Sasha walked into the lobby. For some reason the administrator immediately stopped talking.

"Ask her where the director's office is," Michael said irritably. "I have no intention of leaving it like this. A can of talcum only costs fifteen dollars, but I don't like staying in a hotel where people rummage through my things. I've traveled to more than twenty countries. Nothing like this has ever happened."

Lena interpreted. The administrator looked at her with eyes full of hate.

"Tell your foreign friend that he has no proof," she hissed through her teeth. "The director's office is the third door on the left, down the hall. But he won't be in until the afternoon."

"Fine." Lena nodded. "We'll stop by then. But we will stop by. We haven't made anything up. Why would we? You'll agree, though, it's not nice when someone goes rummaging in your things."

"I appreciate what you're saying," the administrator softened a little. "But if you or he had lost something valuable, we would have checked the maids on your floor and spoken with the women on duty. But over a tin of talcum . . . I don't understand!"

"We'll be out all day again today." Michael would not relent. "Where is the guarantee that this won't happen again?"

"I will personally keep an eye on the maids making up your room," the administrator promised.

"Thank you, of course. But I seriously doubt it was the maids. Where can we get breakfast?"

Lena couldn't stand conflicts with peroxide-blond lady administrators. It was simpler to keep quiet than to yell. For them, arguments like this came with the job. They yelled with skill and pleasure. And nearly always won.

If it hadn't been for Michael, Lena wouldn't have gone to the administrator at all. She knew how the conversation would end.

"The buffets on the third and seventh floors are open now," the lady replied, and she turned away, making it clear that the conversation was over.

"Sasha," Lena called to the driver, who had been sitting in an armchair, leafing through magazines. "Are you having breakfast with us?"

He nodded and stood up. "With pleasure."

The second-floor buffet was deserted. Sasha took a big ham omelet and sausage with peas. Lena and Michael each had a vegetable salad and a portion of sour cream.

"Now we can go to my room for coffee," Lena said. "It's going to be the usual weak slop here."

"What about the clinic?" Sasha asked quietly, sending half of a sausage into his mouth at once.

"You know, I was thinking, no one there is going to talk to me. I'll show them my press credentials and ID and they'll throw me out. People don't much like journalists these days. If I were from Federal Security or the Interior Ministry, that would be a different conversation."

"Do you really need to do this?" Sasha smiled.

"What do you mean?"

"Well, that killer who terrorized these parts in the early eighties, was he something special in some way? Right now there are already so many articles and books about maniacs. What makes your killer so much more interesting than Chikatilo and Golovkin?"

"So there's no point writing about him? There are movies, too. But barely anyone knows about this Siberian serial killer. And what disturbs me isn't him per se but his psychology and his fate. You know, they execute anyone judged sane. But how can a sane man rape and kill six girls ages fifteen to eighteen?"

"You don't think they should have executed him?" Sasha carefully wiped his plate with a crust of bread and put the crust in his mouth. "Or do you think they executed the wrong man?" he added quietly.

"I think," Lena replied just as quietly, "they should figure out who rummaged through our bags yesterday and why."

"You promised us coffee in your room," Sasha reminded her, looking into her eyes.

"Yes." Lena nodded, standing. "Let's go. I have Pickwick herbal for you," she said to Michael in English. "You don't drink coffee in the morning, after all."

She had to make the coffee three times. Sasha drank it by the glassful, and to each glass he also added two cubes of sugar.

"You're not worried about your heart?" Lena asked, sipping her small cup.

"Well, I'm not going to drink out of a thimble like that!" Sasha grinned. "Anyway, your coffee is amazing, and I have no complaints about my heart for now. So how about the clinic?"

"Nothing's going to come of it today anyway. Michael has big plans. He wants to cram the local history museum and a couple of villages into one day. By the way, do you know whether there are still Old Believers living in Zagorinskaya?"

"Yes, there are. But it's more than a hundred kilometers to Zagorinskaya. Ninety minutes there, ninety minutes back. That's three hours just on travel. And it's nearly noon. So we'll have to put off the museum until tomorrow."

Lena interpreted this information for Michael.

"Okay. We'll put off the museum. If I get to talk to genuine Old Believers, I'll be so happy I'll forget about my English talcum."

"Tell him Old Believers generally won't talk. They live a very insular life," Sasha reminded her.

"Michael can talk to anyone." Lena smiled. "Even a deaf-mute, even through an interpreter. When I work with him, the people he's talking to forget all about me pretty fast. They think they're talking to him directly. Michael's a kind of communications genius."

"Well, let's see how he manages with our schismatics."

After coffee, Lena and Sasha had a cigarette.

"I'm going to my room to get dressed," Michael announced.

"I'll wash up as well," Lena said. "It's time to go."

In the bathroom she remembered she'd left the immersion heater on the table. That had to be washed as well. When she went back to the room, Sasha was sitting on the bedside table unscrewing the phone. Glancing at her, he winked through his glasses and shook his head expressively. Without saying a word, Lena picked up the immersion heater and returned to the bathroom.

CHAPTER 31

"Idiot! Jerk!" These were the mildest of the expressions the chubby little man, who was as bald as a billiard ball, directed at his underling, who was standing in the center of the room, eyes down.

The bald man was lying in just his underpants on a trestle bed made up with a white sheet. A strong, shapely beauty in a flirty, light silk robe was gently and powerfully kneading his hairy haunches.

"Well, you know, I thought for sure it was cocaine or something," the rather hefty man jabbered, standing barefoot on the massage room's thick carpet.

"You thought!" The bald shrimp sat up abruptly. "Did I tell you to think? Answer me! What were you told?"

"Drive them around a little"—he drew his head into his shoulders as he spoke, making himself smaller—"and plant a bug."

"Correct," the bald man nodded. "Drive. And what did you do? Why did you go shake down their rooms?"

"Well . . . I wanted to do my best . . . Listen, Curly, maybe, uh, well, I can put the hokum back?"

"Christ!" The bald man rolled his eyes. "Cocaine! It's talcum powder. Talcum powder. It's written right there on the tin."

"Not our letters. How am I supposed to read that? I saw white powder and decided, you know, I should check it out, for sure."

"Listen, are you really such an idiot? Or are you just acting like one?" Curly sighed.

The big man didn't know what to say. He honestly didn't understand what he'd done wrong. The things in the hotel rooms of the old American and his interpreter were just begging to taken. The bags were wide open, and he put everything back neatly. If he'd gone into the rooms to plant bugs, then why not give their things a quick look at the same time? It's not like he made off with the white powder. He brought it to Curly. How was he supposed to know it was crap for keeping your armpits dry?

"Okay." Curly gave up. "Go take the day off."

Curly lay back down with a sigh, and the silent and beautiful masseuse went back to work.

"There, Nina, you see what I have to work with?" Curly complained. "You can't teach guys like that anything. It's this new generation, damn them. They're getting stupider and stupider these days. Stupider and more degenerate. Money decides everything. There is no honor among thieves. Not like before."

Nina scooped a little cream from an open jar, spread it on her palms, and started kneading Curly's shoulders. Shoulders tattooed with a general's epaulets.

"And I don't have anyone to consult with," Curly went on. "There's no one, not a soul I can trust. All the money I spend on stooges, and I barely use them. But just try to stop feeding them, the deadbeats. Oh, Nina," he sighed. "I don't know what I'm going to do about this professor. And the girl, the interpreter. She's not what she appears to be. She visited those two old ladies, had supper with them, and drank tea and chatted with them for three hours. That's where we should have planted the bug. But who knew? This is a real puzzle, Nina. I'd better not mess this up. What do you think? What should I do?"

Nina was pummeling his back. Her soft, round face expressed nothing but peaceful concentration. Her full lips were slightly parted. Curly turned his head and met her kind, devoted look. The young woman's eyes were a heavenly blue and amazingly bright and pure.

Just then, his cell phone, lying next to the bed, rang. Curly felt around on the floor and grabbed the phone.

"They removed the bug," the man on the other end of the phone reported briefly.

"Who?" Curly exhaled.

"Either four-eyes or the girl."

"Where are they?"

"They went to Zagorinskaya, to see Old Believers, they said. Maybe it's bullshit? At first they were talking, and then they removed the bug. Maybe they're bluffing?"

"Double-check. Did you fit four-eyes up with a ride?"

"Not so far."

"All right, keep watching them. But don't get caught. Is someone posted near the old ladies?"

"I've got two men there."

"Add a third. And also, tell Cooper to pick out the best working girl he can find, and make sure she speaks English. The best, understand?"

"Major Ievlev says hello," Sasha had quickly whispered that morning when they'd left the hotel and were outside in the fresh air. "We can't discuss anything in the car. We'll talk afterward. Don't worry about the tails."

"Are there many?" Lena asked in the same whisper.

"We'll count en route."

"Maybe we should change routes?" Lena suggested.

"Under no circumstance."

"Why?"

"Because this way it will be easier to count the tails. And anyway, there's no point spoiling your friend's plans."

It had been six hours since this quick conversation. In that time, she and Sasha hadn't had a chance to speak again. But they'd counted the tails. Actually, there was just one tandem tail, two young guys in a gray Niva.

They ate dinner in the small cooperative café on the edge of the village. They didn't have anything vegetarian for Michael besides cabbage salad and roast potatoes. The flattened grilled chicken Lena ordered was a tough old bird. Their tail, the two young men, took off their coats and sat at the next table, which did nothing to improve her appetite. Sasha ate his huge serving of dumplings with pleasure, though, and wiped his plate clean with a crust of bread.

Michael dozed on the way back. *Something's wrong here,* Lena thought. *Why all this attention? I just went to see Vasily Slepak's mother. But they searched our rooms and planted an eavesdropping device. They could have mistaken the talcum powder for drugs. I need to tell Sasha to check Michael's room. They may have planted something there, too. Why did they rummage around in our things anyway? And these guys in the Niva are nowhere near as discreet. They're watching us openly.*

"There may not have been anything in the car," Sasha said when they arrived at last. "Can you hold out another half hour?"

"In what sense?" Lena said, surprised.

"In the sense that I wouldn't refuse a cup of your brilliant coffee."

"Do you think we can talk openly in my room now? What if there's another bug there?"

"No." Sasha smiled. "Now there definitely isn't. While we were out today, I had every centimeter of your room searched by professionals."

"When did you have time to tell them?"

"This isn't my first job." Sasha chuckled.

Behind the hotel counter sat a different administrator. She gave them their keys and said a polite hello.

"We never went to see the director!" Michael remembered.

"But we're leaving tomorrow anyway," Lena remarked.

"I understand. You'd rather avoid confrontation."

Michael grumbled a little longer, wished them all a good night, and went to his room.

"Listen, do you have anything to eat?" Sasha asked when they were alone. "I always get hungry at night."

"I think you get hungry in the daytime, too," Lena commented. "I hate to disappoint you, but all I have is tea, coffee, and sugar."

"Well, then treat me to some coffee. Here's what I want to tell you. Close down your private detective agency, Lena. It could end badly."

Lena unlaced her boots, slipped her feet into her slippers, and got comfortable in the armchair.

"What agency, Sasha?" she asked.

"Quit pretending. You don't have to play these games with me. I have no intention of signing on as your Dr. Watson."

"Sasha, I'm not pretending. Where did you get the idea I was playing at Sherlock Holmes?"

"Then why did you pay that visit to Malaya Proletarskaya?"

"Why do people pay visits in general? I was just visiting two helpless old women."

"And how do you know them, these little old ladies? How did you meet them?"

"What is this, an interrogation? Where's your warrant? And what's your rank anyway, soldier?"

"First Lieutenant Volkovets, Federal Security Service," Sasha introduced himself and took his identity card out of his pocket.

"Very nice to meet you." Lena chuckled and gave it a careful study.

"I have no intention of interrogating you." Sasha quickly put his card back in his pocket. "But I'm giving you a serious warning. Wind up your investigation."

"Maybe I should apologize to Michael and go back to Moscow? And you can assign him another interpreter."

"The right thing would be to send you both home," Sasha said pensively.

"On what basis?"

"On the basis that neither I, nor my department, nor anyone else can guarantee your safety here. We don't have the means here to supply you with an armed guard."

"And if I tell you that those women on Malaya Proletarskaya are just the mother and aunt of my old acquaintance Vasily Slepak? Would that reassure you or not?"

Sasha's glasses slid down to the tip of his nose. She actually felt sorry for him.

"Fine, then. Once upon a time, long, long ago, Vasya Slepak went to prison for a youthful transgression. Something bad happened to him there. He was sodomized. I met him when a group from my magazine performed at the prison. So I got one of his poems published. I wanted to give a little lift to this humiliated man. And I sent the magazine to his mama. Then Vasya and I corresponded for a while. And now that I was in Tyumen, I decided to visit Vasya's mama. Does that sound like a private investigation?"

It wasn't that Lena didn't trust this Security Service officer. She was just tired of retelling the same story, which accumulated more complicated and confusing details every day. She didn't want to see ridicule and a lack of understanding in a stranger's eyes yet again. She was sick and tired of trying to prove she wasn't crazy.

"Well, did you satisfy your curiosity? Did you find out how your old acquaintance is doing?" Sasha asked after a long pause.

"No. He hasn't been to see his old women for a long time. I should warn you that I'll be paying visits in Tobolsk, too. Since you're planning to go there with us."

"So who exactly do you plan to visit in Tobolsk?"

Lena grinned. "That is my problem. This hasn't the slightest thing to do with the room searches, the missing talcum powder, or our two young tails in the Niva."

Lena picked up the mug and headed for the bathroom to fill it with water for coffee. When she came back a minute later, Sasha was standing by the door.

"It's late," he said. "And I have a busy day tomorrow. During the day, I'll be driving you all over town. And in the evening we'll be going to Tobolsk. By the way, it would be simpler if we drove my car there instead of taking the train."

"All right." Lena nodded. "I'll talk it over with Michael. Good night."

Michael was very enthusiastic about going to Tobolsk in Sasha's car. The train took all night, whereas by highway it took three or four hours.

"But in the train we could at least get some sleep," Lena pointed out.

They'd been on their feet since morning. They'd been to the local history museum and the central library stacks, and they'd met with an ethnology professor from the local teachers college. Their tail followed them the whole time. Inwardly, Lena rejoiced that they couldn't possibly have enjoyed a single moment of that long, boring day.

"There, you see?" Lena grinned when they left town late that night. "I spent the whole day as an innocent interpreter. Nothing more. And you assured me this wasn't your first go-round."

"What are you talking about?" Sasha's eyebrows went up in perplexity.

"I'm talking about the fact that our tails haven't left us for a minute. Your people probably haven't figured out anything about them."

"How can we without your help? You're our chief investigator." He shook his head. "By the way, Ievlev's arriving tonight. And heading straight to Tobolsk. And then I'm handing you over to him. Let him deal with you."

"Listen, why are you so upset? All I did was visit the mother of a former criminal. It's really not such a big deal. By now he's probably an honest, law-abiding citizen, anyway."

Sasha didn't respond. He was staring into the gloom of the snow-drifted highway. They were winding alongside the railroad. Dense, limitless taiga stretched out on all sides.

CHAPTER 32

Moscow was cold again. March was already halfway over, but spring seemed to have changed its mind. By night, the sky had been swept clean, and bright stars were spilling out. Volkov was driving his old black Mercedes down the empty highway. Now he only used this car, alone, without a driver or bodyguard. Lately he'd felt a need for solitude. Sometimes he'd catch himself thinking aloud, talking to Lena, imagining her sitting beside him. Her slender silhouette was everywhere, her scent, the sound of her deep, low voice. He was counting the days until her return.

Now, after a long, hard day filled with meetings, negotiations, bad auditions, and cold, alien faces, he'd decided to spend the night not in his Moscow apartment, where Regina was waiting for him, but at their dacha in Peredelkino. He needed the peace and quiet, the last soft snow, and the clean, almost frosty air.

He was a little chilled, but he ignored it. He drove and delivered a long monologue under his breath to Lena.

What I've earned is enough for us for the rest of our lives. I have a small house in Greece, on Crete, right by the sea. We'll live there. And when your daughter is old enough, we'll send her to America or England to study. We'll grow old together. We won't be apart for a day, an hour, you'll be by my side always. You only think your husband loves you. Believe me, he'll find consolation quickly. And I can be a good father to your child. I already love Liza because she's a part of you. Today I transferred a sizable sum to a Swiss bank. That's our money. That's our future. I'll leave my wife the business. That's the main thing for her. She'll find consolation, too. You didn't want anyone to be hurt because of us. No one will be.

As he drove up, he didn't notice the light burning upstairs in Regina's office. As always, the guard was dozing in the booth. The cook came out to meet him with a smile.

"Regina Valentinovna said she was going to wait for you to have supper," she told him cheerfully.

He shuddered.

"Well," Regina said when she'd kissed his forehead. "You have a fever. You finally managed to pick up that horrible flu. Let's get you straight to bed. Lyudmila!" she shouted to the cook. "Make some tea with lemon and brew some linden."

"I thought you were in Moscow," he said thickly.

"I had a feeling you'd be coming here. Come, let's go. Let me put you to bed."

The thermometer read 102.2. Regina removed his boots, pulled off his trousers, and undid his tie.

"How could you drive with a temperature like that? Couldn't you have phoned? I would have sent a driver or come for you myself."

Only now did he feel how badly off he was. His chill had been replaced by a high fever. He'd broken out in a sweat, all his muscles ached, and his skin hurt. Even the thin sheet was unpleasant, rough against his skin.

Regina's hand brought a glass of a clear liquid full of tiny prickly bubbles to his lips. It was slightly sour.

"What is this?" he asked after obediently draining the glass.

"Soluble aspirin. Now your temperature will go down and you can try to sleep."

She left a small nightlight burning and quickly settled into the armchair beside the bed. When Lyudmila came in with a tray holding two steaming cups of tea and the linden infusion, Regina shook her head and put a finger to her lips. The cook retreated without a sound.

A few minutes later he fell asleep. In his sleep, his breathing was raspy and shallow. Beads of perspiration shone on his forehead, and his mouth hung open slightly. The last time he'd been this sick was four years ago, also with the flu. He'd been kept to his sickbed for a good ten days.

Well, Regina thought as she gazed at his pale, perspiring face. *Isn't this serendipitous! By the time he gets better, it will all be over. He won't be able to stop me. He won't have the strength.*

"Lena," she heard him whisper hoarsely. "Lena, my love . . . I feel so bad . . . this is our money . . . it's warm there in the winter and the sea is calm and clean . . . Help me . . ."

"Venya," Regina called softly. "Can you hear me?"

"We won't hurt anyone . . . no one, ever . . . They'll forgive us . . . The blood sank into the ground . . . that wasn't me, it was someone else, from another life . . . the taiga is so noisy . . . the sea . . . a very reliable bank . . ."

Regina rose from her chair, went over to the bed, and leaned over his pale face.

"Venya, I'm here. I love you," she said in a low, chesty voice, and she passed her hand over his closed eyes without touching them.

His eyelids quivered and slowly lifted. He looked at her with red, inflamed eyes and said, "Regina, stop it. I'm not asleep. Go to your room."

"I should sit with you."

"No. I don't need you. Go to your room."

"Fine." She nodded and put her hand on his forehead. "I think your fever's down. Shall we take it?"

He raised up on an elbow and looked her in the eye.

"Tell me, why did you have plastic surgery?"

"You'd think it happened yesterday, the way you're asking." She smiled. "Why bring this up now?"

"Your face was better before . . . It was dear to me."

"Venya, it was ugly."

"It was genuine. I loved it. Why did you do it?"

"No one could live with that face," Regina said softly.

"No one can live with a stranger's face, a doll's fake face." And he leaned back on the pillow and closed his eyes. "I'm sorry. I didn't mean to hurt you. Go to bed. It's late."

"Regina Valentinovna, should I call a doctor?" Lyudmila asked in a whisper when she ran into her in the living room.

"I'm a doctor." Regina smiled. "Put together something for my supper, please. I'm very hungry."

"Lighter or more substantial?" the cook asked pragmatically.

"Let's have something more substantial. Do we have meat?"

"Lean pork. I went to the market this afternoon."

"That's excellent. Make me a nice chop. And plenty of vegetables."

It was midnight. While waiting for supper, Regina lit a cigarette and picked up her cell phone.

"Hi, Grisha," she said after dialing. "I'm sorry it's so late. Did I wake you?"

"Knock it off, Regina!" Grisha responded in a cheerful falsetto.

"Listen, Venya's got the flu. A temperature of 102. Imagine, he went around all day doing what he had to do sick. Now he's lying here, sweaty and pale, and suffering, and saying he might have messed something up with the bank accounts. He can't remember anything and he's worried. He asked me to call you. Could you look first thing tomorrow and make sure everything is okay? He seems to have lost some contract or something. I didn't understand it myself. I'm an idiot in these matters. You'll check, though, all right?"

"Of course, Regina. I'll clear this up and call first thing tomorrow morning. Is his flu that bad?"

"I'm telling you. A temperature of 102. Aspirin's taken it down a little. You know what this nasty flu is like. You just had it yourself. By the way, how are you feeling?"

"Thank you for asking. I seem to be back on my feet."

"That's great. So I'll expect your call tomorrow morning. Kisses, Grisha. Say hello to Innochka for me."

She hung up and sat for a while, focusing on the flames dancing in the fireplace. When Lyudmila brought in her dinner tray, the phone rang.

"There's no peace for you, Regina Valentinovna." The cook shook her head. "Day or night. Why don't I answer and say to call you back? You should be able to eat in peace."

But the phone was already in Regina's hands.

"You were looking for me?" She heard a voice that made her heart leap for joy.

"Thank God," she sighed with relief.

"Is it that bad?" The man on the other end of the phone chuckled raspily. "You'd think I was your long-lost brother. Didn't we just see each other? All right, come to Sokolniki tomorrow at six thirty. The same pavilion. Remember?"

"Of course I do." Regina smiled into the phone.

The call significantly improved her appetite. She finished the tender, nicely browned chop in five minutes.

In Tobolsk they stayed in the same hotel Volkov had put her, Mitya, and Olga in fourteen years ago. The town was just as cozy as she remembered. Lena had liked it before, too, much more than Tyumen's pollution.

There were lots of old buildings left. Tobolsk's famous wooden citadel had been preserved, along with its exceedingly rich library, which contained many unique and ancient volumes. It had been fourteen years since she'd been there, but Lena couldn't forget that particular, soul-stirring smell of antique folios you find only in quiet, provincial libraries. For some reason, the books in big city libraries smell completely different. It wasn't even about their bibliographic value. As an elderly librarian had told her fourteen years ago, in the provinces time breathes differently, deeply and calmly.

Entering the stacks with Michael, Lena remembered that old librarian, small and withered, with short snow-white hair. Cold, she'd been wrapped up in a large, downy scarf. What was her name? Valentina Yurievna? Or not? So many years had passed, and theirs was a brief, chance episode.

Lena remembered the librarian not only because she'd let her and her young Muscovite companions into the library's rare manuscript archive, but because unlike many provincials, she didn't complain about her out-of-the-way existence. On the contrary, she sincerely believed she couldn't live anywhere else on earth but in the ancient wooden town of Tobolsk. She'd spent her entire conscious life among books. She hadn't ventured farther than Tyumen, though she knew France from Balzac and England from Dickens and assured Lena that she knew the world much better than most who'd had the chance to travel its length and breadth.

At the time she was over seventy. She could scarcely be alive now. Nonetheless, Lena decided to ask.

"Valya . . . Valentina Yurievna is alive," the oldest librarian there told her. "A year ago she had to move to the Veterans Home. She's ninety now and doesn't have any relatives to take her in. She's all alone in the world."

"Well, not all alone," the other librarian, a little younger, interjected. "She does have a daughter in Moscow. They say she's gone far."

"Yes, a daughter." The older woman nodded dolefully. "I've spoken with her on the telephone and by letter. She sends money to support her but hasn't visited once. The conditions at the Veterans Home are fine, of course. Valya has a separate room and we stop by sometimes. You should visit her if you have the time. She's so pleased when people come to see her."

"I doubt she remembers me." Lena shook her head. "So many years have passed."

"She'll remember. She has an excellent memory and an amazingly bright mind. And if she doesn't remember, it will still be nice for her."

"Good." Lena smiled. "Give me the address and I'll drop by."

"You can take your professor along. I don't think anyone knows the history of Tobolsk better than Valya. Not only that, she is fluent in English and French. It will be quite a treat for her to speak English with a professor from New York." The older librarian wrote the Veterans Home's address on a slip of paper and explained to Lena how to get there.

Later, unfolding the slip, Lena read: *Valentina Yurievna Gradskaya.* Lena paused. It wasn't only the last name that put her on her guard, but the name and patronymic as well. Valentina Yurievna was the name the fake doctor had given. But she immediately checked herself. It had to be a coincidence. Right?

Major Ievlev flew into Tyumen in the dead of night. He woke up at eight, did some quick exercises, rubbed himself down to the waist with ice-cold water—an old army habit—had a quick breakfast in the hotel buffet, and headed for the Provincial Prosecutor's Office. He sat in the archive the entire day, studying the thick files from a twelve-year-old criminal case.

Nikita Slepak was a model citizen compared with the serial killers of his day—Chikatilo, Golovkin, Mikhasevich, and Jumagaliev. He didn't do anything particularly horrible to his victims, didn't disembowel them, didn't dismember their corpses, didn't eat their organs, didn't hang them on a rack in a specially equipped cellar. His victims were all girls ages fifteen to eighteen. And there were six of them in all. Four of them were strangled with the killer's bare hands; two were killed with a precise knife blow to the heart. Each had been raped before being murdered, but not in an outlandish, disturbing way.

Slepak was given the title of serial killer with great reservation. His first victim had been eighteen-year-old Galina Kuskova, a resident of Tyumen. The fifth of many children in an underprivileged family, Galina had suffered from a mild form of mental retardation. After completing her special school, she had worked as a prostitute. Her place of residence was listed as the Moscow Restaurant, the most expensive and elegant hotel in town. The mental disabilities that prevented her from attending a normal school and working a traditional job by no means kept her from succeeding at the world's oldest profession.

Her body was discovered in September 1979, in a vacant lot near a construction site on the edge of town. The medical examiner determined that her death was the result of manual strangulation. Before her death, the victim had been in a state of severe alcoholic intoxication and had had sexual intercourse with a man. What was odd about the case was that the murderer hadn't taken her money or jewelry. When her body was discovered, the girl was wearing three expensive rings and a pair of sapphire earrings. Lying next to her was her purse, still fastened, which, besides holding her passport, also contained three hundred and seventy rubles—a considerable sum in those days.

Later it was discovered that a piece of jewelry Galina Kuskova never left the house without—a small gilded pendant in the form of a bell tower—had disappeared.

According to witness testimony, that evening Galina had been propositioned at the restaurant by Mustafa Saidov, a resident of Azerbaijan, and spent close to ninety minutes in his room at the Dawn Hotel. The doorman and administrator on duty said categorically that at 11:20 the young woman had left the hotel alone, alive and unharmed, albeit visibly drunk. She was never seen alive again.

The next victim was discovered seven months later, in April 1980, in Tobolsk. The body of fifteen-year-old Tobolsk high school student Marina Laricheva was found at an abandoned construction site. She, too, bore the marks of death by manual strangulation.

The night before, she'd visited the house of a girlfriend, whose parents were away, to celebrate her friend's birthday along with several of their friends. With no adult supervision, the vodka and port flowed and, according to complaints made by neighbors, the music wailed. At about midnight, after arguing with her boyfriend, a very drunk Marina left without saying a word.

Just as was the case with the body of Galina Kuskova, Marina was discovered with her expensive gold earrings still in her ears. The cheap nickel-silver bracelet she always wore on her right arm, however, had been taken.

Three months later another body was found, this time on the outskirts of Tyumen, in a wooded park not far from the city's summer camp, where older schoolchildren and vocational students went during vacation. Once again, toxicology reports showed that the victim, sixteen-year-old Irina Kozlova, had been intoxicated at the time of her murder.

Kozlova, a ward of the children's home, was learning the painting trade at the vocational school at the time of her death, but wasn't known for her exemplary conduct. She had already had several run-ins with the local police. Approximately two hours before her murder, she had been dancing at a nightclub. Then she got into a fight with two other intoxicated girls. The other two were giving her a beating, but

Irina managed to break free and run away. Marks from a beating were discovered on her body. As were the strangulation marks her killer left around her neck.

Of her numerous cheap adornments, only one was found to be missing—a silver seal ring that Irina wore on her pinky.

One of the girls who'd fought with her told investigators that she remembered seeing "some older blond guy, badly dressed and stinking drunk" standing by the fence outside the club. She even cadged a cigarette—a Pegasus—off him. Though he never spoke a word to her, she noticed a tattoo on his arm—maybe letters, maybe numbers, she didn't get a good look—when he lit her smoke.

The murder was never solved. That this murder might be related to the other two similar ones in the area never occurred to any of the investigators working the case.

Nine months later, in late May 1981, a fourth body was found in Tobolsk, at the same abandoned construction site where a year before the schoolgirl Marina Laricheva had been killed.

Eighteen-year-old Olga Fomicheva was in her second year at the Tobolsk teachers college. Unlike the three previous victims, she had not been drunk at the time of her death. She didn't drink, was an excellent student, and didn't frequent nightclubs. The rapist robbed her of her virginity and knifed her in the heart. The blow was so precise that there was almost no blood and death was likely instantaneous. The murder weapon was never found. Neither was anything else that could have helped investigators solve the crime. A hard rain fell all night, quickly washing away any clues from the ground and the dead girl's clothing. Her large, fake leather bag was found right next to her body. In it were her notebooks, a comb, a mirror, and a small purse with fifty-five rubles.

Olga wasn't wearing jewelry, cheap or expensive. The murderer had taken only her small Dawn watch.

Zakharov was the first to have the idea that all four murders had been committed by the same person. He went to Tyumen and studied the cases carefully. Based on his examination of all the case files, Zakharov created a profile of the killer. In his opinion, the murderer was extremely cautious, although he made no attempt to hide the corpses. He wasn't interested in money or valuables, but he took something—a souvenir—from each victim, which meant these murders had a ritual aspect for him. He was psychologically disturbed, but not a fool. He managed to leave almost no trace of his presence other than the sperm in the dead girls' bodies at the crime scenes. No witness had ever seen him. And this was no accident. He carefully prepared and thought through every crime.

The cases had been looked into by four different investigators. Zakharov was able to get ahold of the forensic reports, which said that the sperm discovered in the bodies of the four raped and murdered girls could belong to the same man. But they hadn't wanted to combine the two Tyumen and two Tobolsk murders into a single case.

In June 1982, a fifth body was found at a construction site in Tyumen. A classmate of Natasha Koloskova, the sixteen-year-old student at Vocational School No. 8 who'd been killed, stated she'd seen a tall, fair-haired man looming in the door during the graduation dance. The girl was raped and strangled. A piece of jewelry was missing—a cheap, heart-shaped enameled pendant with a red rose drawn inside.

She had a low blood alcohol level. During the dance, Natasha drank only half a glass of vodka. She left the dance alone and in a bad mood.

Just ten days later, in Tobolsk, deep in the city park, the body of yet another dead girl was discovered. Seventeen-year-old Angela Nasebulova, unemployed, had been raped and knifed in the heart. According to the forensic report, she was highly intoxicated at the time of her murder. Her blood showed high levels of drugs and alcohol. The murder weapon was never found.

It was not known whether any of the girl's jewelry had been taken. Nasebulova was an orphan, and she lived with her alcoholic aunt, who couldn't remember what kind of trinkets and jewelry Angela owned or wore. What was known was that the sperm found inside her body belonged to the same serial rapist and murderer that had killed the other five girls.

Major Ievlev was starving. He'd been poring over the case files since nine in the morning. And it was now half past one.

In the cafeteria at the Provincial Prosecutor's Office, a man of about thirty wearing jeans and a colorful patterned sweater sat down at his table. The man had a pleasant, round face with a bushy mustache.

"I hate digging around in old cases," he said with a smile.

Ievlev gave him a surprised look.

"Zhenya Kostikov. I'm an investigator in the Provincial Prosecutor's Office." He held out his hand. Ievlev shook it and introduced himself.

"In these parts for long?" his new friend inquired.

"Depends on how it goes," the major growled vaguely.

He didn't feel like socializing. He had some serious thinking to do, and he did that best over a meal. When he was a boy, his grandmother was constantly grumbling and taking away his book when he read at the table. For some reason, complicated episodes of history got learned more easily in the kitchen, over a bowl of soup than in his room at his desk.

The pickled cucumber soup in the cafeteria of the Tyumen Prosecutor's Office didn't compare with his grandmother's, but he thought pretty well over it, too. Investigator Kostikov was a perfectly nice guy, but his chatter kept Ievlev from concentrating.

They left the cafeteria together.

"I'm on my way to breathe dust, too," Kostikov told him, descending into the archive with Ievlev.

The major went back to his reading and soon after forgot about his chance acquaintance. He forgot about everything. Everything but the case.

In the files, he found three typewritten pages of a psychological portrait of the killer. This quasi-official document suggested that the girls had been killed and raped by a man aged forty to fifty with a midlevel technical education. Married, a drinker, psychologically unbalanced. Possibly registered at his local drug or psychiatric clinic. In his adolescence he probably had difficulties in relations with the opposite sex and may have suffered some serious setback or insult, which traumatized him so badly that it left a deep scar on his psyche. The document, which gave a name to the psychological illness of the killer—the so-called heboid syndrome—was authored by "R. V. Gradskaya. Medical student, Serbsky Institute of General and Forensic Psychiatry."

So, in November of 1982, Zakharov had gone to Moscow specifically for this document. For the psychiatrist Gradskaya to compose a psychological portrait of the criminal, she would have had to familiarize herself with the materials of the investigation.

In late December, police arrested Nikita Slepak, age forty-five. Slepak had a midlevel technical education, was married, an alcoholic, and was registered at the local drug and psychiatric clinics. On one of his benders, Slepak had tried to sell women's jewelry and a watch near a beer stall. He'd created a scandal, cutting the line and shoving the baubles under the stall owner's nose and attempting to pay for his beer with them. A duty cop happened to be walking by and responded to pleas for assistance from the stall owner.

Nikolai Ievlev looked at the photographs and the detailed descriptions of the items taken from N. V. Slepak at the time of his arrest. Here was the small gilt pendant in the shape of a bell tower on a silver chain, and the nickel-silver bracelet, and the silver seal ring, and the Dawn watch on the black leather strap, and the heart-shaped enameled pendant with the rose. All of the jewelry taken off the murdered girls.

Slepak was blind drunk, and the report said he'd actively resisted arrest. Later, after he'd slept it off, he said he hadn't stolen the trinkets, he'd found them in the pocket of his quilted jacket.

When his home was searched, they discovered a sweater with blood spots stashed behind the stove. It was the blood of Angela Nasebulova, the latest victim. A small, carefully washed tourist knife with a plastic handle was wrapped in the sweater. The nature of her wound pointed to it having been inflicted by a knife of this type. And Slepak's blood type was the same as the killer's, which had been determined from an analysis of the sperm.

He often went to Tobolsk to stay with a relative; he'd lived there for long stretches. He did odd jobs wherever he could find them. Then he'd drink up all his earnings, sometimes right in Tobolsk with his relative. Sometimes, if they were at odds, Slepak would go back to Tyumen and drink there instead. He didn't have an alibi for a single one of the six murders.

He was tall, broad shouldered, and blond. And he had a tattoo on his left wrist—NIKITA, written in small letters.

For a long time he didn't understand what they wanted from him. Then they nearly beat him to death in the holding cell at the Tyumen jail, smashed his head, and crushed his genitals. After that, he answered all their questions with the same phrase: "I didn't kill anybody."

Slepak never did admit his guilt. But he didn't write any statements or petitions or appeal to any higher offices. His lawyer did his job strictly by the books and with little energy. In the courtroom, the dead girls' relatives rained loud curses on the beast, the pervert, the vile monster Slepak. If anyone had had any doubts about the evidence against him or the nature of his guilt, in the atmosphere of that courtroom, they would have felt foolish, even blasphemous. If not him, who? Everything pointed to him. If they hadn't caught him when they did, who knew how many more victims there might have been?

The Tyumen Provincial Court sentenced Nikita Slepak to death. The sentence was carried out in the spring of 1983. Up until the last hour of his life, he continued to repeat the same thing, like an incantation: "I didn't kill anybody!"

Of the entire large operational and investigative team, only one person expressed any doubts about Nikita Slepak's guilt—First Lieutenant Igor Zakharov. But in late November 1982 he was killed under mysterious circumstances, randomly attacked by hooligans. There were no clues. His murder was never solved.

CHAPTER 33

"Hello. Are you Nadezhda Zakharova?"

"Yes, I am." The plump, gray-haired woman nodded and wiped her floury hands on her apron.

"My name is Polyanskaya. I'm from Moscow. Twelve years ago you sent your son Igor's story to my magazine." Lena pulled the old letter out of her bag and handed it to her.

Nadezhda Ivanovna took it cautiously with her fingertips.

"You're that same journalist? I remember. Of course I do."

"Gran! Who's come?" A child's voice came from the back of the apartment.

"It's for me, Igor," the woman shouted in response.

"Something's burning in the oven!" A sturdy, crew-cut boy of thirteen came into the front hall. "Hello." He nodded to Lena and stared at her curiously.

"Please, come in, take off your coat." Her hostess remembered herself. "Excuse me, I'll be right back."

She ran to the kitchen. It really did smell like something was burning there.

"What's your business here?" the boy asked gravely, not taking his eyes off Lena.

"Personal business." She smiled, took off her jacket, and started unlacing her boots.

Her hostess reappeared, without her apron now, and invited Lena into the room. Lena was immediately struck by a large portrait made from a blown-up photograph of First Lieutenant Zakharov on the wall.

"So many years have passed. Here is my grandson, grown up already," Nadezhda Ivanovna said, sitting at the table across from Lena. She nodded at the boy. "When little Igor was born, big Igor was already gone. Three months later." She sighed, fell silent, and propping her chin in her palm, looked at Lena quizzically.

"Nadezhda Ivanovna, I know your son Igor was on the team working the Slepak case."

"What's this? Have they decided to look for the real killer again? After so many years?"

"Why again?" Lena asked softly, feeling her fingers turn cold.

"An investigator from the General Prosecutor's Office in Moscow came specifically to talk to me about it. A long time ago, in '84, I think. A year after Slepak was convicted. She questioned me, in great detail, about what my Igor had told me and when. I gave her his diary and a few other papers. I hoped they'd find the real killer and at the same time whoever killed my little . . ."

"I'm sorry, Nadezhda Ivanovna. Are you absolutely certain the woman was from the Prosecutor's Office?"

"Please, I'm an educated woman, after all. She showed me her identification. And asked her questions professionally. I did have a police officer for a son, so I do have some understanding of these things."

"Forgive me again, but you didn't ask me for any identification," Lena remarked.

"But I remember you." Her hostess smiled in response. "You performed at the police officers' club. I was sitting in the first row. You have a memorable face. And you haven't changed at all. It's not often anyone comes here from Moscow, especially from such a famous magazine.

And my Igor read your letters to me out loud and the editorial notes you wrote him. And I subscribed to the magazine for years. You were a special correspondent, and your photo was above all your articles. No, don't think I would let just anyone into my home."

"Nadezhda Ivanovna, if you have such a good memory for faces, maybe you remember what the woman looked like?"

"I can't describe her in detail, of course. But you know, she was . . . How can I put it? Outwardly unpleasant, her face . . . Basically, an unpleasant face. But a very fine person. A very charming woman. Now what her name was, I don't recall."

"Did you ever tell any of Igor's colleagues about her visit?"

"Oh no! She warned me from the very beginning that the General Prosecutor's Office was reviewing the case in secret. She said there was reason to suspect the real killer worked for the police. That's why she asked me not to tell anyone anything. She even made me sign a nondisclosure agreement. It was an official form, 'Office of the Prosecutor of the USSR.' She promised to return Igor's diary, but she didn't. I guess the investigation hit an impasse and she forgot about it."

Sure, Lena thought. *She forgot.*

"So there are no papers left?" she asked.

"None. I gave her everything I had. Not that there was much. A notebook, Igor's diary, and some statements he wanted to write. There were drafts of those statements, all scribbled over and illegible."

"Who did he intend to write to? Do you remember?"

"To the General Prosecutor's Office."

"Did he ever actually write and send them?"

"No." Nadezhda Ivanovna shook her head. "He didn't. He wanted to clarify something else before sending anything. And he never got the chance."

Lena didn't spend long with Nadezhda Zakharova. She'd promised Michael she'd be back by six. He was excited about visiting the old librarian.

"Someone who's worked so many years in a book depository has to know a lot," he'd said. "Not only that, she can tell us about the 1920s and 1930s, about dekulakization, about how the Bolsheviks hunted down pagan shamans. She's a living witness. I can't let this opportunity slip by."

Lena planned to find the building where Volkov once lived tomorrow. She didn't know the address, but she hoped to find it from memory. Doubtless there were still people there who remembered him. She'd say she was writing an article about the great producer's youth. But that was tomorrow. Right now she had to catch her breath. She was running on fumes.

She was ten minutes late. Michael and Sasha were sitting in the hotel lobby, and Michael was chatting in English with a beautiful stranger.

The young woman was stunning. Fiery red hair to her waist, slanting green eyes, high cheekbones, and a large, sensual mouth. She was dressed simply and expensively in light gray woolen trousers and a black cashmere sweater.

Approaching, Lena was hesitant.

"Here you are at last!" Michael exclaimed joyously. "I'd like you to meet Natasha."

The young woman cast an appraising glance at Lena, nodded coldly, and continued telling Michael her recipe for preparing authentic Siberian pelmeni. But Michael interrupted her.

"I'm sorry, Natasha." He smiled as he rose from his armchair. "It's time for us to go. We have another meeting planned for today."

"You have such a full program," Natasha crooned, and she rose as well. "So we're agreed, Michael?"

She was a head taller than Lena and looked down at her with an arrogant, incinerating gaze.

"Natasha has antique cookbooks from the last century, with recipes for the local cuisine," Michael explained guiltily when they'd started for the car with Sasha, who'd been silent the whole time.

"And she invited you to her place? Michael, you were the one who gave me a talking to about morals." Lena shook her head.

"Child, I'm old enough that I can allow myself certain liberties, especially in a foreign country, especially at the edge of the world. She's such a beauty, this Siberian Natasha, and the poor thing doesn't have anyone to speak English to. She's forgetting the language and is very upset over that."

"Does she live here?"

"No, she's from Omsk. She's visiting her aunt, who lives in a private house from the last century. A real wooden cottage!"

"What was she doing in the hotel?"

"Drinking coffee in the bar."

"Michael, she's not a . . ."

"No," Michael said firmly. "She's not a prostitute. Prostitutes look completely different. I should know."

"You have a lot of experience with them?"

"More than you, at any rate." Michael chuckled sarcastically.

Right then Sasha chimed in. Not talking, but singing. He started humming a famous song under his breath: "She's just a working girl . . ."

"Sasha, what can we do?" Lena asked quietly. "He's going to go see her."

"Jealous, are you?" Sasha laughed.

"Don't mock me. We have to think of something."

"Serves you right if they kidnap your old American! I warned you."

"Sasha, cut it out." Lena was nearly crying. "She clearly is a prostitute and they obviously sent her."

"What are you saying!" A grimace of comic fright was reflected in the small mirror. "Imagine! I never would have guessed! I'm so naive I thought the beautiful Natasha had sincerely fallen for your old friend. She introduced herself very professionally. I saw it all. High class. Enviably so. The only thing I don't get is whether your professor really thinks she's interested in him. He seemed to take it all at face value."

"He's just sociable. And he'd love an adventure. And here's this beauty. Some men, the older they get, the more gullible they let themselves be about the selfless romantic intentions of beautiful young women."

"I don't think she'll disappoint him or take his money," Sasha noted thoughtfully.

"And you're going to drive Michael right to them?" Lena grinned nervously.

"Of course! I, Sasha, the evil pimp, am going to drive your friend straight into their clutches." Sasha pressed his lips resentfully. "Why this mistrust? If you're so smart, use your brains a little!"

"You want to use her to figure out—"

"We already are."

"You're talking about me being an old playboy, aren't you?" Michael chimed in.

"What else?" Lena chuckled.

Along the way, they stopped at a small market and bought a bouquet of white roses.

The Veterans Home was on the outskirts of Tobolsk. It was a five-story brick building that looked like a hospital. An armed guard met them at the front door.

"Who are you here to see?"

"Valentina Yurievna Gradskaya, room 130."

"Do you have any identification?"

Lena held out her journalist credentials and Michael's navy passport.

"What's this, a foreigner?" The guard raised his eyebrows.

"A professor. From America."

"Go on in." The guard nodded and handed back the documents. "Second floor, down the hall on the left."

There was a thick runner on the hall floor. And pots of flowers on the windowsills. It was clean and oddly quiet. They didn't meet a soul on their way to room 130.

"Yes yes, come in!" a cheerful old lady's voice answered their knock.

It was amazing to see a perfectly homey, very cozy room in such a bureaucratic institution: a round table in the middle, floor-to-ceiling bookshelves, a small antique writing desk with a nice new Unis typewriter and a neat stack of manuscripts, a low ottoman covered with a large knit afghan, an elegant étagère from the turn of the century, and on it, a 1960s-model record player and two rows of records.

Valentina Yurievna had scarcely changed. She had the same snow-white, neatly cut and coifed hair and wore the same silk blouse with the round collar, a small brooch at her neck. She was even thinner, and there was something touchingly childlike about her face. Lena had long noted that the faces of very old people who have lived a long life without growing bitter become almost childlike.

"Looking at you, I'm not at all afraid of growing old," Michael said in English, and he smiled and held out his hand. "Professor Michael Barron, Columbia University, New York."

"Very nice to meet you. As I understand it, my colleagues at the library recommended you pay me a visit. You must be a historian?" She had classical English, without the clipped American vowels and deep snarl. "And you must be his interpreter." She addressed Lena in Russian. "I think you'll be glad at the chance to rest a little. I know what a hard job simultaneous interpreting is. What's your name, child?"

"Lena."

She had decided not to mention to Gradskaya just yet that they'd already met. In forty minutes, Sasha would come pick up Michael and take him to his meeting with the beautiful Natasha. And Lena would stay here. That was their agreement. She wondered where he was actually going to take Michael. How would she and Sasha communicate?

"Lena, dear, you can look at the art books first. And there are albums of old photographs. I've collected them my whole life," Gradskaya said to her. "What interests you most?"

Lena asked for the albums. She loved old photographs. Ladies in hats on a background of painted landscapes, infants in clouds of lace, men with top hats and absurd mustaches, and the perfectly still, serious faces of Siberian peasants. On the next few pages, the same ladies in the starched headscarves of the sisters of mercy, the men in military uniform, the trenches and machine guns of World War I, a Cossack captain sitting on a rearing horse, an enormous hospital ward. Then came very different faces, leather jackets, shorn women—a brutal fire in their eyes—emaciated, raggedy children.

Lena picked up the next album, and a large cardboard photograph fell out. *High School No. 2, Class of 1963.* The faces of the graduates and teachers in separate ovals, pale vignettes of stars, spikes, sickles, and smokestacks. Lena was about to set the photograph aside when suddenly her glance fell on the inscription under one of the photographs: *Regina Gradskaya.*

She was by far the most unattractive of all the female graduates—a broad, flattened nose, buck teeth, a large chin, and small, deep-set eyes. Lena couldn't take her eyes off that face.

Right then she heard a knock at the door. Sasha walked into the room. Michael, expressing his profuse thanks, began getting his coat on.

"I'll come back for you in half an hour," Sasha said, glancing at Lena.

"You don't have to worry. I can get back to the hotel."

"Whatever you say." He shrugged.

"Valentina Yurievna, may I spend a little more time with you? I wanted to talk about these photographs," she said to Gradskaya.

"Yes, child." Valentina Yurievna nodded. "I'd be happy to have you stay. I so rarely have visitors."

When Sasha and Michael had gone, Gradskaya looked at Lena closely through her glasses.

"Tell me, where might I have seen you before?"

"It was a very long time ago." Lena smiled. "Fourteen years ago you let three young Moscow students into the book depository. Then you treated us to tea and cranberry preserves and told us all kinds of interesting stories."

"What do you know." The old woman shook her head. "I don't remember that at all, but I've been looking at you and trying to figure out where I've seen you. Speaking of tea, if you would like some, I have a kettle and all the essentials. Open the buffet. You'll find everything there."

Behind the little buffet's glass door there was a Tefal electric kettle, a sugar bowl, an open box of Lipton tea bags, a jar of cookies, and a few tea glasses in antique silver glass holders.

"You know, this is a very peaceful institution," Gradskaya said while Lena was making the tea. "It's clean and comfortable here and always as silent as the grave. Top-quality medical attention, massage, all kinds of procedures. Only there's no one to talk to. At one time this was a boarding house for Party veterans. Now the local nouveau riche park their old folks here. No more than five rooms are occupied on each floor. It's very expensive to stay here. I held out as long as I could, you know, but age is age. I'm grateful to my daughter, of course, but . . ."

"Forgive me, Valentina Yurievna." Lena held out the large group photograph and pointed to the unattractive girl. "Is this your daughter?"

"Yes." The old woman nodded. "That's Regina."

Lena noticed a shadow cross Gradskaya's face. Her lips pursed slightly and her eyes narrowed—but only for a second.

"Do you have any other photographs?"

"What for, child?"

"You see, I think I've seen this face somewhere. Maybe I met your daughter. Does she live in Moscow now?"

"She's lived in Moscow for a long time. And you may well have met her. The world is terribly small. Only I don't have any other photographs. Not even baby pictures. This is the only one."

"That's odd. You collect photographs. So many pictures of other people."

"Regina destroyed all her photos. And then she destroyed her face." That last sentence came softly, with an edge of irritation. Lena could tell the old woman didn't like this conversation about her daughter, but she had to take it to its conclusion. There was no other choice.

"She destroyed her face?" she echoed quietly.

"Get that stack of magazines there, on the shelf."

She quickly skipped through a few well-known glossy publications and silently handed Lena an opened magazine—the same one Gosha Galitsyn had shown her recently. Smiling dazzlingly from the centerfold was the "sweet couple"—Veniamin Volkov and his beautiful wife, Regina Gradskaya.

"My daughter had a series of plastic surgeries done at a Swiss clinic," Valentina Yurievna said. "She'd suffered her whole life over her appearance."

CHAPTER 34

"Professor Barron, I'm obliged to inform you that the woman who invited you to visit is a dangerous criminal." Sasha's pronunciation was mediocre, but he spoke English precisely and literately, without mistakes.

Michael's eyes popped and his jaw dropped.

"There's an old joke," Sasha went on. "A wealthy English family had a little boy who had never spoken and he was nearly five. His parents were very worried. They took the child to various doctors, but all in vain. Then one day at dinner the boy pushed his plate aside and said distinctly, 'The steak is overcooked.' 'Johnny, darling!' his parents exclaimed when they recovered from their shock. 'Why didn't you talk before?' 'Before this everything was fine,' Johnny answered. So you see, Dr. Barron, before this everything was fine and I didn't talk."

"But what's not fine now?" Michael asked, swallowing hard. "We're not at the dinner table and there's no steak. I'm trying to make a joke, but joking's the last thing on my mind. Please explain what's going on. And you can start with who you are."

"I'm a first lieutenant in the Federal Security Service, and my name is Volkovets."

"Sasha, could you explain, specifically, what is going on? Why is a Security Service agent driving me around Siberia?"

"Dr. Barron, do you know your classic Russian literature well?"

"Oh Lord, Sasha, I asked for specifically!" Michael groaned.

"Remember Gogol's play *The Inspector General*? Well, you've been taken for someone else, too. The local mafia is following you very closely. And it's getting dangerous. I think you should go back to Moscow today."

"What do you mean Moscow? I still haven't been to Khanty-Mansiysk and the surrounding villages. I haven't done half of what I wanted to do. And Lena?"

"She'll go, too. Right now we'll stop by your room together so you can pack. Quickly. Then we'll head straight to the airport in Tyumen. There's a night flight and I want you on it."

"Alone?"

"Why alone? With Lena."

"And if I don't agree?"

"You already have." Sasha grinned. "You're a sensible man and you don't want to risk your life."

"You're right," Michael sighed. "I don't want to risk my life. But I have one condition. I won't go without Lena."

Nikolai Ievlev watched Sasha Volkovets's Moskvich drive away and the dark brown Zhiguli take off after it.

That's all right, the major mentally addressed the four goons in the Zhiguli. *That's all right, shitheads. We'll cut you off at the intersection, and good. Unfortunately, not at the roots.*

It had been dark for a while. There were only a few lights on in the gloomy five-story Veterans Home. Pale yellow patches of lights flickered randomly, falling on the black wall of the snow-drifted taiga.

The taiga came up very close to this side of the building, but they weren't watching it from that direction. They should be waiting for Polyanskaya around here, in the tall, dense bushes that grew along the main drive. And they were. When the sound of the dark brown Zhiguli's engine had died down, Ievlev picked up on a rustle, and the black mass of bushes stirred.

He glanced at his watch dial. In ten minutes, Polyanskaya would come out of the building and walk down this drive flanked by the black bushes. They might let her walk on a little bit, rather than attack right away. But there was another possibility. In their place he would have lost patience long ago.

Ievlev knew that very soon, a hundred meters from here, an army vehicle would stop. He listened to the roar of the infrequent cars going down the highway, trying to pick out the distinctive rumble of its engine. The SWAT team, five men from the local Security Service, were prepared to go into action at a moment's notice. The faintest noise, let alone a gunshot, would be an automatic signal for them.

His old leather boots were soaked through with melting snow, and the cold had permeated his body. Ievlev was dying for a cigarette or a cup of steaming hot tea. He thought about the fact that the bad guys they caught wouldn't talk or give up their boss for all the tea in China. Life's worth more than any tea.

That's the way it was always going to be. The foot soldiers would keep quiet and sweat it out in prisons all across the country. And the bosses would continue to rule their fiefdoms—large swaths of this enormous country, with its gold and oil, its poppy and flax fields, its crooks and prostitutes, its people's artists and members of government—with an iron hand. That's the way it was always going to be. Nothing was going to change just because he, Major Ievlev, was sitting here now, soaked through and shaking, on the outskirts of an ancient Siberian town, waiting—for either a stray bullet or pneumonia to strike him down. Even if he could get the thugs hiding across the way to talk, nothing was going to change.

A faint whistle came from the bushes opposite. In the distance, on the highway, the army vehicle's motor quietly came to life. A long shadow dashed across the pale light of the streetlamp. The butt of a gun smashed into the major's head from behind, sending him sprawling onto the crumbly snow. Ievlev managed to grab his adversary's left wrist in a reflexive motion, and his right hand was fumbling at the safety of his pistol when there was a deafening explosion. A hundred meters away on the highway, something blazed up, for a long second lighting up the low sky over the pines and a corner of the five-story brick building.

For that brief instant Major Ievlev hesitated, and a blade struck his heart. The last thing he saw was a whitish, blurry patch of moon through a layer of night clouds and the black, gnarled branches of shrubbery.

"Thank you, Valentina Yurievna. It's time for me to go," Lena said, standing up and putting on her jacket.

"How can you go alone so late, child? I thought someone was picking you up."

"I'll be fine." Lena smiled. "The bus runs until twelve. It's only ten thirty now."

There was a boom in the distance. For a second, the blackness out the window was lit by a pale light. The windows tinkled.

"Did you hear that, Lena dear? What is it?" the old woman asked, frightened.

"It sounded like an explosion." Lena stopped by the door. "Yes, it sounded very much like an explosion."

"It must be an accident on the highway. Do you want me to call someone to walk you to the bus?"

"Thank you. Please don't bother anyone. I'll get there myself."

After saying good-bye to Valentina Yurievna, Lena went out into the empty hall. *Now it all fits,* she thought as she walked down the runner. *For some reason what's hardest to believe isn't that Volkov raped and murdered those girls or that Regina Gradskaya unleashed this entire operation to erase any traces just for his sake. What's hardest of all to believe is that Regina is Valentina Yurievna's daughter. Her only daughter.*

The floorboards under the thick runner creaked ever so slightly behind Lena. Before she could look around, something hard was resting between her shoulder blades. Even through her sweater and leather jacket, Lena could feel the distinct chill of a gun barrel.

"Don't struggle or yell," a man's voice whispered in her ear. "Keep walking forward, calmly and slowly. Don't do what I say, and I'll shoot. That's it. Good job. Now take your hands out of your pockets. Smart girl. Now down the stairs. Don't look around."

She went down, step by step. Her head was spinning, her mouth had dried up, and her legs were like cotton wool. One flight and then another. The guard should be there, by the entrance. But she wouldn't be able to cry out. No, they were taking her to another exit, the service door most likely.

"Now to the right," the man with the gun gave her a little push with the barrel into a blind, dark opening.

A second later, someone deftly twisted her arms behind her back, and Lena felt something cold and metal on her wrists. The handcuffs clicked.

A car was parked right by the service entrance. They shoved Lena into an enormous SUV, and she found herself in the back seat between two goons she couldn't get a good look at in the dark. What she could tell was that there were five of them in all. When the car started up, one of the ones sitting next to her, with the deft movement of a magician, took a rag out of his pocket and blindfolded Lena, pulling a few strands of hair so it hurt.

"Could you be a little more careful?" Lena said. She didn't recognize her own voice.

"Pardon me," a goon apologized politely.

"You pulled my hair into the knot and it hurts," she told him calmly. "What can I see in this darkness anyway?"

"If you're going to run your mouth, we'll knock you out!" one of her neighbors snapped.

But something came over Lena. For some reason, in this situation it was scarier not to talk than to talk. The sound of her own voice was soothing. Each time she heard it, it was like a confirmation that she was still alive.

"If you planned to knock me out, you'd have done it a long time ago," she reasoned out loud. "But so far you've treated me politely. And I would be grateful if you would both tie that knot more carefully and let me smoke."

"I like this one!" someone sitting up front said. "Listen, Turnip, retie that knot for her and give her a cigarette."

The one they called Turnip fussed with the knot. A minute later she heard the click of a lighter. They brought a cigarette to Lena's lips.

"Are we going far?" Lena asked.

"The more you know, the sooner you die," came the answer from the front seat.

They drove for an hour and a half. That whole long way, not another word was spoken. They popped in a cassette, and a singer from a famous pop group started singing a sad song about prison and love.

If they'd wanted to kill me, Lena thought, *they'd have done it right away. It's probably a good thing they blindfolded me. That means I may still get out of this alive. They don't blindfold dead men. Why bother, it's not like he's going to tell anyone if he sees something. No, these can't be Gradskaya's men. They would have killed me straightaway. She had one goal: to kill me,* Lena reasoned. *I wonder what blew up on the highway? And what became of Ievlev?*

Finally the SUV stopped. Without removing the blindfold, they led Lena out of the car. The snow crunched under their boots.

"Don't forget my purse, please," she asked.

"Go on, go on," they told her and gave her a light shove in the back, with a hand, not a gun barrel.

A weak light leaked through the blindfold. They led Lena out from the cold and into someplace warm, guiding her by the elbow. Only now did she feel how tired her arms were from being handcuffed behind her back. Her shoulders ached miserably. Even though the handcuffs were loose, the cold steel weight of them was repulsive.

"Take the handcuffs off," she asked softly. "I won't run away, and I'm not going to fight you."

"You'll manage," they told her, and they stopped and pushed her roughly into an armchair. "Sit quietly."

A minute later, the door slammed. Lena was left alone, God knows where, handcuffed and blindfolded. She tried to get more comfortable in the chair, but it was impossible. Her shoulders ached more and more, and her hands were numb.

She remembered how once, during the summer semester, she'd studied all night for an exam sitting by an open window in the kitchen that looked out on the Garden Ring Road. That night, right before dawn, was strangely tense and quiet. Suddenly, in that quiet, she heard a distinct tapping. Looking out, Lena saw a man walking down the deserted sidewalk right under her window.

He was walking very slowly, holding a slender cane and cautiously tapping the asphalt in front of him. It was a blind man, but he had clearly only gone blind recently. He was learning how to walk down the deserted streets in the night. Back then she suddenly felt vividly, to the point of horror, the black, desperate loneliness of blindness.

Many years had passed since then, but that lonely blind man on the nighttime Garden Ring was firmly etched in her memory. Now, as she sat blindfolded, her entire being felt the danger emanating from the world around her.

She didn't know how much time had elapsed. She was hungry and her mouth had dried up. It was quiet. She'd thought there wasn't anyone else in the building, but then she heard the click of a door lock. Then quick light steps. Someone was silently untying the knot at the nape of her neck. Carefully, trying not to pull her hair.

At first, Lena thought she really had gone blind. The light in the room wasn't bright, but it killed her eyes. The pain lasted several minutes. Lena squinted and wished she could wipe her eyes, but her hands were still shackled behind her back.

When she was finally able to see she saw a tall, round-faced young woman dressed almost exactly like her, in jeans and a long, loose sweater. She was wearing woolen socks and men's house slippers.

"Please, give me something to drink and take the handcuffs off," Lena asked. "It's not like I'm going to run away."

The girl shook her head and pointed expressively to her ears.

Great, a deaf-mute, Lena thought sadly, and she finally looked around the room in which she'd probably spent a few hours.

The room was tiny and nearly empty. Besides the armchair Lena was sitting in, there was only an iron cot with a striped mattress and not a single window. A bare lightbulb in the low ceiling gave the room its only light.

Lena swallowed hard and jerked her shoulders. The young woman looked at her calmly and thoughtfully. She had clear blue eyes. She went out, locking the door behind her. Five minutes later, though, she returned with a glass of water, which she brought to Lena's lips. It was slightly sour mineral water. Lena gulped it down. Putting the empty glass on the floor, the young woman took a small, flat key out of her jeans pocket, unlocked the handcuffs, removed them, and left. The lock clicked behind her. Lena was left all alone.

She stood up, kneading her numb hands, and walked around the room. The walls were covered in beige oil paint. Up near the ceiling, Lena noticed a tiny round window, more like an air vent. And there turned out to be one more door in the corner. Pushing it cautiously, Lena discovered a tiny toilet and sink. There was hot as well as cold running water.

That means I'm somewhere in town, she thought. *But we left Tobolsk, and we couldn't have gotten to Tyumen in an hour and a half. Actually, I could be anywhere at all. Mafiosi can put in plumbing and hot water anywhere they want if it suits their needs, even the desert or the remote taiga.*

All she could do was wait and see what happened. Lena washed her face and hands with warm water, removed her jacket and boots, and lay down on the striped mattress. She looked at the yellowish ceiling, trying not to cry.

Michael shuddered at the first gunshots. Sasha pushed the car to its top speed. Behind them, at the intersection, a police car cut off the dark brown Zhiguli. Michael pulled a muscle in his neck turning to look out the back window into the darkness of the night highway. He saw gunfire, and bullets flashed in the gloom like trailing falling stars.

"Maybe we shouldn't bother to stop by the hotel for our things," he suggested. "I can see something very bad is going on."

"There's another car waiting at the hotel," Sasha replied. "Don't worry. It'll all be okay."

"Why did you leave Lena there? Why didn't she come with us?"

"That was her decision."

"But you knew everything. You should have insisted, taken her by force!" Michael wouldn't calm down.

"It was her decision. She's a grown woman."

Somewhere in the distance, on the highway, there was an explosion.

"What is it?" Michael exhaled. "I think war's broken out! You, Federal Security lieutenant, can you explain to me what's going on?"

"No," Sasha honestly admitted.

"Your calm astonishes me!"

"That's part of the job." Sasha shrugged and lit a cigarette in the closed car.

Three agents were waiting for them at the hotel. Sasha handed Michael over to them, and they escorted him to his room. It took him three minutes to pack his things. Their Mercedes rushed Michael to the Tyumen airport in two and a half hours. They encountered no pursuit or gunfire along the way.

The plane flew to Moscow through a starry, velvety night, above heavy March clouds, the immense, snow-drifted taiga, and icy Siberian rivers. Michael looked out the black porthole and saw his own blurred reflection. He was thinking about Lena and was worried. He'd realized long ago that asking questions was useless.

On the outskirts of Tobolsk, a hundred meters from the Veterans Home, the SWAT team was working under a searchlight and trying to figure out why, out of the blue, an old empty Volga had blown up on the shoulder of the highway, right in front of five Federal Security agents sitting in a vehicle very nearby. The explosion was powerful, deafening, but they still hadn't found any victims.

Twenty meters from the Veterans Home front door, in the dense, high bushes by the main drive, they discovered the body of Major Ievlev.

Sasha Volkovets woke up the old woman, Gradskaya, and heard her report that Lena had left at about ten thirty, saying she'd take the bus back to the hotel.

Naturally, the guard at the door hadn't seen a woman in black jeans and a brown leather jacket leave the building.

She's got herself in a real mess, the first lieutenant said to himself, and he spat through his teeth at the hard, trampled snow.

When Curly got the call from Moscow and was told the "curious news," he tensed more than he should have.

"For what it's worth," his old friend Regina Gradskaya told him after she'd laid out the story of the American psychology consultant from the CIA and the journalist accompanying him as his interpreter.

"Thanks, Regina." Curly smiled into the phone. "I'll definitely look into it. Valuable news. What's it worth to you?"

As a sober man, Curly didn't believe in altruism. His old friend had to have some personal interest.

"You take everything so literally!" Regina laughed. "What I meant was that the information is uncorroborated and possibly just hearsay."

"Well, we'll check that out. Anyway, what kinds of problems are you having?"

"Well, you see," Regina said listlessly, "that female, Polyanskaya, is pretty darn curious. She sticks her nose in other people's business. Like lots of journalists, she's got a loose tongue and a raging imagination."

"You mean you know her?"

"Not exactly, no. So far we haven't been any serious problems with her. But I don't like her. And traveling with a CIA consultant, I like her even less. So I thought I should warn you because we're old friends."

Curly had very serious organized crime connections in America, which is why he decided the CIA psychologist's visit probably wasn't hearsay. He'd come very close to getting nicked in Boston once, where he'd been stupid enough to show up in person for the opening of a small pharmaceutical company. He'd wanted to take a look at his latest acquisition—purchased through proxies, naturally. He'd managed to slip away, but he'd still gone into the CIA and FBI databases.

Curly tensed up. The first thing the curious journalist did was head to Malaya Proletarskaya to see Blindboy's mother and aunt.

In and of itself, the fact that that punk had become one of Russia's best and most expensive hitmen was insulting to Curly. A punk couldn't, shouldn't become anyone, let alone a killer. That broke the rules. But worst of all was the fact that Curly himself had paid twice for his services.

Blindboy was a true artist. He worked without a guard or armored car. He could kill anyone anywhere. But he only killed big shots, and only those he thought deserved to be killed. He never took a kopek in advance. He always took one shot, and only one, but it was accurate, deadly. No innocent bystander had ever died by his hand. After doing the job, he would disappear, vanish in a puff of smoke. It was as if a bullet had simply materialized out of thin air to shatter the skull of whoever he'd been ordered to kill.

Now Curly had to worry about a wily and uncatchable punk who knew too much, respected no one, and was capable of God knows what. That's why the journalist who'd arrived with the CIA consultant and had talked with Blindboy's mother for three hours had puzzled Curly in a bad way. Regina Gradskaya was right. The woman was too curious for her own good.

After that visit to Malaya Proletarskaya, the odd team consisting of a Federal Security agent, a CIA consultant, and the journalist had gone to Zagorinskaya, deep in the taiga, where just fifty kilometers from an Old Believers settlement was Curly's personal oil field. And what, one asks, had taken them to Zagorinskaya specifically? No, his oil was perfectly legit. Well, almost perfectly. Even if Curly owned the well, the drilling was done by a state company that belonged to Curly, naturally, so they shouldn't have gone there. There was no reason to.

In Tobolsk, for some reason, the journalist had visited the family of a cop who was killed a long time ago. Nothing connected that cop to Curly personally, but the visit wasn't what it seemed. When it turned out that this unholy trinity was planning to go to the Veterans Home, the same one where an entire floor had been set aside for Curly's senile father, the boss's patience snapped. He had to stop them, and fast.

The old man detested his son, didn't want to see him, and would always holler at Curly in his rattling little voice: "Thief! Murderer!"

Curly hadn't had any feelings for his father in a long time. He was just doing his duty. He'd placed his father in a good home, close by, in Tobolsk, and ensured his comfort and excellent care. Before, it wouldn't have occurred to Curly to put a special guard on the Veterans Home. No one would ever dare stick his nose in there. What good was the old man to anyone?

But Curly had no doubt that the trio had gone to the Veterans Home specifically to see his father. Why they had done so, well, he no longer worried about that. Nothing in the world irritated him more than the unknown. Of course, it was too much trouble to nab them both, the journalist and the American. And better not to get mixed up with a foreigner anyway. He decided the journalist was more than enough. Let her explain it all!

He was able beforehand, through his people in Moscow, to get some information about this woman. The fact that she was also the wife of an Interior Ministry colonel didn't dismay Curly one bit. On the contrary, that fact made taking her all the more appealing to him.

The gunmen sent to the Veterans Home kept in constant contact with him. At nine thirty they reported that the Federal Security agent had left with the American. He ordered them to put a small tail on him, but not to touch him, just to follow him. At first, all went well. He even regretted having employed so many people to deal with one woman. But it turned out he'd acted quite correctly.

Almost simultaneously, the group watching the highway discovered a Federal Security vehicle, and those waiting in the bushes by the building entrance noticed a stranger sitting in the bushes opposite them. He wasn't answering nature's call, that's for sure. Later he turned out to be a Federal Security major. The gunman who offed him made sure to rifle through his pockets.

The situation was more complicated now. He had to think of something, and fast. And Curly did. He had an old Volga at the Veteran's Home. It was hidden behind the trees, right by the shoulder—just in case. There were two guys sitting in it. They were the ones who'd noticed that damned military car. Curly ordered the boys to pull the Volga a little closer to the shoulder and blow it up right in front of the military car. At that moment, in the confusion, they'd be able to get the journalist out without extra fuss—assuming everything happened at the same time.

And it did. The boys played it out to a T, note for note. True, there was a little gunfire. A police patrol car cut off his tail on the American at an intersection.

"How many of our boys did they lay out on the highway?" Curly asked in alarm when he heard about the shooting, not directly but from one of his people, a former marine major who was acting as his private secretary—or else as his gray cardinal.

"None," the former major replied cheerfully. "That Zhiguli has a good engine. The boys veered away when they were cut off and disappeared into the taiga. The cops were scared to even get close. They turned their lights on it, saw it was empty, and drove off."

"And the injured man?"

"It's all good. Khottabych's already digging out the bullet."

"Well, that's great." Curly nodded. "What about Moscow?"

"There'll be a cassette tomorrow morning."

CHAPTER 35

He was having Technicolor dreams and was reluctant to wake up. Before, he'd only dreamed in black and white—bad dreams, gloomy dreams. That's probably why he'd always slept so little. But now he was reliving his entire forty-year life—completely differently.

He dreamed of himself as a little boy loved tenderly and doted on by his parents. His mama had cool, light hands. She stroked his hair, kissed him good night, and read him fairy tales. His father was strong and good-natured. He taught him about the taiga, how to guess where the solid hummocks were in the swamp's abyss, how to weave pots out of fragrant spring birch bark and boil water in them over a fire.

There was a great deal of warmth and light in his dream. The scarlet taiga cranberries glowed in the sun and looked nothing like drops of blood. His dark-haired little neighbor Larochka ran down the creaking stairs, smiling gaily and tapping her heels. No one ever raped her in the deserted park in spring. She didn't know how painful and terrifying it was, which meant she was going to live a completely different life.

Sixteen-year-old Tanya Kostylyova stepped out on the bank from the calm nighttime river, shook her long wet hair, and, huddling in the predawn chill, pulled her graduation dress over her damp body.

"Venya, I'm freezing! Why did you talk me into swimming?" she whispered, pressing her warm forehead to his chest.

Tanya Kostylyova was alive, and she was forty. The six other girls were alive, too. He hadn't pursued anyone, hadn't attacked anyone, hadn't strangled anyone, hadn't killed anyone. They were all alive, and each had followed her own path, lived her own life, happy or unhappy, dissolute or righteous—but her own. Four of the six had children. The children were growing up, some of them had children, too. Those grandchildren were girls Venya Volkov had never raped or killed.

Somewhere far away, in another dimension, on another planet, there was an enormous business, Veniamin Productions, an invincible iron horse that fed on intrigue, cruelty, and blood. But he, Venya Volkov, had nothing whatsoever to do with that. He lived peacefully and happily. Lena Polyanskaya looked at him with her clear gray eyes. He wished he could touch her face and feel her long black eyelashes flutter. He reached out, but around him was emptiness, cold, dead air. He couldn't breathe that air. It burned his throat and shredded his lungs. He had to wake up, but he didn't want to.

"Veniamin Borisovich, wake up, please," he heard a voice from far away.

"Venya, the doctor's here to see you. He has to examine you."

He opened his eyes and saw over him two faces—Regina's doll-like face and the soft, round, bespectacled face of an older man he didn't know.

It pained him to pull himself out of his dream. It felt like he was falling straight from his warm, Technicolor world into a dull, icy, black-and-white nightmare. The round-faced otolaryngologist had dry, rough hands. He palpated Venya's glands and looked at his throat.

"I don't see a postpharyngeal abscess. The throat's enflamed, but not badly."

"So you're ruling out angina?" Regina clarified.

"What angina? It's the flu. A perfectly ordinary case of the flu. This should not get to the point where there are complications. But I would recommend a course of antibiotics. In any case, he'll require a thorough examination. You should bring in a cardiologist."

"Yes." Regina nodded. "I think you're right. Thank you, Doctor. My driver will take you home."

She handed him a hundred dollars.

When she heard the car departing, she went back to the bedroom and took a disposable needle and a cardboard box of ampoules filled with a colorless liquid from the nightstand. She sawed the ampoule's neck with a diamond saw, broke the thin glass—and cut her finger. The cut wasn't deep, but it bled. She had to set the open ampoule carefully on the nightstand and go to the bathroom, where she had hydrogen peroxide and iodine in the cabinet.

When she returned to the bedroom, Venya was sitting on the bed, holding the open ampoule in two fingers and examining it in the light.

"Why isn't there a label?" he asked.

"I can see you're already feeling better." Regina smiled delightedly.

"Yes, I am. What were you injecting me with all that time?"

"Antibiotics and vitamins."

"I don't need any more medicines. Or specialists. And stop trying to turn me into an invalid. Bring me the phone."

"Whatever you say, my love."

Lena curled up under her jacket and tried to fall asleep. She didn't know what time it was. Her watch had gone missing. The leather strap had probably broken when they put on the handcuffs. All she could see out the tiny window was a sliver of sky, which had brightened considerably.

Now I know almost everything, she thought, *but what good is that? Even if a miracle does happen and I do get out of here, I can't prove anything.*

I don't understand why Regina Gradskaya needed to take this kind of risk. What is it all for? Is she that in love with Venya Volkov? Or did she decide to tame the monster so he could help make her beautiful and rich? Plastic surgery in a Swiss clinic is expensive. But she has the brains and energy to earn that independently, without the help of a monster. She's taken risks, and not only when she framed Nikita Slepak. She's taken a risk all these years, living with Volkov, and lying down next to him every night. Or did she manage to cure him after all?

What about Mitya Sinitsyn? Why did he only bring this up fourteen years later? And who with? Volkov himself! Yes, he only had a suspicion, but no actual proof.

Lena imagined Mitya's torment as he tried to decide what he should do with his suspicions. He couldn't say nothing and forget it. At first he'd thought of blackmail, but he couldn't do it. He probably found a way to meet Volkov alone and ask him a direct question: "Are you or aren't you a murderer?" Knowing Mitya, she could imagine that. He thought he was acting nobly, that he had no other option. And what did he achieve?

What would I have done in his place? Lena asked herself. *Actually, I am in his place. I know much more than Mitya did when he went to see Volkov. But what's the point? I'm locked up God knows where. My only goal is to get out of here alive and see Liza and Seryozha again. That's much more important to me than some abstract idea like justice.*

Lena had nearly fallen asleep when the door opened and two young goons appeared at the threshold.

"Get up. Let's go," one of them said.

Lena laced up her boots and threw on her jacket. They led her down a dim corridor where she couldn't make out anything other than a few closed doors. Then they went up a short wooden staircase to the second floor. A minute later, Lena was in a large living room. The floor was covered with a light-colored, thick-piled rug, and in the corner a fire flickered in an antique fireplace. The dark, heavy, red drapes were pulled tight. In front of a low zebrawood magazine table, in a white leather armchair, sat a flabby, perfectly bald man of sixty or so with a good-natured, snub-nosed face.

"Hello, Elena Nikolaevna," he said. "Please, come in. Take a seat."

"Hello," Lena echoed back. She took a few steps into the room and sat in the armchair facing the bald man.

The two goons stayed in the doorway behind her.

"Coffee? Tea? Something stronger?" the bald man offered with a polite smile.

"Coffee, if I may."

The bald man's eyes were light brown, almost yellow, small, and lashless.

"Okay, Vadik, get some coffee for us." He nodded to one of the goons. "Don't worry, Elena Nikolaevna," he addressed Lena kindly, even rather paternally. "I'm just going to ask you a few questions, we'll have our coffee, and we'll part on good terms. On one condition, of course. You know perfectly well what that is. You'll answer my questions honestly. Are you ready?"

"Yes."

"Question number one." The bald man grinned. "Who is Michael Barron?"

"Michael Barron is a US citizen, a professor, and a historian," Lena said calmly.

So that's what this is about! They really have taken Michael for someone else. And Gradskaya has nothing to do with it. I wonder where Michael is now. I hope Sasha had the sense to send him to Moscow.

"Elena Nikolaevna, we did agree that you would answer honestly." The bald man frowned slightly.

"I have no reason to deceive you. Dr. Barron really is a professor and a historian. To figure that out, you certainly didn't have to go through this charade of searching our rooms and abducting me. This is as obvious as the fact that there was talcum powder in that tin can, not drugs."

The bald man burst out laughing, though with a wheeze.

"Well, fine. Let's continue. Why did you come here with this, as you say, historian?"

"Dr. Barron is studying the history of Russian Siberia. He's interested in schismatics and the small ethnic groups of the North. He hired me as an interpreter since he doesn't speak Russian."

"And who is the young man who drove you around?" The bald man's eyes became altogether yellow, and his pupils narrowed to a pinpoint.

"We needed a driver. We hired the first one we came across. He asked for very little money."

The goon called Vadik silently walked up to the table with a tray holding two small cups and a sugar bowl.

"Drink your coffee, Elena Nikolaevna, and think a little more," the bald man suggested politely.

"May I smoke?" Lena asked.

"Yes, of course."

Parliaments, a lighter, and an ashtray appeared on the table. Lena greedily sipped the hot, strong coffee and took a cigarette out of the pack.

"Well, fine, and what did you talk about for so long with the two old women on Malaya Proletarskaya?"

"I was visiting the mother of an old acquaintance. It's an old story."

"I'd be happy to hear it."

Lena calmly laid out the story of Vasya Slepak's poems. Curly listened and thought that she was telling the truth. Not the whole truth, of course, but the truth. He knew that the killer really did once write poetry. And one of his poems was even published in a popular youth magazine.

"Was it hard to get him published?" he asked with some sympathy.

"What do you think?" Lena smiled.

"What did you do that for?"

"I felt very sorry for Vasya Slepak."

Right then she heard laughter. The bald man was laughing, though with a wheeze. The two young goons standing in the doorway were laughing hard.

"Sorry for him, you say?" the bald man said when he'd finished laughing, and he wiped tears of laughter from his eyes with his fingertips. "You should have felt sorry for yourself!"

His face hardened. His bare yellow eyes stared at Lena in a way that made her shiver.

"Do you miss your daughter?" he asked insinuatingly.

Lena didn't respond. She felt everything inside her turn cold. The hand holding the coffee cup started shaking noticeably. Lena put the cup down on the table and squeezed her hand into a fist.

"You do," the bald man answered for her, and he quickly licked his thin lips. "Do you want to take a look at her?"

Lena suddenly got very dizzy. *This can't be happening,* she told herself. *He's bluffing. This can't be.*

A remote appeared in the bald man's hand. Only then did Lena notice a large television and VCR on a zebrawood stand in the corner of the room. The bald man pressed a few buttons. The screen turned on, and a minute later Lena saw the broad drive of the Istra holiday house. Liza was running down the drive wearing her bright, colorful snowsuit and her striped knit cap with the pom-pom. In one hand she was holding a red plastic bucket and in the other her stuffed monkey. She was running toward the camera. Her rosy little face now took up the entire screen. Her blond curls poked out from under the cap, and her big blue eyes looked straight at Lena.

"Nanny Vera!" she shouted gaily, then turned and ran off to the side.

On the side, Vera Fyodorovna was standing in her warm jacket and loose woolen trousers. She leaned over to Liza, smiling, straightened her cap, and fastened a snap on her snowsuit.

"Let me look, Liza. Are your little feet wet?"

The scene changed. Now they were looking into the bedroom through the window on the balcony. Liza was sleeping in her pink flannel pajamas. Vera Fyodorovna was knitting, sitting in a chair in front of the television. The glowing screen cast pale patches of light on her calm face. The picture was so peaceful and cozy that Lena wanted nothing more in the world right now than to be in that room, to stroke Liza's silky hair, and to kiss her warm cheek creased by the pillow's folds.

Vera Fyodorovna rose heavily from her chair, went over to the bed, straightened the blanket, and did exactly what Lena so wanted to do— stroked Liza's little head, leaned over, kissed her little cheek, and quietly made the sign of the cross over the sleeping girl. Then, yawning sleepily, she turned off the television and left the room.

The screen went dark. Lena took out another cigarette and lit it, trying to stop her whole body from shaking.

"You have a beautiful daughter," she heard the bald man say. "Who does she take after to be so blond? Your husband? Speaking of the colonel, is he still in London? When will he be back, do you know?"

"What do you want from me?" Lena asked, and she forced herself to look straight into his yellow eyes.

The young deaf-mute woman silently approached the coffee table and began clearing the coffee cups. Lena didn't notice when she'd appeared in the living room.

"You do realize," the bald man continued thoughtfully, "I have much experience in loosening the tongues of people who preferred to keep quiet. Mostly men, though. I don't much like dealing with women. There are all kinds of ways to make a person talk. You're an educated woman, you know how this is done. But each person requires a unique approach. Now you, for example, you'll probably pass out at the first touch. Physical pain is one of the easiest ways to get a person to talk. But I don't like that. You end up with a lot of noise and blood. None of my boys has laid a finger on you yet. And they won't. And, so far, we've only filmed your Liza. We won't harm your child for no reason. But we will if we have to, and you'll have only yourself to blame. Believe me, it will give me no pleasure whatsoever to show you another movie of your beautiful baby in a few days."

Lena suddenly noticed that the deaf-mute had stopped by the table holding the empty cups and was looking steadily at the bald man's lips.

"This is how it is." His stubby-fingered hand lightly chopped through the air. "Give this some proper thought. I'm not rushing you."

"Why do you think I'm not telling you the truth?" Lena asked quietly.

The deaf-mute was focusing her bright blue eyes on Lena's lips as she spoke. No one besides Lena noticed.

"You're a strange woman." The bald man sighed. "You pitied some prison bastard, but you don't pity your own child. Or maybe you haven't completely caught on, eh? Fine. I'll give you another day. You can take the cigarettes and lighter with you. And if there's anything you need, don't be shy. Consider yourself my guest."

They took Lena back to the small room. Only now did she realize the room was in the basement. When the door slammed, Lena collapsed on the bare mattress of the creaky cot and began to weep. She sensed that this wasn't the time for tears, but she couldn't stop herself. Her tears streamed and she angrily wiped them over her cheeks. Yes, if she was ever going to calm down, she first had to get good and angry.

"Pigs, brutes, brainless bastards!" she whispered.

And that really did make her feel better. Her tears dried. Now she could calmly contemplate her situation.

CHAPTER 36

Misha heard the announcement that the plane from London had landed, and he got even more nervous. Krotov was about to deplane, and Misha was going to lay it all out for him straightaway, from beginning to end—Mitya, Katya, the stroller bomb, and the fact that Lena had been abducted by Curly. No one knew where she was or whether she was even alive. All they knew was that Curly didn't joke around. The mere thought of what might happen to Lena Polyanskaya made Misha's stomach hurt. He could only imagine what it would be like for Seryozha.

Krotov was waiting for his bags. He had two hefty suitcases full of presents—for Liza, Lena, and Vera Fyodorovna—as well as souvenirs for his friends and coworkers. The only thing that saddened him was that Lena wasn't going to meet him at the airport. She wasn't due to fly in for another four days. He decided that today he'd catch up on his sleep, and tomorrow morning he'd go see Liza at the holiday house. He'd missed his family terribly.

It was just after midnight when he finally pushed the trolley with the two hefty suitcases into the arrivals hall. And immediately saw Misha. He could tell from his face that something bad had happened. Very bad.

There was a black Volga waiting at the taxi stand. The driver, Kolya Filippov, known by his coworkers for many years as Filya, smiled broadly, got out of the car, and opened the trunk. They stowed the suitcases, got in the car, and Misha continued the story he'd begun in the airport terminal. He tried not to leave out any important details.

Filya made a quick maneuver by the Sokol subway station— stepped on the gas and dashed across the intersection in front of a big black truck.

"We have a tail," he commented without looking around. "There's been an SUV following us since the airport."

"Contact traffic police to cut them off," Krotov said. "Did you get a look at the license?"

"Don't insult me, Sergei Sergeyevich!"

The Volga was already entering the square in front of the Belorussky train station.

"Too bad about Ievlev." Misha sighed. "He was a good guy. Listen, Seryozha. Do you think this was Gradskaya's work, too? Could it just be a coincidence? The Tyumen Federal Security guys are saying that Curly mistook the American for someone else. Curly's got major deals going in America. It's odd that he let the professor go so easily. He's still here, no one has tried to touch him. Poor guy, he's a wreck over Lena."

"Misha, how's your English?" Krotov asked.

"I took German in school. Most of my dealings with Barron have been through an interpreter. But he knows more than I thought. You need to get together with him first thing tomorrow morning."

"Filya." Krotov turned to the driver. "Do you know the fastest way from here to Volokolamsk?"

"I'm on it, Sergei Sergeyevich. The road's empty now. We'll be there in an hour. Do you want to contact the guard at the holiday house?"

"No. The guard has probably been bought off already. Does anyone have a gun?"

"I've got my pistol on me," Filya responded.

"Me, too." Misha nodded. "Listen, Seryozha, where are you planning to take Liza and Vera Fyodorovna?"

"That's the last thing on my mind right now," Krotov said through his teeth. "The main thing is that they're still there. Filya, I think the tail is back!" Krotov noted a cherry-red Toyota behind them.

"Maybe we should call in a support team?" Filya asked.

"Let's try to handle this ourselves, quickly and quietly. Go out on Tverskaya and head toward Petrovka. You'll turn off onto Chekhov Street just for a minute. Misha and I will get out there, and then you'll take the Toyota to Petrovka. Judging from the tails, they know I'm here. The main thing now is that we get there first."

Krotov reached over the seat for Filya's radiophone.

"And lend me your gun," he said, dialing.

Fifteen minutes later, the three occupants of the cherry-red Toyota got worried. The Volga they'd been following had evaporated somewhere after the Mayakovsky station. But they soon heaved a sigh of relief. The Volga was going slowly down Chekhov, probably headed for Petrovka.

At the intersection of the Garden Ring Road and Kalyaevskaya Street, hiding behind two glass and concrete towers, were two prerevolutionary buildings with connecting courtyards. A gray Zhiguli drove into one of the courtyards, barely making a sound. It braked slightly and Krotov and Sichkin got in. Behind the wheel was First Lieutenant Gonchar, whom they knew well. Twenty minutes later, the Zhiguli was racing down the deserted highway to Volokolamsk at top speed.

When they drove up to the tall iron fence around the holiday house, it was a little after two in the morning. They parked the car away from the gates. Gonchar stayed back in the Zhiguli, and Krotov and Sichkin hopped the fence. Skirting the building, they discovered the front door was locked. There was also a door through the kitchen, but it had a padlock on it. Krotov leaned his head back and assessed the rickety fire escape, but right then Misha noticed a small window that had been left slightly open over one section of the dining room.

Vera Fyodorovna slept with one ear open. She woke at the soft, cautious knock on the door, turned on the small sconce over her bed, and looked at the clock. It was 2:40. *Maybe I dreamed it?* she thought, and she was about to turn off the light when the knock was repeated.

She threw on her robe and tiptoed barefoot to the door.

"Who's there?" she asked in a whisper.

"Vera Fyodorovna. It's Seryozha."

"Seryozha! You're back! But what's going on?"

She clicked the lock. Seryozha quickly slipped into the room, followed by Misha Sichkin. They locked the door behind them.

"Vera Fyodorovna, please pack yours and Liza's things," he whispered in her ear and walked over to the balcony door, closed the small window, turned the bolt on the upper lock, and pulled the drapes tightly closed.

"Seryozha, what's happened?" She was already getting the suitcase out of the closet.

"I'll explain everything later. Right now we have to be quick. Get yourself dressed, and I'll dress Liza. And Misha will pack the suitcase."

Liza wasn't at all surprised when she opened her eyes and discovered her papa pulling her snowsuit on right over her pajamas.

"Papa!" She threw her arms around his neck, closed her eyes again, and murmured, "I'll just sleep one minute more. I'll sleep and you carry me. Okay?"

"Yes, Liza. You sleep while I get you dressed." Sergei pulled woolen socks on her bare feet and immediately fell still.

He heard something going on either in the next room or on the next balcony. The building had gone up in the early 1970s, and you could hear a rustle through its thin walls. Picking up the sleeping Liza, Sergei tiptoed out into the tiny hall, where Misha, squatting, was stuffing everything into the suitcase as quickly as he could. A dressed Vera Fyodorovna came through the door to the connecting room.

"Who's staying in the next room?" Seryozha asked her in a whisper and nodded at the wall, on the other side of which sounds could be heard again.

"Some very nice young men. They arrived here a few days ago. They videotaped Liza."

That moment, there was a gentle knock on the other side of the balcony door. When he was going around the building, Seryozha had noticed that the neighboring balconies were separated by low gratings. Hopping from one to another was child's play.

"That's it! We're out of here," he whispered.

"But we're not done packing," Vera Fyodorovna remarked in dismay.

"Nothing will be lost. Just be sure to take your documents." Misha Sichkin quickly latched the suitcase and put it back in the hall closet. "Someone will come for your things later."

"My monkey!" Liza said loudly without opening her eyes.

Vera Fyodorovna stepped over to the bed, retrieved the plush animal out from under the blanket, and reached to turn off the light, but Seryozha stopped her.

"Don't. Keep it on," he whispered.

The glass of the balcony door tinkled softly. On the balcony, someone was trying to look into the room through the tightly drawn drapes.

Trying not to breathe, they left the room for the dimly lit hallway. Misha, leaving last, closed the door without making a sound. But despite his caution, the lock clicked anyway.

"I can't see a damn thing," the thug told his friend in the next room.

He only had his underpants on. He'd just come back from the balcony and was huddling from the cold. He felt like diving back under the warm blanket.

"Quiet!" the second thug sitting on the bed and listening through the wall shouted at him in a whisper.

"Oh, cut it out," the first one yawned. "The old woman probably just went to take a leak. Don't get so worked up! Where are they going to go at three o'clock in the morning?"

"Shut up, I said!" The more conscientious thug leapt silently from the bed, cracked the door, and looked out into the hallway.

It was quiet there. Not a sound. Just in case, he stood there a little longer, listening to the sleepy, nighttime silence of the holiday house. He was interested in the stairs at the end of the hallway. He wasted no time reaching them and leaned over the railing. But it was quiet there, too.

That's ridiculous, he told himself. *They couldn't have made it down to the first floor already. I would have heard them.*

The thug knew Curly would rip his head off if anything happened to the child or the old lady. But everything was calm for now. It was true, where were they supposed to go at three in the morning? Just because they'd made some noise, what did that mean? Sometimes old women can't sleep, and sometimes children wake up in the middle of the night to go pee or to get a glass of water. He went back to the room, where his friend was snoring peacefully.

The conscientious thug listened to the silence in the next room. "They've been asleep for a long time, for sure!" he growled, gave a relaxed yawn, and went back to bed.

The stairs and elevators were to the right down the hallway, but to the left, at the other end of the hallway, there was a small sitting area with armchairs, a magazine table, and a television. The small niche was separated from the hallway by two narrow screens. Right now it was completely dark there. Krotov had decided to wait there in the darkness for a bit just in case and not to go directly to the stairs. Whoever was rustling in the next room and trying to look in from the balcony was bound to check the stairs as well. And it was virtually impossible for the four of them to descend swiftly and silently from the eighth floor.

Vera Fyodorovna heard the cautious steps and pressed her hand to her mouth. The steps moved away as the man walked toward the stairs. It was quiet for a few minutes. Then they heard the steps again. They were getting closer. Vera Fyodorovna's heart was pounding madly. But the steps died down in the middle of the hallway. Somewhere near their room a lock clicked. They waited a few more minutes and then quietly headed for the stairs.

"Well, where to now?" Gonchar asked when they were finally all in the car.

"I have to think," Krotov said.

Liza had slept soundly through the whole escape, her arms around her papa's neck.

"Maybe to my place?" Misha suggested.

"They'd find us." Krotov shook his head. "It wouldn't take them long to figure out we were there."

"Seryozha, why can't we go home?" Vera Fyodorovna asked.

It was time, Krotov knew, to explain what was happening to the woman who up until this moment had acted courageously and hadn't asked any questions. Only now, in the car, did her voice start to quake.

"Vera Fyodorovna," Krotov began cautiously. "I'm in trouble. It is related to my work. For a while, it would be better if you and Liza stayed somewhere safe."

"I knew it." Vera Fyodorovna sighed. "In the courtyard on Malaya Gruzinskaya . . . it was Liza's stroller that blew up. That's all the neighborhood is talking about. I kept hoping maybe . . . My old school friend lives not far from here, on Lugovaya. She lives alone, and the house is big and warm. She gave her apartment to her son and moved into their dacha. We can go there. She'll be happy to have us."

"Yes." Seryozha nodded after a second's thought. "That may not be a bad idea."

"Seryozha, they won't hurt Lena, will they?"

"Don't worry, Vera Fyodorovna. They won't get to her. She's far away," Sichkin answered for Krotov. "By the time she gets back, all will be well."

"Are you sure?"

"We'll do our best."

Lena could tell something had happened. It had been evening for a while, but they seemed to have forgotten about her. She didn't know whether that was good or bad, whether it was better to remind them she was here or to sit tight.

She'd already thought through the broad strokes of her conversation with the bald man. But only the broad strokes. Of course, Gradskaya might well know the bald man. But she couldn't imagine her hiring such a high-level figure as a killer. She could hire one of his hitmen, but then Lena would just have been shot.

Gradskaya had probably called in a favor and asked him to deal with Lena. But those kinds of requests require explanations. And laying out the truth to the crime boss was the last thing she'd do. She'd probably had to make up a story for the bald man that suggested that Lena and Michael represented a danger for him personally. For example, she could have said Michael was a big American mafioso, a competitor with his eye on Russian oil and gold. No, that was ridiculous. Lots of Russian crooks were in America, but there weren't any American gangsters here yet. And a story like that would be easy for the bald man to verify; it wouldn't require kidnapping her. What wouldn't he be able to verify through his criminal networks? Say Gradskaya hinted that Michael was a CIA agent. Now that made more sense.

Why did I ever accept Volkov's offer to drive Michael around Moscow? No, I didn't, she immediately objected to herself. *I was just keeping the game going. I had no choice. But as a result they found out where I was going and who I was going with. But they would have found out eventually. They would have found a way. None of that matters now. What's important is to decide whether to tell the bald man the whole truth. But what if they don't believe me? It's a serious and unexpected accusation. I wonder why my visit to Malaya Proletarskaya raised such a reaction—with Sasha and with the bald gangster? Vasya Slepak, the convict known as Blindboy. What makes him so interesting?*

The door opened. The deaf-mute rolled a cart into the room. On it were two open-faced cheese sandwiches, an apple, a banana, and a large cup of strong tea.

"Thank you," Lena said.

She had no appetite, but she needed her strength, so she forced herself to eat nearly all of it. The young woman stood there, leaning against the wall, observing her. But Lena didn't mind her gaze, which seemed warm, sympathetic even. Before taking the cart away, the deaf-mute touched Lena's arm and nodded at the tiny toilet nook. At first,

Lena didn't understand her, but the young woman took a contoured lipstick out of her pocket and nodded again.

They went into the cramped nook together, and the young woman closed the door and started writing quickly in lipstick on the white tile. *Your daughter is all right*, Lena had time to read.

The deaf-mute immediately wet her handkerchief and wiped off the letters. Lena wanted to take the lipstick out of her hands, but the young woman shook her head and moved her lips expressively. Lena understood her. In a slow whisper she said, "Thank you. What's happened?"

Last night someone took her away. Searched all day. Didn't find her. The letters disappeared again.

Lena's heart beat fast and joyously. *Of course! Seryozha was supposed to arrive last night. Misha Sichkin managed to tell him everything. Seryozha understood and acted.*

Don't let them see you know, the young woman wrote.

"Yes, of course," Lena whispered, and all of a sudden she asked, "Who is Blindboy?"

Killer.

The letters immediately disappeared. Lena realized the conversation was over. Without looking at her, the young woman quickly took the cart out. The lock clicked. Lena took off her boots, sweater, and jeans. She sat down on the bed in her jersey and tights and lit a cigarette. She felt as if she'd just been let out into the open air from some dusty black sack where she couldn't breathe. Now she felt like washing herself from head to toe, brushing her teeth, and getting some sleep.

She washed with soap and warm water, gargled, put her folded sweater under her head, and covered herself with her jacket. *Did Vasya Slepak really become a killer?* she thought, and then she fell asleep. The light of the bare lightbulb in the ceiling didn't keep her from sleeping. When they woke her up, it was nearly morning.

"Get up and get dressed," she heard the crude male voice of the thug Vadik and opened her eyes.

"I need to wash up and brush my teeth," Lena said after pulling on her jeans and lacing her boots. "Please be so kind as to bring me a new toothbrush and toothpaste."

For a few moments Vadik said nothing, just looked at her stupidly and blinked. Then he went and got her what she needed to get ready.

She took her time. She enjoyed brushing her teeth and carefully and slowly combed out her tangled hair with that idiotic comb meant for a close crew cut. Vadik stood there and waited patiently.

The bald man was back in the living room sitting in the same white leather armchair. Once again, the heavy dark drapes were drawn tight. Whatever was outside the windows—a town, a village, or a remote taiga—Lena couldn't see.

"Good morning," Lena said, and she sat across from him.

"Hello." He nodded. "Well, have you come to your senses?"

"Before we begin, I would appreciate it if you would introduce yourself. If I'm going to talk to you, I have to know what to call you." Lena looked him straight in his yellow, unblinking eyes.

"You can call me Vladimir Mikhailovich. Or Curly. Whichever you prefer."

"Pleased to meet you, Vladimir Mikhailovich." Lena tried to smile graciously. "I have to warn you that this conversation is going to be long. And confidential," she added, and she nodded in the direction of Vadik.

The thug, standing in the doorway, snorted contemptuously.

"And because of that," Lena continued, "you and I should first drink some coffee. And breakfast wouldn't be a bad idea, either."

"You're getting ahead of yourself." Curly shook his bald head. "But, okay, we'll do it your way. Hey, Vadik," he said to the thug. "Get us coffee and something to eat."

"Tell me, Vladimir Mikhailovich," Lena asked when they were alone. "Did Regina Valentinovna Gradskaya tell you about my trip?"

Attack is the best form of defense. She would try to ask him the questions and not wait for him to ask his own. Watching his reactions was the only way she could survive this conversation.

His first reaction was a rather long and tense silence and a hard stare. But she withstood both the silence and the stare.

"That, little girl, is none of your business," he rasped at last, quietly, and he coughed into his fist.

Excellent, Lena thought. *He did get his information from Gradskaya. Let's keep going.*

"Regina Valentinovna, as an old friend, informed you that a mysterious American, most likely connected to the CIA, was coming here. And he would be accompanied by an interpreter. Not just any interpreter but one with her own connections to law enforcement. Am I right?"

Curly took a cigarette out of the pack and lit it while looking silently at Lena.

"Being a smart and cautious woman," she continued. "Regina Valentinovna did not go into detail. She said the information was vague, possibly just a rumor. By doing that, on the one hand, she sparked your curiosity, and, on the other, she was insuring herself against the possibility of you finding out that Michael Barron wasn't a CIA agent after all. Actually, it's very hard to verify something like that. But you never know . . . Life is full of surprises. And Regina Valentinovna by no means wants you to think she is deliberately misleading you."

Vadik appeared with a tray. The smell of eggs and bacon filled the room. While he was putting plates, cups, and the hot coffeepot on the table, Lena said nothing. Nor did Curly, though he continued to look hard at Lena. In another situation she might have curled up into a ball under that kind of icy, penetrating gaze. But right now she couldn't allow herself the slightest hint of fear.

"Thank you, Vadik. It's delicious," she said as she sent a forkful of eggs into her mouth.

"Go," his boss growled at him. "And close the door."

"I would like to note," Lena continued once Vadik had left the room, "that in fact it's not at all hard to verify this information. You don't even have to do anything, just think about it." Lena sipped her coffee and started buttering a piece of white toast. "A real CIA agent would be much younger. He would speak excellent Russian. He would work quietly and discreetly. And no one—not Regina Valentinovna or anyone else you know—would have informed you of his arrival. Even if she were in possession of such information, she'd hardly be telling you. You're not her husband, right? Why would she take such a serious risk? For the sake of your friendship? My point is that this affects her personally. Well, her and her husband, Veniamin Borisovich Volkov. The CIA, FBI, and our Federal Security have absolutely nothing to do with this."

Lena finished her buttered toast and her coffee, lit a cigarette, and told the crime boss everything she knew, starting with the events of fourteen years ago, and ending with her conversation the day before yesterday with Regina Gradskaya's mother. She cautiously skirted any personal details and just set out the facts as she knew them. Curly listened silently and intently. When she finished, a dense, almost explosive silence reigned in the room.

It was an eternity before he said a word.

"What you've told me is very serious. I'll have to verify it."

Lena nodded. "I understand."

"You're going to have to stay here in the meantime."

"What about my daughter?" Lena asked, remembering what the deaf-mute had communicated to her earlier. "Are you going to stop threatening her?"

"We'll leave your daughter in peace." He relaxed back into his chair and added, "For now. Then we'll see. By the way, when does your husband get back?"

"Tomorrow night," Lena told him without blinking. "Vladimir Mikhailovich, if I am going to stay here while you verify my story, I have a few personal requests."

"Go ahead."

"A hot shower, clean sheets, slippers, and a mirror," Lena listed. "Yes, and a blanket and pillow, too."

"No problem."

"There, Nina. Now we need to get everything we can from her. She's a gold mine."

Nina's strong, warm hands kneaded Curly's hairy back in smooth, practiced movements. A beautiful cathedral with three cupolas tattooed in many colors of ink was clearly visible through the gray fluff.

"You know what I realized when she told me all that, puss? You can't know, you can't even guess!" He groaned and turned over on his back, caught Nina's hands, and squeezing her strong wrists, pulled the young woman toward him.

Her kind face came very close. Her straight, light brown hair tickled his shoulder.

"I'm getting old, that's what," he exhaled into her soft, mute lips. "Kiss me."

She slipped out of his hands and began calmly unbuttoning her long silk blouse.

"Ten years ago, Nina, I would have finished off that viper with my own hands. It's a thief's code of honor," he continued, watching the blouse fall to the thick rug. "There isn't room on this earth for snakes like that, to say nothing of in prison. Six girls! In prison they don't forgive even one. They sodomize him right off."

Nina was chilled, standing there naked. But he kept talking.

"You know how much their business is worth?" He squeezed his eyes tight. "And it's all going to be mine! Right down to the last kopek. They'll hand it over without a murmur. When they find out who I have here, they'll hand it over immediately. They aren't afraid of the court or the prosecutor. They're afraid of the disgrace, which is worse than death for them. And here's their disgrace, alive and unharmed, sitting with me and asking for a blanket and pillow."

Nina quietly started dressing, but Curly didn't even notice, carried away as he was by his own monologue.

"Regina's problem is she thinks there's no one smarter or cleverer in the world than her. She thinks she can outwit anyone, even me. Fuck that!"

He shook his heavy, hairy fist in the air. "She's outwitted lots of people. But not me. Fuck it!"

His fist slammed into the hard edge of the bed and fell still. His fat-fingered hand unclenched and fell limp.

"But I'm getting old. In the old days I would have smeared Regina and her pervert all over the wall, and that would have been sweeter than all their wealth. I would have spat on their wealth. To an honest thief, honor is more precious than anything. I'm not that man anymore. I'm getting old. And times have changed. These aren't my times. They're for other people."

CHAPTER 37

His room in the Sovetskaya Hotel on the Leningrad highway wasn't bad at all. Michael could have stayed there and worked for several days. He could have gone back to the Tretyakov, and the Pushkin Museum, and the Bolshoi Theater. But he didn't feel like going anywhere. Or working. He couldn't listen through the tapes of his Siberian conversations. All he heard was Lena's voice as she interpreted the stories of scholars, art historians, Old Believers, and museum curators. And Michael would feel sad and frightened all over again. What if Lena didn't make it? He was the one who'd talked her into going to Siberia.

For the second day in a row, Michael lay on his hotel bed with Oscar Wilde's fairy tales. It was an old, well-worn edition that had belonged to his mother, and he'd carried it around with him wherever he went. When he felt sad, he would choose a tale at random and read it. But right now he couldn't even read. He looked through the lines he'd known since he was a child and thought about what had happened in Siberia.

The nice Russian police officer with the funny name Sichkin had paid him a visit. And his name was Michael, too—Mikhail, that is, Misha for short. He didn't speak a word of English so he had a very young interpreter with him. Their conversation was brief and confused.

"Dr. Barron, we would like you to stay around a few more days," he said, and Michael noticed his embarrassment as he said that. "We don't have the right to demand this of you. We're just asking. For Lena's sake."

"Yes, of course, I have no intention of leaving until I see Mrs. Polyanskaya with my own eyes. I have to know she's all right. I was the one who asked her to accompany me to Siberia. It's my fault all this happened."

"We suspect she was abducted," the Russian police officer told him gloomily.

First they'd rummaged through his things and stolen his tin of talcum powder, then they abducted his friend. He wondered what that Chekist Sasha, the Gogol lover, was thinking. Did he appreciate the danger? He'd spirited Michael away but left Lena at the mercy of some unknown thugs. All these young men from the KGB inspired no trust in Michael at all. He liked the police officer Sichkin much more, but Michael placed his main hopes on Lena's husband. He was a colonel, and that's no joke. He must have serious resources, and most of all, he wasn't searching for just anyone—he was searching for his wife.

When a tall, fair-haired man in a formal suit appeared in his hotel room and said in quite decent English, "Hello, Dr. Barron. My name is Colonel Krotov, I'm Elena Polyanskaya's husband," Michael breathed a sigh of relief.

Entering the room behind Sergei Krotov was the same young interpreter.

"You speak good English," Michael quietly commented. "Why do you need an interpreter?"

"My vocabulary isn't large enough. We have much to talk about, and I would hate to miss a single word of what you will say." Sergei smiled.

The interpreter slipped into their conversation only rarely, only helping Sergei with the odd word.

"I don't understand why the Federal Security Service, knowing the danger, didn't avert it," Michael said agitatedly. "I have the feeling they set Lena up, although I absolutely can't imagine what good that would do anyone."

"Michael, please, tell me in detail about everything that happened in Siberia," Sergei asked him.

"I think we have to start with Moscow," Michael said agitatedly. "Before I didn't give it much thought, I didn't see any connection. But now . . . someone tried to break into the apartment one night."

Sergei noticed the professor's detailed story of his time in Moscow made no mention of the entire day they were driven around the city and taken to a private club by a wealthy man in a Mercedes. He himself knew this from Misha, who had learned it from Major Ievlev.

The old man doesn't want to tell on Lena. Sergei chuckled to himself. *He thinks, what if this involves something other than friendly relations? So he's keeping quiet about Volkov, just in case.*

"She visited an old librarian, at the Veterans Home." Sergei pensively repeated the professor's last sentence. "Valentina Gradskaya."

"Yes." Michael nodded. "Sasha never should have left her there."

From odd individual details, a more or less comprehensible picture finally took shape. Michael's story added the last missing fragments. Only one thing was still unclear: where did Curly, the legendary boss of the taiga, come in?

Late that evening, they moved Lena to a different room. This must have been the guest room. It had a separate shower and a complete array of toiletries. Lena discovered not only shampoo but also conditioner, face moisturizer, and hand cream on the glass shelf, a terry robe, and a shower cap. In the drawers of the antique-style bureau was a pair of new stockings and underpants, a nightgown, two knit shirts, and a loose hand-knit sweater.

How touching. Lena grinned to herself. *Have they put me up here permanently or something?*

The main advantage of the new room was the big window. It was solidly shut with only a small vent that opened. Solid, snow-drifted taiga came right up to the window. The first night, Lena slept like a log. In the morning the deaf-mute came and brought breakfast—a piping hot omelet, strong coffee, and bread and butter. There was also a pack of cigarettes on the small serving cart.

"Thank you very much. You must have given me your things, am I right? Did you buy all this for yourself? It's all new except for the sweater."

Lena tried to articulate precisely to make it easier for the young woman to read her lips.

"How long are they going to keep me here?" Lena asked in a whisper, and she nodded to the bathroom in hopes that the deaf-mute would have a tile dialog with her again.

The young woman frowned and shook her head no.

"What's your name?" Lena asked.

The deaf-mute got a pencil out and wrote right on the cart's white plastic surface: *Nina.*

"Very nice to meet you, Nina. My name is Lena. Although, you probably know that already."

Nina nodded and smiled.

"Nina, please sit with me. Let's have coffee together. I won't ask you any more hard questions."

Nina looked at her watch, nodded, went out for a minute without even closing the door behind her. She returned a minute later with a second coffee cup and an ashtray.

"Thank you again," Lena said.

But there wasn't anything for them to talk about. All she had were hard questions, and Lena was afraid of scaring off her companion. They drank their coffee in silence and then both lit up.

"Do you live here all the time? Or do you just come for visits?" Lena finally brought herself to ask.

But Nina frowned again and shook her head.

"I'm sorry. I don't know what I can ask you that you can answer. When you leave, I'll be left alone. What am I supposed to do then? Are there any books here? Or newspapers, or magazines? I could at least read. I can't do this—eat, sleep, look out the window at the snow, and wait."

Nina nodded and took out her pencil again.

There are books, she wrote on the white plastic.

"What kind?" Lena asked.

I don't know. I can bring them all.

She stubbed out the cigarette and left quickly, taking the serving cart with her. She reappeared half an hour later. On the same cart there was a stack of books. Nina neatly unloaded them onto the bureau, gave a friendly nod in response to Lena's "thanks," and left.

The usual black-market books from the late seventies, Lena determined, examining the spines. A gentleman's assortment: *Angélique, The Three Musketeers*, Pikul's *Word and Deed*, and a few novels by Maurice Druon. Books obtained in exchange for pulp fiction or else bought through connections. "Proper" homes were supposed to have them. Not that anyone actually read them. The colorful covers just adorned the shelves of imported bookcases, like mother-of-pearl china from East Germany and Czech crystal.

It was obvious no one had ever touched these books. They had never been opened, though they'd been on the shelf for nearly two decades. Lena didn't feel like reading *The Three Musketeers* or *Angélique*. The only thing that drew her attention was the collection of Ivan Bunin's works.

Lena lay down on the bed, on top of the blanket, in her jeans and a T-shirt. After the first two pages of "Antonov Apples" she forgot where she was. It was as if she could smell the apples.

That afternoon Nina stopped by to bring food—a small piece of baked sturgeon, a vegetable salad, two apples, and a bunch of bananas.

"They're feeding me well," Lena noted. "You don't know whether they're planning to let me out of here alive, do you?"

Nina turned away and headed for the door.

"I'm sorry. That was a stupid joke," Lena said as she left.

Nina wasn't looking at her, so Lena may as well have been speaking into the void.

Night fell imperceptibly. Lena shut Bunin's selected works. She had read the fat volume from cover to cover, including the foreword and notes.

She walked over to the now-black window. She could try to open it or break the glass. She was only on the second floor, and the snow would cushion her landing if she jumped. But there was probably a guard out there, and beyond him, the taiga.

The wind was wailing softly, and the trees' black silhouettes were bending and creaking. Somewhere close by, dogs were barking, and judging from their heavy, low voices, they were big, German shepherds or wolfhounds. In the distance, in the taiga's deep, dense forest, wolves howled to the cold night wind.

Either they'll kill me in an escape attempt, Lena reasoned calmly, *or else I'll get lost in the taiga. But more than likely they'll shoot me before I can take even a single step. Curly has probably decided to use the information I gave him for his own benefit. He is going to blackmail Volkov and Gradskaya to become the sole owner of their business. I wonder how long this is going to take? For now, he needs me. I am his primary weapon against Volkov and Gradskaya. He's decided to keep me in good condition so that he can present me to them at any time—not only alive but well, clean, fed, and capable of speaking coherently.*

And after that? Then I'll just vanish. Seryozha will look for me. At the last moment, special ops will fly in on a helicopter and take the building by storm. Yes, of course. Hope and wait! Lena grinned. *Federal Security Sasha knows exactly who's following us. Is it even possible that they don't know about this building? But what if Curly paid them all off? Why spoil their relationship with him? A bad peace with a crime boss is better than a good quarrel. His own colleagues will make sure Seryozha doesn't find me.*

Before going to bed, she headed for the shower. She washed her hair slowly, stood under the hot shower for a long time, and then carefully combed out her wet hair in front of the mirror. Nina hadn't missed a single detail and had equipped her with virtually everything a woman might need. *I wonder for how long? This isn't for life, after all! Though how much longer do I have to live? A week? A month? Probably not more. But in a month they'll find me. Seryozha won't rest until he does.*

After stepping out of the shower and putting on the borrowed robe, leaving her wet hair loose, Lena lit a cigarette and pressed her back up against the black window. The smell of early spring came through the open vent. Soon the snow would melt in the taiga, and the Tobol and Yenisei would overflow their banks. It was probably warm in Moscow already. Liza had grown out of her snowsuit. Lena would have to buy her a new one for next winter. Or would a little coat be better? She wondered whether her new boots leaked.

The barking of the dogs grew loud and then turned into a howl. There were several of them, at least three, but they fell silent—one after the other. Then it got quiet, and in that silence she distinctly heard a soft thump, as if something big and heavy had fallen to the ground right in front of her window.

All of a sudden the lights went out. Throughout the building. The yellowish light that had just been cast from the neighboring windows disappeared. Lena froze and peered into the darkness. The light of her cigarette flared up in the glass. A minute later she heard steps and voices outside the door.

"You go check!" Lena heard the voice that belonged to Vadik shout. "Let me go outside and I'll check the fuse."

Someone replied, but Lena could no longer make out the words. The voices and steps moved away, and then it got quiet again. Lena's heart started pounding. Without knowing why, she dressed quickly in the darkness, feeling for her jeans and knit shirts. She zipped up and used her lighter to find her boots.

And then she thought, *What for?*

The building was quiet. Her boots were under the bureau. She'd pulled on one boot when she heard voices again.

"Maybe something's wrong with the wiring. I can't see a fucking thing!"

"The boss'll come and you'll see everything plenty fast!"

"Hey! Who the hell do you think you are?"

"I'll show you who I am!"

"Okay, fellas, enough shouting." a third voice interjected.

A key turned in the lock. Lena managed to quickly kick off her boot. The door opened. The flashlight's powerful beam struck her in the eyes.

"Were you sleeping?" he asked her evenly.

"Nearly." She nodded, squinting from the flashlight. "What happened?"

But the door had already slammed shut.

"Have you seen the dogs?" Lena heard.

"They're asleep. Everyone's asleep." Vadik said, and then yawned loudly and groaned. "It's the middle of the fucking night. We'll figure out what's up with the electricity in the morning."

The steps and voices died down and a door slammed somewhere.

Lena couldn't calm down. *That means the bald man is gone. He's not here. All that's left are the guards. How many of them are there? One would be plenty for me. But they said they were going to bed now.*

She put on her boots just in case, laced them up, and pulled on her sweater. The moon was shining brightly out her window. Lena lit another cigarette. She couldn't understand why she was so nervous.

"Does this mean I want to escape? Do I really want to escape into the taiga? With no jacket and thin-soled boots? I could put the other sweater on top of this one, but it's still colder than ten below at night in the taiga. I'll just get lost and freeze or starve to death. The wolves will eat me. And how can I get out? If I break the window, they'll hear." She noticed she was speaking out loud, in a quick, nervous whisper.

At that moment she fell silent. She heard a rustle right outside her door and the lock click quietly. The handle turned slowly. Lena jumped back and pressed up against the wall. The door cracked open and shut immediately. A short male silhouette slipped quickly into the room. He moved lightly and silently, like a cat. His flashlight blazed up for a second, rested on Lena, and went out immediately.

She had nothing to lose. She flicked her lighter. In the trembling, unsteady light she made out powerful shoulders under a dark leather jacket, a blond crew cut, deep-set, almost-white eyes under bare eyebrows, deep, rough pitting on his cheeks, and the traces of a young man's unhealed blackheads.

"Vasya Slepak," she whispered, and she dashed to the window. "Vasya, have you come to kill me?"

CHAPTER 38

Regina Valentinovna liked to make money and spend it. It wasn't that she was too lazy to count it—she just couldn't bear to. Long ago, when she'd had very little as a young student, she'd counted every kopek.

But now, everything that had to do with banking and bookkeeping made her yawn. Naturally, the company had an entire staff of book-keepers, lawyers, and managers. She didn't have to worry about their qualifications. But their trustworthiness, that was always in question.

Veniamin Borisovich, on the other hand, liked to count money as well as make it. The business's gigantic financial mechanism was under his vigilant and keen control. He trusted his colleagues, but he was constantly checking on them. You could wake him up in the middle of the night and he could answer how much money there was in each account and how much was invested in securities. He always knew what was going on in the markets of Europe, Asia, and America and understood stock prices as well as a professional broker.

Over the years, Regina had gotten the hang of bookkeeping, though. Gradually and imperceptibly—even to her husband—she'd made up for lost time. It's always better to know than not to know, she thought. Anything could happen. What Venya, still not recovered from the serious flu, was doing with the bank accounts she learned from the bookkeeper Grisha, but confirmed with a few other sources as well.

And here she was, sitting with one of her secret consultants in a small restaurant, sipping on Baileys from a shallow glass and looking thoughtfully into the young lawyer's clear, brown eyes.

"There's something else, Regina Valentinovna," the young man said. "But I'm afraid this information . . ." He coughed and fell silent.

"Don't be afraid." Regina smiled gently. "Call a spade a spade. Are you trying to say this information will cost me more?"

"What do you mean?" The young man blushed. "That's not what this is about."

"Then what is it?"

"The information is still vague but dangerous. But for your sake, Regina Valentinovna, I'm prepared to take the risk."

"Come on, Anton, spit it out." She leaned back in her chair and suddenly winked merrily. "What do you want in exchange for your burning secret? You don't have to be shy with me."

But Anton was shy. He blushed and felt his shirt treacherously soaking through under his jacket.

"I think we'd do better to talk about this somewhere else," he said softly. "If you don't object."

"Where are you and I going to talk?" Regina shook her head.

"If you have no objection"—he filled his lungs with air and blurted out—"at my place!"

For two weeks a quiet rumor had been circulating among the employees that the boss had a new love interest. People had always been surprised by the iron faithfulness of the couple. Neither Volkov nor Gradskaya had allowed themselves any outside distractions. People were used to seeing them as a single unit, whole and indivisible. And now someone had heard from someone else who knew for a fact that the boss was head over heels in love with another woman.

The most interesting part was that the object of his desire was not some film star or model, but a modest, middle-aged journalist. People were burning with curiosity. If the boss had started something with one of the famous beauties that circled around him, no one would have been surprised.

People said that Volkov was very serious about the journalist, he'd fallen in love in his old age, and he was planning to divorce Regina and marry the journalist, who no one knew or had even laid eyes on.

After cautiously verifying the business's financial affairs on Gradskaya's instruction, Anton Konovalov had become more and more convinced that his boss was busy dividing up their joint property. He had to give his boss his due. He was dividing up the business's immense wealth between him and his wife fairly. From what he was able to see, Volkov intended to put the entire business in Regina Valentinovna's full control, leaving himself with several houses and money in the form of cash deposits in a few Swiss banks. It was clear that Gradskaya was losing almost nothing. The business yielded huge profits, and in five or six years Regina Valentinovna could fully recover what her husband had taken with him.

Regina Valentinovna would be rich and powerful as well as available, so naturally there were several young men prepared to ease her solitude. If previous attempts to flirt with the older but still attractive woman had been doomed to failure, now there was a real chance. And Anton Konovalov had decided that he had the most realistic chance.

This was the second time he'd been alone with his boss in a dimly lit restaurant. What he'd reported to her today unambiguously confirmed the vague rumors of an impending divorce. But there was one other piece of news, quite unpleasant news. Anton believed he'd learned of this dangerous information in time, and it was probably worth a lot. But this had nothing to do with money. His boss should be grateful to him. She could express her gratitude at his place. Then he would tell her what he had discovered.

"Okay." Gradskaya smiled tenderly. "I'm burning with curiosity."

His two-room bachelor pad on Vernadsky Boulevard seemed to have been specifically designed for intimate encounters. The floor in the living room was covered in a very soft rug that begged to be walked on barefoot. There was only a low, wide, L-shaped sofa to sit on. The guest had no choice but to sit beside her host. Out of his extensive music library, Anton chose Mozart. A scented candle was quickly lit on the round coffee table, and two tiny cups of strong Turkish coffee were brewed.

"I'm listening, child," Gradskaya said wearily when her gracious host finally stopped fussing and sat down beside her on the sofa.

"Regina Valentinovna." He tried to make his voice low and a little raspy. "Aren't you tired of talking about business?"

"All right, Anton, quit playing these games." She frowned. "Tell me what you know."

"I'm afraid," he murmured in confusion. "I'm afraid you'll leave the moment I tell you everything. And I want you to stay here a while. It's so nice to have you here."

"Don't worry." She reached out and ruffled the hair on the back of his head.

He caught her hand and kissed her firm, broad palm, and said in a whisper, "You really won't leave?"

"I promised," Regina whispered in reply and tenderly ran her finger across his cheek and touched his lips.

"I discovered entirely by accident that someone has taken an active interest in the business's financial affairs." His hands explored under her narrow suede skirt. "At first I thought it was the tax police, but it isn't. It's someone entirely different." One of his hands slid across her hip and the other unzipped her skirt.

"Who?" Regina took his face in her hands and looked closely into his eyes.

"Crooks," he exhaled. Pulling off her skirt, stockings, and panties simultaneously, he started to unbutton her silk blouse.

"Can you be more precise?" Regina asked.

"Curly's men." Her blouse fell to the floor, followed by her bra. In the candle's weak light, he couldn't see Regina Valentinovna's face turn deathly pale.

"What specifically were they interested in?" she asked in a whisper.

Anton, who had been undressing himself as he undressed her, was almost completely nude.

"Everything. Absolutely everything. Not only that, they did it brashly, almost proprietarily." He took off the last thing—dark blue socks with little white stars.

This is the end, Regina thought, barely responding to the young lawyer's energetic caresses. *Curly is going to take everything. All he needs there is Polyanskaya and Blindboy. In Curly's place, that's exactly what I would have done. But what am I going to do in my place? Or can't I do anything? Is this truly the end? The end could be even worse, but never dumber. Lord, is Sinitsyn's unlucky verse going to surface again?*

Anton Konovalov was already moaning quietly, and Regina noted distractedly that she'd been wrong to reject the advances of these young peacocks for so many years. Although she understood perfectly well that it was exclusively a matter of money and career, nonetheless, she'd missed out on a lot. She couldn't catch up now.

Things were approaching their denouement. The violin wailed high and passionately, and the cello's deep, low voice began affectionately echoing it. Regina was surprised to discover that she was well on her way. All of a sudden there awoke in her such a bitter, insatiable thirst for life. She dug her nails so hard into her partner's muscular back that she nearly drew blood. She arched her head back and she was off somewhere above the sparking waves of the violin solo.

The tub in Konovalov's apartment was round and roomy and had a whirlpool. Anton carried his lady there and got in himself.

"You know, I think I'll stay here until morning," Regina said, and she closed her eyes. "I need to get good and relaxed."

"Really?" He was overjoyed.

"It's I who should thank you. Your secret is indeed worth a lot. You're right, the information is indeed both unpleasant and dangerous. Be cautious with it, please."

"Of course! Not a word to anyone! The silence of the grave!"

"That's the truth." Regina nodded pensively.

The lighter's flame flickered and went out. Lena flicked it one more time, but it had run out of fuel.

"Hello, Lena Polyanskaya. Please get dressed as quickly and quietly as you can," the killer whispered.

With trembling hands, Lena pulled the sweater Nina had left over her own. Blindboy flashed his flashlight on her.

"Do you have anything warmer?" he asked.

"No."

"All right, then let's go." He took her by the hand.

His hand was iron.

He's worked out and is twice as wide as he was then, Lena thought. *He's a killer.*

They slipped out of the room and stole down the hallway. The building was filled with a sleepy silence. A minute later they were in some kind of a room. Looking around, Lena realized it was the kitchen. The flashlight flashed again, lighting a small, inconspicuous door next to the giant refrigerator. Through the door was a wooden staircase.

They climbed it and ended up in the attic. Moonlight fell through a small dormer window. Stepping cautiously over the creaking wood floor, trying not to make any noise, they went to a window which Blindboy had left half open. Outside was the steep incline of the metal roof. Blindboy gave Lena a boost, she crawled out the window, and her feet immediately slid on the icy metal. Vasya crawled out and managed to grab her hand.

"I'm going to jump first," he whispered in her ear. "And then you. Don't be afraid, it's not high. I'll catch you. Why is your hair wet?"

"I washed it," Lena whispered in reply.

"That's bad. You'll catch cold. Okay, I'm going. When you jump, watch you don't yell."

He slipped almost silently off the edge of the roof. Lena began creeping after him. She was scared to look down. Easy for him to say it's not high! It was every bit of five meters. Lena squeezed her eyes shut and jumped, imagining all her bones breaking, but she landed right in the killer's iron arms. He had an odd smell.

"What is that smell?" Lena whispered.

"Ether. For the dogs," he answered and cautiously set her down on the snow.

There was a noise in the building. A flashlight ran by a first-floor window. Grabbing Lena's hand, the killer dragged her to the other side of the building. It was hard to run through the deep snow. Lena realized they were running away from the road.

The building was surrounded by a concrete wall at least two meters high. From her window, she hadn't been able to see that past the trees. Right by the fence there was something dark in the snow. Lena could see that it was a dead body and that Vasya was taking the short pea jacket and scarf off it.

"Put this on," he said. "Faster! Put the scarf on your head!"

Lena obediently zipped up and threw the wide knit scarf that had been taken off the dead man around her head. The scarf smelled of tobacco and men's cologne. Blindboy pulled her by the arm, and they quickly ran along the wall. There was a narrow gap between concrete sections with fat pieces of steel armature sticking out of it.

"I'll go first, you follow. Be careful going over the barbed wire. Don't get snagged."

"Is it electrified?" Lena asked.

"It was. It's not now." He climbed deftly, like a cat, onto the two-meter-high wall and immediately disappeared down the other side. Lena grabbed onto a piece of steel and pulled herself up. Even as a child she hadn't climbed walls. Her foot looked for a hold and slipped over the concrete.

Voices and footsteps could be heard coming from the house.

"Stop!" a voice shouted from very close by. "Stop or I'll fucking shoot!" And a few shots rang out.

Lena flew over the wall like a bird. And found herself back in the killer's arms. The moon was shining brightly. They ran into the taiga, slogging through the deep snow, tripping on roots. It was getting harder and harder to run. Behind them, the guards were shooting at random.

Blindboy pulled a small, short-barreled submachine gun out of his jacket as he ran, looked back, and fired a round. The shots behind them stopped for a second. Then they rattled again.

"Get down!" Blindboy ordered.

Lena fell onto the snow. She couldn't see a thing. She heard only continuous gunfire and cursing. Someone was running heavily over the deep snow. Vasya was shooting off rounds. Lena suddenly realized he was taking out one thug after another with his submachine gun. She didn't know how long this had been going on, but it seemed like an eternity. She was cold lying in the snow. A trembling struck her. The locks of her hair that escaped the scarf turned into icicles.

Finally it was quiet. She decided to raise her head and looked around. Vasya was sitting on the snow, squeezing his right shoulder with his left hand.

"That's it," he said. "We're going."

"What happened to you? Are you okay?" she asked.

"Just grazed. I'll be fine. Shake off the snow." He stood up. "Let's go. We have to get as far away from here as possible."

They didn't run now. You can't run through the deep taiga, there's no solid ground underfoot. You might step into a swamp at any moment. That's not so bad in winter, when the ground is frozen solid, but by spring the ice is very thin. A taiga swamp will suck you down instantly.

They moved forward, stepping over the trunks of fallen trees. It started growing light. Lena could make out a dark stream of blood on Vasya's right sleeve.

"We have to stop the blood. Let's sit down on a trunk and I'll look at the wound."

"No." He shook his head. "We have to get to the hermitage."

"What hermitage?"

"There's a place near here, an abandoned hermitage from the Schismatics."

"You shot them all. Who's going to be chasing us?"

"Not all of them. When it gets light, they'll send a helicopter. We have to get to the hermitage, which you can't see from above."

"Is it far to this hermitage?"

"A couple of hours at least."

"Does it hurt?" Lena asked. "Does your shoulder hurt?"

"Don't talk," he replied. "Conserve your strength."

She barely had any strength left. Lena kept rubbing her face with fistfuls of snow. Her feet slipped over the iced trunks of trees. Her head was spinning she was so weak. They walked for three hours without halts or stops. Despite his wounded shoulder, Blindboy walked easily and swiftly over the treacherous terrain. He walked through the taiga as if he had asphalt underfoot.

They didn't say a single word for the rest of their long, agonizing journey.

CHAPTER 39

"Regina, we have to talk," Venya Volkov whispered as he sat in his audition hall watching a young boy leap across the stage. His sweet caramel face was red from exertion, and his weak falsetto produced the standard dreck.

Regina wasn't there. She'd disappeared. She hadn't spent the night at the dacha. He knew she hadn't been at their Moscow apartment, either. *Well, that's excellent,* he thought. *She has enough sense to understand.*

"We have to talk," he whispered yet again, trying to get used to the sound of the cliché on his lips.

He'd wanted to say it last night, but Regina wasn't there, and he'd heaved a sigh of relief. It was probably best to wait. He had to launch this last project. He couldn't leave without finishing what he'd started.

A month ago he'd decided to create a young superduo. A boy and a girl, no more than eighteen, but who looked like teenagers. Not today's teenagers, racing on rollerblades with bandanas around their empty heads. They had to have the touching love of children, outside of time, outside any crudeness or worldly cynicism. A Romeo and Juliet for the new millennium. The main thing was to figure out the precise types.

He'd already found the girl. He'd chosen a first-year drama student, skinny as a rail. She had waist-length, ash-brown hair and huge black eyes set in a slender, almost translucent little face. Without makeup, she didn't look more than fifteen. Her name was Yulia. She moved very well and her voice wasn't too bad.

The boy had been harder to find. Today he'd decided to pick someone. This caramel one was the seventh one he'd auditioned today. Listening to his weak falsetto, Venya suddenly clapped and said loudly, "Stop!"

The boy stopped.

"Can you recite a poem?"

"A poem?" The boy batted his long eyelashes in confusion.

"Didn't you study Pushkin, Lermontov, and Tyutchev at school? Recite something. Whatever you remember."

"Uh-huh." The boy nodded, thought a second, and began:

> Uncle, tell me something.
> Did Moscow burn for nothing?
> Handed to the Frenchie . . .

"Oh my God." Venya frowned. "Don't you get it? Something about love. Well? 'Shall I compare thee . . .'" he hinted.

"'To a summer's' . . . um . . . way?" the boy continued in confusion.

"'Day!'" Venya raised his voice. 'To a summer's day.' That's all. You can go. Okay, who's next?" he shouted, turning toward the door.

As soon as the next boy came in, Venya heaved a sigh of relief. Dark chestnut curls, round eyeglasses, big, bright blue eyes. Before the boy could climb onstage or open his mouth, Venya already knew he'd found his boy.

"Where's Yulia?" He looked around.

"Here I am, Veniamin Borisovich!" came a delicate voice from the back row.

The girl had been sitting in the room the whole time. He'd totally forgotten about her.

"Go up onstage. Stand next to him." Here it was, his final project. Romeo and Juliet. The rollout would take six months. He wouldn't be here then. If Regina needed help, he'd help. He himself would do just the first two videos and choose what songs they would perform. And that was it.

"Regina, we have to talk," he whispered for a third time.

"Veniamin Borisovich, did you say something?" Yulia asked from the stage.

"No. Nothing. Do you both know a good ballad?"

They whispered together. A minute later they started a duet:

Never leave me, springtime,
Never leave me, hope.

The boy turned out to have a decent voice, low and deep. And he had a good ear. Closing his eyes, Venya leaned back in his seat. The words and melody didn't arouse any fire or trembling in him. He liked a ballad performed well, only . . .

He decided he wouldn't say that hard cliché to Regina tonight. He needed a little longer. He knew Regina would hear him out calmly and wouldn't make a fuss. She would treat his decision with understanding, sympathy even.

"Oh well," she would say. "If that's what you want, if that's better for you, I'm prepared . . ."

And then she'd kill Lena.

She'd find a way. She wouldn't miss again. Something unexpected would happen. An accident. For instance, the plane from Tyumen to Moscow would blow up in midair.

Let Lena get back and have a talk with her husband. Venya didn't doubt for a second that she'd agree to his proposal. She belonged to him and him alone. Who else could his happiness, his youth belong to?

The whole long, terrible stretch of life called his youth compressed in his memory down to a few days, a few happy days in June 1982. There was nothing but that one vital love. Now she would come back to him. She already had. Lena Polyanskaya loved him. They'd be together. He was healthy. He hadn't killed anyone.

"Oh, golden days, go on and on," the boy and girl on stage sang with utter abandon.

"That's it. We're here," the killer said hoarsely, and he fell on the snow.

Lena looked around. There wasn't any hermitage, just a small, snow-drifted mound. Vasya was lying on the snow with his eyes shut. The morning sun was pounding his face. Lena sat on a fallen trunk, feeling dizzy.

The last section of the journey had been almost easy. She'd gotten her second wind. She started to think she wasn't even tired and could go on as long as need be. Only now, having stopped, did she realize she was dead on her feet.

The killer lay on the snow with his eyes shut for ten minutes. He knew how to relax completely and give each cell in his body a respite. Even the pain in his injured shoulder didn't bother him. Lena shut her eyes, leaned against a tree trunk, and fell instantly into a deep sleep.

He didn't attempt to wake her. He picked up a suitable birch branch and used it to sweep clear the dugout's entrance. The job took him less than half an hour. When the entrance was cleared, the killer collected fir-branch litter and spread several layers of it on the bottom of the refuge. Only after that did he wake up Lena.

She opened her eyes and for a moment couldn't understand where she was. She felt a little better after her brief nap, but her body ached and demanded more rest.

"No helicopter so far," the killer said. "You have to look and see what's happening with my shoulder. We'll sit at the entrance, and as soon as we hear a helicopter, we'll hide inside."

"Fine." Lena nodded and immediately thought, *But what if it's a different helicopter? Not the crooks'?*

But she didn't say a word.

From the many pockets of his leather jacket, the killer retrieved a small flat flask, a Finnish knife in a thick leather sheath, and a bar of chocolate. Neatly removing the wrapper, he broke off four squares, gave two to Lena, and put two in his own mouth.

"Eat slowly. This is all our food for the next few days," he said. "Later, I'll try to boil some snow for water."

Under his jacket, Blindboy was wearing a thick sweater, and under his sweater he was wearing a striped T-shirt that made the bloody hole in the upper part of his right shoulder look particularly nasty. Lena was amazed at how easily he moved the injured shoulder, pulling the sweater and T-shirt over his head.

"You're not cold?" she asked when he'd undressed to the waist.

"Look at my shoulder," the killer replied.

"I don't know. I'm not a doctor," Lena warned as she examined the bleeding wound.

"I know. But we don't have a doctor. Use snow to wipe away the blood."

"What do you have in your flask?"

"Alcohol."

"Then why snow? It could get infected."

"There's not much alcohol. It'll come in handy. But the snow here is clean, so pure it's basically sterile. Just do what I tell you."

Lena dug a handful of soft snow out from under the hardened ice crust and began carefully wiping the blood around the wound. The killer didn't even wince.

"The bleeding's not bad; it's nearly stopped. I think I can feel the bullet," Lena told him. "Do you have a handkerchief? It needs bandaging."

"No. It does need bandaging, but that comes later. Right now you're going to take out the bullet."

"I'm sorry, what?"

"You're going to make an incision and pull out the bullet. Then you'll bandage it up."

Lena examined the wound one more time. She could feel the bullet right under the skin. A doctor could probably have pulled it out in ten minutes, even in these conditions. But Lena had never pulled out anything more than a splinter, but she knew Vasya was right. She had to pull out the bullet. Otherwise infection could set in.

"Don't be scared," he said gently. "I know human anatomy pretty well. There aren't any major arteries there. I can feel it right under the skin. There's no one but you to do this. And it has to be done."

All Lena found in the pockets of the stranger's peacoat was a pack of cigarettes and a lighter. She unzipped the inside pocket and searched it. Five hundred dollars, that was it. She needed a clean handkerchief. She took off the peacoat and pulled the hem of her long knit shirt out of her jeans and cut off a strip of fabric about thirty centimeters wide with the Finnish knife. Then she cut a few smaller scraps from that strip. And then she carefully rubbed her hands, the knife blade, and the edge of the wound with alcohol. Taking a deep breath and crossing herself, she stretched the skin around the wound a little and made a precise cut with the knife.

"Well done," the killer praised her. "Do you see it?"

"Yes."

Lena saw the dark metal tip. The bullet was smaller than she thought it would be. She tried not to think about the pain she was inflicting on Vasya Slepak. Her fingers were slender and deft, but for the first time in her life she regretted she didn't have long nails. They would have helped her snag the bullet.

Finally she got ahold of it, and she showed the killer the small, elongated piece of lead.

"You can throw it away," he said.

She soaked another scrap with alcohol, carefully wiped the wound, and used the last long piece of fabric to tightly bind his shoulder.

"Very nicely done, Lena Polyanskaya. With skills like that, why didn't you become a doctor?" the killer asked, pulling on his T-shirt.

"I'm not asking you why you don't write poetry anymore, Vasya Slepak, and why you became a killer, am I?" She smiled weakly in reply. "Can you give me another piece of chocolate? A very little one."

"Here." He broke off two squares and held out both to her. "You earned it. Wash it down with snow. Only don't swallow it right away. Let it melt in your mouth. It'll be a little like cold cocoa."

"Yes, an excellent breakfast." Lena took out the pack of cigarettes from the coat pocket.

Parliaments again. That's probably all the crooks in the taiga house smoked. She held the pack out to Vasya, but he shook his head.

"I don't smoke. Now tell me, who framed my father?"

He asked the question so simply and ordinarily that Lena was taken aback.

"Gradskaya," she said quietly after a long pause. "Your father was framed by Gradskaya. Volkov killed the girls."

The killer's face turned to stone. His eyes turned completely white. Lena turned away.

"And now all of it in detail," he said. "In great detail, from the very beginning."

That was when they heard a helicopter in the distance.

"Get into the dugout," the killer ordered.

A few seconds later they found themselves in pitch darkness, on the soft fir litter. The helicopter was getting closer.

What if it's not the crooks? Lena thought. *What if it's Seryozha?*

"I'm listening," the killer said quietly.

Lena started telling him everything from the very beginning. She talked for a long time, and the helicopter kept circling. The sound would move away and then come back. Every time the helicopter flew close by, Lena fell silent. But Blindboy hurried her along.

"Go on!"

She finished her story, lit a cigarette, and quietly asked, "How did you find me and why?"

"Gradskaya put a hit on you," he said after a long silence.

"You accepted the contract?"

"I didn't take any money."

"But you didn't refuse?"

"If I'd refused, she would have hired someone else. Or tried to do it herself again."

"Why didn't she come to you straightaway?"

"I don't kill women with small children. She knows that. In Moscow you had your daughter, but here you're alone."

"Did you kill Mitya?" Lena asked.

"Yes."

"Were you supposed to stage my death, too?"

"No. Not you."

"How did you do it . . . to Mitya?"

"I did it the way I was ordered. I climbed in the window, knocked him out while he was sleeping, injected a large dose of morphine in his wrist, dragged him out of bed. The rest you know."

He spoke so calmly and in such an ordinary way, it was as if he were sharing a recipe.

"You made just one mistake," Lena said thoughtfully. "Just one. You injected the morphine in his right wrist. But Mitya wasn't left-handed."

"I injected it in the arm that was hanging from the bed. It was easier that way. I didn't think about which it was, right or left."

"What if his wife had woken up?"

"I wasn't hired to do the wife. But she couldn't have woken up. She was too high, and I did it all very quietly."

The helicopter had flown away while Blindboy was talking. It was quiet now. The killer peeked out of the dugout.

"I'm going to light a fire now," he said. "Help me gather tinder. Only don't take fir. Fir smokes a lot."

He cut a layer of bark off a young birch, rolled it into a neat cone, and deftly secured it with a flexible twig. Sitting by the fire, Lena watched the killer make a pot from birch bark.

"Are you planning to boil water in that?" she asked.

"What else?"

He filled the birch pot with snow and secured it over the fire between two forked sticks. The snow melted and he added more. Half an hour later, the pot was full to the brim with melted water, which quickly boiled.

"Why didn't it burn?" Lena said, surprised.

"I don't know." He shrugged. "That's what the Khanty taught me." Carefully removing the pot from the fire, he held it out to Lena.

They sat there taking turns sipping the hot water, handing the bark pot back and forth.

"Didn't you feel sorry for Mitya?" Lena asked cautiously. "You must have recognized him."

"Yes," the killer nodded. "I did recognize him. But this is my job."

"Why did you take pity on me?" Lena tried to keep her voice from breaking. She spoke slowly and softly, almost in a whisper.

"Because you once took pity on me."

CHAPTER 40

Venya woke up very early. It was still dark outside. He knew the only morning flight from Tyumen arrived at 9:15. It would be foolish to rush just to watch Lena enter the arrivals hall only to be met and embraced by her husband. But he couldn't stop himself. He was dying to see her. The ten days had stretched out like an eternity. And now today she was flying back.

He wouldn't get too close. He'd just look at her. And tonight he'd call her and ask her to have a talk with her husband. He hoped he could see her first thing tomorrow. But he wasn't going to rush her. Let things go however she wanted, so that no one got hurt, her husband above all.

Regina was sleeping in her office. He slipped past the closed door, but she immediately appeared in the doorway in a short nightgown.

"What's got you up at this ungodly hour?" she asked, yawning.

"Business," he said, and he headed for the bathroom. He emerged from his shower cheerful and fresh. His face was glowing. While he was putting his boots on in the front hall, Regina appeared again. She was carrying his favorite mug full of steaming coffee with cream.

"You don't have time for breakfast," she said, "so at least have some coffee."

"Thank you." He took the mug from her.

It was true, hot coffee wouldn't hurt right now. Regina knew how to prepare it the way he liked—very strong and sweet, with lots of heavy cream. Right now it seemed especially delicious. Venya drank down the entire mug, gave Regina a peck on the cheek, grabbed the keys to his old Mercedes, and left.

Regina stood there a little longer, waiting for the sound of the engine to fade, headed for the kitchen, and washed out his mug very carefully with baking soda and chlorine.

It was a sunny morning. Volkov drove his favorite car and thought about the best way to get to Domodedovo.

On the way, he passed a small flower market, stopped, and bought a bouquet of large tea roses. He wasn't going to go up to Lena and give her the bouquet. But still, they were for her.

Stopping at the light, he slipped a cassette into the tape deck, an old Beatles album, *Help!*

He sang along with the first verse, barely understanding the words.

The light turned yellow. He felt a strange, nasty tingle all over his body. A moment later, a sharp, burning pain filled his chest.

Seven girls were looking at him from far away, through a bloody fog. Looking at him gravely and sadly. One was Tanya Kostylyova, and her long, wet braid was tossed over her naked shoulder. The other six remained nameless. He hadn't wanted to know their names.

Behind him, cars were honking. The light had turned green. He didn't hear their impatient honks. The pain mounted. It was unbearable. His right hand fumbled desperately over the dashboard. His eyes saw nothing but the bloody fog and the seven young girls' faces.

His head slammed into the steering wheel. The old Mercedes honked desperately, then immediately fell silent. Venya Volkov's head had slipped off to the side.

"Hey, buddy, what's with you?" A truck driver asked after looking into the open window of the black Mercedes, which was blocking his way. "Yesterday" was playing softly in the car. A bouquet of large tea roses lay on the front seat. The man at the wheel was dead.

When the phone rang, Regina looked at the clock.

"Regina Valentinovna Gradskaya?"

"Yes."

"Your husband, Veniamin Borisovich Volkov . . ."

"Where should I go?" she asked hoarsely after hearing the news.

"The Botkinskaya Hospital morgue."

"All right. I'll be there in an hour." Her own voice seemed dead to her.

She hung up, lit a cigarette, and was surprised to see that her hands were trembling.

"Venya, Venya, my love," she whispered. "I had no choice. It was the only way to save the business. Curly would have gobbled us up. And what then? Do you think it was easy for me to pour poison into your coffee? Making the decision, that wasn't hard. Getting a poison that wouldn't leave a trace in your blood was even easier. But opening the vial, pouring it into your coffee, and then handing you the mug and watching you drink it—that was completely different. You're gone now. And no one is going to be able to prove a thing. Ever."

After their break, they were again walking through the taiga. Lena kept hearing a noise. It would get closer, then move away, and sometimes disappear altogether. The noise seemed to be in her head, from exhaustion and hunger. But the killer explained it was a drill.

"Where are we going?" Lena asked.

But he didn't answer. She suddenly had the thought that he himself no longer even knew where they were. They were lost. How much farther could they go without food? There was only a small piece of chocolate left. It was getting dark. The twilight was gloomy, and the sky grew overcast. If the moon didn't peek out, it would soon be pitch black.

Her ears were ringing. Lena no longer felt her own body, which had become light, almost weightless. And the gloom kept thickening. The wind was noisy in the tall firs' crowns. Snow dust was hitting her in the face. A snowstorm had kicked up. Lena felt like she was flying along with the tiny snowflakes. The ringing in her ears was deafening, and vomit was rising to her throat. The black tree trunks started spinning before her eyes. The heavy, pulsing gloom pulled in everything around her.

Lena fainted.

The special ops team scaled the two-meter stone wall one after the other. The four doghouses were empty.

The house was silent. The team scattered to their positions. A military helicopter hovered over the roof. Two men dropped down a rope ladder and entered the attic through the dormer window.

It soon became clear that the stone house was empty. A thorough search yielded nothing. No weapons, drugs, papers. Nothing.

Or almost nothing. In one of the closets Colonel Krotov found his wife's leather jacket. The jacket was hanging neatly on a hanger, and her checked woolen scarf was poking out of one sleeve. In the pockets, the colonel found a clean handkerchief, thirty-thousand rubles in small bills, and a key for the Tobolsk Hotel.

On the floor of the same closet lay Lena's purse. All her documents were there—passport, international press card, an opened pack of cigarettes, two hundred dollars, makeup, and a hairbrush.

The smell of Lena's perfume lingered in the scarf. The colonel buried his pale face in it.

༄

At first, Lena heard a slow, rhythmic rumble. Then she sensed light through her closed eyelids. Then she smelled something odd, not unpleasant, exactly, but odd. Still not opening her eyes, she realized that somewhere very nearby a train was rumbling. A freight train, probably. There was the smell of cinders and coal, that special railroad air you can't mistake for anything else.

She was a little cold. She discovered she was lying on a pile of black and yellow rags, wearing someone else's peacoat, and covered with a ragged quilted jacket. Cautiously rising, she scanned her surroundings.

Around her, wooden walls bore scraps of torn wallpaper. Lying on the floor were pieces of iron, scraps of newspaper, a broken stool, a few empty cans, and a vodka bottle. In the corner was a half-collapsed stove. A gentle morning light poured through a broken window. The door creaked and flapped in the breeze.

The rumble of the train fell silent in the distance.

"Vasya!" she called out.

But no one responded. She went outside. Directly in front of her was a rail bed with a single track. Deep taiga on either side. Not a soul to be seen, just the trackman's small, abandoned hut.

Lena scooped up a handful of clean snow and wiped her face. Her clenched stomach hurt; she was so hungry. Sticking her hands in her pockets, she discovered a small piece of foil. She took it out and unwrapped it. Of the four squares of chocolate, Vasya had broken off only one for himself.

She vaguely remembered the killer carrying her on his back. She even remembered him saying, "Hold on just a little longer, I'm begging you."

She didn't know how long they'd traveled to get to this abandoned hut, but she did remember him laying her on the rags and covering her with the quilted jacket.

The chocolate melted slowly in her mouth. Lena washed it down with clean snow. She didn't hurry. The killer had taught her to eat slowly. "Cold cocoa." Chocolate with taiga snow. She felt better, and the pain in her stomach eased up.

Lena brought out the quilted jacket, spread it right by the rails, and sat down. A train would have to come down the track. One already had. There'd be another. She'd hear the wheels knocking from far off and would go out on the rails. The engineer would notice her and stop the train.

The cold sun peered through the thin clouds. The taiga silence was deafening. She could hear tree trunks creaking.

Lena didn't know how much time had passed. She sat curled into a ball, gradually losing heat. She was afraid to go back into the hut and miss the train. The sun was slowly crossing to the west. No train. Not a one. She closed her eyes. She was so sleepy. She understood she shouldn't sleep, but she couldn't do anything about it. *The train will wake me up,* she thought. *It has to wake me up.*

But there was no train.

The helicopter circled above the taiga without any hope. Colonel Krotov's face was pressed up to the porthole.

If they took her away, he thought, *her jacket wouldn't have been hanging there. If they've already killed her, I would have found something else, her boots, for instance. She might have run away. Yes, she must have run away.*

He sensed there was little logic to his reasoning.

Let's assume she ran away. How much time has passed? Twenty-four hours? Forty-eight? No more. It hasn't been intensely cold. It is March, after all. She could have gone toward the sound of the drilling or the railroad. But there's a phone at the drilling site. They would have let us know.

"It's going to get dark soon," the pilot commented. "We're going to have to go back."

"Just a little more," the colonel asked, not tearing himself away from the porthole.

At first Krotov saw a level cut-through, and then the slender stripes of rails. Then a solitary hut, tiny, like a toy.

"Almost no one uses that single track anymore," the pilot told Krotov. "Only the occasional freight train comes through with timber from Tovda. If the trackman's hut is still there, it's abandoned."

"Lower, please, just a little!" the colonel requested.

He himself couldn't understand why his heart had suddenly started beating so loud.

The helicopter began to descend. From not very high up, he could clearly see a small, dark figure in the snow. It was a woman, and she was lying there, curled into a ball, right by the tracks.

Lena was trying to keep warm. She didn't want to wake up. But sleep blocked out the loud noise and cutting wind that made the bottom of her short loose pea jacket flap. Slowly, heavily, she opened her eyes. It took tremendous effort. The wind was beating at her face, her eyes teared up, and she couldn't see a thing. With a last heroic effort, she raised herself up on one elbow. She saw Seryozha and some other men running toward her through the deep snow. Nearby the helicopter's huge rotor was turning.

Colonel Krotov picked up his wife.

EPILOGUE

"Regina Valentinovna, you may find the question I'm going to ask difficult. How did you manage to jump right back into work after suffering such grief?"

The TV reporter, a young man with a beard, looked at Regina with his light gray, slightly squinty eyes. Written on his face was sincere sympathy.

"What else can I do?" Regina smiled sadly. "Veniamin Productions is my life. My child, if you like. Veniamin Borisovich's and my child. It would be a betrayal to stop now without completing the projects my husband started."

"Your next project. I've heard it's going to be big, a major revolution in the world of pop music."

Lena poured tea in the cups. Seryozha and Misha Sichkin were sitting at the kitchen table.

Liza ran in and climbed into her papa's lap.

"Mama, may I have some tea?" she said. "I want it with lemon. Is it going to be *Nighty Night* soon?"

"Soon, Liza, soon," Lena answered, and she got out another cup, still looking at the television.

"Well, let's not get carried away," Regina smiled into the camera again, this time a little embarrassed. "It's just that Veniamin Borisovich had fresh, vivid ideas. And this one is his last. Unfortunately."

"No, I can't anymore!" Misha Sichkin couldn't stand it. He stood up and switched channels.

It was a cheerful old comedy.

"Uncle Misha! What are you doing?" Liza was indignant. "*Nighty Night*'s coming on soon!"

"Not right away, little one." Lena cut a slice of lemon and put it in Liza's tea. "In about fifteen minutes."

"I can't believe there's nothing we can do! I can't believe it," Misha said through his teeth.

"Why are you getting so worked up again?" Seryozha shook his head. "We can't prove anything. It's impossible! Forensics did everything they could, the works. There was no trace of poison. Acute cardiac insufficiency. According to the experts, Veniamin Volkov died a non-violent death."

"But she did poison Volkov." Misha wouldn't let up.

"Of course she did." Seryozha nodded. "But she used a poison that doesn't leave any traces, and that means no evidence."

"To hell with evidence!" Misha was nearly shouting. He couldn't calm down. "What about Nikita Slepak? Mitya and Katya Sinitsyn? Azarov? And the stroller bomb? I would . . . I would pay a hitman myself, word of honor! I'd kill her with my own two hands!"

"Uncle Misha," Liza said sternly. "What are you saying? You shouldn't kill anyone! Do you understand? It's time for *Nighty Night*!"

⁂

In the South, on the Black Sea, in the dim living room of his own three-story house, Vladimir Mikhailovich Kudryashev—Curly, the boss of the taiga—sat staring at the television screen.

"You outwitted me, Regina," he said pensively, devouring the beautiful, chiseled face on the screen with his eyes. "Business above all else for you. You needed Volkov, so you got him out of a sure death sentence. When he got in your way, you finished him off, even though he was your husband. I never expected that of you. I thought this was it, you weren't going to wiggle out of this one. But you did. Respect!"

Nina approached silently, sat down on the floor by the boss's feet, and lay her light brown head in his lap.

The long black Lincoln, its windows mirrored, embarked silently from its designated parking spot next to the Ostankino Television Center.

"Well, Anton, I think the live broadcast went pretty well." Regina leaned back in the soft seat and closed her eyes.

Anton Konovalov tenderly kissed her cold, soft cheek.

"Yes, Regina. You looked stunning. I saw you on the monitors. The cameraman didn't even have to choose his angles. You're beautiful no matter how they shoot you!"

"I'm not talking about that, child." Regina frowned.

"What then?"

She didn't deign to respond.

A small, dirty Zhiguli kept tightly on the Lincoln's tail. The lights from oncoming cars occasionally picked out the face of the man behind the wheel: deeply pitted cheeks and strangely light, almost-white eyes under bare, eyebrow-less brows.

Vasya Slepak was preparing to do his usual job. Not for hire. And not for money.

This was personal.

ABOUT THE AUTHOR

 Dubbed the "Russian crime queen," Polina Dashkova is Russia's most successful author of crime novels. She's sold fifty million copies of her books and has thrilled readers in countries across Europe and Asia. A graduate of Moscow's Maxim Gorky Literary Institute, she has been active as a radio and press journalist and has worked as an interpreter and translator of English literature. Her books have been translated into German, Chinese, Dutch, French, Polish, Spanish, and English.

ABOUT THE TRANSLATOR

Marian Schwartz translates Russian classic and contemporary fiction, history, biography, criticism, and fine art. She is the principal English translator of the works of Nina Berberova and translated the *New York Times* bestseller *The Last Tsar* by Edvard Radzinsky, as well as classics by Mikhail Bulgakov, Ivan Goncharov, Yuri Olesha, and Mikhail Lermontov. Her most recent publications are Leo Tolstoy's *Anna Karenina*, Andrei Gelasimov's *Into the Thickening Fog*, Daria Wilke's *Playing a Part*, and half the stories in Mikhail Shishkin's *Calligraphy Lesson: The Collected Stories*. She is a past president of the American Literary Translators Association and the recipient of two National Endowment for the Arts translation fellowships, as well as prizes including the 2014 Read Russia Prize for Contemporary Russian Literature and the 2016 Soeurette Diehl Frasier Award from the Texas Institute of Letters.